$\mathcal{D}uring$ the $hour$-$long$ drive back home, they fell into a brooding silence broken by fits of conversation as new thoughts struck them.

Owen mused aloud, "I can't see it. I can't believe that Bruce is a rapist."

"I know. But it's just as hard to believe Emily would make this up."

"True. But Emily's romantic. Dramatic."

"But she's never been a liar. And she's not crazy."

"I'm not saying she's crazy. But she is in a psychiatric ward."

"She's *in* a psychiatric ward because she was *raped*. She's in a psychiatric ward because she wanted to spare us, but keeping it secret was killing her."

"But I just can't see Bruce *raping* anyone. . . ."

"ANYONE WHO WANTS TO GET INSIDE THE SKIN OF A CONTEMPORARY WOMAN SIMPLY HAS TO OPEN NANCY THAYER AND START READING."

—Elizabeth Forsythe Hailey

St. Martin's Paperbacks titles
by Nancy Thayer

BELONGING
THREE WOMEN AT THE WATER'S EDGE
AN ACT OF LOVE

An Act of Love

•

Nancy Thayer

St. Martin's Paperbacks

AN ACT OF LOVE

Copyright © 1997 by Nancy Thayer.

Library of Congress Catalog Card Number: 97-14404

ISBN: 0-312-96535-4

Printed in the United States of America

St. Martin's Press hardcover edition / September 1997
St. Martin's Paperbacks edition / January 1999

St. Martin's Paperbacks are published by St. Martin's Press, 175 Fifth Avenue, New York, NY 10010.

10 9 8 7 6 5 4 3 2 1

For Mimsi Harbach
My Calliope
With Love ·

Acknowledgments

Many people have helped me with this book,
and I would like to thank them:

Katie de Hertogh at Nantucket Cottage Hospital; Tim
Thompson, who directed me to A Safe Place; Sheila
Coffin, for help with police procedure; attorney Kevin
Dale; the members of the Wednesday Night Study
Group, especially Marilyn Whitney; psychologist, family counselor, and brother-in-law *par excellence* Chuck
Foshee. I would also like to express my gratitude to my
agent, Emma Sweeney, and my editor, Jennifer Weis,
who kept me turning the kaleidoscope until the pattern
came clear.

And Charley,
thanks for making me happy,
all day, all night.

An Act of
Love

Chapter One

❧

She was *aware* only of murky darkness, a tilting horizon splintered with light, and then all at once Emily surfaced to air and white brilliance, her throat burning. The tube in her mouth and her throat prevented her from speaking, but she moaned from deep in her chest and twisted on the stretcher, struggling to get free.

"Blood pressure one-forty-five over ninety-five. Heart rate one-hundred."

The glaring emergency room light burned her eyes. Someone had removed her clothes and stuck her into a skimpy cotton hospital gown that scarcely covered her body. She was tubed and wired like a sci-fi creature, from her breast and both arms and her finger and her mouth and her nose and, hideously, from between her legs.

"Let me go," she insisted, but only garbled sounds came out.

"It's all right," someone said. "You'll be fine. You'll be all right."

A nurse wearing blue scrubs bent over Emily. She had a pleasant face, a grandmotherly face. The doctor looked pissed. Emily knew he was thinking: stupid bitch. She *was* a stupid bitch, so why wouldn't they leave her alone and let her die?

The nurse was saying: "You'll be all right. We're

almost through pumping out your stomach and rinsing it with saline fluid. When it's clear, we'll remove the tube."

Emily thrashed and bucked. With one hand she tried to rip the needle from the vein in her arm, but the nurse gently checked her hand.

"You need that. That IV is carrying necessary fluids to your system. Don't do that, dear. Those wires are for the heart monitor, and your heart rate's a little faster than we'd like right now. The tubes in your nose are for oxygen. This is just a blood pressure cuff, you know about that. The thing on your finger that looks like a giant paper clip is a pulse oxymeter . . . it measures your oxygenation. We've put in a Foley catheter so we can collect some urine for tests. Settle down for us now and we'll be able to disconnect you from most of it."

In despair, Emily wept. The nurse leaned forward with a tissue and wiped the tears from Emily's face and the mucus from around the tubes in her nose.

"Okay, charcoal," the doctor said.

Now thick, ink-black liquid flowed through the tube into Emily's stomach. "This will bind with your system to absorb any bits of the drugs we didn't get pumped out of you. You'll be having a little diarrhea later in the day. Just a few more seconds and we'll have this tube out."

"Ninety-nine percent O_2 sat," another nurse said. "Blood pressure one-twenty-five over eighty-five. Heart rate eighty."

Her head hurt hideously. They began removing things. Bending over her, the nurse removed the bits of sticky paper connected to the wires stuck just beneath her clavicle and beneath her left breast. She felt a tug in her crotch when they took out the catheter. As the tube came up her esophagus, Emily involuntarily made retching noises.

The doctor left the room. The nurse bent over the equipment.

Emily threw herself off the bed and bolted for the door. She raced down the hall, aware of cold on her back, on the soles of her feet, toward the exit sign. She was almost there when they caught her and brought her back.

Last night's storm had torn away autumn's wrenching brilliance, and now the forest circling the farm that had for weeks seemed to shimmer with flame was merely a skeletal, ghostly gray. Beneath an overcast sky the pond rippled darkly in the dying wind. But in the field the horses were playful in the bracing air, nipping and teasing each other. Linda found herself leaning on the windowsill, just staring, savoring the sight, while her computer hummed industriously, waiting. She relished these first cold, dreary days of winter when the heart turned toward inner comforts and joys.

Owen appeared in the doorway of her study. "Want to make love?"

Surprised, she laughed. Certainly her husband was compelling, lounging there in his jeans and flannel shirt, short and compact and sturdy, his thick hair gleaming as brightly as spun copper. His pale brown eyes were flecked with gold and amber, like currents of light in his tanned, freckled skin. His hands were massive and hard and sure. As was his body.

"Yes. Let's."

"Good. Take the phone off the hook."

With only a twinge of guilt, Linda lifted the receiver and stuck it into a drawer. It would make disturbing noises for a few seconds, then go mute. Anyone calling would get a busy signal. She switched off her computer, rose, and followed Owen into his bedroom.

After the first year of their marriage, they agreed to have separate bedrooms. Linda was a hopeless insomniac, waking at all hours of the night to read. She never had enough time to read; she often thought she had insomnia just so she could grab an extra hour in the deep heart of the night to spend with books.

While Owen needed solitude. His antidote to the news of the contemporary world was to listen to classical music. The farmhouse was large enough for them to have separate bedrooms, and it added a bit of spice to have different rooms, to enter, as she did now, her husband's lair.

Owen's room was dark, with heavy Empire furniture, and his parents' old mahogany sleigh bed was almost regal. Owen liked the past, liked old things, did not like change. Linda had come to accept this as a good sign; he wouldn't grow tired of her.

She undressed and slid between the sheets, which were cold and sleek against her skin.

"I love it that we don't have to shut out the light, don't have to draw the curtains."

"And the better to see you, my dear," Owen growled wolfishly, crawling into bed and nuzzling her neck.

Languorously they rolled together, entwining their arms and legs. They had all the time in the world. Their pulses slowed, they took deep breaths, and for a while they didn't kiss, but only stroked each other, learning once again the warm, smooth span and fold of shoulder, hip, and thigh. Then Linda forced Owen onto his back and knelt between his legs so that she could feel the erotic friction of his wiry red hair against her cheek, eyelids, lips. Turning her head slowly from side to side, she grazed in the long deep bowl of his belly. He ran his hands over her arms and shoulders and back. His penis grew long between her breasts. He was always very clean, with a cool scent like redwood emanating from his skin. Linda felt almost drowsy, drugged, as if browsing among poppies, and then he turned her over and prepared to enter her but withheld himself, making the tension mount. She arched up toward him. The room was full of light and skin and breath. When he finally penetrated her, she wrapped herself around him in a kind of bliss. She was more in love with Owen now than she was when she first met him.

Finally they subsided, curled together, fell into an easy sleep.

Owen woke to see by his bedside clock that two hours had passed. Within the curve of his body, his wife lay sleeping. Almost impersonally, he noted the crow's feet at her eyes and the slight incipient sag of flesh around her jawline, and all at once he was stabbed through with sorrow at the realization that she was growing older. He wanted to protect her from age, from death. He wanted his love to be a shield.

Sap, he chided himself, and scratched his naked thigh. But the truth was that he was amazed by their marriage. He had never thought a woman would be able to love him as he really was, reclusive and sardonic and pessimistic, struggling to write novels about the environment that garnered praise but little money, angry most of the time at what men were doing to the planet, often sinking into black moods that made everyone around him, including his son, Bruce, and their old dog, Maud, miserable.

But Linda accepted him. Perhaps because she was a novelist, too. She understood that writing was his sanity . . . and his insanity as well. He was haunted by the characters who seem to pummel his brain, by the way the world was headed toward hell in a handbasket. He would write day and night if he could.

Now he was restless. Quietly he slipped from the bed and padded down the hall, thinking as he went how few women would be content to be stuck out in the country in this place. Old, rambling, and eccentric, with Victorian touches lacing a good solid colonial foundation, six fireplaces, wide board floors, and a wraparound porch, the house had been passed down from his father, who received it from his father before

him. Owen loved the house and the land surrounding
it; he would never leave it; he would pass it along to
Bruce some day.

Linda loved the house, too, although she occasionally went into fits of distress over its state of disrepair.
She wanted to have the rattling, cracked windowpanes
fixed; to have the two blocked fireplaces opened up; to
have the faded wallpaper dimming the high expanse of
walls in the front and back halls steamed off and those
walls freshly painted. Some of the work he could do
himself, and all of it he could supervise, but it would
take time away from his work, which would mean a
loss of income, and with Bruce facing four years of
college, right now was not the time even to think about
that.

In Linda's study, Owen dropped the phone receiver
back into its cradle, then headed to the bathroom. As
he stepped into the old claw-footed bathtub and turned
on the shower, he acknowledged to himself he was
comfortable with the house as it was, a little shabby,
and crowded. All the rooms were crammed with books
on shelves or on tables or in piles on the floor or the
stairs. Linda liked this, too. Most of the books were
Owen's; but many were hers, many the children's. He
and Linda were always reading, always talking. If one
of them came upon a perplexing thought or clever
metaphor, they'd wander through the house, searching
each other out, and finding one another, lean against
a doorjamb and talk for hours. They talked over dinner, over breakfast. They talked as they walked
through the damp rock-strewn woods. Or they walked
in silence. Linda was the only woman he'd met who
was comfortable with silence.

It was as if they had become two halves of a whole,
a pretty amazing thing considering how they'd all
started out, two divorced adults, each with a divorced-
scarred child. The first year they'd all lived together he
hadn't been certain they could make it. But now, after

seven years of marriage, it seemed that his son and Linda's daughter had gotten so accustomed to each other and to their way of living together that all distinctions of blood and law had blurred and they were at last a real family.

This was purely a miracle. This was more than he'd ever expected from life.

As he stepped out of the shower, the phone rang. For a moment he toyed with the thought of not answering. Then he wrapped the towel around his midsection, went down the hall, said hello.

"Mr. McFarland? It's Bob Lorimer here. I'm sorry to have to tell you this, but I'm here at Basingstoke Hospital with Emily. She's going to be all right, but it seems she attempted to commit suicide today."

Chapter Two

*W*hat happened?" *Owen* asked.

"Emily swallowed a number of pills as well as a quantity of alcohol. Her roommate Cordelia Analan wondered why she wasn't in class, went to their room, and found Emily comatose. She notified us, and we had Emily brought to the hospital by ambulance. We found empty aspirin, Sleepeeze, and Midol containers on her bed, and a half-empty bottle of vodka. Emily's stomach has been pumped. Physically she's out of danger now, but emotionally she's . . . upset."

"Did she tell you why?"

"No. Emily's not—coherent. Cordelia appeared as surprised as we are. Perhaps she'll talk to you."

"We'll come at once. We'll be there in an hour."

"Good." Mr. Lorimer hesitated, then said quickly, "I'm sorry about this."

Linda had come into the study and stood waiting, listening. When Owen put down the phone, he told her, "Emily's in the hospital in Basingstoke. She tried to commit suicide."

Linda blinked and took a step forward. "She—"

"She's going to be okay. She's in the hospital."

"I don't understand. Are you sure? *Emily?*"

"We've got to go there now. I'll call Celeste and ask her to take care of the place while we're gone."

Linda nodded, but did not move. "What did they

say? Who called? Are you sure it's not . . . a prank?"

"It was Bob Lorimer. He said Emily swallowed a bunch of pills and some alcohol."

"What kind of pills?"

"Midol. Aspirin. They pumped her stomach. Cordelia found her in her room. She was comatose."

"I don't understand."

"Let's get moving."

Linda nodded and headed for her bedroom to dress. Owen called after her to remind her to pack a bag. They'd probably have to stay the night in Basingstoke.

*T*here was no direct way to get from the farm outside the small town of Ebradour in central Massachusetts to Hedden Academy, situated on the north side of Boston. The scenic route through rolling mountains and sleepy villages took about forty-five minutes longer, more if they got stuck on the two-lane road behind a truck hauling livestock. Today they took Route 91 down to the Mass Pike, then headed east to 93 North.

The unsettling flash of cars at the periphery of their vision always took some getting used to after the pastoral pace of their farm and the country roads curving moatlike, protectively, around it. Now the frenetic traffic sounds of horns and brakes and radios and the hurtling rush of air seemed appropriate to the moment. Everywhere the land swept off in all directions, the occasional orange or red leaf flashing like a message of alarm.

"Sit back," Owen said.

"I can't imagine why Emily would do such a thing."

"It's not like her."

"She seemed in great shape this summer."

"Both kids did."

"She seemed happy to return to school."

"Something must have happened there."

"You think I was right about the braces, don't you?"

"Absolutely."

"She didn't want them put on now. She said a boy liked her. She wanted to look good. Probably she was thinking about getting kissed."

"You were right to make her get them now."

"It's just that . . . I can remember what it's like when you first fall in love. The first time you kiss a boy."

"Now she can have two first times, one with braces, one without."

Linda glanced at her husband. Usually he was not so sanguine, and in spite of his words his face was grim. It was possible that he was concerned, as she was, that they had been wrong to send Emily to boarding school. Just because Bruce flourished there didn't mean Emily would. But Emily had wanted to go, had begged to go. All the things Owen and Linda loved about the farm, the silence and privacy and peace, the vast stretch of air and sky and rolling fields, the long shared walks through the sweet high wet grasses with only the flash and dart of birds for company, only the fragrance of alfalfa and pine perfuming the air . . . all that bored Emily.

Emily loved people. She was an extrovert and an optimist. She didn't want solitude, she wanted the giggles of her girlfriends and the rumble of boys' laughter, the jolt and thud of music from a boom box, the smell of sweat and shampoo and chewing gum and illicit cigarettes in the hallway. She wanted the sight of boys' bodies, their crooked grins, their ambling figures coming toward her down the hallway. Linda knew what her daughter wanted.

Thought she knew. Obviously she was wrong. It seemed she didn't know her child at all.

*B*ruce heard the siren when he was running toward the fieldhouse, but it didn't signify anything to him until the moment he stepped out of the shower to find Coach Parker waiting by his locker.

"Bruce. Lorimer wants to see you. Now."

"What's up?"

"Something about Emily."

"Emily? What about her?"

"You've gotta see Lorimer right away. That's all I know."

Bruce yanked on his khakis and striped shirt and sweater, slid his feet sockless into his shabby loafers, then set off at a run toward the dean's office in the administrative buildings, turning things over in his mind. If the siren had meant an ambulance, and that had come for Emily, well, what could have happened? She wasn't a jock, she wouldn't have gotten hurt playing. He took the steps up to the entrance to Tuttle Hall two at a time. In the lobby he stopped to brush back his hair and tuck in his shirt.

The dean's secretary, Mrs. Echevera, sat at her desk, pounding away on the computer, but the moment Bruce stepped into the office, she swiveled her chair toward him. "Hello, Bruce. Go on in, dear. He's waiting for you."

Dear, Bruce thought, there was an ominous sign. After rapping sharply at the door, he went in.

Dean Lorimer was six foot three and had a Teddy Roosevelt kind of gruff charm. "Bruce. Sit down," he growled. "How are you?"

"Fine. I'm fine, sir." Bruce settled uneasily on the edge of the chair facing the desk.

"We've got a little problem you should know about. I wanted to tell you before you heard it elsewhere. Your sister's been taken to the hospital. If appearances don't lie, she attempted suicide this afternoon."

"*Emily?*" Bruce asked, incredulous.

Lorimer nodded. "Her roommate Cordelia found her. In time, I should add, thank God above for that. An ambulance came immediately and she should be in the hospital right now. I want you to know I've called your parents. They're on their way to the hospital. I thought you might like to go over there, too, later on. I'm giving you permission to be off grounds for the rest of the day."

"Well, thank you, sir," Bruce said, automatically polite. "But—are you sure it was a suicide attempt?"

"Unfortunately, yes. She had a bottle of vodka and a variety of pills with her. Seems she waited until the dorm was empty after lunch."

"But she'll be okay?"

"We think so," Lorimer replied cautiously. After a moment he asked, "I don't suppose you can help shed any light on what would be bothering Emily?"

Bruce shook his head. "She's two classes behind me. Well, you know that. I hardly ever see her."

"Can you remember when you did see her last?"

Bruce thought. "Probably at assembly. She seemed all right then."

Lorimer shook his head. "It's not like her."

"No, it's not."

"I'll walk you to your dorm," Lorimer said, rising. "Something like this . . . I need some exercise."

"I, uh, I'm not sure I'm going to my dorm right now," Bruce told the dean. "Unless you thinks it's necessary."

Lorimer looked at him.

"I'd kind of like to talk to a friend right now," Bruce explained.

"Of course, son," Lorimer said. He waved his hand. "Go on."

"Well, uh, thank you, sir," Bruce said awkwardly. He left the room, making a polite grimace to Mrs. Echevera, then hurried down the hall. When he stepped out into the cold freshness of the day, he began to run toward Shipley Hall, Alison's dorm.

From his window, Bob Lorimer stood, watching Bruce run.

*   *   *

Emily felt like shit. Was made of shit, actually. The stuff they called charcoal kept making her run for the john. She was sure every sound she made could be heard throughout the ward. People must think she was really disgusting.

Her intestines were cramped, her stomach hurt, her mouth was dry, and her face felt swollen. She lay on her side on the bed, finding what relief there was in sleep.

Then she heard the door open. Someone entered the room.

"Emily? Do you know where you are?"

Someone was looking at her. A woman.

"Emily?"

"Hospital."

"Good. Do you know what day it is?"

The woman smelled like the incense Zodiac liked to burn in their room, against dorm rules. Sandalwood and cinnamon. A clean smell.

"Monday. Thanksgiving week."

"Good. I'm Dr. Travis. I thought you might like something to drink. I've brought a 7UP for you. With ice."

Emily rolled over, sat up, rubbed her eyes, reached out for the paper cup. "Thank you." She could not believe how great the first sip tasted, cool and wet and soothing to her throat.

"I thought I might stay here a while and talk with you." Travis settled into a chair at the other end of the room. She was a heavy woman, fat like the "before" photos you'd tape to your refrigerator to keep you on a diet, yet pretty in spite of it all. Her clothes and jewelry, even her hair was sort of beautiful in a rococo way. "Rococo" was a new vocabulary word in English, one of Emily's new favorites; she was surprised it popped up in her brain just now.

Travis continued, "You'll stay in this room overnight. It's comfortable enough, don't you think?"

As if now her comfort mattered. She snorted. "Right."

"The door does not lock, as you may have noticed. Nurses will be checking in every so often during the night, just to see how you're doing. Tomorrow we'll start talking about how long you might like to stay here. And we can wait until then to talk about what brought you here." She paused. "Unless you'd like to start talking about that now."

Emily snorted again. "I fucked up. That's what brought me here."

"Fucked up how?"

"Didn't take enough pills. Didn't do a good job."

"A good job of . . ."

Emily flashed the woman a look of impatience. "A good job of killing myself, what do you think?"

"Why would you want to kill yourself?" Travis spoke as if she were discussing a book Emily had chosen, or a dress. Her voice was calm.

Emily sipped the rest of the 7UP. Travis sat quietly. After a while, Emily said, trying to be as calm as Travis, "Because I don't want to go on." Then the words came out as if they were entities on their own, moving from her throat without her consent. "Because I don't deserve to go on. Because I'm too gross to live."

"And why is that?"

Emily looked at Travis's face. "Why should I tell you? You'll tell my parents and then everyone will be miserable. Why can't people just leave me alone? There are too many people in the world, anyway."

"Oh, I see. It was a philanthropic act."

A talent for sarcasm had always appealed to Emily, and now she looked at the doctor again, more carefully, surprised that such a barbed statement would come from such a plump, mild-looking woman.

Travis continued, "As far as telling your parents anything, I won't, unless you give me permission. I'm here to help you. I'm here as your advocate. Whatever you tell me is entrusted into my safekeeping, and I am obligated by my oath to keep your secrets safe."

Emily looked back at the floor, finishing the 7UP.

"Unless," Travis went on, "you make another suicide attempt, or try to leave the ward without permission."

Emily's eyes flashed up at Travis. "I'm imprisoned here?"

"Not at all. You have been brought here involuntarily, of course, since you were unconscious at the time and the emergency room physician treated you and referred you to us. You are not obligated to remain, but if you do remain, we will want you to sign a form stating that it is your voluntary act, and we'll want a commitment from you that you will work on the problem that brought you here."

Emily was listening carefully.

"You will also pledge that while you are on this ward, you will not attempt to harm yourself, and that if the urge to do so arises, you will tell us, so that we may help you."

"How?"

"A number of ways. Medications often help. Often it's sufficient to know that the nurses are alerted and will keep a fifteen-minute watch on your room, to be sure you're not doing anything harmful."

"This place must be expensive."

"Is that relevant? If it is, it might help to know that your school health insurance will probably cover everything."

After a moment's pause, Emily got it. "You've had Hedden students here before. You know the drill."

Dr. Travis only smiled and recrossed her legs, sending her voluminous skirts into a flurry. "If you decide to stay with us, you'll have a complete physical checkup tomorrow. You'll meet the various people on the team who will be helping you. You'll be given a schedule that we'll work up for you. You'll be restricted to the ward until the team decides you're ready for other privileges, such as—"

"You mean I can't go back to school?"

"Do you want to go back to school?"

"What about Thanksgiving?"

"I'm sure the dining room will serve turkey, cranberries, and pumpkin pie on Thursday."

"So you're saying I have to stay here for a while."

"You have committed an act that indicates that you can't function on your own right now. Something is bothering you. We're here to help you work on that. There are other adolescents on this ward who are working on their own problems and you might find it helpful to hear what they have to say."

"No one can help me."

"I know you feel that way now. But if you'll give us a chance, I think you'll find that we can help you. You're not hopeless. You are not without choices in your life. We might help you find a new way to look at your problems, or a new way to defeat that which seems to be defeating you."

Emily stared at the psychologist, then bent her head over her 7UP, making a gross sucking noise as the straw hit ice. She flushed with embarrassment.

"Emily, your parents are going to be here fairly soon. As you can imagine, they're worried about you."

"I don't want to see them."

Travis waited for Emily to say more, and when she didn't speak, continued, "I'm sure they're worried about you. I'm sure they want just to see that you're okay. I'll be with you when they come in. The important thing you need to do now is to decide whether or not you'll sign yourself in, voluntarily, for treatment here."

"For how long?"

"We don't know yet. I can say that it often takes a while to work things through."

"I'll sign the form," Emily said.

Chapter Three

❦

Basingstoke Hospital stood at the outskirts of the historic town of Basingstoke, home of Hedden Academy. A small building, only five stories high, it was constructed from stone and cement and glass, very practical and no-nonsense looking. A sign directing traffic to it from 93 North pointed the McFarlands toward a long driveway and instructions to a parking garage that was as large as the hospital and apparently as automated. Owen stopped the Volvo and took a ticket from a machine, then steered upward through the dark, low-ceilinged, Stygian aisles until he found a space.

Linda's door was open before Owen had the key from the ignition. He ran to catch up with her and together they passed through the sliding glass doors and into a lobby bright with color and people and sound. While Linda spoke to someone at a desk, Owen looked around. An elderly woman nodded off in a wheelchair, head drooping on her chest. A couple sat side by side on a vinyl sofa, staring out in terrible shock. A pair of blissfully ignorant children fussed over a bag of candy while their parents consulted each other in sharp whispers.

"This way," Linda said. "She's already in the psychiatric unit."

They found the elevator, ascended three floors,

walked down a long yellow hallway until they were
halted by wide double doors bearing a sign in huge red
block print:

STOP. NO ONE ALLOWED ON WARD WITHOUT DOC-
TOR'S PERMISSION. THIS DOOR LOCKED FROM MIDNIGHT
TO 8 A.M.

Pushing through, they entered a world of glass-
walled cubicles. They couldn't hear the people inside
talking, but they could see them seated on plush sofas
and chairs, sipping coffee. Everyone was wearing street
clothes; the only thing that differentiated patient from
doctor was that one person held a clipboard and pen
while the other sat empty-handed, or with a wad of
tissues.

They found the nurse's station.

"We're Emily Scaive's parents," Owen said to the
nurse.

The woman was small-boned, with feathery light
brown hair and bright tiny black eyes; she looked like
a sparrow. "Oh, right. I'll get Dr. Travis for you. Just
a moment." Smiling, she left them and disappeared toward an area of offices walled off from view.

As the McFarlands waited, another nurse came
around the corner pushing an old man down the hall
in a wheelchair. He was dressed in a suit, with his
white hair carefully combed. Around his neck hung a
stethoscope.

"Where are my charts?" he yelled.

"The other physicians are consulting them," the
nurse answered.

"He'll need a tracheotomy!" the old man declared.

"They're setting up the operating room now, Dr.
Martin," the nurse assured him. Smiling at Linda and
Owen, she wheeled by, mouthing, "Alzheimer's. We're
just going for a little stroll."

"Where's my black bag?" Dr. Martin whined quer-
ulously.

"In your office, Doctor."

"Where's my office?" he demanded as they went around the corner and out of earshot.

Sparrow-nurse reappeared followed by a short woman, nearly as wide as she was tall, flowing toward them in a flurry of loose silky tunics and beads.

"Mr. and Mrs. McFarland? I'm Tina Travis. I'm the ward psychologist who will be coordinating the team that will be working with your daughter."

Linda asked, "How is she?"

"Subdued at the moment. It's natural. She's had her stomach pumped and she's had to ingest charcoal, so she's not feeling too good right now."

"Did she tell you why—" Linda began and could not finish.

"She's said very little. But again, remember, she feels physically out of sorts."

Owen asked, "Can we see her?"

"Of course. I'll take you in now. First, I need to tell you that I will be in the room with you when you see her. Hospital rules. I suggest that you remain calm and especially that you ask her only what you need to know. For now. Only what you need to know."

Meekly, Owen and Linda nodded.

Travis lead them to a room, opened the door, ushered them in, entered behind them, and shut the door.

It was a small bland room with blue walls, no windows, three chairs, and a narrow bed. On the bed lay Emily, eyes closed, hands crossed over her chest, fully dressed in loose sweatpants and a plaid flannel shirt. No shoes. White socks with dirty soles.

"Oh, Emily," Linda whispered, going toward her daughter, sinking down on the bed next to her.

Linda and Owen last saw Emily when they drove her and Bruce to begin the new year at Hedden in mid-September. Since then Emily had hacked off her lovely long golden-brown hair and dyed it dead black. Tufts sprouted jaggedly in all directions from her scalp. The skin around her eyes looked strained and shadowed.

Her lips were chapped. Her fingernails were peeled and bitten to the quick.

"Emily," Linda said again. Emily didn't open her eyes but her eyelids quivered. "I love you, babe." Gently Linda put her hand on her daughter's. Linda's hand was warm; Emily's, cold, and Linda realized with a start that in addition to all the other physical changes, Emily had gained weight. Her thighs, hips, belly, and bosom were pudding soft beneath her loose clothing. Even her hands were fat: soft and plumply yielding, like bread dough.

Weight was such a volatile issue with young women, Linda knew; the necessity of being thin was hyped in magazines, on television and movie screens, in ads. It could not be ignored, but Linda had tried to deflect it by joking about it, and by pointing out standards of beauty in other societies and ages, while at the same time taking care to serve reasonably healthy meals with plenty of fruit and few junk foods.

Emily had never before been fat. When she was about eleven her body took on an odd Humpty Dumpty amorphousness for several months and then almost overnight her breasts sprouted, her period began, and she shot up three inches and developed a long, lithe waist. Not really athletic, this summer on the farm she'd swum and ridden the horses, and as always the sheer expense of energy on talking and giggling and whispering with her friends seemed to use up each day's calories with ease.

So this new plumpness was unusual. A sign?

"Perhaps you'd be more comfortable in a chair," Travis suggested, seating herself in the one chair near Emily's bed.

"Sweetheart," Linda whispered, gently touching her child's cheek, and then she rose and moved to the chair near the opposite wall.

"I'm sure you have some questions you'd like to ask," Travis prompted.

Linda cleared her throat. "Emily. What's wrong?"

Emily didn't reply.

"Please, Emily, tell us this much. Was this an accident? Or were you really trying to . . ." Linda looked to the counselor for help, but Travis remained silent.

The last time Linda was in a hospital with Emily had been when she was born. She had been a breech baby and in some amount of distress, and so they had taken her from Linda and kept her in an ICU for twenty-four hours. Linda had slipped from her bed and shuffled down the hall and leaned against the window, peering in at her tiny endangered daughter, weeping with hope and fear.

Now she said, "Emily, we love you. Whatever you did. And we want to help."

Emily didn't answer.

Quietly Travis spoke: "Emily's probably too tired to talk right now. We'd like her to stay with us for a while. She'll need to sleep today, but she'll probably feel up to seeing some visitors this evening. You could return then, and bring her some necessities while you're at it. Toothbrush, toothpaste, and so on."

"Is there anything special you want?" Owen asked. "A book . . . ?" He waited, but Emily did not respond, so he rose. "Well, then, we'll leave you to rest. We'll be back later."

" 'Bye, Emily," Linda said. "I love you."

Emily's eyelids trembled, but she didn't speak.

In the hall Linda and Owen waited as Travis went behind the nurses' station to gather up some papers, then they followed her into her office, which after the impersonality of the corridor nearly exploded upon their senses with shapes and color. The furniture was standard issue: metal desk, metal filing cabinets, inexpensive brown armchairs, oatmeal-colored rug and drapes. But the walls were plastered with posters covered with stars, rainbows, blue skies, fluffy clouds, and quotes:

*"Nobody can make you feel inferior without your
consent."*
—ELEANOR ROOSEVELT

*"It is always one's virtues and not one's vices that
precipitate one into disaster."*
—REBECCA WEST

*"Well, if I called the wrong number, why did you
answer the phone?"*
—JAMES THURBER

Travis sat behind her desk and indicated with a
graceful gesture the small armchairs facing her. Knowing he was thinking critically, even cruelly, in a way
that would anger Linda, Owen observed that the psychologist weighed close to two hundred pounds. Her
hair, an unusual color, sort of orange, flew off her head
like curly ribbon.

How smart is this woman, Owen wondered. How
stable? Certainly her manner of dress—gypsyish colors,
flowing skirts, ropes of beads—seemed peculiar. Would
that perhaps make those with emotional problems feel
at home with her?

"First," Travis began, reaching across the desk to
hand Owen and Linda each a pamphlet, "I'd like to
give you a booklet to read about West Four. This unit
is called, simply, West Four, because it's the west wing
and the fourth floor of Basingstoke Hospital. This way
there is no description—thus, no judgment—attached
to the name of the wing."

Obediently Owen looked down at the slender leaflet.
The cover read: WELCOME TO WEST FOUR.

Linda asked, "How long will Emily be here?"

"We can't say definitely yet. A few days at the least.
We'll see."

"Can you tell us what happened?" Owen asked.

"Only the little I know. A little after noon Emily's roommate Cordelia found Emily comatose on her bed. Cordelia called the dorm parent, who notified the dean of students, and Emily was brought here by ambulance. She was admitted by Dr. Gable, the emergency room doctor, who treated her and sent her up here. I don't yet have the entire lab report, but I can tell you that on admittance this morning Emily's blood alcohol level measured point thirty-three." She paused, then added gently, "Point four is comatose . . ."

Owen said, "Dear God."

Travis continued. "There was no note. When she was brought to the hospital and revived, she tried to run away. When I spoke with Emily, she told me she had attempted suicide because she considers herself 'too gross to live.' Do you know of any reason for her to feel this way?"

They responded together. "No."

"Clearly she is a danger to herself. We want to keep her here. We haven't had a chance to evaluate her yet. We'll be doing that today. I'll need some information right now, however." She looked at Linda. "You're Emily's mother?"

"Yes."

"And you are her father?"

Owen shook his head. "Stepfather."

"Her father lives elsewhere?"

Linda answered. "Pennsylvania. He's a cellist. He doesn't communicate much with his daughter."

"Are there other children?"

"Just one," Owen replied. "My son, Bruce. He's seventeen, almost eighteen. He's a senior at Hedden."

"And his mother?"

Owen shrugged. "She's usually traveling. We seldom hear from her."

"How long have you two been married?"

Linda and Owen spoke simultaneously. "Seven years."

"Happily?"

"Yes."

Travis looked at Owen. "What's your relationship with Emily like?"

Owen considered. He tried in all things never to lie or exaggerate. "Good. I'd say good."

"And you, Mrs. McFarland? With your daughter?"

"We're very close. We've always been. I thought—I thought we still were."

"Do you have any idea why Emily did all this?"

"No. I'm completely stunned."

"Can you give me a profile of your daughter?"

"Of course." Linda leaned forward, eager. "She's like the sun. She's bright and energetic, full of ideas and plans. She loves school and her friends. She loves books and movies and food and animals and music and her teachers. She's a very happy person." Her words made her pause. "At least I thought she was. I can't imagine why this happened."

"Have you anything to add?" Travis asked Owen.

After a moment's deliberation, Owen said, "Emily can be impulsive. Impetuous. She often acts without fully thinking things through first."

Linda shifted in her chair. "Owen, that's part of the basic definition of an adolescent."

Owen looked at his wife, then proceeded. "She's ambitious. Too tough on herself. Drives herself hard, sets standards that are hard to keep."

"But she's hardly the type to kill herself over bad grades!" Linda objected.

"No," Owen agreed. "I'd say Emily's an optimist. A fighter as well. She likes a good challenge. But she does tend to take on more than she can handle."

Linda pondered this. "But at any rate, it's too early in the semester for her to be worried about her grades . . . It has to be something else."

Dr. Travis asked, "Has Emily ever spent time in a psychiatric ward before?"

"No!" Linda realized she felt vaguely insulted by the question.

"Has she ever seen a psychiatrist or therapist or counselor?"

"No."

"Has she ever been prescribed medication for problems such as mania, depression, anorexia, anxiety, that sort of nervous disorder?"

"No."

"Has she ever attempted suicide before?"

"No, absolutely."

"How about blackouts, fainting spells, memory loss?"

"No. No, she's just been completely normal."

Travis wrote in her folder, then looked up at them both, smiling. "I think that's enough for today. I'll talk more with Emily this afternoon, after she's rested a bit."

"Can we do anything?" Linda asked.

"Yes, actually. As I said, we'll need for you to pick up some things for Emily from school. Hygienic necessities, perhaps a book, pajamas, a change of clothing."

Owen and Linda nodded.

"When you return with her things, you'll need to give them to a nurse when you come in, so they can be checked over." Reading their expressions, she hastened to explain. "Often we can spot something that the parents might not realize is potentially dangerous."

"Potentially dangerous," Linda echoed.

"Emily is here on a voluntary basis. That means she has signed herself in. She will be seen by a multidisciplinary group of professionals, including the psychiatric director of the team, the counselors and nurses, our social worker, and myself. I am the program coordinator. After we speak with Emily, we'll determine how we can be of help to her, and how long we'll want her to remain with us. For the time being, she will be restricted to this ward. She will be kept safe here. If she stays here long enough, she will be gradually given privileges to leave the ward and go out for a walk on the grounds."

Puzzled, Linda asked, "When will she be allowed to return to school?"

"Let's take this one step at a time, shall we?" Travis suggested. "Your daughter has some problems that are interfering with her ability to stay alive. We've got to sort all that out first."

"Can we visit her?"

"Of course. Visiting hours are printed in the brochure I gave you. We especially like the parents to be here on Wednesday nights for Family Group."

"Can we call her?"

"Certainly. The three pay telephones are down the hall. They're turned off during group session and after eleven at night. You will probably want to write down the numbers. You'll need to fill out the insurance forms at the desk. We'll need that done immediately."

Travis rose and ushered them to the door. As dumb as a pair of sheep, Owen and Linda let themselves be herded out of the office and to the nurses' station, where sparrow-nurse handed them a long questionnaire.

"There are desks at the other end of the hall for writing," she said as she pointed them out.

Owen sat watching as Linda filled out the forms. Emily's father's university covered her health insurance. Linda had the health insurance card in her wallet.

Linda furrowed her brow. "I hope it covers this particular kind of illness in this particular kind of hospital ward."

"If not, then the school insurance will kick in," Owen reminded her.

Inscribing the necessary information in a wavery hand, Linda completed the form and returned it to the nurse, and then she and Owen stood befuddled, staring around. Travis had disappeared. The nurse was on the phone. Through the glass of the walled "living room" three people stared zombielike at a soap opera.

"Let's go over to the school and get Emily's things and make some appointments," Owen said.

Linda nodded. Together they walked down the linoleum hallway and out through the ward's wide doors.

Chapter Four

When Dr. Travis opened the door, Emily came awake instantly.

"How are you feeling?" the doctor asked.

"Better," Emily admitted. "I didn't read the pamphlet," she apologized. "I guess I just fell back asleep."

"That's good. That's what your body needed to do. You'll have plenty of time to read the brochure." Travis didn't enter but instead stood in the doorway, holding it open. "I thought you might like to come see some of the ward."

Emily sat up and was overcome by a wave of dizziness.

"Take your time," Travis advised, as if she could see into Emily's body. "When you feel like it, we'll go to the dining room and you can have a little snack. You must be hungry."

In response Emily's stomach growled furiously. She cringed and clasped her hands over her belly. Traitorous belly. Like the shrink would believe she really wanted to die when here she was, a fat pig ready to eat.

"You won't want much," Travis continued, "but you need something to keep your blood sugar level up. Come on. I've convinced them to send you up some toast."

Dutifully Emily rose. At the doorway, Travis lightly put her hand on her back, guiding her.

"Nurses' station, offices, conference rooms." Slowly they went down the corridor. "Here's the bedroom you'll be in tomorrow."

Emily stuck her head around the door. "Looks bare."

"You'll be able to put cards, photos, on the bulletin board above your bed."

"No TV. No phone."

"There's a television in our common living room, just down this way. And there are three pay phones in this hall. This is where you'll receive and make all personal calls."

"Not much privacy."

Travis smiled. "That's right. You may place calls between seven A.M. and eleven P.M., but we ask you to keep the conversations short, no more than fifteen or twenty minutes, because there are so many others who will need to use the phones. And they will be shut off during group sessions. Here are the bathrooms. Your parents will bring you a toothbrush and toothpaste, which you may keep in your room and bring to the bathroom with you. The dining room."

Emily looked into a large cheerful room set with long tables and chairs, empty now of people. "Where does the food come from?"

"The hospital cafeteria. I've heard that it's edible, but a strong incentive for getting well."

For the second time that day, Travis's gentle sarcasm made Emily smile, made her feel not quite so . . . so fucking *pathetic*.

Travis walked over to a metal cart. "Here's your toast. And some more 7UP. If you go through this door, you'll come to the ward's own little kitchen. We don't prepare entire meals here, but we do have a microwave for popcorn, and a stove and oven so the patients can make desserts for our family nights."

They sat together at a table looking out a picture window at the grounds. To the right all was pastoral—sweeping lawns, walking paths through low hedges, trees valiantly clinging to their last shreds of leaves—but to the left, behind a high retaining wall, the bright metal of speeding cars glittered from the highway.

"We have twenty-seven beds here," Travis informed her. "At the moment there are twelve patients. Five of them are around your age, the others are young adults in their twenties. None of the people is dangerous. In fact, I think you'll like them."

Emily looked around. "Where are they now?"

"Most of them are in task-oriented group therapy. Quite a few are in chemical dependency rehabilitation programs, especially for those involved with drug abuse and alcohol. The chem depps, which is what they informally call themselves, have their own specific problems. But each person has here a schedule worked out especially for her."

The toast was cold, the butter or margarine congealed in yellow globules on the surface of the barely browned bread, but when Emily spread it with grape jelly from a little plastic packet and took a bite, she was amazed at how good it tasted.

"We've found that working in groups is helpful to everyone, so when you read our pamphlet you'll see that most of our meetings are group. Many of the problems that bring people here are shared by others."

"Not mine."

"I wouldn't be so sure," Travis disagreed. "Adolescence can be a difficult time. And all families have problems of one kind or another."

Emily sipped her 7UP and did not reply.

"Through? Shall we go on?" Travis rose, showed Emily where to toss her trash and where the cart was for her plate and utensils, and then they walked on down the corridor.

"The smoking room."

"I don't smoke."

"Good. The small group discussion room. The crafts room. Exercise room. The kitchen. Wednesday evenings the patients usually make some kind of dessert to be eaten during Family Group."

"Family Group?"

"Parents are invited to join us on Wednesday evenings, to discuss general problems, to ask questions about the hospital, and so on."

"What if you don't want to have your family come?"

"Let me answer that in a roundabout way. Tomorrow after you have a complete physical, you'll meet with the adolescent team psychiatrist for some tests, and you and I will talk some more, intensively. We'll see if we can discover what brought you here, what your special concerns are, what goals you'd like to achieve while you're here in the hospital. On your pamphlet you'll see we've left space for you to record your goals and the progress you're making toward them. What you write won't be judged; it won't even be read. It's for you to keep notes about what's going on with you. We find it's helpful for the family to visit, once a week, to remind our patients of the life they will be returning to, so they might start discussing and thinking of options for changing their lives, often in relation to their families."

They had walked in a rectangle and now were back at Emily's room, and Emily was glad, because suddenly she was exhausted. Travis was nice enough and certainly eager to help. It wasn't *her* fault that no one could help, that nothing could ever fix Emily's life.

"I'm tired."

"Then rest. Someone will wake you for dinner. And you might have visitors this evening."

"I don't want to see anyone."

"Your parents are going to return with some of your clothing and personal necessities. At that time you can ask them to bring you anything else you might need. And after Thanksgiving vacation, they can bring you your homework and school books."

"You think I'm going to be here for a long time."

"We don't know that yet."

"Will I go home for Christmas?"

Travis looked at Emily for a long moment before replying, "Let's not think that far ahead until we've done a more thorough intake on you, okay?"

Emily shrugged. Weak with fatigue, she sank onto the bed, put her hand over her eyes to block out the light, and hurried back into the protection of sleep. She heard Travis close the door.

They drove toward Hedden, stunned.

"She looked pale, but otherwise all right. Not ill."

"There's so much we don't know. So much they didn't tell us."

"Owen, she's gained so much weight."

"Perhaps she has an eating disorder."

The entrance to the school was marked by a stone lion rampant with a plaque in its mouth inscribed HEDDEN ACADEMY. A private road wound through evergreens past a pond and over a rushing stream until it arrived at what looked like a miniature Oxford. The eight stone buildings were built around a courtyard and ornamented with corner turrets and gargoyles on the waterspouts. The chapel with its grand rose window and soaring spire towered at the front while the new plebeian gymnasium hunkered down at the far end of the campus.

"Where do you want to go first?" Owen asked.

"Emily's dorm."

It was early afternoon. As they parked in the visitors' lot and walked across the fields toward Shipley Hall, students rushed past them toward the football field or the crew house. Others tossed Frisbees or stood talking in clusters beneath trees. Occasionally a student stared at them, then glanced away, embarrassed.

"They've heard about Emily."

"I'm sure they have," Owen replied, and took his wife's arm.

Shipley Hall was built especially as a women's dorm in the late sixties when Hedden, formerly a single-sex school, went coed, and consequently it was cursed with the boring boxy lines of many institutions, but blessed with many large bathrooms.

Emily's room was on the first floor. She shared it with Cordelia and Zodiac, and because they'd agreed to take a threesome, they were given the largest room on the ground floor. When Owen and Linda brought Emily in September to begin the new year, the room had been a mess of packing boxes, suitcases, and black plastic bags bulging with new linen and pillows and clothing.

Now it was neat, attractive. Using the modular desks and chests provided by the school, the girls had managed to divide the room into three areas. Zodiac's was the most obvious because of the posters of constellations and astrological signs hanging above her bed, which was brilliant beneath a spread of purple silk sprinkled with moons and stars. A gleaming black CD player squatted on her shelf, portable cases of CDs next to it, and on her desk were a camera and a Macintosh computer. All the high-tech equipment was decorated with cosmological signs and surrounded by twists of herbs and clay bowls of what looked like old grass.

Cordelia's area could have belonged to a much younger girl. Her bedspread was flowery, and several stuffed animals had been carefully tucked against the pillows. Her bureau top was littered with dainty perfume bottles, lipsticks, and small china bowls filled with rings and necklaces and bracelets. Romantic perfume and makeup ads were tacked to the wall.

Emily should have had posters of Jason Priestly and Brad Pitt on her walls; Linda remembered carefully rolling them and fitting them into a long cardboard tube for the drive down. Scarves should have been draped dramatically over the bedposts and lamp, and clothes should have been flung everywhere, because Emily was always in a hurry.

But her walls were bare, except above her bed, where from one nail a silver cross hung on a metal chain.

"What on earth?" Linda sank down onto the dark green duvet cover she had bought for Emily during a special trip to Boston the past summer. Emily had begged Linda to take her to a sale at Jordan Marsh. Emily had chosen a sky blue duvet cover and matching sheets when she entered Hedden a year ago, but this year she yearned for "a whole new look." She wanted to be "sophisticated."

But her space did not look sophisticated. It looked, except for the rumpled bed on which earlier today she had lain, stark. Bare.

"Penitential," Linda whispered. "Why?"

Last year Emily's area had been a mess, a flurry of clothes, books, cassettes, journals in pastel notebooks, letters scented with perfume. Now her electronic typewriter and cassette player were lined up on her desk, right angles matching exactly those of her tidily stacked textbooks. Next to the typewriter lay three pens in rigid line. Her bureau top was bare except for—Linda rose to make certain—a Bible, bound in white leather, the one Linda's mother gave Emily several years ago.

"Linda."

Linda turned. Owen had lifted the duvet to expose, beneath Emily's bed, boxes of cheese crackers, bags of chips, a pile of chocolate bars, a litter of empty wrappers.

"Owen. What's going on?"

Grim-faced, Owen shook his head.

"Clothes," Linda murmured. "She needs a change of clothes. Pajamas. Underwear. Toothbrush."

Emily's bureau drawers were so neat it was as if she had folded the clothes and lined them up with the edge of a ruler. The drawer of underwear, which just this summer Emily had begun to call her lingerie, was full of—underwear. Plain white waist-high, full-cut cotton briefs, the kind that were sold in packages of three or twelve. And sports bras. Only sports bras.

"Where," Linda wondered aloud, "is Emily's lingerie?"

She found it stuffed away inside a brown duffel bag meant for dirty laundry, all Emily's pink, lavender, or flowered panties and bras, as well as some shirts and skirts Linda had thought Emily loved. Upending them into a pile on the closet floor, Linda took the duffel bag and filled it with underwear, white flannel pajamas, socks, sweatpants, and sweatshirts, noticing how large everything was. In the top drawer of Emily's bureau she found her travel kit with toothbrush, deodorant, and soap. Clean hunter green towels and washcloths were stacked on a closet shelf; Linda took one of each.

"Should I take a book?" she asked Owen.

"Maybe a novel?"

Linda scanned the bookshelf and found only texts.

"Mrs. McFarland?"

Cordelia Analan entered the room, her large blue eyes dark with emotion, her brow furrowed.

"Oh, Cordelia," Linda said, gathering the girl into her arms, "are you all right?"

Cordelia was the protected only child of two wealthy professionals who had had her late in life. A picture-book girl, as pale as a Botticelli, as sweet and sentimental as a Whitman's Sampler, Cordelia played piano, dressed in flowing ankle-length dresses, and wore her blond hair to her waist, often tied up in elaborate braids.

Now her large eyes shimmered with tears. "Is Emily going to—be okay?"

"She's out of physical danger. But she has to stay in

the psychiatric ward for a while, until we find out what's going on with her. Do you have any idea, Cordelia?"

"No."

"Anything at all would help."

Cordelia turned from Linda and sank onto her bed and with one hand twisted a strand of hair that had escaped from the braids. "She was different this fall."

Linda sat down next to Cordelia. Owen quietly settled on Emily's bed, leaned forward, rested his elbows on his knees. "Different, how?"

"Well, like, this summer she was so much fun? And when school started she was all serious."

"Were her classes difficult?" Owen asked, and Linda asked at the same time, "Were her teachers tough?"

Cordelia shrugged. "Kind of, I guess. They're all hard."

"What about boys?" Linda queried.

Cordelia's eyes flew to Linda's face. "Jorge Avila."

"Yes?" Linda prompted.

"He liked her." Cordelia shrugged. "But she stopped liking him."

"Why?" Linda pressed. "Did he do something?"

"No. I don't think so. I mean, she stopped talking to everyone, even to me. She just, I don't know, she only wanted to be by herself."

"Did you talk to her about it?"

"Sure. I tried to. But she wouldn't talk. She was kind of weird. And she hid food and skipped study hall and sneaked back into the dorm and ate it. Sometimes we even heard her rustling around in the Doritos in the middle of the night." Cordelia blushed. "I'm sorry."

"Cordelia, we need to know."

Owen asked, "Did she talk about killing herself?"

Cordelia flushed and her eyes streamed with tears. "No! Never!" Sobbing into her hands, she cried, "She was my best friend and I don't know anything!"

Linda reminded her, "You saved her life today, Cordelia."

"I just came back for a book. It was so scary."

Owen said, "We should go. We have an appointment with Lorimer."

"Will you be okay?" Linda asked Cordelia.

The girl nodded shakily.

Linda flashed a look at her husband, then said, "I'm not sure which building is Tuttle Hall. Can you show us?"

"Sure." Cordelia blew her nose and took a few deep breaths, then stood up. "I'll take you there."

The campus grounds were still beautiful. Well-tended lawns swept down to tennis courts and playing fields while in the distance giant evergreens watched the campus like sentinels. Yellow mums in stone urns adorned the entrance to Tuttle Hall. The walk and the fresh air revived Cordelia and she said good-bye with a smile.

Bob Lorimer was waiting for them. After shaking hands, he gestured toward the chairs facing his desk.

"How is Emily?" he asked.

Linda answered, "Out of danger, physically. But she won't talk to us. She won't even look at us. They want her to remain at the hospital."

Bob Lorimer was a kind man, well liked by the students and parents as well. Perhaps because he was so large, he spoke with a soft voice, and in that gentle voice he assured the McFarlands that this sort of episode was more common than they might think, especially among adolescent girls.

"I've spoken with several of her teachers, and they all tell me that Emily started the school year in good spirits. She worked hard and was alert. Responsive. Recently, though, her work was beginning to suffer, and she seemed inattentive in class. Again, this is common among adolescents. It seemed no cause for worry. One thing"—he cleared his throat—"I mention it only because it is one thing we can pinpoint as a change in Emily's behavior—she has been attending church in Basingstoke. The Methodist church."

Linda was puzzled. "We didn't know that. We don't attend church regularly at home, except at Christmas."

Owen added, "The last we heard, Emily wanted to be a pagan."

"The school holds a nondenominational service every Sunday morning," Bob Lorimer continued. "People attend mostly for the music. I sing in the choir. I don't think I've ever seen Emily there. I don't know what relevance her church attendance has, if any, but I thought you should know."

"Of course. Thank you."

"Emily is a good student. Everyone likes her. We're concerned about her, and what we'd like to propose is simply that we put her on medical leave for a few days. I've spoken with the Head about this. As I said, Emily's grades have been on a downhill slide during the past few weeks, but we know Emily is an intelligent and responsible girl, certainly capable of missing some classes and still passing the courses. If she needs to remain at Basingstoke for a while, we will need to consider some other options. Is there anything else . . . ?"

"We need to find Bruce," Owen said. "We want to tell him about Emily and find out whether he knows anything that might help us."

"Actually, I called Bruce into my office earlier this afternoon. I didn't want him hearing gossip from the students. You can imagine how fast word flies around here." Lorimer rose. "Come out to the main office. I'll have Mrs. Echevera look up his schedule for you." Holding the door open, Lorimer said to Owen, "Your son is a great guy. He's really come a long way in three years."

"The school has been good for him," Owen replied.
But not quite so good for her daughter, Linda

thought, at once chastising herself; Bruce was her step-son. She should be happy for him, proud of him. And she was. She'd never thought Bruce and Emily were in any kind of contest. And she didn't think that now.

Chapter Five

As Owen and Linda crossed the campus, they were so engrossed in their thoughts that it took a moment for Bruce's voice to register.

"Dad! Hey! Linda!"

Coming toward them from the library beneath a canopy of shadows were a trio of healthy young men: Lionel with his shining blond hair, Terry in madras trousers, a flowered Hawaiian shirt, and heavy black Buddy Holly glasses, and Bruce in a sweater and khakis, looking so tall and fine and strong that Owen's heart lifted with pride and Linda exclaimed, "Oh, Owen, isn't he handsome!"

Owen and Linda waved. Bruce spoke briefly to his friends, then began to run toward his parents, a great wide spontaneous smile on his face. Then he stopped, remembering why his parents were there, and his smile dissolved.

"Hey," he said somberly when he reached them.

"You've heard about Emily?" Owen asked.

Bruce nodded. "She okay?"

"Yes. But she has to stay in the hospital. Psychiatric ward."

Bruce flinched. He looked stricken, his face at odds with the helplessly cheerful gleam of his uncontrollable curly red hair and the sparkle of sweat in the curly hairs on his arms. "Sucks."

Linda asked, "Do you have any idea what could have caused this?"

Bruce shook his head. "I don't see much of her. I mean, all our classes are different. Her dorm's across campus from mine."

"Have you heard anything? Could you ask around? She won't talk to us at all."

"Man, she *must* be sick if she's not talking." The words burst from his mouth before he stopped to think. Grimacing, he quickly added, "Sorry."

"No," Linda told him. "You're right."

They walked toward Bates Hall, passing beneath the shadows of great-limbed copper beeches and extravagant maples and oaks. Several students, enclosed by headphones in worlds of their own, jogged past. A golden lab lumbered along beside one of the students and by the entrance to the dorm another dog lay blissed out in the late afternoon sun. From one direction came the throb of rock music, from another, a capella singing.

They entered Bates Hall through massive oak doors. Hedden had once been an all-male school, a stronghold for the elite, and the architecture reflected that. From the large foyer, wide stairs wound upward toward a landing baroquely radiant with stained-glass windows. The newel post was a carved and beaded shining gloss of mahogany. Oblivious to such elegance, Hedden boys rushed past the McFarlands, up the stairs to change from sports and prepare for dinner, nodding or mumbling greetings as they passed Bruce.

"Uh, you want to come up to my room?" Bruce asked. "It's kind of a mess."

"No thanks," Owen replied. "We're going to spend the night in Basingstoke. We'd better get over to the Academy Inn and get a room. Want to go out to dinner with us?"

"Well . . ." Bruce hesitated. His neck turned pink. "Could I bring a friend?"

Owen began, "I don't think this is the appropriate—"

Linda intervened. "Sure. As long as you don't mind that your friend knows about Emily."

"Everyone knows about Emily by now," Bruce said with blunt honesty. "It's just the way it is here."

"Linda and I will check into the hotel and get organized and come back for you in, how about an hour?"

"Great," Bruce said. "See you then. Oh, uh, Dad—I know this is the wrong time to ask about this, but did you bring my clothes for New York?"

"We didn't even think about it," Owen told him. "I'll go back to the farm tomorrow and get them to you sometime in the morning. Will that be okay?"

"Sure. Thanks."

"What time do you leave on Wednesday?" Linda asked.

"Vacation starts at noon sharp. Whit's parents are springing for a limo to the airport," he added, unable to check a grin.

"*Very* nice," Linda told him.

Just then a tall, exotically handsome boy entered, clad in tennis whites, carrying a racket. His glossy black hair was held back at the neck in a ponytail, accentuating his olive skin and dramatic cheekbones.

"Hey," he said to Bruce.

"Hey, Jorge," Bruce replied, all at once looking gawky and innocent, a boy in the presence of this man.

The man's name set off a warning bell in Linda's mind: Jorge. Cordelia had said Emily liked someone named Jorge.

The man took the steps two at a time. When he was out of earshot, Linda asked, sotto voce, "Who was *that*?"

"Jorge Avila."

"Good Lord. Bruce, I think Emily had a crush on him."

Bruce shrugged. "Every girl here has a crush on Jorge."

"So we'll pick you up in an hour?" Owen asked.

"Great." Bruce looked up the stairs, half turning to go, then looked at his father and asked, "How long will Emily be at the hospital?"

"We're not sure."

"Can I visit her? Would it, uh, help?"

Tears sprang into Linda's eyes. "Oh, Bruce. Thanks for offering. I don't know what will help Emily. But why don't you come to the hospital tonight. It might cheer her up to see you."

"And Bruce," Owen added, "try to think of anything, no matter how insignificant, that would help us figure out what's troubling Emily."

"Sure."

Bruce headed off, up the stairs, leaving Owen and Linda to themselves as they stepped out into the dimming light of early evening.

Basingstoke, once a colonial village, was now a bedroom community for Boston. The Academy Inn was situated on the main street of the small town of Basingstoke and existed mainly because of Hedden Academy and Basingstoke Hospital. A charming, stately Greek Revival building, its many small rooms were pleasantly decorated. The dining room in the front parlor served a limited menu of delicious food. One of the first things the McFarlands learned when Bruce was admitted to Hedden was to reserve months ahead of time for rooms during Parents' Weekend. Those who didn't were relegated to one of the many chain hotels situated off Route 93.

So it was with a satisfying sense of familiarity that the McFarlands checked in and carried their bags through the wide hall to the curving, carpeted front stairs. Their room was pleasantly furnished in reproduction early American. Owen dropped into a wing chair; Linda sank onto the bed, near the bedside table with the telephone.

After a moment's silence, she looked at Owen. "Do I have to call Simon?"

"I think you should."

Linda called her ex-husband so rarely that she had to look through the small black address book in her purse in order to find his phone number. She didn't expect him to be home; he traveled a great deal with his chamber quartet. But his newest wife answered and when Linda told her there was an emergency, she didn't hesitate but quickly carried the phone to Simon; Linda could hear the other woman's movements through the house, and then the sound of cello music as she entered Simon's studio. For an instant Linda was surrounded by that life again, where everything was devoted to Simon's music.

"Yes?" As always, his greeting was brusque.

"Simon, Emily's in the hospital. In the psychiatric ward. She took some pills today and drank some alcohol, in what we think was a suicide attempt. She's okay, but they want to keep her there for observation."

"You have the information for the health insurance."

"Yes, I do. But I also thought I should let you know." Linda's throat convulsed. "Simon, perhaps it would help her if you came to see her. If you showed her you care—"

"I can't. My schedule's packed."

"Perhaps you could call her, then. Would you like the number of the hospital?"

"No. I don't think I could help and I don't have the time."

There was nothing more to say but good-bye.

Settling the receiver back onto the phone cradle, Linda hissed, "I *hate* him." A thought struck her. "Do you think Emily hates herself for being, at least genetically, this man's daughter? Or because he has ignored her all her life, do you think she feels rejected? Oh, I could kill him."

"If that's what's going on with her," Owen replied sensibly, "then it's a good thing she is where she is. She can work it through, get some help." He rose. "I'm going down to the newsstand to buy a newspaper. Need anything?"

"No, thanks. I'll just . . ." What? What could she do now that could be of any use? "I'll just lie here a while."

She settled back onto the pillows, taking deep breaths, trying to calm herself, but her mind was a scattered thing, mercury from a broken thermometer. Was that how her daughter felt? From this vantage point she saw that here and there on the ceiling the paint was curling off. This was oddly comforting. The same was happening to the ceilings on the farm. Humidity, old age. She had always felt at home with imperfection. She'd always admired peculiarities, change, eccentricities, challenges, found them more interesting than finished flawlessness.

So why did she feel so bleak and frightened for her daughter now? Perhaps because she had no control here. Her daughter's life had been saved by strangers . . . and it would be strangers who would, with luck, heal her daughter's soul.

Dark.had fallen by the time they returned to Bates to pick up Bruce and his friend. It was colder now, and the wind had risen, and when the car lights flared over the lawn, they illuminated two figures: Bruce in his overcoat, and a young woman, her hair tossing in the wind.

"It's a girl," Owen said, stupefied.

Linda laughed. "You didn't guess?"

"How did you know? He didn't tell us."

"Well, Owen, he blushed," Linda whispered the

words, for the young people had rushed to the car and were crawling into the back seat.

"Dad, Linda, this is Alison Cartwright."

The girl was lovely, with long blond hair and enormous blue eyes.

She lived in Manhattan. "I'm hoping when Bruce comes for Thanksgiving at Whit's that he'll be able to come by my place. I'd love for my parents to meet him."

"Where do you live?" Linda asked.

"Park and Sixty-fifth, only a few blocks from Whit's." She smiled conspiratorially at Bruce.

At the restaurant, their hostess, a tiny woman wearing very high heels with her hair whipped up like topping on a sundae, showed them to their table.

"Here you are, dawlings," she growled as she handed them their menus.

Alison was a vegetarian, and to Owen and Linda's surprise, Bruce was now, also.

Owen thought vegetarianism was bunk. "Now what made you—" Owen began, but Linda flashed him a warning look, and Owen turned toward Alison and finished the sentence "—choose Hedden Academy?"

"My dad went there, and my granddad before him. So I sort of had to go. But I'm glad I did. I love it."

"Where are you applying to college?" Linda asked.

"Westhurst. It's *the* new hot liberal arts college. I'm a pianist and if I go there, it will open all sorts of doors for me. But it's super hard to get in. So many people are applying."

That, Linda thought, explained why Bruce had surprised them this summer by talking about applying to Westhurst. For Bruce was smitten, it was obvious. Linda's heart ached for him. She wanted to take him aside and advise him not to look quite so lovestruck. As she recalled, young women could be fickle and cruel to someone so obviously enamored. But as the evening went on, she saw the way Alison looked at Bruce, and was reassured, and then moved. Good Lord, she thought, could this be love, the real, passionate, tormenting, overwhelming first love that sent one's world reeling? Of course she had known it had to happen sometime for both Bruce and Emily; she just hadn't realized it would happen so soon. Could Owen sense it, too?

Bruce and Alison split a pizza; Linda and Owen each ordered pasta primavera and a glass of red wine. Bruce and Alison kept up a steady chatter about their courses, Christmas plans, school gossip.

"The school paper has a Christmas poem in it," Bruce told them. "The first letters of each line spell out—"

"Don't say it, Bruce!" Alison burst out, laughing.

"They're old enough, they can handle it."

"It's too embarrassing, let them read it."

Linda watched the two argue, laughing, their faces glowing as they looked at one another.

"You're not eating anything," Owen quietly said to his wife.

"I'm not hungry."

"You should still eat."

"My sister was in West Four when she was at Hedden," Alison said suddenly.

Owen and Linda stared. Bruce said, "No way."

"She was. For about three weeks. They're really nice there."

Linda asked, "Why was your sister—"

"Bulimia. You know, she made herself vomit."

"Did they help her?"

"Oh, yes. She's still working on it, though." Alison looked down at her empty plate. "I'm the youngest, so I get to be the spoiled baby. I guess since she's the oldest she has to be perfect."

"Sounds right to me," Bruce said. "I'm the oldest and I'm perfect."

"Right." Alison nudged his arm and grinned.

"Do you still want to see Emily?" Owen asked.

"Sure. If it's all right. If you think . . ." Bruce's voice trailed away.

As they drove back to the school to drop off Alison, leaves whirled down through the dark, splattering against the windshield. Owen had to turn on the wipers to scrape them away.

As they neared the school, Alison said, "I thought I might tell you . . . you might ask Emily . . . I saw her with Jorge Avila."

Linda turned to look back at the girl. "Where?"

"In the woods. At night." She shrugged apologetically.

"What were you doing in the woods?" Bruce asked, an edge in his voice.

"Smoking. And just Salems!"

"What about Emily?" Linda prompted.

"She . . . she was upset."

"How? Why?"

"I don't know why. But . . . but I heard someone crying and yelling, and then Emily ran across the lawn to the dorm, and Jorge came out from behind the trees and followed."

"Was he chasing her?"

"No. No, he went the other direction."

"I'll smash his face in," Bruce muttered.

"Bruce, don't talk like that," Alison said quickly. "I wouldn't have said anything . . . I don't know what happened. I just thought you might . . ."

"It's helpful to know," Linda assured the girl. "Thanks for telling us."

They stopped in front of Shipley Hall, Alison's dorm. As Alison got out on her side of the car, Bruce opened his door.

"I thought you were going to the hospital with us," Owen said.

"I changed my mind."

"Please do, Bruce," Linda said. "Emily might talk to you. She won't talk to us."

"I could help her more if I stay here and find out what's going on," Bruce retorted, leaving the car and slamming the door.

"Thanks for dinner, Mr. and Mrs. McFarland." Looking anxiously at Bruce, Alison tugged the collar of her coat up around her neck and headed off into the wind toward her dorm.

"Don't do anything stupid, son," Owen said, but Bruce had already run off, and was too far away to hear.

Chapter Six

❧

Travis had gone home for the day, and it was a huge black man named Beldon who led Emily into the dining room at five o'clock. He wore street clothes—baggy trousers, a striped jersey, high tops. His pock-marked face was vaguely familiar, like a retired sports celebrity selling aspirin on TV; he looked like he could be strong when necessary.

"Ladies and gentlemen," Beldon announced when they entered the dining room. "We have a new guest with us tonight. I'd like to introduce Emily Scaive from Hedden Academy. You all be nice to her, hear?"

Perhaps six people looked up at her. About six others stared gloomily at their plates. They all looked normal to Emily, but then she guessed she probably looked pretty normal to them.

"Sit with me," suggested a guy about Emily's age, rising.

He was massively handsome, Emily thought, suddenly nervous.

"Keith Wight." He held out his hand and Emily shook it, then followed him to the table set near the stainless steel cart. "See, here's the deal: we can't be allowed to go down to the cafeteria, so they send up a menu every morning and we check what we want from their awesome list of delectable gourmet meals. Of course since you're new here, you'll have to take what they sent you tonight."

Emily stacked her tray with utensils, a paper napkin, a plate of macaroni and cheese, broccoli stewed into submission, a carton of milk, and a bowl of apple crisp. Beldon grabbed up a bowl of apple crisp and ate it as he strolled around the room.

"The only way to convince your palate this is edible is to smother the food with salt," Keith was saying, "and salt *of course* as we all know makes you retain water and *that* makes you depressed, but since the main purpose of this hospital is to provide fine working conditions for the kitchen crew, things aren't about to change." As they sat down at the table, he asked without taking a breath, "So what are you here for?"

Emily just looked at him.

"Don't pay any attention to him," said the woman sitting next to Emily. Her hair was lank, her eyes lusterless, and she was only turning her food over and over. "He thinks he's the Kathie Lee of West Four."

"All right, I'll guess," Keith continued, unfazed. Folding his arms, he leaned back in his chair and studied Emily. "Okay, it's not bulimia or anorexia."

"Definitely not chem depp," added the guy seated next to Keith. He was in his early twenties and lean, with black circles around his eyes and a slight tremor to his hands.

"And we all know it takes one to know one," said Keith.

The chem depp stuck out his hand. "I'm Arnold."

"Hi, Arnold." Emily shook his hand.

"I'm Cynthia."

Emily returned Cynthia's shy smile. "Hi."

"Cynthia's manic-depressive," Keith said. "She gets great drugs."

"Why are you here?" Emily asked.

"Split personality," Keith answered archly. "*I'm* gay but my parents' son isn't."

Cynthia said, "She looks situational to me."

"Yeah, I think she's not endogenous," Arnold agreed.

"What does that mean?" Emily asked.

"Girl, you will learn such great words in here! Endogenous means you're here for a problem in your system, like chem depp or neurosis or manic-depression. Situational means you're normal but something happened. So that's what we think you are. Are we right?"

Emily nodded.

"What happened?" Cynthia asked.

Emily shrugged and looked down at her plate.

"You go to Hedden?" Arnold asked.

Emily nodded.

"Must be nice to be rich," Cynthia muttered.

Emily looked at her. "We're not rich."

"Right," Arnold said.

"We're not. It's just that we live on a farm in the middle of Massachusetts and the schools there . . ." She couldn't find the energy to continue.

"Do you hate Hedden?" Cynthia asked.

"No. It's a great school."

"In-ter-est-ing." Keith stroked an invisible Freudian goatee. "So it's not the school."

"Is it love?" Cynthia asked.

Emily shook her head, but Arnold leaned forward. "You're lying. She's lying. I can tell. It is love. Look at her!"

Emily raised her eyes to his. "It is *not* love."

"Oooh," Keith cooed. "Honey, you're turning red. I do believe you're lying to us."

"And I do believe you're a bunch of morons," Emily snapped back, angry. "Believe me, you don't have a clue. You aren't even *close*."

"Children," Beldon said from behind her back, "play nicely."

"We've got to hurry." The seriously overweight,

pasty-skinned man at the end of the table spoke in a monotone. "We'll miss the beginning."

"*Star Trek* reruns at seven o'clock," Keith informed Emily.

"We all have to watch them," Cynthia added, grinning. "Bill gets unruly if we don't."

"He's got a little problem with reality," Keith said under his breath.

"We've all got a little problem with reality," muttered Arnold.

"We've got to hurry," Bill said.

Emily hadn't touched her food, but when the others rose, she rose with them, scraped her debris into a trash barrel, stacked her tray on the cart, and followed Bill as he lumbered out the door and down the corridor toward the glassed-in living area. The television was mounted up high, out of reach, near the ceiling, but there was a remote control, which Bill grabbed up.

"Hurry," Bill said.

She dragged a chair into the spot Keith and Cynthia had left for her between them. Somehow, she realized, she'd joined a group, this collection of peculiar characters who seemed to be the elite of West 4, for as the others entered the room, they sat in chairs scattered elsewhere instead of joining the semicircle Emily was in. Bill had gotten a chair with arms and she could see from the corner of her eyes how his hands clutched the ends of the arms, as if for support during turbulence.

She settled back in her own chair and surrendered to the hypnosis of television.

It was a little like being back in her dorm, watching television with her friends, and when *Star Trek* ended, and Emily looked around, she was startled to see her parents standing patiently outside the glass wall.

Bill, Cynthia, Arnold, and Keith rose.

"Where are you going?" Emily asked, alarmed.

"We've got group. You will, too, later," Cynthia assured her.

Keith darted forward. "Tell me what you're in for and I'll stay here with you, give you moral support."

Arnold grabbed Keith's arm and lightly twisted it behind his back. "You terrible little ferret. Get out of here."

They half shuffled, half wrestled from the room. Some of the other patients remained, two engrossed in a chess game, another one reading, another just staring at his hands.

Linda smiled and waved at Emily as if she were on a train arriving from another country. She looked so pitifully hopeful it made Emily want to weep. Emily wished the glass were some solid material from *Star Trek* technology that could not be shattered, that would keep them apart forever.

In fact the door was standing open, and Linda and Owen entered the living area.

"Hi, honey," Linda said. "How are you?"

Emily shrugged. Her mother smelled so good, so familiar, like cinnamon and flowers, it made Emily feel weak and childish. But the perfume was a lie. Emily was not a child, and her mother had not protected her.

"Shall we sit down over here?" Linda suggested brightly.

They settled in an empty corner of the room around a card table. Emily folded her arms over her chest defensively and stared fiercely at the floor, fighting back tears.

"You look good, honey," Linda said gently.

"We brought you some clothes," Owen said. "The nurse has the stuff. It's in your duffel bag."

"Cordelia said to tell you hello."

"We're staying at the Academy Inn."

"We had dinner there tonight. It wasn't bad. A little on the heavy side, what I suppose they call 'traditional.'" Suddenly Linda reached across the table and put her hand on Emily's. "Sweetie, sweetie, Emily. Can't you tell us what's going on?"

Emily didn't want to look up; she couldn't bear to see her mother's expectant face, her furrowed brow, eyes open so wide, as if they were spotlights shining on Emily's darkness. When her mother touched her hand, Emily snatched it away and hid it in her lap. She was one inch away from screaming at her mother. From hitting her stupid face.

Owen cleared his throat. "We took Bruce out to dinner. He says hello. He said he'd come tonight, but we didn't know . . ." He let the sentence trail off.

"He brought a *girl* with him!" Linda exclaimed, sounding as if she were talking to a preschooler. "Alison Cartwright. Do you know her?" When Emily didn't respond, Linda babbled on. "She's lovely. Good sense of humor. She lives in New York. Bruce will get to see her when he goes to New York with Whit. Maybe that's *why* he wanted to go to New York with Whit. I mean he hasn't been close to Whit before this year, and suddenly . . . Emily, I wish you would talk to me. I'm so worried about you."

Owen said, "Emily, we want to help you. We'll do anything we can to help you."

"Please, honey," Linda urged. "If you could just talk to us . . . Emily, you're my brave, strong darling girl! What could be so bad—"

Emily stood up so fast her chair fell over. "Leave me alone!" she shouted. "I don't want to talk to you! Can't you *get that*?" She glared at them, teeth bared, hands clenched. "I don't want to talk to you ever again! I don't want to see you ever again. I *hate* you!" Her mother's face withered, her eyes were full of pain. Emily ran from the room.

Beldon found her in her little cell of a room. She was crying again, the horrible retching, ripping-up crying that she sometimes thought would eviscerate her with its strength. Beldon shut the door and leaned against it. "You okay?"

"No, I'm not okay!" Emily yelled. "Does it look like I'm fucking okay? I want to die, all right? I don't want to live another moment!"

"Why don't you lie down and rest a bit? We've got adolescent group/young adult in half an hour."

"I don't want to be in your stupid group! I don't want to be anywhere!" She dragged her fingernails down her cheeks, drawing blood. "I just want to die. Why won't you let me die?"

"Oh, honey, now look what you've done," Beldon said, coming over and taking her hands in his.

Sitting next to her on the bed, he wrapped his arms around her and held her while she cried. He was so large and strong and sexless. Emily wanted to dissolve into his body.

After a while, when she'd exhausted herself, Beldon said, "I'm going to get a nurse now to put some ointment on those scratches. We don't want you getting infected. And she'll give you something to help you rest a bit."

"Make her give me a lot," Emily said. She collapsed onto the bed. The pain in her belly was so great she wanted to gnaw it out with her teeth. Her hands burrowed under her sweatshirt. She clawed at the flesh of her fat stomach. That pain was clear, brilliant; it distracted her from the other pain. For a while.

After a while a fat old nurse came in with two pills and a paper cup of water. Emily sat up to take them, then sat docilely as the nurse gently washed her face and dotted it with antiseptic cream. The nurse smelled like vanilla and was restfully quiet. She didn't say a word, but hummed a waltzy kind of tune under her breath. When she left, Emily curled up on her bed in a fetal position, saying to herself, "It will stop soon. It will stop."

And in a while the pills took effect and she slept. At

some point she was aware that Keith stuck his head in the door. "Hey." He gave her the thumbs-up sign. "Looks like you got some good drugs. Way to go."

Later the humming nurse came in to escort her to the bathroom where she listlessly pretended to brush her teeth, then back to her cell where she helped Emily change out of her clothes and into her pajamas. Then she tucked Emily into bed as if she were a child. Emily knew that if the old nurse had a clue about how filthy Emily really was, she wouldn't treat her so gently. She wouldn't even touch her.

All the rooms of the Academy Inn had a kind of old-sweater-and-lavender smell that over the years had become so familiar to Linda that it was homey, and in the very early morning light sifting through the curtains, she floated on the tide of wakefulness, incorporating that aroma into her dream.

In her dream she and Owen and Emily and Bruce as well were together at Linda's grandmother's house and in the logic of dreams Linda was young, even younger than Emily, which made a kind of sense, because her grandmother had died when she was thirteen. They were waiting for her grandmother's cinnamon buns to come from the oven. They were safe. They were all safe. Her grandmother's cat was purring erratically and Linda knew with the liquid knowledge of the dream that the noise was really Owen snoring in the bed next to hers.

The phone rang, shattering the dream.

Linda lurched upright in bed, her heart thrashing in her chest.

She stared at the instrument on the bedside table. Its imperative shrill was different from those on the farm, more electric, a kind of electronic bleat.

The clock on the bedside table said 7:30.

Owen picked up the phone.

Chapter Seven

The blood hammered so loudly in Linda's ears that for a moment she couldn't hear, could only see Owen's face, which was like thunder.

Owen slammed down the phone. "That wasn't about Emily. That was Dean Lorimer. About Bruce."

"Bruce?"

"There's been an incident at school. Last night Bruce assaulted Jorge Avila and beat him up. There were witnesses. They say Jorge hit Bruce, too, but in self-defense; Bruce started it. Because of what's going on with Emily, they waited until this morning to notify us. They want us to come to the school as soon as we can."

"Good Lord. That's not like Bruce. He's the least violent boy I know."

Throwing back the covers, Owen said, "Not anymore."

Hastily they dressed and hurried to the dining room to grab Styrofoam cups of coffee, which they drank as they drove to Hedden Academy.

When they arrived at Tuttle Hall Mrs. Echevera immediately announced them to Bob Lorimer. They entered his inner sanctum to find Bruce waiting, slumped in a chair, all elbows and knees and ears. His right eye was black and swollen; his upper lip was cut and puffy. He looked exhausted.

Lorimer reached across the desk to shake the Mc-

Farlands' hands with great solemnity, part of a ritual, Owen suspected, meant to indicate to Bruce that the three adults were allies. They all sat.

Owen looked at his son and asked, "What happened?"

Bruce stared at the floor. His parents stared at him.

Over the past four years Bruce had gone through many radical physical transformations, the most dramatic during his second year at Hedden, when he grew his hair past his shoulders and let it fall over his forehead so that it veiled his face. Owen and Linda hadn't made an issue of it and neither had the school, because he was proving to be an exemplary student. This summer while outwardly Bruce resembled his friends more than ever before with his J.F.K. Jr. haircut and clothes, he seemed somehow lost in those clothes. Part of this was from his adherence to the current style: at Hedden the boys were not allowed to wear blue jeans, although, oddly enough, the girls were, and except during sports were required to tuck their polo or button-down cotton shirts into their khakis or flannels or trousers, so for all the boys it was a symbol of rebellion to wear their shirttails out. This led to their buying shirts of larger sizes so that when the shirttails were out, they were aggressively out, like flags or banners of independence hanging nearly to their knees. Also they wore their pants low on their hips so that the hems dragged on the ground, to be eventually ripped and worn and ragged, which coordinated with their scuffed, ripped, and withered leather loafers; Bruce bought a new pair of Top-Siders at the beginning of the year and tried his best to make them look old immediately. He was proudest of them when they were not merely worn but ravaged, so that the sole was a lacework of holes that flopped loose from the upper part of the shoe with every step. All the boys wore their shoes that way; one could hear them coming down the halls by the flapping.

This morning Bruce wore a blue button-down oxford cloth shirt tucked into his khakis. With his bruised face he looked like a boxer in banker's drag.

Staring at Bruce, Lorimer said, "Last night around ten o'clock, Bruce went to Jorge Avila's room, grabbed him up from his desk, shook him, called him a few insulting names, and punched him in the nose." He shot a look at the McFarlands. "I have this from Jorge's roommate, who witnessed the entire thing." Looking back at Bruce, he continued, "Jorge tried to defend himself without actually entering into a brawl, but Bruce was persistent, and the two young men ended up exchanging several blows."

"Is Jorge okay?" Linda asked.

Lorimer replied, "He's all right. Bruised here and there."

"Bruce, what's going on?" Owen demanded, his voice not unkind.

Bruce didn't reply.

Lorimer said, "I'm sure you're aware of the rules set down in the school handbook about altercations of this nature. Of course over the four years they're here, young men do occasionally engage in this kind of dispute, and we try to overlook it, especially if the men can shake hands and apologize. But if it happens too often, we will find it necessary to suspend the instigator. Mr. Phillips, the dorm parent, heard the brawl, separated the young men, reported the incident to me. This morning I had both Bruce and Jorge in my office, and they apologized to each other and shook hands. But I'm not satisfied. I would like to know what caused Bruce to start the fight."

They waited. Bruce stared at the floor, his face adamantine. Linda knew that look well; she'd seen it on Owen's face often. Both men could be monumentally stubborn.

"Does it have anything to do with Emily?" Linda

asked. Glancing at Lorimer, she explained, "Emily had a crush on Jorge."

Bruce wouldn't reply.

His voice lowering to a growl, Owen said, "Answer your stepmother, Bruce."

"No." Bruce spoke to the floor.

For a few long moments they all sat in an uncomfortable silence. Then Lorimer stood. "Very well. We don't have any thumbscrews at this institution; we aren't going to try to force Bruce to tell us what set him off. But I will tell Bruce, here in the presence of his parents, that if anything like this happens again, he will go directly before the disciplinary board, and my recommendation will be suspension. Which, I might remind you, would not look good on college applications. I won't put up with violence and recalcitrance in any of my students. Bruce, you're excused. Go to your class. Mrs. Echevera will give you a late slip."

Bruce rose, and without looking at his parents, slouched from the room.

Lorimer shook his head. "I have no idea what's going on," he admitted. "I don't need to tell you that this behavior isn't typical of Bruce."

"It must involve Emily," Linda said.

"Perhaps. But maybe not. We've had many sets of siblings pass through Hedden Academy, Mrs. McFarland, and you'd be surprised at how separate their lives and their intrigues and dramas can be." Pulling off his glasses and taking his handkerchief from his pocket, he polished them, put them back on, and said with a smile, as if he now could see the world more brightly, "How's Emily?"

Owen equivocated. "We're taking it day by day."

"Well, good luck." Lorimer rose and they were politely dismissed.

*T*he *Basingstoke Café* had always been a favorite place for breakfast for all four of them. The food was excellent, and over the years they had come to appreciate the high-backed booths that let them talk in privacy. Now Linda and Owen sat across from one another in a booth next to a window box of artificial geraniums, over plates of food they knew was delicious but scarcely had the heart to eat.

"I don't understand what's going on with either one of them," Owen said.

"I'm sure Bruce beating up Jorge had something to do with Emily. It would be too much of a coincidence otherwise."

"Whatever his reason, his behavior was way out of bounds. The school might be indulgent but I'm in no mood to be. He's not going to New York."

"Owen. Wait a moment. Let's talk this over."

"What's to talk over? Bruce beat someone up. He's got to learn that his behavior has consequences."

"All right, I agree, but let it be different consequences. Owen, this trip means so much to him."

"He should have thought of that before he got into a fight."

Linda looked down at her plate and counted to ten. Then she said, "Eat something. We both need to eat something."

Whit Archibald was a fairly new friend of Bruce's. Over the past three summers quite a few of Bruce's gang from Hedden had come to stay on the McFarland farm in the summer, riding the old horses and hiking up the mountains and swimming in the pond. When Linda and Owen had met Whit at Parents' Weekend in October, they'd been a bit surprised. A tall, handsome, poised young man, Whit could have posed for Ralph Lauren ads, and he seemed so much more sophisticated than Bruce that Owen and Linda were a bit baffled that Whit would want Bruce as his guest over Thanksgiving.

There was no doubt that Bruce wanted to go. "Let it be my Christmas present," he'd urged.

"It would have to be," Owen had replied. "Round-trip plane fare to New York, money for cabs, we're talking three hundred dollars."

"His parents will pay for theater tickets—"

"No. We'll give you money and you'll pay for your own."

"Great! Then I can go!"

Linda said, "I'm afraid you'll get up to something wicked in the city."

Bruce laughed. "Linda, we'll be with his parents every minute. Oh, it'll be so cool! Thanks, you guys. You're the best."

Now Linda took a deep breath. "Owen, there are several other ways to impress consequences on Bruce. But I don't think we should take this trip away from him. He's worked hard; he's been an exemplary student for three and a half years now. Guys get in fights all the time. Remember your own adolescence, remember some of the stuff you told me you got up to, and I'm sure you didn't tell me everything. Think of what some of his friends have done . . . pot, drinking, smoking in the bathrooms, hotel parties . . . Bruce hasn't done any of that. I think he deserves some credit. Some points."

"You're always too lenient," Owen said.

"You're always too harsh," Linda countered. "Make him muck out the stalls when he's home for Christmas. Or cut a cord of wood. Something useful. Owen, I feel strongly about this."

"All right," Owen said. "Fine." After a moment's thought, he added, "I have to bring him his dress coat."

"Let's do it tomorrow. We have to be back at the hospital tomorrow evening for Family Group with Emily. If we get Bruce his clothes by late tomorrow morning, that should be time enough. Their vacation doesn't start until noon."

"We might as well go home. There's nothing left we can do for Emily today."

"Wait, Owen. I think there *is* something we can do."

"What?"

"Talk to the people at the Methodist church. Find out if she confided in anyone there."

"Good idea."

"You could do that. While I talk to Jorge Avila."

"Why don't we *both* talk to him?"

"Because you would intimidate him."

"I doubt it."

"Come on. You know he'd react differently if he spoke to me alone. If I enlisted his help in a nonthreatening way. He might be willing to tell me anything he knows about Emily. But with you standing there glowering . . ."

"I won't glower."

"Please. We'll save time, too, if we do it separately."

"All right," Owen conceded. He wasn't pleased, but he could see Linda's point. He was beginning to experience a bit of the old stag/young stag tension with Bruce; he'd only get Jorge's back up if he questioned the young man about Emily. To say nothing of how his own blood would rise.

They had weighed her and tapped her and cuffed her and taken more blood, as if through scientific analysis they could discover a suicide-provoking microbe that they'd extinguish with the proper antibiotic. Now Emily sat in yet another office, facing Dr. Brinton, the ward psychiatrist. A bald man with a bulging cranium, he looked almost extraterrestrial and the eyes behind his glasses were not kind. Why had they chosen this creep to interview her? He had little tiny bloodless lips. Couldn't they see how spooky he was? Who would ever tell *him* anything?

He asked, "Have you often had thoughts of suicide?"

Perhaps if she answered some questions, he'd let her out of the room and away from him. Probably that was why they'd chosen him. She could lie. How would he know? Although if anyone had the power to read minds, this zombie did.

"No."

"Have you ever harmed yourself before?"

"No."

"Want to tell me about those scratches on your face?"

Emily didn't reply.

His chair squeaked as he leaned back. "Do you have friends at Hedden?"

"Of course."

"Close friends?"

Emily nodded.

"Do you confide in them?"

She nodded again.

"If they ask you—and know they will—why you attempted suicide, what will you tell them?"

Emily looked down at her hands. The room seemed to swell with silence. "Maybe I won't see them again."

"Don't you want to see them again?"

Emily shrugged.

"I guess they're not really close friends."

What right did he have to say something like that? She was trying to ignore his words, but they got to her, they were stirring her up inside.

"So. No close friends at Hedden." He wrote something down.

Angry, she snapped, "I didn't say that."

"How about your relationship with your parents and your brother?"

"Stepbrother."

"Are you close to them?"

She didn't answer.

"You and Bruce get along okay? Parents treat you both fairly?"

This time she let the silence swell. The silence had no power, and Dr. Brinton had no power. Nothing mattered.

"Emily, I'd like you to look at the picture and tell me what you see."

He was holding up a black-and-white abstract of a bunch of blobs. Did he think she was totally uneducated? That she didn't know about Rorschachs?

"Julie Andrews in the *Sound of Music*."

"And in this picture?"

" 'The Brady Bunch.' "

He displayed no impatience with her answers but continued through a set of ten, and when he was through, he swiveled in his chair to place the set on the table behind him. Then he turned back to face her.

"I'd say we've got a little issue avoidance going on."

I'd say you look like Frankenstein's brother.

"One more thing. We've got a little test we'd like you to take. I'm sure someone as smart as you will have no problem with it. It's multiple choice. One answer only. We'd like, of course, for your answers to be honest. Take your time."

Emily took the pencil and papers he handed her. She was sitting in a student's desk with a writing table curling around her, and without a word she bent over the test.

I often feel I don't belong in any group.

    Always.   _____

    Never.   _____

    Sometimes.   _____

My friends keep secrets from me.

    Never.   _____

    Sometimes.   _____

    Always.   _____

My body is ugly.

    Yes.   _____

    Parts of it.   _____

    No, it's just fine. _____

As fast as she could, without reading the rest of the questions, Emily sped through the test, checking off the first line of every question. She handed it back to him.

He took it without looking at it and leaned his forearms on his desk, earnestly peering at her from beneath his Cro-Magnon bulge.

"I'd say you are as angry as you are sad."

She felt her face flame.

"Further, I'd say you're as angry with yourself as you are with anyone else. And you think no one can help. And you think you are the only person in the history of the entire universe who has ever had the particular problem you're having."

She glared at him.

"Isn't that a little arrogant? A little solipsistic?"

"I don't know what that word means."

"Self-centered. Unaware of the rest of the world."

She shrugged. "Fine, just add being solipsistic to the rest of my sins."

"You've got *sins*? A pretty young girl like you?"

"Sometimes people are just born bad."

"I see. *The Bad Seed* sort of thing."

Emily nodded.

Brinton leaned back in his chair for a moment and stared at the ceiling, humming tunelessly. Emily wished there was a clock in the room.

"Now what bothers me," he said, suddenly turning to her, "is that in these reports I've read, interviews with your parents and the dean of your school, I've come across nothing that indicates any kind of sinning on your part."

Emily didn't reply.

"No suspensions from school. Nothing but glowing remarks from your teachers. So what's up? I mean, come on, help me out here."

"Maybe it's something in the future."

"I see. Something that hasn't happened yet, but will. Something bad, planted inside you."

Emily nodded. "Like a time bomb."

He looked sad. Shaking his head, he said, "What an awful burden you are bearing, carrying a time bomb within you, thinking you are the only one who can avert disaster."

Emily wrapped her arms around her stomach. "I don't want to talk any more." Pain was swelling through her stomach and chest. "Please."

Brinton stared at her a while, considering. When he looked at his watch, Emily felt oddly offended.

"All right. It's almost time for the fitness hour anyway. We'll talk again tomorrow." He rose. "I'll escort you to the exercise room."

He rose, a tall, ungainly, Ichabod Crane of a man, all bones and joints. It couldn't have been easy for him as a boy. He could never have been handsome. He couldn't help having that bulging forehead, those little eyes. She thought of Kafka's story they'd read part of in school, where the man turned into a cockroach. Dr. Brinton was like a cockroach turned into a man. He was hideous, as she was, and still a human being. There was almost comfort in that thought.

Chapter Eight

❧

"H*ey, Mrs. McFarland!*"

Owen had dropped Linda at Hedden, and as she entered Bates Hall, Bruce's good friend Pebe lumbered down the stairs toward her, a bulging backpack over his shoulders.

"Looking for Bruce?"

"Looking for Jorge, actually."

Pebe seemed surprised. "I think he's in his room. Want me to tell him you're here?"

"That would be great."

"You can wait in the lounge if you'd like."

"I'll do that."

The lounge was a beautiful room, with long casement windows, a fireplace ornamented with marble wreaths and vines, mahogany paneling, a parquet floor. Over the years it had been democratized by its furnishings: several sofas and armchairs sagging and misshapen from use, card tables set up among the claw-footed antiques.

Crossing to the window, Linda gazed out at the lawn sweeping out to the woods, crisscrossed by streaks of shadow.

"Mrs. McFarland?"

Jorge entered, wearing khakis and a white button-down shirt with the sleeves rolled up over his muscular forearms. His black hair was freed of its band today and hung down around his face in an ebony curtain that partially obscured his puffy, blackened right eye but could not hide his split, swollen lip.

Linda shook his proffered hand. "Thanks for coming down, Jorge. I won't take up much of your time."

"How is Emily?"

"She's going to have to stay in the hospital a while. We don't know what her problem is. Can you help us?" When he didn't answer at once, she gently pressed, "Anything. We would be so grateful."

Jorge leaned one hip on the windowsill. The sun fell over his face like a spotlight. His gaze was clear, direct. "I don't know if this is significant."

"Tell me."

"Well. Last spring Emily and I became friendly. She's really nice, Emily. Really smart." His face softened. "We hung out together. We wrote a few times over the summer. Then this fall, we hung out together again. Saturday night, there was a dance here, and we danced. Then Sunday night we decided to meet in the woods for a cigarette—" Jorge glanced at Linda, judging how much this particular bit of information disturbed her.

"Go on."

"Everyone does it. I mean, smokes, or if you're part of a couple . . ." Jorge fiddled with his watchband, unfastening it and fastening it as if it were too tight. Looking at his wrist, he said, "I kissed her. She kissed me back. She wanted me to kiss her, I mean, she wouldn't have gone to the woods with me if she didn't. I mean, that's why we go to the woods, everyone knows that." Color was spotting his cheeks.

"I understand." Linda kept her voice impassive.

"So we kissed, and I liked it, and she liked it, I know she did. I mean, a guy knows. So we were near trees, you know? And I just kind of—" Jorge coughed. "I kind of leaned against her so that her back was against the tree, and I put my arms around her. I didn't touch her anywhere, you know? I just wanted to hold her. But suddenly she freaked. She just went apeshit. She shoved me away, she yelled, 'What are you doing? What do you think you're doing? What kind of girl do you think I am?' I couldn't calm her down. I tried to, but she just was, like, deranged. Like that!" He snapped his fingers. "She went from romantic to nuts. I tried to talk to her, but she was crying and saying stuff, I can't even remember the stuff, she was saying it so fast, I think some of it might have been religious stuff. Being clean, wanting to be clean." Jorge looked directly at Linda, his dark eyes concerned. "She ran off. She ran in the direction of her dorm. I started to follow, then decided not to. I guess I thought I had overstepped some kind of boundary. But honest to God I don't think I did anything wrong."

Linda studied his face. "Is that all?"

"Absolutely."

"You didn't . . . have sex with her."

"No. I swear."

Linda had been standing, but now she sank into a brown leather sofa patched in places with silver electrical tape. "Have you *heard* anything about Emily? Anything else at all that might explain or even give us a clue about what's going on with her? We're so worried, and we just can't figure her out."

Jorge settled into a chair across from her, and leaned forward, resting his arms on his knees. "I know she's been more serious this year than last year. Intense. But that happens a lot. I mean, each year you learn more stuff you have to deal with in life. I think she was finding her classes more difficult. Or not as much fun. She was more quiet."

"Do you think she was doing drugs?"

"No. Absolutely not. She's not interested in that stuff. Besides, usually drugs make you skinny, and she was—" His face darkened with embarrassment.

"She'd gained quite a bit of weight over the past two

months," Linda agreed. After a moment's thought, she decided: "So Sunday night is why Bruce tried to beat you up."

Jorge nodded. "Right. I mean, people saw Emily running from me. And I know she was upset. Zodiac told me. But she didn't say why. I mean, I only kissed her. I guess Bruce put two and two together and got eight."

"I'm sorry."

"Hey. A guy's bound to be protective of his sister."

They sat a few moments in a broody silence, then Linda rose. "I'm grateful to you for talking with me, Jorge. I really appreciate it."

"No problem."

"If you think of anything else, will you call me?"

"Sure."

"My phone number—"

"It's in the facebook."

"Oh. Right." Linda let herself scrutinize his face. "You seem older than the other students."

Jorge smiled, abashed. "I am. Two years older. Because of my English. It's okay now, but it held me back for a couple of years."

"I think your English is superb."

"Thank you."

"Thank you, for talking to me."

"I hope, you know, that everything turns out okay."

"Yes. So do we."

T*he grounds of* the campus were quiet as Linda cut through the quad toward Shipley Hall. The dorm was empty, yet the air seemed to shimmer, so full of the laughter and calls and emotions of young women that particles of hope and haste seemed to hang suspended, like dust motes, in the large bright rooms.

Someone had gone to the trouble of making Emily's bed. The green duvet was perfectly aligned and smoothed, the pillows plumped, and next to them lay a pile of envelopes.

Picking one up, Linda saw that it was addressed to Emily, and sealed. Running a fingernail beneath the flap, carefully she opened it. A long white sheet of paper was folded inside. It was covered in different colors of ink and in a variety of handwriting with get-well greetings and expressions of support.

> "Hang in there, Emily!"
> "Merde! Emily, depeche-toi! I can't do my French without you!"
> "Wishing you much health and a speedy return, Gila Silvia, your dorm custodian."

Linda examined the other envelopes. All were addressed in different hands, all to Emily, decorated with flowers or hearts or kisses or funny faces. Nothing threatening. Nothing helpful. She refolded the large card, returned it to the envelope, and carefully sealed it so that it looked as if it hadn't been opened. Then she turned her attention to the rest of Emily's space.

Everything was so wretchedly tidy. The white leather Bible seemed to glow on the bureau. Linda picked it up, and at once it fell open to Psalms 51. Emily had underlined certain lines so fiercely that the paper was nearly sliced through.

Have mercy upon me, O God, according to thy loving-kindness; according unto the multitude of thy tender mercies blot out my transgressions.

Wash me thoroughly from mine iniquity, and cleanse me from my sin.

Behold, thou desirest truth in the inward parts; and in the hidden part thou shalt make me to know wisdom.

Purge me with hyssop, and I shall be clean; wash me, and I shall be whiter than snow.

Create in me a clean heart, O God; and renew a right
spirit within me.

Fear surged in Linda's chest. This was just not like Emily. Should she take this to the hospital, confront Emily
with it? This *had* to be linked to whatever Emily's
problems were. Surely someone at the Methodist
church could shed some light on Emily's condition.

There were three churches in Basingstoke. The
Catholic was built of red brick and featured a statue
of the Virgin Mary set into the front wall. The Epis-
copal towered in a mountain of gray stone topped with
a bell that tolled the hours. The Methodist was the
most modest, a white clapboard structure with modern
stained-glass windows. Demure signs, white script on
blue wood, directed Owen to the rector's office in the
white house next door to the church.

Owen knocked, then stepped in through the unlocked door. He found himself in a hall furnished much
like the hall of any house, with a coat-rack and carpet
and mirror and a long polished table covered with
pamphlets, brochures, pledge cards. Three doors
opened off the hallway. He chose the one designated
REVEREND CARTER, and knocked.

"Come in."

An attractive older woman in a blue dress and car-
digan was seated behind a desk against which leaned
a handsome gray-haired man with a salt-and-pepper
mustache. They were perusing a sheet of computer
print-outs.

"Sorry to interrupt you," Owen said.

"Not at all. Come in, come in!" the gentleman
urged.

"I was wondering if I could talk to you, Reverend
Carter," Owen said to him. "About my daughter."

The man smiled, graciously displaying his perfect

false teeth. "This," he indicated with a sweep of his hand, "is Reverend Carter."

"Sorry again," Owen said.

"Don't worry," the woman reassured him with a smile. "It's a common mistake, believe me. Especially since my husband looks so much more ecclesiastical than I. How can I help you?" Her eyes were a brilliant periwinkle that matched her sweater, but Owen thought he caught a bit of ice sparkling there.

"I'm Owen McFarland. My stepdaughter, Emily Scaive, is a student at Hedden Academy, and she's been attending your church services this fall."

Reverend Carter interrupted him. "Won't you sit down?" She gestured toward a chair.

Owen sat. "This past week she has gone through a rough patch. I mean, she has made a suicide attempt, and now she is in Basingstoke Hospital, in the psychiatric ward, and I'm trying to find out what exactly her problem is. She can't seem to tell us."

"Would you like me to visit her?"

"Oh, well, I'm not certain—I was wondering—do you know her? Have you talked with her? Is it possible that she has come to you with her problems?"

Gravely Reverend Carter shook her head. "I wish I could help. But I'm sorry to say that no young woman has approached me. I only wish one would. We've been trying to sustain our Young Methodist Fellowship programs on Sunday evening, but so few young people have time for Church these days. It's possible your daughter has attended Sunday morning church services; we do get a group of young people from Hedden. But they all seem a little wary of personal contact." She smiled slightly. "Probably afraid I'll try to inveigle them into some dreary church duty."

"What they see as dreary," her husband corrected.

Owen rose. "Well, thank you for your time."

"If you'd like me to visit her—" Reverend Carter offered again, eagerly.

"I'll ask her. If she does, I'll call you."

He shook hands with the woman and her husband, then made his way back out into the sun.

On the way to the farm, Linda and Owen compared notes on their morning interviews, and then Linda read the hospital brochure aloud to Owen as he drove.

"West Four is a short-term psychiatric unit for patients ages fifteen and older. It is a voluntary unit. You will be assigned a key person or primary clinician who will talk with you on a regular basis about the problems and issues that brought you to the hospital. Your family will be part of the process and will take part during Family Group every Wednesday night. You will be taking part in a number of groups, which will be assigned to you, and you are responsible for checking in with your key person during each shift.

"Some of the groups available are Fitness, Small Group, Adolescent Topic Group, Activity/Task Group, Crafts Group, Relaxation/Assertiveness, Family Issues, Art Therapy, Dessert Preparation, Chemical Dependence Education . . ."

"Dessert preparation?"

Linda read, " 'Voluntary cooperative group activity focused on preparing dessert for the Wednesday evening Family Group.' There's a schedule on the back of the letter to the parents. Apparently Emily's every moment will be accounted for."

"That's good."

"There's also study time and quiet time. And a series of privileges: 'Restricted to Unit, Unaccompanied Hospital and Grounds, Accompanied Passes Off Grounds, Day Passes, Overnight Passes.' Following this it says in bold face that they may be asked to submit to random blood or urine tests at any time. There's a dress code, and provocative or inappropriate clothing is unacceptable. Owen, this is sort of comforting."

"I hope it is for Emily."

They fell silent, brooding, while the miles clicked by. The sky was clouding over, turning the horizon dark, even though it was early afternoon.

As they pulled into the long gravel drive, the farm looked so beautiful that Linda was stabbed with pleasure, and immediately with remorse. She and Owen had been lucky; they were wealthy. They had this enormous old house, and acres of gorgeous land Owen inherited from his parents. They had books and friends and music, and they had healthy, happy children. They had each other, best friends, best lovers.

Perhaps they had been too lucky for too long.

Chapter Nine

Tuesday afternoon at four fifteen Emily entered the small conference room and took a place at the oblong table with ten other patients and Tina Travis, today clad in a green jungle print.

"All right, ladies and gentlemen," Tina began, "we've got some work to do. Whose family is coming tomorrow night?"

About half the group raised their hands.

"Emily?"

Emily was studying the scarlet and emerald parrots swinging from Travis's ears. "Yes?"

"Aren't your parents coming tomorrow night?"

"I guess."

"Could you raise your hand, then, please? Good. Now can anyone tell Emily about the topic block we're focusing on?"

Across from Emily, Cynthia sat slump-shouldered, aimlessly twiddling a strand of her hair. Arnold was gnawing on a thumbnail. Fat Bill sat motionless, in his own world. Everyone else was staring impassively at the table or dutifully at Travis except Keith, who had his head cocked like a bright little puppy, ready to play.

Travis rose and wrote on the blackboard behind her.

POWER
PRIVACY
PEACE

"Every family on the planet deals with these issues. Power is obvious. Who sets the rules? Who gets the car keys? Who decides how you dress? What college will you attend? Minor issues, major issues. Monday Cynthia told us she feels that her parents suffocate her. She has no privacy. No sense of independence." She looked at Cynthia. "Want to talk about this?"

Cynthia shook her head.

Keith leaned forward, aiming his words at Emily. "Cynthia doesn't like the way her drugs make her feel, so when she lives alone she goes off them, and then she gets manic, and do you know what she did last time?"

"What?"

A smile crept over Cynthia's face. "I catalogue-binged. Used my dad's Visa and bought about six thousand dollars worth of stuff."

"She had to repackage it and mail it all back," Keith said.

"My parents had to," Cynthia said, her face sobering. "They came over to see my new apartment, and the next thing I knew, I'm in here."

"So for Cynthia," Travis said, "privacy and power are only going to come when she makes peace with herself about taking her meds regularly. Faithfully. Every day."

"One day at a time, baby," Arnold said. "One grisly day at a time."

A woman at the other end of the table who had not yet spoken to Emily leaned forward and skewered her with a piercing gaze. "So, Scratch-Face, why are you here?"

Immediately all eyes were on Emily. She felt them like weight. She knew her face was red. She stared down at the table.

"Emily was admitted yesterday," Travis said mildly. "Emily, take your time. We're ready to listen when you're ready to talk."

Emily nodded.

"Keith," Travis said, "your parents are coming."

"Lucky me."

"Would you like to tell Emily a bit about your particular problem with privacy and power?"

"No, thanks."

"Come on," Arnold growled. "Or I'll do it for you."

Keith shrugged, then suddenly went camp, limping his wrist and widening his eyes as he spoke. "Oh, well, I *thought* I was going to get through high school and out of the house before Mere and Pere Wight found out I was gay. Then one day my mother searched my room, found some homo porn beneath my bed, and, like, totally freaked out. Now they want to send me to a Christian deprogramming camp in the Midwest, where I'll learn that I'm not gay after all. Where I'll learn to repent. And you know, I just don't see that I'd have a very good time there." He shrugged, nodded, and lightly concluded, "That's it."

Arnold muttered, "Not quite."

"Tell Emily what you did in response," Travis prodded.

"Hung myself. With a belt. Calvin Klein, of course." The room was very quiet. "They'd gone to a movie, but Mother thought it was too violent, so they walked out in the middle and came home and found me. Five more minutes and . . . they could have had the son they wanted."

"Well, *fuck them*," Arnold said, hitting the table with his fist. "That's what I say, just fuck them. How old are you, Keith?"

"I'll be eighteen in January."

"Why hang around for the punishment? Hell, move out of the house. Get a job. Get a life."

"I want to go to college. I can't pay the tuition myself."

Arnold disagreed. "Of course you can. If you really want to."

"You're avoiding the issue," Cynthia said.

"Look, if your parents won't change, it's a hopeless situation. Ditch the shits."

"Let's remember that Keith is an only child," Travis reminded them. "His aunt and cousins live in Australia. So his parents are his family. And we all know, no matter how difficult the situation may be, our family is woven inextricably into our lives. If we're going to be adults, we have to come to some kind of peace with our families."

"There's no escape," Cynthia said.

Emily began to cry.

It was so lame, having classes on Wednesday morning, Bruce thought, when all anyone could think about was getting out of there at noon. Why didn't they just let everyone go Tuesday night? Other schools did.

He jogged full speed from trig class to his dorm. If his parents didn't take forever giving him his stuff, he'd have time to see Alison before she left for the airport. She was taking an earlier shuttle than Bruce and Whit. Probably he wouldn't see her until Friday.

Bates was in chaos. Parents and drivers milled around the entrance hall, guys collided on the stairs, and the air was filled with the hyena laughter of students freed for vacation.

Bruce found his parents in the lounge. One good thing about them, they weren't like a lot of other parents who assumed a guy's dorm room was theirs to enter because they paid the tuition bill. There were guys in Bruce's class, *seniors*, and their mothers came right into the room and opened all the drawers and closets and packed and unpacked their clothes and even "tidied up" the clutter.

Bruce had always known his parents were cool, good-looking, and youthful for people as old as they were, and it was a shock as he approached them this morning to see how they'd aged overnight. Especially Linda, whose face looked sunken on the bones.

"Hey, guys," he said.

They'd been sitting on chairs by the fireplace, both of them staring at the grate as if a fire burned there. At Bruce's words, they turned, rose, and gave him absentminded smiles.

Owen handed him a leather suitcase, his *good* leather suitcase, which he'd refused to let Bruce use since sophomore year when Bruce went to a friend's house for spring break and someone at a party had vomited on it.

Linda handed him his camel overcoat. "You may not need this," she said. "The forecasts are for an unusually warm weekend."

"I'll take it anyway. You never know."

Owen was peeling bills from his wallet. "One hundred fifty dollars. I wish it were more. But with the plane ticket . . ."

Bruce took the money. "Thanks, Dad. Thanks, Linda. This is great."

Linda put her hand on his arm. "Look into my eyes and repeat after me: *I will call my parents to let them know I'm safely in New York.*"

Good-naturedly, Bruce echoed, "I will call my parents to let them know I'm safely in New York."

"You could call other days, too," Linda added. "We'd love to hear about your trip."

"Yeah, sure." He didn't want to be rude, but he wished they'd leave now.

"Your lip looks better," Owen observed. "But your eye's pretty spectacular."

He *knew* his father wouldn't let the matter drop. "Yeah, well, I'd better finish packing."

"If it were up to me, you wouldn't be going on this

trip," Owen continued. "Linda convinced me to let you go, but I want you to be aware that your actions the other day will have consequences. You know we never have condoned violence."

Bruce gritted his teeth and stared at the floor.

"If you could just tell us what it was about . . ." Linda suggested.

"Nothing. Something stupid." Why wouldn't they just *go?*

"You're sure it wasn't about Emily?" Linda pressed.

Exasperated, Bruce said with clenched emphasis, *"It wasn't about Emily."* Out of the corner of his eye he saw his father's jaw set. Quickly he added, "How is she?"

"Not so good," Owen replied.

Linda continued, "They called us this morning. They had to sedate her last night. She can't seem to stop crying. We were going to see her tonight, at Family Group at the hospital, but they think she's at a crisis point and it might help if we came in to talk to her today."

"Weird," Bruce said.

"Would you like her phone number?" Linda asked him. "Maybe if you called over the holiday, toward the weekend, just so she knows you're concerned . . ."

"Yeah. Sure."

So of course Linda had to go sit down at a table and root around in her purse, dredging up a pen and a piece of paper and her little address book, and doors slammed and guys yelled as they ran down the walk and Bates was getting that echoey hollow feel that happened when it emptied out. Bruce's leg jiggled with nervousness.

"Bruce! There you are, man. You ready?" Whit burst into the lounge, radiating energy. He'd changed into his gray flannels and navy blazer and even a tie.

"Don't you look handsome," Linda said.

"Thanks, Mrs. McFarland." Whit turned to Bruce.

"We've got forty-five minutes before the limo arrives."

"I'm almost packed. I just have to throw stuff in the suitcase." Desperately he looked at his parents.

"Here's the number," Linda said, handing him a slip of paper.

"Great." Bruce stuffed it in his wallet next to the cash. "Okay, I'd better go."

Linda grabbed his shoulders and pecked a kiss on his cheek. "Have a wonderful time."

He shook hands with his dad.

"Call," Owen said.

"I will," Bruce promised, then grabbed up the empty suitcase and raced to his room.

They sat in the small conference room: Linda, Owen, Emily, and Dr. Travis, who today was arrayed in orange tights and a nearly knee-length sweater in a fall leaf design. Small metal leaves in rust and gold and scarlet swung from her earrings, and Linda found herself staring at them as they sat in a miserable silence, waiting for Emily to talk. She could scarcely bear to look at her daughter's face, so ravaged by the long angry scratch marks on each cheek.

"From the tests we've been able to do so far," Travis said, "we feel certain that Emily's problem is not physiological. From taking a family history, we also feel that in all probability nothing in her childhood aggrieved her, remained hidden, and is surfacing now. It's most likely that something has happened to Emily within the last few months, something frightening, something harmful. Traumatic."

"Is that true, Emily?" Linda asked. "Darling, please. Let us help you."

Emily did not speak.

They sat in silence for a few more minutes, and then Linda said, "I don't know what's happened. I really don't. Everyone seemed fine. Now this with Emily, and then Bruce beating up Jorge, it just seems so—"

"Bruce beat up Jorge?" Emily's face was red.

Owen nodded. "Yesterday morning. Dean Lorimer—"

"Bruce beat up Jorge? I don't believe it!" Fury transformed her face and she clutched her hair with her hands, as if to pull it out by the roots.

"Emily," Linda whispered, frightened, rising, wanting to take her child in her arms. Travis signaled Linda with a look, and she sat back in her chair.

"Why does he hate me so much? Does he want to take everything from me? I really loved him. Why is he doing this?" Emily pounded her legs with her fists. "God damn him! Damn him! I *hate* him! I wish he would die!"

"Emily," Travis asked, "are you talking about Jorge?"

"No! I'm talking about Bruce!" Spittle formed at the corner of her mouth and her eyes were wild. "I won't hide it anymore, I don't care, I don't care anymore, I don't care what happens, he can't take everything from me."

"Emily, what about Bruce?" Linda implored.

Emily lifted her tear-streaked face toward her mother. "You want to know? All right, I'll tell you! It's all your fault, anyway!"

"What's all my fault?" Linda asked.

"Bruce raped me!" Emily spat. She was overcome with shuddering sobs.

Chapter Ten

Linda and Owen looked at each other, dumb-founded. Travis reached over to a small table holding a box of tissues and handed the box to Emily, who tore them from the box and pressed them to her face.

When Emily's sobs had subsided, Linda leaned forward. "Honey, I don't understand."

Hugging herself, Emily looked at her mother. "It's all your fault. You went away. You left me there."

"Emily, *when?*"

"When you and Owen were at that writers' conference at the end of August."

"Em, we've left you and Bruce alone before," Linda said. "And we were only gone three days."

"Yeah, well that's long enough. Long enough to be raped more than once."

"More than once?" Linda could hardly take in what Emily was saying. At the same time she could not stop staring at her daughter's hands. Emily was clawing herself, repeatedly dragging the jagged ends of her finger-nails deep into the skin of her hands and arms, leaving reddish welts. "Emily, your hands, honey."

Dr. Travis seemed to shake her head once, briskly, at Linda. At the same time, she said to Emily, "Go on. Start at the beginning. Tell us everything."

"It was terrible. He was so mean." Emily was trembling. As she spoke, her left thumb dug deep into the skin around her right thumbnail. She found a tiny tab of skin and grabbed it and pulled. And pulled. A transparent sliver of skin came away.

"Tell me, Emily. Please."

"That first night, I thought he was just, oh, you know, like, being friendly." A scarlet blush mottled her neck and chin.

"The first night."

"The first night you were gone. The first night you left me alone with him." She took a deep breath, and now the words poured out. "We watched a video and then I went to bed and he came into my room. I was almost asleep. I was just under a sheet. It was hot. You know. And he lay down next to me, but on top of the sheet. Just sort of threw himself down next to me like we were watching TV, except on the ceiling. You know."

"I know."

"He kept touching me. I mean we were talking about school starting and stuff and he said that Terry had a crush on me and I told him Cordelia had a crush on him. And he just, well, first he turned on his side and kind of bumped into me with his, um, against my leg, and he put his hand on my arm near my breast. Touching my breast. I pulled away. Told him I was sleepy. After a while he left."

Owen interrupted. "If *that's* all—"

"The next night he raped me." Emily stared at her stepfather. Her entire body shook. "I know what *rape* is. He came in my room and this time he got under the sheet, just like it was normal, and I go, 'Hey, Bruce, what are you doing?' and he goes, 'Take off your clothes.' And I said no and pushed him and suddenly he was like, strong, and *mad*. He held me down with his arms and hands and I twisted and tried to kick him and he shoved me down into the mattress and tore off my pants, and I was just wearing a big white T-shirt and underpants. I screamed at him to stop—"

"Take your time," Travis said.

Emily's forehead creased in anguish. "I yelled, 'Bruce, don't be so rough, you're scaring me. I didn't know you wanted, I didn't know you liked me!' " Emily's eyes flew to Linda's. " 'Cause I always thought, whenever I saw a scary show? How if that happened to me I could talk them out of it? So I thought I could talk Bruce out of it, but he said—" The next words were distorted by sobbing.

Linda asked, "What did he say, Emily?"

"He said, '*Like* you! I hate you, you fucking bitch!' " Shuddering, nearly retching, Emily said, "Then he stuck his penis in me really hard and fast and I was screaming no but he held me down."

For a few moments the three adults sat aghast while Emily sobbed.

"Then what happened, Emily?" Travis asked.

Emily struggled to control her breathing. "When he was through he just got off me. I pulled the sheet up over me. He said, 'If you tell Dad and Linda, they won't believe you. And I'll make it hell for you at Hedden.' "

"Oh, sweetie," Linda said.

"I waited till I heard him shut his bedroom door. I ran into the bathroom and locked the door and stayed there all night. The next day I called Rosie to see if she could use me for a baby-sitter. I said I'd do it for free, my last chance to be with Sean before I left for school, but she said no, Sean was sick, I shouldn't come over. So I took food and went out in the woods and stayed there and read all day and that night I took a blanket and hid in the barn, but he found me, and he laughed at me. He goes, 'You stupid little sack of shit, don't you know I'll always be able to find you? This is my farm.' And . . . he did it again. He raped me again. I was crying and fighting the whole time. When he was through, he went up to his room. And I stayed there till you and Owen came home."

Linda remembered returning to the farm on that brilliant day. Summer was not yet gone, but there had been an autumnal clarity and a light to the air, as if the landscape were gilt-edged. Owen and she had spent three nights together in a cabin in Maine at a writers' conference, and three days of talking with other writers about their work. They were closer than they'd been in a long time, and happier. It had been really idyllic, the romance of the ocean, the luxury of all meals prepared, no housework looming, the exhilaration of discussing their work, the pleasure of talking with people whose lives were centered on books.

Linda had been hoping that Bruce and Emily had finished packing and organizing their things for the new semester at Hedden. She'd been hoping that they'd done the dishes and left the house in a reasonable state of disorder. She'd been wondering what was in the freezer she could thaw out for dinner.

Where had Emily and Bruce been? The horses had ambled up to the fence and bobbed their heads and Maud had waddled out to greet them.

Linda thought hard: Bruce was in his room, grumbling over his laundry, and Emily was in her room, yes, that was right. They hadn't come down to say hello or ask how the conference had been, and Linda had just assumed they were preoccupied, thinking of the next day, when they would leave for school.

Now Emily lifted her face to her mother. It was a terrifying, heartbreaking sight, so contorted with emotion, her lips pulled down and back in a hideous grimace, saliva bubbling as she wailed, "Mommy, he *hurt* me!"

Linda rose and in three steps was next to her daughter. Bending over, she wrapped herself around Emily and held her as she cried. "Oh, baby," she murmured, stroking her back.

"Emily, why didn't you tell us this before now?" Owen asked.

"Yes," Linda agreed. "You should have told us the moment we got home."

Emily cringed. She dug at her hands. "I was embarrassed. I was afraid of what Bruce would say. I didn't want to make you guys unhappy. I thought if I got pregnant, then I'd have to tell you. I made a deal with God that I wouldn't tell you if He wouldn't make me pregnant."

Linda's knees went weak. "Are you—"

"No."

Linda reached for her chair and sank back down into it.

Softly Owen asked, "Why are you telling us now, Emily?"

"Because I don't know what else to do. Because Thanksgiving is here and I don't want to go back to the farm anymore. It scares me."

"The farm scares you."

"Yes. Because of what Bruce did."

Owen cleared his throat. "Are you sure . . . are you sure it was rape?"

Linda said, *"Owen."*

Emily leaned forward, hands clenched into fists. "You see, Mom! You see how you let him talk to me? How you let him speak to me? *I hate you both!*"

"Emily, please, we're just trying to understand . . ."

"*I fought him.* I yelled and told him no, and tried to get away, but he held me down. *He hurt me.* He told me he hates me."

Linda shook her head as if to clear it. "I can't take it in. It's impossible."

"It's the truth!" Emily yelled.

"I'm not implying that you're lying, Emily," said Linda hastily. "It's just that this is so *difficult* to believe. It's like hearing that the world is flat." Looking at Dr. Travis, she continued, "Bruce is a *nice* boy. He's always been easygoing. A really good kid. He's never been violent before, not that we know of. Perhaps he was rough with Emily when they were playing when they were children, when we first all moved in together, but nothing like this . . . I don't understand."

Owen looked at his watch. "Perhaps he hasn't left Hedden yet. What if I go get him and—"

"Owen, I'm sure they've left by now. Whit said the limo was on the way."

"All right then. Look, Bruce returns Sunday night," Owen told Dr. Travis. "Is there any chance we can have a meeting then?"

"I'm afraid not," Travis replied. "The soonest would be Monday morning." She flipped through an appointment book. "Ten o'clock. Would Bruce be allowed to leave classes?"

"I'll make sure he is."

"Go ahead," Emily said bitterly. "Ask your precious Bruce what *I did* that made him rape me!"

"It's not that," Linda said. "We just . . . we just need to hear what he has to say."

"Yeah, and you'll believe him and not me. You only care about him. Your perfect Bruce. You hate me for telling you, don't you?"

"God, no, Emily," Linda said. "Honey, we don't hate you. We're just so completely shocked."

All at once Emily was overtaken by a yawn so enormous her whole body spasmed with it.

Dr. Travis said, "I think this would be a good time to break for the day. It is tremendously hard work, dealing with these powerful memories and emotions. Telling you—telling you *both* what happened took incredible courage. It was a significant step for Emily, and a necessary one."

"Honey," Linda said, "Bruce is in New York for Thanksgiving. If you could come home . . ."

"I want to stay here."

"Shall I come in? Take you out to dinner at the Academy Inn . . ."

Emily shook her head.

Travis interceded. "Emily is dealing with a trauma. You wouldn't expect her to go out with a broken leg. She needs rest, and she needs to work on healing in a safe place, with people trained to help her."

"I understand that, but can't I do *anything*?"

"Trust us. Let her rest." Travis rose and opened the door. "Emily, you probably would like a nap."

Emily yawned again and stood up. When her mother rose to embrace her, Emily recoiled, turning her shoulder toward her mother. Emily's face was dark, sullen. Owen had arisen, too, but he stopped dead, warned away by the anger in his stepdaughter's eyes.

Linda said, "I love you, Emily."

"I do, too," Owen said.

"Yeah, right," Emily muttered, and went out the door and down the corridor to her room.

After a moment of uncomfortable silence, Owen said, "She's angry with me."

"She's angry with you, and her mother, and Bruce, and herself," Travis replied. Opening the door again, she led them out into the hall. "I have some brochures in the other room that might be of assistance to you."

They followed her to her office and stood awkwardly just inside the door, as obedient as drugged creatures. Dr. Travis closed the door and motioned them toward chairs.

"I can't understand this," Linda said. "It's too much. Too terrible."

"Sit down," Dr. Travis said. "Let's talk a moment. I know this is difficult for you both. And I imagine it's going to get worse for a while. You might want to get a therapist for yourselves." Turning, she picked up some brochures from a shelf behind her desk. "I'd like you to take these home with you and read them. They might help you; they might help you in understanding what has happened to Emily."

Owen stared at the brochures in Dr. Travis's hand.

Printed in black and white with vivid purple graphics of a hand on a wrist, they hurt his eyes.

After You Are Raped
When Someone You Love Has Been Raped

Taking them would seem an act of conviction. It would mean that he believed Emily had been raped by his son.

Linda looked at Owen, then reached out and took the brochures. "Thank you."

"One more thing," Dr. Travis said evenly. "A common reaction among men whose loved ones are raped is anger. Intense anger."

"I'm not angry," Owen said. "I'm just . . . completely bewildered. I can't believe that Bruce . . . that Bruce *raped* anyone."

Travis asked, "Is there any reason why we should not believe Emily? For example, is she a habitual liar? Or has she lied about a truly significant matter in the past?"

Linda said, "No."

"Has she ever attempted suicide before? Or done anything to act out, such as running away from home? Any extreme, attention-seeking behavior?"

Linda and Owen shook their heads.

"What about sexuality? Have you discussed it as a family?"

Linda and Owen looked at one another. Linda said, "As the children were growing up, we talked about it. Of course. Where babies come from, how they're made. Then, later, we talked about contraception, and diseases, AIDS, herpes, and so on."

"How about emotions? How about feelings of desire? Inappropriate feelings of desire?"

Owen said, "I'm not sure I follow."

"Human sexuality is a complicated thing," Travis said. "Research shows that in stepfamilies, inappropriate sexual feelings are common. There is nothing *wrong* with them, but they should not be acted upon. The incest taboo applies in stepfamilies as well as in families. Perhaps you have seen or sensed that Emily has had a crush on her stepbrother. Has been in love with her stepbrother."

"No," Linda said. "I haven't been aware of anything like that."

"Sometimes the person feeling inappropriate love and desire is ashamed, and masks these feelings with a pretense of hatred for the other person. Has Emily, in the past, irrationally lashed out in anger at Bruce over seemingly insignificant matters?"

"Not any more than he has toward her," Owen admitted fairly.

"Has she behaved violently toward him? Conversely, have you ever seen her acting in a seductive way toward him?"

"No."

Dr. Travis opened a folder and looked through it. "We've collected a family history from you. Think carefully. Is there anything you've left out? Has, for example, Emily ever had a period of mental instability? Has she ever hallucinated? Blacked out? Has she ever accused another man of raping her? Accused anyone of anything that wasn't true, or done anything similar to call attention to herself?"

"No." Owen was growing impatient. "But still . . . Bruce hasn't done anything like that, either. He's a good boy. He's always been a good boy. I don't understand why you believe Emily."

Very calmly, Dr. Travis said, "I don't understand why you don't."

"It's not that," Linda hastily interceded. "It's just that it's so confusing. Surely you must see that."

Travis leaned back in her chair. "I'll admit that I'm not one hundred percent without doubts. In a situation like this, of course, there is no one but God who knows the full truth. But let me tell you why I believe Emily. First of all, we have given her a battery of diagnostic tests. We've found nothing to indicate psychosis, dementia, any kind of physiological or biochemical dysfunction. Her family situation has been not optimal, but certainly, without a doubt, good. She has always been well cared for. Loved. She has grown up in a healthy environment. She was performing well at school. She had friends. Good grades. Nothing to indicate any underlying chronic psychiatric problem. Now. Emily came to us because of a suicide attempt, which indicates a serious emotional trauma. She has evidenced feelings of shame, self-hatred, depression, a sense of hopelessness. She told Dr. Brinton that she was carrying the seeds of destruction for your family within herself. I would say this announcement fairly well fits that bill, wouldn't you? I might also add that a great deal of research has been done on rape victims, and Emily's response fits the patterns found in that research. She displays certain identifiable signs of a rape victim. For one, she is angry at her mother for not protecting her."

"But how could I—"

"Emotions are not rational. This is how she *feels*. Also, she displays obsessive behaviors. In the short time she's been with us, she's made her bed probably fifty times. She can't get it smooth enough, she says, can't get the wrinkles out. Can't get it to look right. You've remarked on her overeating. Her recent weight gain. She's been medicating herself with food. And the self-mutilation. Her face. Her hands. Those also are common signals. She hates herself. Punishes herself."

Owen interrupted, "But if she really was raped, why does she punish *herself*?"

"Again, I need to stress that emotions are not rational. This is what studies show is the common behavior of victims of rape."

Owen could keep silent no longer. "I don't think it's

fair to discuss this when Bruce isn't here to defend himself. Who is protecting his interests here?"

"Well," Dr. Travis coolly responded, "I am, for one. I need for both of you to know that I am bound by federal law to notify the police about any report of rape."

"Good God!" Owen exploded. "You can't do that! How can you even think of doing that? You have no proof! You haven't even talked to Bruce. You haven't even set eyes on him!"

"If I may finish. I'm going to take a risk here and not report the accusation of rape for two reasons. First of all, for the reason you mentioned. We have no proof. We need to hear from Bruce. This is an extremely personal and volatile situation for the entire family. More important, I think that bringing in the police would not be the best thing to do therapeutically at this moment in time for my patient. I'm making a clinical judgment call here and I want you to know that I'm doing it."

"Thank you," Linda said, thinking that Owen should have said it.

Owen was thinking furiously. "Look," he said. "These two have always tattled on one another. Why didn't she tell us when we got back from the writers' conference? When we could perhaps have found proof, one way or the other, taken her to the doctor, that sort of thing."

"Keeping her silence is not unusual. She thought she could bury it. Hide it. Make it go away, as if it never happened. She was humiliated, angered, confused. She knew that disclosure of it would be a divisive element in your family. She hated herself because it happened to her. She blamed herself for it. It is common, it is *textbook*, for a rape victim to feel guilty. Emily tried to hide it, to bury the fact of it, and the pain and anger worked inside her like an acid, eating away at her, until she no longer could contain it. She tried to protect you from the pain of knowing, but that was an impossible task. Her only recourse was a suicide attempt." After a moment's silence, she said, "Now Emily can move on. Now she can own her anger. Deal with her grief. Work it through. Begin to heal."

"How can we help her?" Linda asked.

"For now, just give her time. Don't be surprised or angry at her anger with you. With both of you. That also is common. Right now Emily is a very intensely distressed young woman."

"So there's nothing I can do until Monday?"

"You could call her. She might not talk to you." Travis rose. "I'm sorry. I have an appointment now."

It was when she was opening her office door that Owen said, "I'm not sure exactly how to say this but . . . I would hate it if any talk about this got out. Especially to Hedden. For Bruce's sake. Emily's too."

Dr. Travis drew herself up. "Mr. McFarland, we do not divulge our patient's private concerns to anyone." She shut the office door firmly behind them. "I'll see you on Monday." She walked down the hall and around the corner.

"Yes, all right." Linda said into the emptiness.

Together they left the hospital, walking slowly, as if the rules of gravity had been suspended and the halls were turned into mazes, as if they had suddenly become old and frail and strangers in the world.

Chapter Eleven

❦

They found their old Volvo in the garage and got in.

Owen looked over at Linda. "You okay?"

She nodded. "I guess so. You?"

"I feel like I've been hit in the stomach with a bat."

"Me, too."

"What should we do now?"

"I don't know."

"I guess we'll just go back to the farm."

"I guess." The brochures Travis had given them were lying in her lap, staring up at her like a curse.

What if Emily were telling the truth?

Dear God, what if she were lying?

"Owen," she said, "hold me."

They shifted across the seats, the leather creaking as they moved, and wrapped their arms around one another.

"It's a nightmare," Linda said.

"We'll get through this," Owen said. "Somehow."

For a moment Linda took solace in the familiar bulk of her husband's body, the reliable pounding of his heart, the comforting rumble of his voice in his chest as he spoke. In the way their car curved around them, enclosing them in a safe and familiar world.

Then they heard the brisk click-clack of someone's high heels. Next to them a figure moved, opening a car door. They broke apart, fastened their seat belts. Linda brushed back her hair with her hands. Owen put the key in the ignition and started the engine and steered the car from the garage.

During the hour-long drive back to Ebradour, they fell into a brooding silence broken by fits of conversation as new thoughts struck them.

Owen mused aloud, "I can't see it. I can't believe that Bruce is a rapist."

"I know. But it's just as hard to believe that Emily would make this up."

"True. But Emily's romantic. Dramatic."

"But she's never been a liar. And she's not crazy."

"I'm not saying she's crazy. But she is in a psychiatric ward."

"She's *in* a psychiatric ward because she was *raped*. She's in a psychiatric ward because she wanted to spare us, but keeping it secret was killing her."

"But I just can't see Bruce *raping* anyone."

"Me, either. Still, Bruce's a young man. A lot of hormonal changes are going on inside him . . ."

Owen was quiet for a while, considering, and after a few moments, he said, "I know. There was something different in the air this summer. When the boys were visiting."

The boys, Terry and Doug and Pebe, had come to stay for a month, as they had for the two previous years, but this year they'd not been as boisterous. They spent more time secluded in the attic or the woods and no time at all with the horses or in the pond. As always, the guys had taken over the attic for a makeshift clubhouse and guest room, playing poker late into the night, sleeping past noon, and this year Owen and Linda had assumed, from the choked laughter they heard, that they were discussing women. Owen suspected they were sneaking off to smoke cigarettes; he'd reminded them every time he saw them that if he

caught them smoking near the barn or if he came
across an uncrushed butt anywhere he'd send them
back home on the moment. He'd worried all summer
about the possibility of fire. He'd been alert, kept pretty
good watch. He suspected they'd smoked some pot
down by the pond, but he hadn't told Linda; she would
have freaked out. It was also possible that they'd
sneaked some alcohol into the attic. But adolescent
boys acted bizarrely enough when sober; Owen and
Linda hadn't been able to guess by their behavior
whether or not they'd been drinking.

Mostly Owen had been aware that this year the boys
were bored by the farm. The pond, the woods, the hills,
the horses, all had lost their charms. Day after day
Bruce and Doug and Terry and Pebe had risen after
noon to straggle down the stairs bleary-eyed and sit
with cups of coffee on the side porch, staring out at
nothing. After a while they'd strolled in to collapse on
the various sofas in the den where they'd watch television with the glazed eyes of lobotomy patients. When
the coolness of evening fell, they might rouse themselves for a long walk in the woods, and then sometimes they had grown lively again. They'd returned
laughing and shoving each other and muttering behind
their hands. Owen didn't know how their time had
passed; they'd been so inactive. He remembered his
own adolescence, how his parents had yelled at him for
being absentminded and forgetful. He remembered his
first sessions with liquor, how violently ill he'd been.
When the boys were out in the woods, Owen had made
surreptitious inspections of the attic, looking for bottles
of booze or signs of drugs; he'd never found anything
suspicious.

Owen came out of his reverie. "I asked Terry why
they'd all gotten so quiet. One morning when he came
down before the others woke up."

"He was always the easiest one to talk to. What did
he say?"

"Just that they were getting older, heading into their last year of high school. They were all worried about applying to colleges and waiting for the results. They were facing the most difficult semester of their lives. Everything hung on the grades they would make."

"Well, we know Bruce is anxious."

"Terry said the college advisor told them that it's harder now for prep school students to get into colleges. Universities are trying to redress the balance of earlier years when prep school kids sailed into any school they wanted, but parents still expect the same accomplishments their parents had expected of them."

"Did you ask about girls?"

"Yup. Terry said people didn't date anymore. They went out in groups, or else they met as really serious couples in the woods surrounding the school. He also told me the girls at the school liked the jocks, or else the radical grungy guys. Although Pebe had a girl-friend."

Linda smiled. "Pebe would." He was drop-dead handsome as well as brilliant. "Did he mention Alison?"

"Not that I recall."

"She likes Bruce, it's obvious. And he likes her. There's a real sweetness between them."

"They must have been involved before the summer. Bruce never particularly cared about which college he got into before this summer, and suddenly he was adamant about getting into Westhurst."

"Where Alison wants to go. Right."

"It just doesn't seem to fit that Bruce would be so . . . smitten . . . with Alison and yet—" Linda paused. It was hard to say the word. "—and yet rape Emily."

"I know. It doesn't make any sense."

"But then I can't believe Emily would lie." Linda rubbed her temples. "I'm getting a headache."

"Want to stop for a cup of coffee?"

"No. I'll be all right. We're almost home."

They finished the ride in silence, and when they turned down the long gravel drive to their house, Linda realized with a jolt that this beautiful farm, their sanctuary, their home, looked different to her now. The bare branches of trees darkened the ground and the buildings with tangles of shadows. Was this the house where her child was harmed?

"I'm going to cut some firewood," Owen said. "Maybe it will clear my head."

"All right."

As Linda entered the house, their old dog, Maud, snorted forward, wagging her tail as well as she could. Linda stooped and scratched her behind the ears. On the old desk wedged between the refrigerator and the door, the answering machine blinked. She hit the button: a message from her friend Janet, wondering when she was coming to Boston for their annual Christmas shopping spree. Linda just stared at the machine. She'd call Janet later.

The house felt cold. For once she wouldn't fret over the money spent on heat. She needed heat. Perhaps she'd take a long hot bath. But when she reached the second floor, she found herself wandering into her daughter's room where she simply stood in the silent air, looking around.

Emily's room could scarcely keep up with her personality changes. Her canopy bed still dripped with pink chintz, but her dolls and stuffed animals had been heartlessly shoved beneath the bed, along with a lone sock and a paperback of Shirley MacLaine's *Don't Fall off the Mountain.* Barrettes, earrings, and tiny rubber bands from Cordelia's braces left during her summer visit glittered on her bureau. An opened box of cassettes was stacked on the satiny linen chest Linda's mother gave her. An incense holder full of ash slanted atop a pile of *Sassy, Dance,* and *Cosmopolitan. Cosmopolitan!* A little advanced for her.

Or maybe not.

Opening her desk drawer, Linda made a desultory search for Emily's diary and was relieved not to find it. She wouldn't have violated Emily's privacy before, but now might be an appropriate time. If only there were some *proof* . . . But of course there couldn't be, not when the rape had taken place almost three months ago.

She looked back at *Cosmopolitan*. Picking up the magazine she looked at the front cover. She could tell the model was very young, perhaps not even Emily's age, and made up to achieve a perfection real life never saw. Images like this, which once would have titillated young boys from the inside of porn magazines, now flashed out from all magazines, and from catalogues as well. Sex was advertised everywhere, like a kind of food or product. Certainly it was a confusing time for young people just growing into their own sexuality.

But Emily was not naïve. She wasn't insane. She knew the difference between imagination and reality. If she said that Bruce had raped her, then that was what had happened.

The afternoon had grown dark with a glowering late November sky and a steady wind. From the windows Linda could see Owen ferociously chopping wood. She should do something physical as well to use up her nervous energy, but in spite of her nerves, what she felt most was a terrible fatigue.

She left Emily's room, went back downstairs, wandered into the front parlor, which after her marriage to Owen had become a den. Sinking onto the worn, welcoming old brown sofa, she remembered how, when they were younger, Bruce and Emily used to watch the same television shows from opposite ends of this sofa. During the coldest parts of the winter they'd pulled the afghan Owen's mother had made down from the back of the sofa for warmth, but it hadn't been long enough to cover them both. They never had snuggled up against one another. Instead they'd yanked the afghan, played tug of war with it, and sometimes this had escalated into a kicking battle. Finally Linda had put another blanket there, over the arm of the sofa. But they had both preferred that ratty old afghan, and time and time again as Owen and Linda had sat reading, they'd heard the children yelping with laughter. Sooner or later would come a thud and a yowl as one kicked the other onto the floor.

"Settle down in there!" Owen would yell. "What do you think, you've been raised on a farm?"

Linda and Owen would look up from their books and smile at one another. It was as if Bruce were her son, Emily Owen's daughter. As if they were a family.

Chapter Twelve

Whit's family's Manhattan townhouse was all old furniture and old paintings and old books and Whit's parents were so old they looked more like his grandparents. Mrs. Archibald wore her gray hair stuck up in a sort of bun on top of her head, held there with what looked like chopsticks, and at Thanksgiving dinner she also had a number three pencil stuck through the clump. Mr. Archibald had terrible posture and yellow teeth and went around in a tweed jacket with holes in the elbows; if you saw him on the street you'd think he was one of the homeless. Bartholomew, the oldest child of six, was twenty-one years older than Whit. He came with his wife and four children, the oldest of whom was thirteen. Some of his cousins came to Thanksgiving dinner, too, and various friends of the family, so there were twenty-one people for Thanksgiving dinner, which was served by a couple who looked straight out of Monty Python. After dinner they all had to play charades in the living room, the maid and butler, too.

"Don't you think we could slip out and no one would notice?" Bruce asked Whit.

"Not tonight," Whit whispered back. "We can do whatever we want Friday and Saturday."

So Bruce had to be content with that. He could have

called Alison, but he didn't want to appear too eager, or like a pest.

He called her at noon on Friday.

"My parents are going to a party tonight. Come over about nine," she said.

"That's so late."

"Yeah, but they won't be home until two or three in the morning."

"Cool. See you at nine."

"Just give the doorman your name."

Bruce spent the day with Whit at the Metropolitan Museum of Art, seeing new exhibits Whit's parents had told them they really shouldn't miss, and then they ate at a Russian restaurant, where Bruce memorized lots of stuff on the menu so he could tell his parents. They liked stuff like that. Then since Bruce wasn't familiar with New York, Whit walked Bruce to Alison's, which wasn't very far from his own apartment, and went off by himself to a movie.

Alison looked unbelievable. She wore tight red plaid pants that started just below her belly button, and a tight black sweater that stopped just above her belly button. Bruce could hardly keep his eyes off that strip of skin with its seductive indentation.

"Come in," she said, and curled herself around him right there in the doorway. She gave him a teasing kiss, then pulled back. "Let's get something to drink."

Alison's place was extreme. Everything was black, white, chrome, with splashes of red and lots of enormous windows with all of New York glittering.

"Look." She spread her hands to indicate the wealth of choice behind the curved bar.

Bruce didn't want to expose his inexperience with alcohol. He wanted to be cool, but he also wanted not to get drunk and puke all over her house like he knew he'd do if he had more than two or three drinks of hard stuff. He looked for beer but found none.

Alison was opening a bottle of Perrier-Jouët champagne, the kind that Linda was always cooing about.

"Want some?"

"No, thanks." He poured himself a rum and Coke. He'd had some experience with that.

"Want to see the house?"

What could he say? *I want to see your bedroom?* "Sure."

For a while he got distracted from Alison's midriff by the amazing place she lived in. It was more like a museum than a home, with massive murals and realistic life-size dummies seated at a table playing cards in the hall and clear Plexiglas bridges crisscrossing between bedrooms on the second floor; not the place for someone with a fear of heights.

"This is really wild," he told Alison.

"I know. Dad's *the* architect in New York. Let's get more to drink."

With fresh drinks in hand, they invaded her brother's room, which was like the control center of a spaceship. The guy had a state-of-the-art computer, CD player, VCR/TV, and every CD ever made. His bed hung by silver ropes from the ceiling and swung gently when Bruce and Alison leaned on it.

"The help hate it. Hate to change the sheets," Alison said.

"It's cool."

"Want to try it?"

"Sure."

They fell onto the swaying bed and, using the remote control, played CDs. Pearl Jam. Soundgarden.

"Not Hootie and the Blowfish. I'm so tired of them," Alison said.

Bruce had finished his second drink and felt too lazy to get himself back down to the first floor and the bar, so he let Alison pour champagne into his glass from the bottle she'd brought along. Then she finished it, holding it above her mouth so that the last few drops dribbled down onto her tongue. Bruce thought he'd lose his mind seeing that, being this close to her, and on a bed.

"Wait a minute," Alison said. The bed rocked as she got out. "I wish he'd alphabetize these. I don't know how he finds anything. Here it is." She put on a Mazzy Star CD, and the room filled with the slow, dreamy, slurred music.

"Comfy?" Alison asked.

"Um." Bruce set his glass on the floor and curled toward her. "Alison." He put his mouth on hers. He put his hand on the naked strip of flesh beneath her breasts. He felt her muscles tighten. Her skin was hot.

She tasted like champagne and something sweet and minty. The inside of her mouth was like strawberries. She pressed herself against him and did not pull back when she felt his erection pressing on her belly.

"God, you're so beautiful," he said, and sort of wished he hadn't, because Alison stopped kissing him and drew back.

"Do you think so?" she asked. "Do you really think so?"

"Of course I do. I think you're the most beautiful thing I've ever seen in my life."

She smiled and ran her hands through his hair, one hand on each side of his face. It made him shiver. "Sweet boy," she said.

But the bed was swinging slightly, more every time they moved, and it was disconcerting. In fact it was making Bruce dizzy.

"Where's your room?" he asked. Hoping her bed was stationery.

"I'll show you." Taking him by the hand, she led him from her brother's room. "Want some more to drink?"

"No." His voice broke, and she smiled at him knowingly. She was so much more sophisticated than he was. She'd probably done it before. Lots of girls at Hedden had. She might even be on the pill. But he had two condoms in his wallet, thanks to all the safe sex courses.

Her bedroom was kind of a disappointment, like any girl's room anywhere. Twin beds, flowery, frilly spreads, tons of lacy pillows and what Linda called frou-frou.

"It's my own little world," Alison said. "Now that my sister lives in California. My own little kingdom."

"The magic kingdom." He pulled her down onto the bed with him. It was a big wide bed with a high white wooden headboard painted with flowers. The quilt was soft.

If he told her he loved her, would she let him do it? He did love her; it wouldn't be a lie. She was being very provocative, arching her hips toward him, rubbing against him, pushing his bum with both her hands. It was all he could do not to come in his boxers. What could he say?

He said, "Please." Groaned it.

"Oh, Bruce, Bruce," she answered, blowing in his ear.

He rolled her beneath him.

A crash resounded all around them. For one terrible moment Bruce thought a bomb had gone off.

"What?"

"Oh, jeez, my parents." Sighing, Alison rolled off the bed and went to the door of her room, opening it a crack.

"You *knew* she would be there, and you *did it on purpose*!"

"Don't be so fucking paranoid."

"Don't call me paranoid. *I'm not paranoid*. You just wanted to rub my face in your shit."

Alison shut the door and leaned against it. Her face had gone white. "You'd better go."

"But I thought . . . you said they wouldn't be back till after two."

"Yeah, well, sometimes . . ."

"Why don't we both sneak out? We could—"

"I can't. I have to stay here and help out."

"Help out?"

"Mom calms down better if I'm around." Something smashed against the wall. Alison straightened her clothing and leaned over to put on fresh lipstick. "Come on. I'll let you out."

Bruce followed her. What choice did he have? He felt like crying like a girl.

"Womanizing shit!"

Alison's mother caught sight of them as they were tiptoeing to the foyer.

"And who's this?"

"Bruce McFarland, Mom. A friend from school. From Hedden."

Bruce held out his hand, trying to be courteous, but Mrs. Cartwright put her hands on her hips and leaned forward aggressively on her high heels, saying in a sarcastic voice, "I *see.* I see. Come over to get a little action off my daughter, have you?"

"Honoria, for Christ's sake," Mr. Cartwright said.

"Mom."

"Well, it's true. That's all you males think about, isn't it? Isn't it?"

Alison put her hand on Bruce's arm and led him to the door. "I'll call you tomorrow morning," she said. "Sorry," she whispered.

Then Bruce had to go outside and hang around Whit's apartment in the cold for a whole hour until he saw Whit coming home from the movie, so he could get into the Archibalds' house without having to knock and explain why he was alone.

*N*othing much happened on Thanksgiving. No group or private sessions, no occupational therapy, although the chem depps did meet in the evening. The hospital cafeteria sent up a reasonable facsimile of Thanksgiving dinner with turkey and pumpkin pie, and at three o'clock one of the floor nurses arrived with a stack of new videos. So they made it through the day. Emily's mother called and talked to her quite a while about neutral stuff: seeing Rose and baby Sean at Thanksgiving dinner, Barn Cat's new litter, and the latest hysterically funny letter from Emily's grandmother, who lived in a retirement home in Florida and at seventy-eight found herself besieged by suitors in their eighties.

Most of the time Emily slept. Felt she could sleep the rest of her life.

On Friday Dr. Travis was back and after breakfast and a fitness hour, Emily had to meet with her and some of the other patients in a small group session. For a while Travis focused the talk on holidays and the approaching Christmas season and its perils, and then when Emily wasn't expecting it, she said, "Would you like to tell us how you feel about Christmas this year, Emily?"

Emily shrugged. "I don't want to go home for Christmas."

"Tell us why."

In a tiny voice, Emily said, "You say."

"It's for you to say," Travis insisted gently. "Trust me. You'll feel better if you say it."

Emily's hands found one another. The sharp pain of her nails in her skin helped shroud the deeper, more powerful pain burning inside her every moment, spurting acid through her body with each heartbeat. "It's embarrassing." When no one spoke, she took a deep breath and said in a hurried monotone, "I don't want to go home for Christmas because my stepbrother raped me." Her skin went hot all over and tears began to prickle her eyes. "I don't ever want to go back to the farm again." Looking up at the circle of faces around her, she rushed on, "If I weren't so incompetent, I'd just run away somewhere. Get a job, start a new life. But I don't know how I'd make any money.

I've thought about it, and you need a high school diploma even to work in a fast food joint—"

"Wait a minute!" Keith said. "Hang on. Did you say your stepbrother *raped* you?"

Emily nodded.

"That's brutal," Keith said. "What happened?"

Emily covered her face with her hands. "I don't like talking about it."

"How old's your stepbrother?" Arnold asked.

"Seventeen. Two years older than me."

"Is he cute?" Cynthia asked.

"Oh, *please*!" Keith snapped. "Who cares. He raped her."

"Well, I just thought maybe . . ." Cynthia let her voice trail off.

"Go on," Travis prompted Cynthia.

"Well . . . that if Emily liked him, maybe it wasn't so bad."

The words were like slaps. When she could get her breath, Emily said, "It was bad. It was *terrible*. I didn't want to have sex with him. He forced me. He was mean to me. He held me down. He said hideous things to me. He squeezed the breath out of my throat with his arm. He called me a stupid bitch. I hid in the woods all day and tried to hide in the barn at night and he hunted me as if I were some kind of nasty *game* he was playing, and he did it again. He called me a *stupid sack of shit*." She was shaking again. "He told me it was his farm. And it is his farm. And I have nowhere to go."

"What about Hedden?" Keith asked.

"Bruce's at Hedden, too. And he's probably telling everyone that I'm cheap. Easy. 'I did her, you can do her, too.' And the thing is," Emily's voice rose; she was almost laughing, "now I know I'll never ever want to have sex again in my life. I just feel . . . ruined. Like this guy Jorge, he's at Hedden, he's really nice, and I liked him, and he liked me, but when he tried to kiss me, I went berserk, 'cause I got so scared, it was like all of a sudden I thought I was going to die, having a guy so big and strong with his hands on me . . . I can't stand it! It's too scary! So I'll never be able to . . . have any children. Everything's gone! Everything in my whole life is gone."

Cynthia said, "I bet your parents freaked."

"I didn't tell them. It would have been horrible. My mom . . . I thought I could just pretend it didn't happen. I mean, Bruce's going away to college next year. If I could stay away from him . . . but then . . ."

"But man, why try to off *yourself*?" Arnold asked. "I'd go after *him*."

Emily dug at her hands. "I *loved* him. He must *hate* me to do that to me. He must have hated me all these years when I thought . . . I mean, he's my *brother*." Sobbing overtook her.

"All rapes rob the victim of their sense of having control over her life," Travis said. "Many victims react to being raped with feelings of self-disgust, feelings of failure. Many times the victim turns her anger inward on herself rather than outward toward the rapist. This is what you did, Emily. What you're still doing. This is why you're here with us." She looked at her watch. "All right, group. This is a good time to break for the day. We'll meet again at four, right?"

Keith came to stand by Emily. "Want to go to the O.T. room? We're going to start making some really exquisite Christmas decorations out of old toilet paper rolls."

Emily sniffed. "I'm tired. I just want to go to bed and sleep."

"Want me to wake you for lunch?"

"Sure."

"Emily," Dr. Travis said, "let's go to the nurses' station and get some bandages and antibiotic ointment for your hands."

Chapter Thirteen

❧

The night before Thanksgiving, the wind swooped down from the north like a marauder, setting the branches of all the trees into frenzied swaying, shredding the few remaining leaves and plastering them against the windows and the side of the house, battering the bushes until they bent double. The noise was terrible. Sometimes it seemed to come all in one block like a wrecking ball slamming into the side of the house. Sometimes it divided itself into shrieks and lamentations.

After listening to the onslaught for an hour or so, Linda rose and slipped barefoot through the dark out of her room, down the hall, and into Owen's room. He was snoring. He was asleep. He could sleep through this storm, and Linda smiled: he was her good, sane, rational husband, steadfast, reliable, undaunted by the storm. She slipped into his bed, comforted immediately by the warmth and bulk of his body.

"Mmm?" He didn't really wake.

"Sleep," she answered, snuggling her back to fit against his. At once she felt warm, safe. She slept.

In the morning, she woke to find herself alone in the bed. The clear light of a sunny day fell through the windows. She dressed and went downstairs. Owen was at the kitchen counter, scooping dog food from a can into Maud's bowl. Linda stood behind him, wrapped her arms around his warmth, leaned into his back, rubbing her cheek against the soft flannel shirt, inhaling Owen's scent of soap and heat.

"Nightmares?" he asked.

"The storm. I can't believe you didn't hear it."

They sat with their coffee at the table, across from one another.

Owen yawned and rubbed his whiskery jaw. "Do you feel like going today?"

"Not really. But it would be more trouble not to go, don't you think? We'd have to give them some kind of excuse. And at least it might be a diversion. My mind just keeps going in circles."

Owen nodded.

She went on. "I keep thinking how lucky we've been. Until now. Do you think everyone gets an equal amount of good and bad in their lives?"

"I don't know about that. But I'm sure no one ever gets only good." He rose and set a pan on the stove. "Oatmeal?"

"No, thanks." She wanted to continue her train of thought. "For one thing, I've always thought how fortunate we were not to have either Michelle or Simon causing problems. You know the way Carla's husband does, trying to set their daughter against her, playing games with their schedules, showering the child with gifts."

"Was it Doug who said when his mother gave him a Dalmatian puppy for his birthday, his father went out and bought him a Dalmatian puppy that would live at *his* house?"

"Right. That sort of thing. So our kids didn't get pulled in two different directions. On the other hand, they each have one parent who has totally rejected them, and that's got to hurt."

"Are we out of brown sugar? Oh, here it is. I don't know, Linda, I don't have much patience with that. It's gotten to be a national fad, who's had the worst life. Who has the weirdest kind of misery. You and I have provided Emily and Bruce with a damned good life if you ask me."

"I'm not arguing that. I just think that at some level, Emily and Bruce must feel . . . unwanted."

Owen spooned the oatmeal into a bowl and brought it to the table. "Look, they're both smart, educated, thoughtful kids. They know about life. They know they've got a good home, two parents who love them, and that's a lot more than a lot of other kids have."

Linda reached over to dip her finger into the oatmeal. "Mmm. Good."

"I made enough for two."

She rose and got a spoon, then ended up just staring at it. "Owen, I can't stop thinking about Emily."

"I know."

"I keep wondering if Bruce—"

"Look. There's nothing we can do until Monday. We won't know everything until then."

Linda bit her lip. It was always this way with them, in small crises as well as large. Linda fretted; Owen didn't. When something was wrong with the children, her life was interrupted to the very fibers of her nerves; his was not. When they were waiting to receive letters of acceptance or rejection from the various private schools, Linda had said to Owen, "My blood pressure rises every time I open our post office box."

"How can you tell when your blood pressure is rising?" Owen had asked.

Linda had snapped, "I could kill you for that."

Now she rose. "I'd better get busy. I've promised to bring two pies."

"Pumpkin?"

"And deep-dish blackberry." Taking an apron from a hook on the pantry door she tied it around her, then dug into the cupboard for the rolling pin.

"Great." Owen rose and put the bowl in the sink.

"Look, Linda, I've been thinking. I'd rather we didn't tell anyone about all this. Not just yet."

She carried the canister of flour to the table and set it down. "Fine. Except, what will we say when they ask where the kids are?"

Owen shrugged. "They're both spending Thanksgiving vacation with friends."

Linda nodded. "All right."

"And I don't think you should tell Janet, either."

Surprised, Linda studied her husband. Since before she'd even met Owen, the Friday after Thanksgiving was the day that Linda met her best friend, Janet, for a day of serious Christmas shopping.

"I'm not certain I'll even go shopping," Linda said. "All that seems so trivial now . . ."

"You should go. It would help you pass the time. And we've got to have Christmas, somehow, this year."

"I know. Still. But Owen, about Janet . . . I really would like to talk this over with her. She's known Emily since she was two years old. She knows how much I love you, how much I love Bruce. She might be a good sounding board for me."

"She would find it impossible to be impartial," Owen said.

"Impartial," Linda repeated, letting the implications of the word loose inside her mind. She lifted down her beloved English mixing bowl and held it against her stomach as she thought. "All right. Then I'll tell her about Emily's suicide attempt, and the fact that someone raped her, but that we don't know who."

Now Owen's voice was tense. "Look, Linda. If you tell Janet that Emily says she was raped, one way or the other you'll let it out that Emily has accused Bruce. And Janet will tell her husband, and one of her children will overhear, and it will get back to Hedden and Bruce will be found guilty before he's even had a chance to speak."

"Owen, Janet loves Bruce. She—"

"Please. Even Travis admitted she's not one hundred percent certain. Let's keep this in the family for now."

Her heart cramped at the sight of anguish in Owen's eyes. "Yes. All right." She had been thinking of Emily, of herself. But she would do anything to shelter Owen from pain, and if it would make him feel better for her to keep quiet about Emily and Bruce, at least for the next few days, that was little enough to do. She would postpone the shopping expedition. "We'll keep it in the family."

And we are still a family, she thought.

And so they went through their day as if it were any other normal day. Linda baked and Owen worked outdoors, picking up fallen branches and twigs and stacking them in a pile for kindling, raking leaves, turning the horses into the outer pasture. In the late afternoon just as Owen came into the house, Linda said, "I'm going to call Emily. Want to get on the extension?"

Owen collapsed into a chair and began to unlace his workboots. "I'd better get in the shower or we'll be late. Tell her hello for me."

Linda always talked longer to Emily on the phone than Owen did; she talked longer to Bruce as well. It was simply the way they were, the way it always had been, and it implied nothing, Linda told herself, that Owen didn't want to speak to Emily now. It didn't mean he was angry with her, was avoiding her . . .

"Hi, darling," she said when her daughter's voice came on the line. "How are you?"

"Okay."

"Did the hospital serve a Thanksgiving feast today?"

"I wouldn't exactly call it a *feast*."

"Well, did you have turkey? Stuffing? Pumpkin pie?"

"Sure."

And did you enjoy it? Linda wanted to ask. Are you

eating, are you sleeping, are you taking care of yourself?

"Well, we're getting ready to go to the Burtons'. It's at their house this year. We're going to tell them you're with friends today, by the way. Just . . . because it's too complicated otherwise."

"Fine."

"I made a pumpkin pie. And a deep-dish blackberry." When Emily didn't reply, Linda went on, her voice cajoling, encouraging. "We had a letter from Grandmother. She has a new suitor. His name is *Oswald*." Linda waited to hear Emily's laugh. Usually Emily loved hearing about her grandmother's life in a retirement home in Florida, besieged by suitors with antiquated names and old-fashioned dating customs. But what was Linda *thinking*? Probably any talk of men and women wasn't appealing to Emily right now. "Owen says hello. We had a terrible storm last night. Amazing wind. Did you have it there?"

"I guess."

"Well, what are you doing today? Anything special?"

"Watching videos. One's on right now."

"Oh, what is it?"

"Some chainsaw murder thing."

"That doesn't sound very . . . appropriate. Do the staff know you're watching it?"

"They're watching it with us."

"Oh. That's okay then. Well, I guess I should let you get back to the movie."

"Yeah."

"Emily . . . darling. I love you, babe."

"Yeah. I love you, too, Mom."

Linda sat staring at the phone for a moment after they disconnected. On the one hand, Emily's voice was so spiritless, drained of her usual ebullience. On the other hand, she seemed rational, composed. She was watching a video.

She was safe. For now, for today, Emily was safe. That was enough to be grateful for.

Linda thought of her daughter. She could envision her clearly, a glowing ember of life encircled by the hospital staff, enclosed by the hospital walls, encompassed by highways and roads that Linda could travel on to reach her, surrounded by webs of telephone lines so they could communicate at a moment's notice. So many layers of protection. With that image fixed clearly in her mind, like a garnet set within elaborate holdings of gold, like an amulet Linda could look at whenever she needed to, Linda knew she could continue with her day.

Still, she felt frivolous as she dressed in a velvet skirt, high-cuffed suede boots, and a long loose sweater. She felt *irresponsible.* How could she care what she wore, what she looked like, when her daughter was in the psychiatric ward of a hospital? Then Owen appeared in the doorway, handsome in his tweed jacket and corduroys but still strained-looking through the eyes, and her heart went out to him.

"You look beautiful," he told her, and she understood that he saw the anxiety in her face, too, and was trying to cheer her.

"Hungry?" she asked.

"Not really," he admitted.

She took a bracing breath. "You will be once we're at the Burtons' and you smell the turkey."

And so they gathered up the pies and drove off to share the Thanksgiving meal with their friends.

The village of Ebradour nestled at a curve in the mountains just about fifteen miles west and a little bit north of Northampton. It served a population of around seven thousand scattered residents, three-fourths of them Massachusetts natives whose families had made their living in the area for generations in farming, logging, trucking, and millwork. The newcomers were an educated, solitude-hungry elite who had bought up deserted farm houses and renovated old hunting cabins in order to live in a tranquillity and natural beauty that was disappearing from larger towns.

The town had a post office, a redbrick church the McFarlands occasionally attended, two cafes, a grocery store, an insurance agency–real estate office, and an old-fashioned five-and-dime store with a pharmacy. The Ryans' convenience store and gas station was just on the McFarland's side of Ebradour.

For years, the McFarlands had shared the holiday with the same group of friends, rotating houses each year, everyone bringing something. This Thanksgiving the meal was held at the Burtons', a retired couple in their early seventies. Both were professors emeriti, Irene of English literature, Bud of anthropology. Their home was full of books and journals and reviews and correspondence; their conversation about worldly rather than personal matters.

The Ryans were there, bringing vegetables from Rosie's garden. Riley Ryan and Owen had known each other from childhood, although they hadn't been buddies because Owen was ten years older. But after Riley grew up and married, the difference in their age leveled out. Linda and Rosie had become good friends and Emily loved baby-sitting for one-year-old Sean. Linda knew that Rosie would be enormously concerned about Emily, and she yearned to talk to her. But she wouldn't, not yet.

Celeste was at the Thanksgiving dinner, too. Celeste was always there. Her family's farm bordered Owen's, had for decades. As children Owen and Celeste had been intimate, best friends, comrades, remaining loyal through adolescence, nursing each other through the turbulence of early love and then through marriage and divorce.

It was after her divorce that Celeste had realized she

loved Owen, had loved him all her life. Unfortunately for her, Owen did not reciprocate those feelings. He was fond of her. He cared for her. But for him that sexual and romantic spark just did not ever flare or even flicker. They managed to remain friends; they dealt with any awkwardnesses with the diffusing device of humor.

When Linda came on the scene, Celeste treated her with a swaggering candor that was supposed to make up for its substance: she envied Linda and wished she'd drop dead, or at least just leave. After Linda married Owen and moved to the farm, Celeste reduced the voltage of her death-ray smile and adopted a kind of brusque big sister–camp leader bossiness with Linda that really was the best she could do, given the fact that Linda had gotten the man and the farm as well.

Tall, bony, angular, agile, Celeste was the one woman Linda had ever met in all her life who could have carried off couture fashion, and she was the one woman Linda knew who disdained clothing. Her farm was everything to her. She bred quarter horses and golden labs. She kept bees and sold their honey. She had inherited enough money from an aunt to keep the farm in tiptop shape forever and to travel as well if she wished, but she didn't want to. She'd tried traveling, and discovered she preferred to be on her farm.

Or on the McFarlands'. One of the enduring arguments between Owen and Linda concerned Celeste's habit of walking into their home without knocking or calling first to see if it was a good time to come over. Over the seven years of their marriage, Linda had found Celeste's habit intrusive and arrogant, not to mention occasionally awkward and embarrassing. Celeste had walked in to find Linda weeping over a bad review or yelling at the children or arguing with Owen, and Celeste hadn't had the good sense or manners to leave but had instead said, "I'm out of salt," and opened the cupboard—she knew what was in each one—and taken it out. "I'll bring it back later." Linda didn't begrudge her the salt—or the dog food or rope or aspirin—she begrudged her the act of entering their home without first knocking and waiting for someone to open the door and invite her in.

"But Linda, she grew up treating our house and farm as an extension of hers. And I did the same at her house," Owen contended.

"It's not appropriate now," Linda insisted. "God, Owen, you place so much significance on privacy, on boundaries, on propriety. I don't see how you can't see how invasive it is to have her just barge in whenever she wants. It's as if she thinks she has a claim to this place."

"I think you're overreacting. She's merely a good neighbor. You have to admit, she comes in handy whenever we go away."

That much was true. Celeste knew where the fuse box was and how much medicine Maud needed at night and how to toss out the hay for the horses so that Fancy didn't get it all. Because of her, the McFarlands had been able to make overnight trips to Hedden for Parents' Weekend. Linda had tried to teach Rosie Ryan the routines of the house. She liked Rosie more; she trusted her. But Rosie was busy now with her baby. Owen was right, it was just easier for Celeste.

The seven neighbors gathered around the Burtons' long mahogany table, and Bud Burton stood to say a Thanksgiving prayer. As Linda listened, head bowed, she looked through her lashes at the table, covered with linen and set with china and silver and a centerpiece of fruit spilling from a silver bowl. Candles set in long holders all up and down the length of the table threw a soft glow over the faces of her friends, and she thought how fortunate they all truly were. And how they also were strong, persevering, in their individual ways. Irene was battling Parkinson's disease, and sometimes was almost defeated by it, which in turn sank her husband into the depths of misery. No one knew how he would live without Irene. But today she was in a good period, smiling, gracious, and this, Linda knew, was something to be thankful for. Each good day was something to be thankful for. The Ryans were always near financial disaster; Riley worked hard, but the little convenience store brought them only a tiny income, which he augmented by selling firewood from the few acres of land he'd inherited. They had to work hard, scrimp and save; yet this was the life they'd chosen, and they loved it. No pity needed there, Linda thought, and looking at Rosie's face, she decided that her friend looked especially pretty today, with Sean nestled on her lap. Motherhood suited Rosie. And Celeste . . . Celeste must be lonely. But Owen said that she liked her solitude, so Linda wouldn't worry about her, either. She would just try to appreciate the day, the delicious food, the company of friends.

But at every moment Linda was thinking: Emily. Emily. Her first Thanksgiving apart from her family. Linda had known, of course, that this would happen some day, but never had she imagined it would happen like this.

After the enormous meal the group dispersed. Rosie carried Sean up the stairs to the Burtons' guest room for a nap; Riley and Bud turned on the television to check out the football games.

Linda and Owen settled in front of the fireplace with cups of coffee and Celeste sank into a chair across from them.

"What's up?" she inquired. "You've been away."

Linda looked at Owen.

"Had to get to Hedden. Take Bruce dress clothes. He's going to the big city."

"Come on. There's more. You're in a black mood, I can tell." Celeste leaned toward Owen, speaking as if Linda were not in the room.

"Just minor kid stuff," Owen hedged.

"Oh, come on, tell me. It couldn't be any worse than some of the stunts we pulled as teenagers." She ran her hand through her short blond hair. She cut it herself, and it fell in a shaggy golden mop over her shapely skull, framing her enormous blue eyes.

Owen looked at Linda. He cleared his throat. "Bruce got in a fight with another boy. Wouldn't say why. We had to meet with the dean of students. He was given a warning this time. He'll be suspended if it happens again."

"Good for Bruce!" Celeste exclaimed. "High time he got into a little red-blooded trouble."

"I'm not sure I agree with you," Owen said.

"Come on. Remember what we did at his age."

"I think I'll see how the game's going," Owen said, and rose, heading for the den and the group around the television.

"Huh!" Celeste sat back, surprised. She arched a brow at Linda. "Where's his sense of humor?"

"I suppose we all lose it when our kids are concerned," Linda told her.

"I guess," Celeste replied halfheartedly, and rose and followed Owen into the den.

"It's sort of pitiful, isn't it?" Rosie asked in a low voice as she entered the room.

"You mean Celeste?" Linda asked, looking over her shoulder to be sure the other woman was far enough away. A roar exploded from the den and Bud yelled, "Touchdown!"

"They can't hear us," Rosie assured Linda, and settled in next to her on the sofa. "I just feel so sorry for her. Trailing around after Owen like a lovesick puppy."

"She's a beautiful woman. You would think she'd have hordes of men after her."

"She doesn't want hordes of men. She wants your husband. Besides, how would any man find her? She

never leaves her farm." She snuggled close to Linda.
"Anyway, guess what?"

The glow in the other woman's eyes confirmed
Linda's suspicion. "You're pregnant."

Rosie nodded. "Only just. Riley knows, but I'm not
telling anyone else for a while."

"I'm so glad for you, Rosie."

"Thanks. It's just what we wanted. It will be good
for Sean to have a sibling around."

The fire was warm and crackling, the room filled
with its golden glow. Rosie was telling Linda about
baby clothes, baby furniture. Linda listened, smiling,
nodding, and thought of Emily.

They returned home late in the evening. No mes-
sages on the answering machine; thank God for that
much.

Linda was slightly melancholy as she moved around
her bedroom. For a few moments she stood at her window, looking out at the night, thinking how everything
had changed. Usually this time of year filled her with
satisfaction and anticipation for the season to come, as
if darkness and cold were luxuries. But it could be any
season now. It could be spring or summer, still she
would be numb with cold. What could she do to sort
through the puzzle that her daughter had become? Her
head ached from thinking.

She heard Owen enter. He was naked, and he
crossed the room and took her in his arms. For a moment she held back, feeling irrationally that if she did
not at this moment enjoy pleasure, somehow that de-
nial would balance out a mysterious scale and keep her
daughter safe from future harm.

But Owen mattered, too, and she could feel his need,
here, now, physically real, more indisputable than su-
perstition.

Everything else fell away. She let it fall.

The floorboards creaked as they moved to the bed.

Linda lit a candle, and the flickering light threw all the aged, familiar sections of her room, the fading draperies, the scuffed floorboards, the cluttered bureau, the half-shut closet door, into shadow. This was their home. This was still their home, and here there existed many kinds of love. As she moved beneath Owen's body, she was filled with certainty. She was exactly where she belonged, doing the one thing she should be doing in all this world. So ordinary, so profound: she was making love with her husband, in a bedroom of their home.

Chapter Fourteen

Friday Emily had to see Dr. Bug-Man again. Well, why not? It was already a gross day. The windows were streaked with rain. The sky was gray, bleak. The leaf-stripped tree limbs shivered in the wind like living things, living things in pain. It was creepy.

"How are you doing today, Emily?" Dr. Brinton asked.

"Okay."

On days like this on the farm, her mother would pull on old boots and a rain slicker and stalk off into the wind, exhilarated. She'd climb the hills, yelling at Emily: "Take a deep breath! Doesn't it smell *rich*? Leaves and pine needles and wet earth and fresh air. The *planet*. Yum." Later, she'd shower and build a fire and bake cookies and cajole everyone into a game of Scrabble or Pictionary. Those thoughts glowed inside her like little fires. She missed her mom.

Dr. Brinton looked at a folder. "So tell me. What's the deal with your father?"

Emily shrugged. "No deal. He's an asshole. I never see him."

"How do you feel about that?"

"I don't feel anything."

"No anger? No regret?" When Emily didn't reply, he prodded, "How did your parents get together? Do you know?"

"Yeah, a little." She stirred deep into her memories. "Mom was getting her masters in English lit. My father's a cellist. He's on the music faculty at Leeds University." This was like talking about a book her mother had read her as a child. She could conjure up the images in the same way, the way she'd envisioned things when she was a little kid, curled up in her mother's lap at bedtime, both of them smelling of baby shampoo, her mother's voice dreamy, spinning out a tale that Emily made pictures to in her mind. She had shown her photographs, too. Her mom had been pretty, in a kind of humorous way, in her dorky clothes, like shirts with long pointy collars and swirly vests, and her hair had been cut in a shag that surrounded her head like a fuzzy box.

"Where's that?"

"Huh? Southern Pennsylvania somewhere. They fell in love, got married, had me, got divorced." Her mom had one album, padded blue leather, heavy pages, with photos carefully placed and annotated: Linda in an ivory wool suit, Simon in corduroys and a tweed jacket, and an ancient couple, friends from the music department who witnessed the marriage. A few photos of Linda and Simon on vacations, on the beach, in New York. On holidays, decorations for Christmas or a birthday cake in the background. Lots of photos of Simon in his tux with his chamber group before a performance. Linda huge with pregnancy, Simon with his arm around her and his mouth primped up with disdain. Linda with her newborn baby. Simon with his infant daughter, holding it out from him as if afraid it would pee on his clothes.

"Got divorced because of you?"

"No. Well, maybe, kind of. My father doesn't like children. But Mom would have left him sooner or later anyway. He's nuts."

"Nuts? Certifiably?"

"No, just narcissistic." She flashed a glance at Bug-

Man, checking to see if he believed she knew what that meant. "Arrogant. Selfish. Ask Mom. She doesn't talk about him much."

"Do you miss him?"

"How could I? I never was with him. I mean, Mom left when I was, like, one year old."

"You must wish now and then that you had a father . . ."

"Sometimes." Emily squirmed in her chair. "When I see friends at school with their dads. Or those TV commercials of, like, a wedding with a father all happy to see his little girl getting married. But I don't think about it much."

"Have you ever tried to communicate with him?"

Emily snorted. "You don't *get* it, do you? The man plays by his own set of rules. He doesn't give a shit about having a daughter. He doesn't want to know. I don't exist for him. And all right, sure, sometimes I get all pathetic about it, but I mostly don't even think about it. He doesn't exist for me, either. It's like having a father who's dead."

"What about grandfathers?"

"Don't have any."

"Why not?"

"They're both dead. So's Simon's mother. I've got a grandmother, though. Mom's mother. She's kind of cool in her own bizarre way."

"Where does she live?"

"Florida. We visit her sometimes." Just the thought of her grandmother flushed Emily with warmth. Inches of sweet thick icing on cake, mashed potatoes, Jell-O salads, creamed corn, creamed everything. The constant beat of heat against the walls and windows. The drowsy exhalation of the air-conditioning. Shades and curtains pulled to dim the brassy sunlight, and pillows everywhere, the wall-to-wall carpet feeling three feet thick, everything so soft, as if you could fall asleep anywhere, any time.

"So, Emily, not a whole lot of males in your life, huh?"

She returned to the present. Shifted in her seat. Thought about the question. "Well, there's Owen."

"What kind of stepfather is he?"

"Okay." She braced herself to be pried for more detail, but Dr. Brinton said, "Tell me about life in . . . what is it, Ebradour."

Emily shrugged. "It's okay."

He leaned back in his chair, arms crossed behind his head, relaxed. Not hovering over a pad of paper, poised to write stuff down. "Do you like living on a farm?"

"I guess. Mom *loves* it."

"So you tried to love it, too, right?"

"I'd rather live in a neighborhood on a normal street. Where I could walk to friends' houses or to a coffee shop or to school. And Ebradour is a stupid town. You can't do anything there without everyone knowing. Can't buy cigarettes, can't even buy a candy bar without Rosie knowing and making some kind of deal out of it."

"Not much privacy?"

"Well . . . when Mom and I lived in Arlington we had to live on the second floor of an apartment house above a wicked mean nurse. She worked at night and slept during the day and totally freaked if we, like, walked on our floors." Day and night traffic hurtled past their house at such dangerous speeds that Linda wouldn't allow Emily to roller-skate or ride a bike even on the sidewalks. There was not much of a front yard, and the back yard was small and perpetually darkened by neighboring garage walls.

"So it must have been nice to live in a house."

"Mom thought it was paradise, all that space, all those rooms."

"And you thought . . . ?"

"Boring."

"How'd you get along with Bruce?"

She considered, then answered honestly. "When I first moved there, we both really hated each other for a while."

"How old were you?"

"I was eight, he was ten. I don't mean real hate. It was just, suddenly we had no choice, there I was in his house, we couldn't avoid one another, and we had all these dumb rules."

"Rules?"

"Yeah, Mom and Owen made a list and sat us down and talked it over with us, like it was the United Nations peacekeeping laws or something. They kept it on the refrigerator. We had to help clean the table and do the dishes every night. Take turns feeding the old dog. Mom even kept track of who rode to the grocery store with her and helped carry in the groceries. She'd go, 'Bruce, Emily helped me last time, it's your turn now.' "

"Doesn't sound like a bad idea to me."

"Maybe not. It was kind of anal. I mean, each week we all had to make plans for when we'd watch TV."

"Probably kept the friction level down."

"I guess."

"So you and Bruce were adversaries then?"

"Not adversaries. Just . . . strangers."

How could she explain it? That first year, the new place, the males so large, so loud . . . even when they were just talking normally, their voices boomed. They were like extraterrestrials. They didn't shut doors, they slammed them. They didn't put the bread in the bread drawer, they tossed it in from across the room, as if they were making goals in a basket, and her mother didn't stop them. Their movements were fast, jerky. That first year she'd still played with dolls and stuffed animals, and Bruce teased her relentlessly about that, crying *wa-wa-wa-wa* like a baby, making farty noises when he passed by her room. Once when he said he'd

play with her, he put pants on her baby's head and a
hat on the bottom and went into a frenzy of laughter
that accelerated as Emily grew more and more angry,
until he was rolling on the floor laughing, accidentally
kicking over her carefully arranged dollhouse.

But it wasn't that they were bad or anything, it was
just that they were *there*. They were always there. She'd
had her mother to herself all her life, now suddenly
Linda was either gazing cowlike up into Owen's eyes
or going into raptures over Bruce's homework. The
very air around her smelled different: their apartment
had smelled so pretty, a mixture of perfumes and
scented soap and almond body lotion and Cling Free
sheets from the dryer. Owen and Bruce and their house
smelled like sawdust and hay and male sweat and old
dog with an underlying acrid tang like wild grape jelly
that Emily eventually figured out was from the constant
scratches, scabs, and cuts on Bruce's skin. At first Linda
had fussed over him, but Owen had said, "For God's
sake, Linda, leave the boy alone or you'll make him a
sissy."

Until they lived on the farm, Emily had thought her
body was all one soft and supple piece, like a wide
ribbon of flesh, but once she was around the men with
their knobby, bony, hairy limbs, her own body had
transformed itself into parts, parts that needed to be
kept covered, parts that suddenly possessed undertones
of meaning. Even her clothes took on different significance. Suddenly she found herself sick with mortifica-
tion if she left her underpants on the bathroom floor
instead of in the clothes hamper, and now Emily remembered a humiliating time when she first moved to
the farm when she had gotten all agitated to discover
her clothes in the hamper all shoved together with
Bruce's. It had seemed too intimate to bear, yet impossible to explain in words. Her mom had come through
that time, though. Her mom had understood. She'd
gotten each person a plastic clothes basket for them to

keep in their rooms, and she made them help her do their own laundry separately in spite of the fact that Owen complained it was not energy efficient.

Yet after that first year of getting accustomed to the males, a transformation had occurred. Instead of being suspicious of Bruce, Emily had become his ally. And he hers.

She remembered one summer morning, opening the bathroom door to see Bruce with his jeans down around his ankles as he bent over with a washcloth in his bloody hands, blotting the blood on both lacerated knees. His white Jockey shorts had bagged around his butt. His hands had been bleeding, too.

Hey, retard, ever heard of knocking?

Ever heard of locking the door? And then, *Are you all right?*

Sure. I fell out of the loft.

Wow. You aren't supposed to be there.

They looked at one another.

They connected.

Don't tell Dad and Linda.

I won't. They were conspirators. *I'll get Bactine from the kitchen cupboard. What was it like?*

It's cool. I'm trying to rig up a rope swing. An appraising look. *I bet if you ask Dad, he'll let us.*

Now she said to Dr. Bug-Man, "We were friends, for a while."

"Buddies?"

Hurry up, Horse breath!

"We had good games. Make-believe games, dress up, making forts and secret hideaways in the woods. One summer we dragged stuff from the attic, blankets, pillows, dishes, a Styrofoam chest for food, and made a hideout near a bunch of big rocks. And we lugged out old bales of hay and covered them with branches and leaves to make a tunnel we had to crawl through to get into it. All summer we sort of, like, acted out different fantasies."

"Like what?"

"Oh, like rich orphans hiding from kidnappers, scientists hiding from the government, good aliens hiding from bad scientists . . ." Emily flushed with pleasure at the memory. "That was the best summer. We invented these elaborate signals we could use in front of Owen and Linda and they wouldn't know what we were saying."

"And what were you saying?"

"Just dumb stuff like *Meet in one hour,* or *Don't say a word.* We created money from Owen's sacred number two pencils—that's what he uses to write with." She laughed. "We were so *into* it! We kept a record in a notebook of who managed to steal or smuggle a pencil from the house and whoever did got to be the chief that week. Owen used to go apeshit, roaring through the house, 'Where in the hell have all my pencils gone?'" She laughed again. "I can't believe I can remember all that." She made a fist, touched her thumb to her nose, then to her mouth. "That means *Don't say a word.*"

"So you took turns being the leader?"

"Sometimes. Usually Bruce was the leader. It wasn't a male-female thing, it was that I was younger. He just knew more than I did. Had a better imagination."

She was in a pocket of memory now, the memory surrounded her. How often she and Bruce had lain together in their hideaway, plotting. They'd raced through the woods on secret missions. Hidden in trees, spying on Owen and Linda weeding the garden. If Linda finished tying up the tomatoes before Owen had mown the walking paths around the garden plots, that was a message to hide the secret amulet. If Celeste came plodding over on her horse Rock with Bubalu ambling along, they had to run as fast as they could through the woods and over the pasture to her place, where they retrieved the stolen key to the government code, cleverly disguised in the shape of an apple or a berry.

Once they'd even braved Celeste's house—she always left the doors unlocked—and unable to find a pencil, had stolen a ballpoint pen.

Her skin had been a mosaic of scratches, bruises, and scabs that summer. When she ran, her breath, Bruce's breath, filled the air around them, became one breath filling her ears, her mouth, her chest. One time she tore apart one of his shirts to make into a pretend tourniquet, which she wrapped around his arm after some imaginary injury. His chest had been like hers, ribs and bones, knobby, his skin as warm and familiar as Maud's fur. When they lay together in their fort, she couldn't distinguish between his smell, her smell, and the smell of the hay and leaves and mildewing old blankets. He didn't smile much but when he did it was like a comet blazing through the night.

Brinton broke into her reverie. "You and Bruce didn't fight?"

She switched gears. "Of course we fought. All the time. Bruce could be way mean." Another grin possessed her. "But I could be mean, too."

"Did he ever hit you?"

"Sure. I hit him, too. When we were kids. Sometimes we fought just for something to do when we were really bored, like in the car. But when we were kids, we were, like, really close." The good walls of memory were beginning to dissolve. "I thought we'd always be close."

"When did it change?"

"You know once," Emily continued, not hearing him, "once Bruce did the coolest thing. When I was eleven, I was *dying* to see Bon Jovi when they played at the Centrum but Mom and Owen didn't want to take me. They said it was too much trouble, and none of my friends could go and they didn't want me going alone, and I was, like, *suicidal*. And Bruce told Owen and Mom that he wanted to see them, too, even though he thought Bon Jovi was gruesome. So they drove us there and he went with me. That was really cool."

"Tell me what happened when Bruce went away to Hedden."

Now the easy memories totally vanished. "I missed him," she confessed. "A lot. The house was so empty. Mom drove me everywhere after school to see friends, but it was a drag; it all had to be arranged, everyone lived so far apart."

"Did you two write? Talk on the phone?"

"I guess maybe I wrote him a letter. He never wrote me. He was, like, totally into his new world. I mean, when he came home that first Thanksgiving, he was like a million years older. Then in the summer he started having guys come visit, and it was like they all thought I was just a baby."

"And when you went to Hedden?"

Emily looked away. "What about it?"

"How did you feel about Bruce then?"

Shame beat against her chest and fluttered in her throat. "I don't want to talk anymore."

"Why not? What do you have to hide?"

Emily hugged herself tight. No matter how clever the shrink was, she would not tell him that. Not him. Not anyone. It was too confusing. Too humiliating.

"Emily, Dr. Travis tells me that your stepbrother raped you."

She stared at the floor, mouth locked.

"Could we discuss this?"

She did not answer but began picking at a bandage around her thumb. She could slide her thumbnail under the rubbery covering and find the raw, opened cut. She could dig her nail into that open, angry flesh, hard.

"You know, if you felt physically attracted to Bruce, that doesn't mean you caused the rape."

She shook her head. She whispered, *"I'm guilty."*

And no matter what he said to her, she did not reply

but sat staring at the floor, letting Dr. Bug-Man's words blur into buzzes and drones until at last he sighed and rose and said, "Okay, Emily. Let's call it a day."

Chapter Fifteen

After breakfast Saturday Owen grabbed his jacket and leather work gloves and headed outdoors. The fence around the perimeter of his land needed checking before winter set in; he would do it today while his thoughts were clotted and frayed. Often when he was blocked on a book, a day spent in strenuous physical labor provided him with a new twist, the necessary scene, right down to the dialogue, as if all along the material had been tucked away in his muscles, and had needed only a sufficient amount of outdoor exertion to free it.

Perhaps, if he worked hard enough, by the end of this day his mind would find some ordering principle to guide his thoughts about Emily and Bruce.

He started up the sputtering old tractor, drove it out of the barn, then hauled the flatbed wagon out and hooked it on. From the shed he took a roll of barbed wire, a dozen metal fence posts, his sledgehammer, the box of metal brackets, the wire cutters. He threw them all on the flatbed, climbed onto the tractor, and headed out to the far pasture.

The grass all around was tall and silvered with frost, the air clean and crisp. Owen felt in his element here, clear-minded, able. Beneath him his tractor rumbled and chugged, an ancient but reliable machine, which he loved as if it were human.

He arrived at the far corner of his land. Here the fence sagged in several places and from the barbs, tufts of cinnamon or tan hair hung; his horses and Celeste's liked to rendezvous here, standing nose to nose like gossipy neighbors, leaning toward one another, the barbed wire not really making much of a statement against their tough hides. Owen took off the old wire, cut new wire and strung it, then walked the rest of the fence line, checking the tension of the wires, the steadiness of each post.

He liked the way the ground kept its hold on the posts: *this is mine, and I will not let go.* This fiercely, this firmly, had Owen's grandfather and Owen's father possessed the farm. It was McFarland land. The farm now belonged to Owen; someday it would be Bruce's. Every acre, every rock and tree that someday would be his son's had once been fenced in by Owen's grandfather, years ago, decades ago. They had never sold any of the land, and if Owen had anything to do with it, they never would. It was like a living thing to him. He was its guardian. It was his responsibility and his refuge.

Thank God Linda understood this. Thank God she was happy here.

Michelle had hated the farm. *Hated* it. He'd known that from the start, and it had been pigheaded of him to insist that they live here, although at the time, when his parents died and he and Michelle were both starving young artists, it had seemed the solution to all their financial problems.

But Michelle thrived in cities, among people, anywhere she could be seen and admired. Even her artistic creations, brittle, witty, colorful dioramas, were all urban scenes: elaborately detailed miniatures of public sites and buildings—the Boston Public Gardens, Harvard Square—with real faces cut from magazines and painstakingly affixed next to mythological creatures dressed in human garb. Centaurs. Griffins. Gargoyles.

She hadn't enjoyed the company of real animals; she'd hated dogs, cats, horses.

While he generally preferred animals to people.

Their marriage had been doomed from the start. They should have known that. Perhaps they did, and if they did, they reveled in even that. They both were proud, ambitious, rebellious. No one was going to tell them how to live their lives.

They'd been young. They hadn't known a thing. When Michelle got pregnant, they'd thought it was all some kind of lark, one more clever thing they could do, something new to celebrate. Perhaps if they'd stayed in Boston it would have worked out. They could have hired a nanny; Michelle could have rented a studio space so she could escape the cries and demands of an infant. But they'd been on the farm, and isolated. Owen had known Michelle was miserable. He hadn't been surprised when she'd left.

He'd been surprised at the happiness he felt after their divorce. All at once life had seemed reasonable, orderly in a way it hadn't been for years. He'd hired a local woman, Elaine Cumbie, to help with the cleaning, the cooking, and caring for Bruce. She was a genial woman, plump in the grandmotherly way that most grandmothers no longer were, and she adored Bruce and infused a real warmth into their home. Her death three years ago had been a great loss, but Owen knew, and Elaine knew, that she'd made all the difference during those early years when Owen was bumbling through his life, trying to be both parents to a boy of three while at the same time keeping up with the farm work and writing his novels in order to keep everything going, to buy food for him and Bruce, oats for the horses, to pay the doctor and the vet, to buy clothes and toys for Bruce and gas and oil for the tractor. The farm no longer provided any kind of income, only fields of sweet alfalfa and grasses for the horses in the summer and hay in the winter. Firewood for the house.

Rocky hills crowded with glorious old maples waiting
for Riley Ryan to tap every spring for the syrup he
boiled down and sold in his store. He gave Owen thirty
percent of the profit, a whopping five hundred dollars
a year.

So Owen had to work hard. What else was new?
His son had to learn the realities of life. Owen had built
a miniature desk for Bruce and put it in the kitchen
with a child's chair, next to the kitchen table where he
wrote. He'd stocked the bottom of the kitchen cupboard with paper and crayons and coloring books and
stickers, and while Owen worked, Bruce "worked,"
too. Every day they went out for walks, or clambered
up over Babe's bare back for a ride. They planted a
vegetable garden and weeded it. They swam in the
pond and fished in it. They made snowmen and skated
on the pond. They watched television together and
every night Owen read to his son before bed. They
subsisted on peanut butter sandwiches and spaghetti
and fruit and an occasional full-course meal at Celeste's
or the Ryans or the Burtons. And Elaine had always
been around.

A child could have a much worse life. Owen loved
his son past telling; Bruce always knew that. Owen had
always endeavored to be a good father, and to this
moment he believed he had succeeded.

Still, he couldn't kid himself. He loved solitude. Silence. For a little boy it must have seemed bleak much
of the time. He was aware that he could lose himself
in fugues of pensiveness. Linda often accused him of
enjoying his melancholy and Owen knew that Bruce
would not have known how to interpret that.

There had been many winter days when Bruce as a
little boy was stuck with his father in the kitchen while
cold wind rattled the windows and the ancient furnace
in the dank basement clanked and moaned away to
itself like a beleaguered phantom. Owen would have
been lost in his work, deep in thought, Bruce would

have been dutifully sitting at his little desk, being quiet, being good. He was always free to go to his room to play but it would have been a lonely time for a little boy and in the winter the halls and all the rooms of the house were layered in shadows. Bruce seldom stayed upstairs by himself when he was young.

Linda always said that if any two females were ever meant to enter the lives of any two males, Emily and she were destined for Owen and Bruce. "We were like *The Sound of Music* bursting in on a Strindburg play," she'd say, laughing. And it was true that the females brought laughter and color and movement and life into the males' lives.

In return, he had made Linda and Emily happy.

At least Linda, that much he knew with complete certainty. He had changed her life as much as she had his, perhaps more, and more significantly. He was in his deepest heart profoundly proud of what he had brought to her life as her lover, her husband.

When he first met Linda, he had been attracted to her immediately by her ease and pleasure in the world, by her full, rich, musical laugh, her sumptuous beauty, so different from Michelle's gaunt frame and cool poise.

Yet when finally he took her to bed, he'd been surprised by her reserve. She hadn't wanted the lights on, and she'd been so passive he'd been puzzled. It was a conundrum, how she could cuddle her daughter and carelessly wrap her arm around Bruce's shoulders, hugging him against her, yet come into their bed with a shyness that was almost a dread.

He'd been in love with her from the start, but her sexual reticence concerned him. He didn't know if a long-term relationship would last with what was unspoken between them, and so he broached the subject one night as they lay together after an especially unsuccessful moment of lovemaking. She had come to bed with him eagerly, then turned into a different creature, something spiritless, and he could not bear it.

"Did you enjoy that?"

They were lying in the dark, spoon-style, and he felt her shrink in his arms.

"Did I do something wrong?"

"No. No, not at all. I, well obviously I enjoyed myself. But you seem . . ."

Her voice was very small when she said, "Perhaps I'm frigid."

He considered this in silence. He must be careful. He didn't want to insult her. "Have you been with many men?"

"Only Simon."

"You're kidding."

"No, why should I kid about that?"

"It's just that . . . you're so lovely. Men must have wanted to take you to bed."

"I married Simon when I was twenty. Divorced him when I was twenty-seven. Emily was only two. I was teaching freshman English at community colleges, and tutoring foreign language students, and trying to write my second novel at night. I didn't have a lot of time or energy for men."

"But still . . ." He went quiet as he realized that she was weeping. He felt her ribcage shudder beneath his arm.

He tried to turn her to face him, but she pulled away.

"Linda, I'm sure you're not frigid. Let me show you."

"All right," she whispered, but she stiffened in his arms.

He tried to ease the tension by lightening his voice. "It'll be a real sacrifice on my part, you understand. It'll take a lot of my valuable time. Lots of practice."

With his voice he had eased her as if she were a nervous animal, and that night they spoke no more about it, but over the next months she came to bed with him with an innocent apprehension that in turn excited him. He had only to pull her down on the bed with him to feel her pulse flutter in her throat like a hummingbird's wings.

At first she lay in his arms curled and guarded, and so he soothed her with stroking and gentling words. He kissed her, slowly, softly, lightly, everywhere, taking his time, taking infinite care. His mouth softly touched her shoulders, the fragile ladder of her spine, her soft buttocks, muscular thighs, the silky back of her knees. As the nights went by he was rewarded when she sighed with pleasure. He did not press her for more. It was enough, he thought, for that moment, to hear her sigh, to feel the ease of pleasure relax her body.

Owen caught himself staring down at a splintered, weathered post. He shook his head to clear it. That span of fence was satisfactory. He climbed back on his tractor and drove toward the far eastern boundary of his land.

Once again he stopped the tractor, turned it off. The engine pinged, then all was silent.

As the fence line neared the ascent into the forest, an abundant cluster of wild grapevines coiled up the fence posts, spilling leaves over the fence. The grapes were gone, the large leaves rusty and rattling with autumn. Long ago he had helped his father clear a path between the fence line and the trees wide enough for a man to pass through on a horse. Two feet, all the way up the hill. He began to walk, his hands checking the tension of the wire, his mind churning on other thoughts.

He was a good father to his son, a good husband to Linda. Was he a good stepfather? On the whole, he would say, yes. Yes he was. Although it had taken him a while to get used to the little girl.

Emily had been seven years old when she moved to the farm. She'd been a chatterbox and pretty much of a baby. Just about everything on the farm frightened

her: the horses, the attic, the farm implements. But to
give her credit, she'd adjusted fairly easily. She'd been
anxious about starting school in a new place, then
quickly she made friends, got invited to their homes to
play, and invited them to the farm. Her quarterly
grades were excellent, the comments from teachers at
family nights and conferences glowing. She and Bruce
bickered a lot, over normal family issues: who got to
hold the remote control, whose turn it was to do the
dishes or take out the trash, whose friends were geek-
ier. But almost from the start she slept well at night,
ate well, laughed a lot, and with each day had seemed
to feel more at ease with Owen, who, she had once
confided to Linda, sort of scared her with his booming
voice.

He had tried to be a good stepfather. He had kept
his distance; he'd been available but not pushy. Every
night of that first year he and Linda lay whispering in
bed, going over the day, calculating how happy each
child was and how comfortable, how close, they were
each becoming to the other's child. They'd agreed that
since both kids had been taught to call the stepparent
by his or her first name, they'd keep it that way, unless
the child specifically asked to call Linda "Mom" or
Owen "Dad," and that hadn't happened, and that was
fine.

They developed a ritual for bedtime. Owen would
tuck Bruce in; Linda, Emily. They'd spend a few moments with their own child, giving them a chance to
talk privately, to be together intimately before sleep,
and then they'd visit the other child. Owen would sit
on Emily's bed, talk a few moments, kiss her good-
night, and Linda would do the same to Bruce. Owen
and Linda would cross between the bedrooms like
dancers in an elaborate ceremony, and Owen always
did think there was something slightly affected about
it, something stilted. But Linda had felt strongly about
this, and he'd agreed to it. After two or three years, as

the children grew older and their bedtimes began more erratic, the ritual had changed, then disappeared completely.

But that first year Owen and Linda had kept to it religiously, just as they always sat together at the dinner table every night, eating the slightly elaborate meals Linda insisted on, talking about their days or, when one of the kids was in a bad mood, sulking, preoccupied, pretending to.

He and Linda had tried hard. Had felt they were doing well.

Now, suddenly, a memory, an important memory, slid out of the vault of his mind and clicked into place.

When Emily was younger, she had lied about something of significance.

What year had she been in school? Third grade. He remembered Mrs. Tenner, Emily's teacher, with her high Minnie Mouse voice. She'd asked them in to a private conference after school to tell them that Emily was inventing a series of ever more elaborate lies about the way her father died, rescuing her from a sinking boat in the middle of the lake.

Linda had not been alarmed. "I guess that's what happens when your parents are writers."

"I'm concerned," Mrs. Tenner had said, "not because of the lie, which is understandable—most children in this school are fortunate enough to have both parents living with them. We have a low rate of divorce in this county. So perhaps Emily is embarrassed by her particular situation. It is the elaborateness of the lie that troubles me. And perhaps *troubles* is too strong a word."

Linda asked, "Do you think Emily needs to see a psychiatrist?"

"Oh, I don't think so. No. I don't want you to be alarmed. I just thought you two should be aware of this story, and perhaps discuss it with Emily. Some-

times children can get themselves boxed in by their
own fantasies."

That night they'd gone together into Emily's bedroom. Emily had been wearing her pink-and-white
nightgown, and she'd held a grimy stuffed rabbit in her
arms. Her two front teeth had been missing. Her hair
had been still slightly damp and smelled of baby shampoo.

Linda had sat on one side of the bed, Owen on the
other.

"Honey," Linda had begun, "we talked with Mrs.
Tenner today. She told us how well you're doing in
school. You have so many friends. And your schoolwork is great. But she's concerned because you told the
class that your father is dead. That he died in a lake,
rescuing you."

Emily only looked at her mother, wide-eyed.

"You know that's not true, don't you, sweetie?"

Emily nodded solemnly.

"You know your birth father is alive, and living in
Pennsylvania, and is a cellist."

Emily nodded again.

"And you know I'm your stepfather now," Owen
said softly. "I'll help your mother take care of you."

Emily looked at him. "On the television," she said,
"a house was on fire and a little girl was trapped inside
and the daddy ran in and rescued the girl."

Linda said, "Oh, honey, we take great precautions
to see that this house won't burn down. That's why we
have smoke alarms everywhere."

"But what if the house did burn down?" Emily insisted. She was kneading her bunny. "Or what if I was
in a boat and it tipped over?"

"Well, I'd be there, silly, and I'd save you," Linda
said.

"But what if you weren't there? You go away a lot.
You go to Boston. You go to England. What if I'm in
the house with Owen and Bruce? What if I'm in a boat

with Owen and Bruce? Owen will save Bruce, but who would save me?"

Linda looked at Owen. There was a moment of silence. Owen was proud of the fact that he never lied, never made easy promises, always kept his promises, every single time.

And so he meant it when he said to Emily, "If the house burns down, I'll save Bruce and I'll save you. At the same time. I'm strong enough, I can carry you both at once."

"What if we're in a boat?"

"Then I'll swim and get Bruce and you both."

"How can you swim if both arms are full?"

"You and Bruce can hang onto my shoulders."

Emily looked at Owen's shoulders, as if measuring their width.

"Okay," she'd said finally. Simply.

Standing at the edge of the woods with a strand of barbed wire in his hand, Owen remembered the radiance of Linda's face as she looked across her child's bed at Owen, at Owen, who would rescue her child.

That was the night he felt her body relax, as if her bones were melting inside her skin. That night he at last had brought her to an arching, moaning, sexual release.

"Oh, oh, that's what it's all about," she had sighed when she had caught her breath. "Owen, I never knew. Owen, Owen . . . why, that is *rapture.*"

She'd thrown her naked, sweat-dewed body around his, she'd wrapped her legs and her arms around him, she'd kissed his face, his neck, his chest, his shoulders, she'd been laughing and crying at the same time, and though the lights were off he could feel a radiance steaming from her skin. She had been happy. "Owen," she'd said, nuzzling him greedily. "Owen. *I want more.*"

And he had given her more.

And now it seemed that the meaning of his world

resided in her body, and the meaning of her world in his. They were soul mates; they were comrades; they were husband and wife.

There'd never been one single event during which Owen had saved Emily's life, but over the years Owen had *been* there for Emily, and he was proud of that. Over the years he'd driven her to a friend's house when Linda was gone, or driven into town to pick up a prescription or a liter of 7UP when Emily was sick. He'd led Babe or Fancy Girl around the pasture with a gaggle of giggling little girls on their backs at one of Emily's birthday parties. He'd spent hours looking at Emily's homework, helping her with math, admiring her artwork, listening to her read her essays.

Did he *love* Emily?

Yes. Unquestionably. He hadn't loved her at first. At first he'd only accepted her into his life because he loved and needed Linda. But over the past seven years he'd come to care for the girl, to enjoy her company, appreciate her humor, admire her strong points, and wish her well in all she did.

And, damn it, he *would* save her from a fire if he had to, and he'd rescue her if a boat tipped over.

He would give his life for hers.

But how could he help her now?

He'd come to the far boundary line that ran over the ridge of the hill. He'd work on that another day. Most of the fence around his land was in good shape for the winter; he'd accomplished something with his time.

He only wished the troubles they were facing with Emily could be so easily mended.

Chapter Sixteen

Monday morning while Linda made breakfast, Owen called Hedden and arranged for Bruce to be excused from his classes and to be waiting in front of Bates at nine-thirty.

Linda prepared a mug of coffee for each of them to drink during the drive to Basingstoke; they needed the warmth and the boost of caffeine. They were both anxious, and the weather suited their moods. The sky was low, iron gray; the temperature frigid. Their sleep had been restless and in the hush of the rushing car they were awkward with one another. Finally Linda twisted the dial on the radio until she found a Beethoven symphony that filled their silence.

Owen thought they'd arrive early at Hedden, but because of Monday morning traffic, they pulled into the drive in front of Bates Hall with only a few moments to spare. Bruce stood in front of his dorm as straight and radiant as a flame, his red hair shining in the gray day. He hopped into the back seat of the car.

"Hey, guys!"

Owen asked, "How was New York?"

"Awesome. Except, Dad, we saw some homeless people? Sleeping on grates, you know? One guy was about my age. I gave him a dollar, but Whit says not to, they just buy booze or drugs."

"Did you like Whit's parents?" Linda inquired.

"Oh, man, you've got to meet them! They are like Mr. and Mrs. Albert Einstein. Their house is like a museum. They have more books than we do."

Owen searched for something, anything, to keep things seeming normal until they got to the hospital. He and Linda had agreed not to discuss Emily's accusation with him beforehand. "Did you see Alison?"

"Yeah. Twice. Her place is *extreme*. Ultramodern, like a space station. She and Whit and I and a bunch of their friends went to dinner at the Paramount. I brought you some postcards. It is such a cool place. New York is the best. So, how's Emily?"

Cautiously, Linda said, "Well . . . better, I think. I guess we'll find out in a moment, won't we?"

Today the counseling room seemed too small. Travis had to bring in another chair. Bruce, smelling of sunshine and fresh air, dressed in baggy sweatpants, a rugby shirt, and his J. Crew anorak, his feet enormous in sneakers, seemed to overwhelm the room with his masculinity.

Emily came in after everyone else was settled. Her face was blank in that hateful way all adolescents had of barricading themselves from adults.

"Hey, Emily," Bruce said, easily, naturally.

Emily didn't reply, but sank sullenly onto her chair.

Owen watched his son carefully. Bruce was relaxed and good-natured. Innocent. If he weren't, wouldn't he be just a little nervous?

Travis began. "Thank you for coming in, Bruce. We need your help. We're getting to the root of Emily's problem, and . . . I'll let Emily speak."

Emily's eyes were dry, but as she spoke her face flushed. She looked across the room at her stepbrother with anger in her eyes. "I told them. I told Mom. I told Owen. What you did."

Bruce had thrown himself down carelessly on his

chair, bum on the edge, long legs sticking out in front, arms crossed over his chest. At Emily's words he looked puzzled. He glanced inquiringly at Owen, at Linda. "What I did?"

"I knew you would do this!" Emily growled. She turned to Linda, face creasing. "Mom, I knew he would do this. He is such a liar."

"Do what?" Bruce asked. He looked genuinely puzzled.

Owen said, "Emily says you raped her."

Bruce's head jerked back. "What? No way!" He looked at Emily. "Hey, Emily. Come on."

"*It's true!*" Emily said vehemently. "You know it's true. When Mom and Owen were at the writers' conference. You came into my bedroom the first night, and you *raped* me the second night in my bed, and you *raped* me the third night in the barn."

Bruce looked at his father. "Dad, why is she saying this stuff?"

Before Owen could speak, Emily shouted, "Because it's true! Because you scared me and you raped me and you hurt me and I thought I could forget it but I can't, I never will!"

Bruce looked puzzled, then certain. "This is because of Jorge," he said.

Emily cried, "You *shit*! *No!*"

"What about Jorge?" Owen asked.

Bruce shrugged. "You know. What Alison said. *Everyone* knows. Emily went apeshit at Jorge. Then she tried to off herself. Figure it out. If anyone raped her, he did."

"No!" Emily said.

"That's why you beat Jorge up?"

"Well, yeah. Because"—Bruce shrugged, looking abashed—"I mean, I heard that he'd frightened her, and I wanted him to leave her alone."

"That's not true!" Emily protested. "You're lying about everything."

"Hey, Emily, they can ask anybody at school. Casey and Merrit saw you screaming at Jorge." Bruce looked at Owen. "Ask them. Ask Casey Mestapapoulos and Merrit Frobisher."

"Mom, Owen, he's lying," Emily cried. "I mean, part of it is true. That night Jorge tried to kiss me, he just put his arms around me, and I don't know why, I freaked. I mean, I've had a crush on Jorge, and I still really like him; I don't know what happened, I *thought* I wanted him to kiss me, but when he put his arms around me I got all scared, it was like he was going to rape me like Bruce did, and I started hitting him and telling him no." Tears spilled down her face. "It was so embarrassing. He must think I'm a retard. He'll never talk to me again, I know it. I hate myself, I just want to die."

"You want to die because of what happened with Jorge?" Owen asked sharply.

"No!" Emily lifted her head and confronted them all, Travis, Owen, Bruce, Linda, with her reddened, blotchy, anguished face. "I wanted to die because of what Bruce did to me. It ruins everything, it ruins Mom and Owen, it ruins the farm for me, it ruins Hedden, it ruins everything I do, everywhere I turn. *I've lost everything!* Don't you see? Now when a guy I really like tries to kiss me, it only makes me scared, it makes me want to puke, all I can think of is Bruce and how he held me down, how he raped me!"

Now Bruce was as angry as Emily. "What is your *problem*? I didn't *rape* you, and you know it. I don't know why you're saying this stuff, but it sure as hell just isn't true."

They stared at one another, enraged.

"Take your time, Emily," Dr. Travis said.

Emily took a deep, cleansing breath. She looked directly at Bruce. "I tried to *die*. I thought that would be the easiest for us all. But I didn't die, and I'm not going to try again. You raped me, Bruce, and I'm not going to lie anymore. I'm telling everyone, Mom, and Owen, and I'm going to tell Zodiac and Cordelia, and *everyone* at Hedden will know . . ."

"You fucking psycho, don't you dare."

Emily's head whipped back at the sudden venom in Bruce's voice. Owen and Linda and even Dr. Travis recoiled in surprise.

"Bruce," Owen said warningly.

"You just want to ruin everything for me, don't you, you stupid bitch."

"*Bruce*," Owen said again.

"Bruce, your language is not acceptable," Linda told him.

Bruce glared at his stepmother. "My *language* is not *acceptable*? Emily's trying to ruin my fucking life and you're all worried about my *language*?" He turned to look at his father and now his calm had disappeared. His face was red, sudden tears glimmered in his eyes, and his jaw contorted as he tried to keep from crying.

A slight shadow of satisfaction crossed Emily's face as she watched Bruce's agitation. Bruce saw it.

"Look at her!" he said to his father. "Now she's happy. She's fucking with my *life* and now she's happy."

Emily cried, "I am *not fucking with your life*. I just want *my own life*—"

Bruce interrupted her. "You've always been jealous of me. Now you want to take everything away from me." He turned to Owen. "Don't you see, Dad? She's just a conniving bitch. She wants to keep me from getting into Westhurst. She wants to stop Alison from liking me. She wants to stop *everyone* from liking me. Christ, Alison will freak out if she hears this shit!"

"Bruce, Bruce," Linda said, as if calling to him across a sudden void. "Honey, why are you saying this? Why would Emily want to hurt you?"

Bruce looked at his stepmother, anguish in his eyes. "I don't know! Maybe she's pissed off because I never hang out with her anymore. You know, like on the farm, this summer, I think Emily and her friends . . ." He looked away, suddenly embarrassed.

"Had crushes on you guys?" Linda suggested.

"*Yeah*. And you know, we weren't interested. I mean they're all so young. Like they wanted us all to go on a picnic at the hilltop. And we wouldn't. But we weren't cruel or anything. We just ignored them . . ."

"You are such an asshole," Emily said.

Bruce glared at Emily. "You have always been on my case, ever since you moved to the farm. You hate it that it's *my* farm, that you don't have any place that's yours. You're like some kind of spook, following me everywhere, wanting anything that's mine."

"You are so sick," Emily spat.

"Yeah, well, I went to Hedden first. Where did you go? *You* had to go to Hedden, too, *didn't you*? I mean, did you seriously even consider going anywhere else? No. And now you can't stand it that my friends are higher-classed than yours . . ."

"Oh, please," Emily snarled.

"And I'm more popular than you, my grades are better . . . you just can't stand it! You want to do some damage to me. Admit it! You want people to think you're better than I am."

"Oh, you're clever, Bruce, you're really clever," Emily retorted. "Turning it around, making people think I'm crazy, but it won't work, because I'm *not* crazy. They've tested me. I'm not nuts. I'm *angry*. And I'm a fucking survivor. You probably wished I was dead, but I'm not. I'm not going to die and I'm not going to lie any more about what you did."

"You stupid bitch," Bruce growled, shaking his head in disgust.

"Stop this," Linda ordered.

Then they all were silent. Bruce's leg jiggled frenetically. Emily tore at her thumb.

Linda looked at Travis. "What now?"

Travis cleared her throat. "Now we take a break. Give ourselves time. Emily has come a long way today. She has overcome great difficulties and accomplished a major task by confronting her rapist."

"I didn't rape the stupid b—"

"Bruce." Owen's voice was iron.

Travis continued. "This took an immense amount of strength and courage. But that doesn't mean Emily's through with her work yet. She's got to confront all the emotions engendered by such a violent act. She's got to deal with her rage and her sorrow and her sense of betrayal. She's got to talk through her feelings. Her strong sense of guilt."

Owen pounced. "Wait a minute. If Bruce raped her, why does *she* feel guilt?"

Travis answered, "As I've said before, it's common for rape victims to feel guilty. To feel that they caused the rape somehow. Brought it on by, perhaps, their physical attractiveness . . ."

"Yeah, right," Bruce snorted.

Owen shot a look at his son.

"By her own fantasies of romance. By being weak. Just by being *there*. It's not rational, but I assure you, it is common. Now Emily has to learn where she can find her power, power to return to the world, power to deal with men, especially power to love. To love herself, to love her family. An enormous task is before her. *Enormous*. Later perhaps she'll be able to take part in sessions with you and one day even Bruce, but not yet. And frankly, Bruce is going to need some counseling, and the sooner he faces this, the better."

Owen said, "In spite of everything Bruce has said, you believe Emily."

Dr. Travis looked at him levelly. "Yes."

"I'm out of here," Bruce said, rising. "I don't need to sit and listen to this shit."

"Yes, I think it would be best if you left now," Travis coolly agreed. "Our time is almost up."

Owen rose. "I'll drive you back to Hedden." Looking at Linda, he said, "Then I'll come back here." A thought struck him. "Dr. Travis, again I have to remind you that I am adamant that this . . . this *accusation* doesn't leave this room. If my son's reputation is ruined, I'll take legal action."

"Mr. McFarland, I can assure you as I have before, no one discusses our patients outside of this ward."

Owen looked at Emily. "And what about you, Emily? What are you saying, what will you say, to your friends?"

Emily's face contracted into a sneer. "That's all you care about, isn't it, your precious son's precious reputation. You don't care that he raped me. You don't care at all!" She began to cry again.

Owen held out his hands, palms up. "Emily, I do care a great deal about you. I'm terribly upset about this. I want to help you as much as I can. But at the moment I'm not sure what I can do to help. In the meantime . . ."

"Oh, go on," Emily spat. "I won't tell anyone at Hedden. I promise." Then she cut her eyes at Bruce. "*Not yet.*"

Owen looked at his wife. "I'll drive Bruce to Hedden, then come back here, okay?"

Linda asked Travis, "Is there anything else we can do here today?"

"I don't think so. Emily needs to rest, and to spend some time with the group in therapy. Let's keep in touch by phone. Oh, and Linda, we have Family Group every Wednesday evening. Could you come?"

Before anyone could reply, Emily said, "I don't want Owen to come."

Owen and Linda looked at one another.

Linda said, "Emily, honey . . ."

"Forget it. I don't want either of you to come."

Linda said, "Emily. Look . . . I'll come." She glanced at Owen whose face was like thunder. "I'll come alone."

"I'm taking Bruce back to Hedden." Owen put his hand on his son's shoulder and ushered him out of the room. To Linda, he said, "I'll meet you out front when I return."

Linda nodded.

Then the three women sat in silence.

Linda turned to Dr. Travis. "Is there any way we can make Bruce admit . . . what he did?"

Travis shook her head. "There's no way to provide absolute proof. If Emily had reported it to the police immediately, and they'd been able to take a sample of the semen, and photographed the bruises, then there would be proof. As it is now, even a doctor's certificate saying that Emily is no longer a virgin is not sufficient proof that she was raped."

Linda took a moment to gather her thoughts, to put them in order. Then, taking her daughter's hands in her own, she said, "Emily, I need to say this, just once. You must forgive me for asking, but I think you understand the magnitude of your accusation. Are you telling us the truth when you say that Bruce raped you?" Before Emily could reply, she rushed on, "If you were lying, I'll forgive you, you know I will. It would be such a relief."

Emily said, "I *am* telling the truth. Bruce really did rape me. I swear he did. What do you want me to do? How the fuck can I prove it to you?"

"It's all right, Emily. I won't ask you again." Linda tried to put her arms around her daughter. "I'm so sorry."

Emily shrugged away. "Go on. Leave," she said, her

voice harsh. "Just get out of here. Go off with *your husband* and *leave me alone*."

There was no choice. At the moment that was exactly what Linda had to do.

First she used the pay phone to call Dean Lorimer, who assured them that Emily's homework would be sent to the hospital.

"We're close enough to the end of the semester. And Emily's a bright student," Dean Lorimer told her. "Her teachers have agreed that she can finish the courses if she does the required reading and writes the necessary essays."

"Thank you," Linda said.

"No problem. And good luck to you all."

As soon as they'd slammed the doors of the Volvo, shutting themselves into their private world, Owen said, "What's going on, Bruce?"

He turned to his father, his face creased in distress. "Dad, honestly, I don't know!"

"Did you make Emily mad? Is she trying to get back at you for something?"

"*No*. This is just a nightmare. It's like Kafka. I wake up and she's telling lies about me."

"There must be a reason."

"Well, I *told* you. She's jealous of me."

"I can't see that."

"Great. So you believe her."

"I didn't say that. I just don't see Emily as so jealous of you that she'd do something like this."

To Owen's dismay, Bruce's shoulders buckled and he bent over, head nearly touching his knees.

"Son." Owen reached over to rub Bruce's shoulders.

"I can't believe you don't believe me. I swear I didn't do anything," Bruce cried.

"All right. All right."

"I don't know what's going on. I don't get it. It's just fucked."

"It doesn't help if you swear."

"What does help?" Bruce asked, his voice savage. Raising his head, he took the handkerchief his father offered and blew his nose. "I've got a shitload of schoolwork to do. I've got to write a really great essay for my application to Westhurst. I've got the interview coming up in December. I've got to keep my grades up. Everyone says it's the hardest semester of my school career, and now Emily does this . . . this psycho act." Roughly he blew his nose, then continued, "Plus, shit, I really like Alison. I mean, Dad, I *really like* her. If Emily fucks this up for me . . ." Bruce's knee was jiggling with nerves and suddenly his voice broke as it had when he was younger. "Dad, what am I going to do?"

They'd arrived at Hedden. The grounds were empty; it was lunchtime. Still, Owen only put his hand on his son's shoulder though he wanted to hug the boy up against him.

"We'll get through this. Try to forget it for now."

"Sure," Bruce said dejectedly and left the car.

Owen called out to him, "We'll call when something changes."

"Right."

Owen watched Bruce race off toward his dorm. When his son was out of sight, he still sat, working to control his breath, not sure when he'd been so close to tears.

Linda was waiting for him under the hospital portico when he returned.

She sank into the car. "I'm exhausted."

"I know. What now?"

"I guess you and I return to the farm."

"And?"

"And Emily will remain in the hospital, working

with Dr. Travis and the other staff. I called Dean Lorimer. He's going to see that her homework is brought to her every few days."

"Who's going to bring her the homework?"

Linda shrugged. "Her friends. She is allowed visitors."

Owen's jaw tensed. "If Emily tells her friends . . ."

"Owen, Emily has promised not to discuss the rape with anyone at Hedden."

"Can we trust her?"

"She promised us . . ."

"Still . . . she's so angry at Bruce. She seems out to get him."

"Owen, it was Bruce who harmed Emily." She softened her voice. "But I'm sure she won't talk about this to anyone at Hedden. I do trust her."

"Do you think she's telling the truth? About the rape?"

Linda sighed and rubbed her temples. "I think so, Owen. How can we ever know for sure? I can't believe she would lie about something like this. But I never would have believed that Bruce would have spoken to her as he did."

"Well, he has a right to be angry."

"Maybe. Maybe not. Oh, Owen, what's happened? I thought we'd done such a good job! I never dreamt there was such animosity between the two of them. It's absolutely shattering!"

"I suppose a certain amount of rivalry and antagonism exists in any family. You and I were only children, so we don't have the experience, but I can remember how my friends in high school used to get into wicked fights with their sisters or brothers."

"Well, sure, and Bruce and Emily did, too; they had plenty of squabbles, that's normal. But this . . . this is incomprehensible."

They rode for a while in silence, occupied with their

own thoughts, and then Owen said, "So what can we do?"

"I guess we can only wait."

They said nothing else during the ride home, but kept cold company with their own separate thoughts.

Chapter Seventeen

❦

After lunch, Bruce found Alison waiting for him in their usual place, a soundproof practice room in the basement of the theater arts building. Alison was a pianist, so she had access to the rooms, which unfortunately had small windows in the doorway through which mistrustful school staff often peered, hoping to find someone smoking pot or committing some other kind of crime. Alison perched on the piano bench while Bruce sat on the floor in the far corner, hidden from the window by the piano.

"You weren't in biology."

"My parents came for me. Took me to see Emily."

"How is she?"

Bruce shrugged. "Not good. She's—" To his chagrin, tears filled his eyes. "She's hallucinating or something. Making up weird stories about people. I think she's nuts."

Alison left the piano bench and knelt next to Bruce, taking his hands in hers. "Oh, poor Bruce. You're so sweet. Don't be so sad. She'll be all right." She wrapped her arms around him and suddenly Bruce found his head nestled against her breasts. She smelled of some wonderful perfume.

"Sometimes I think my entire family is crazy," Bruce said.

Alison laughed. He could hear the laugh inside her

chest. "I know *my* family is. That's why God created boarding schools." She began to kiss the top of his head. "It will be all right. I promise."

He let himself be consoled. He tried to believe she was right.

*D*essert that night was not more stale pumpkin pie but ice cream and sauces they could heat in the microwave, and two cans of whipped cream as well.

They sat at their table, Keith, Cynthia, Arnold, Emily, and fat Bill. Those gathered around the other table were quiet, tranqued, or flipped into a world of their own.

"Come on, Cynthia," Keith teased, waving a spoon of hot fudge sauce beneath her nose. "Remember, chocolate is a drug."

"Get out," Emily said.

Bored, Cynthia intoned, "Chocolate metabolizes into the same chemicals as marijuana."

"Hey, we grown-ups don't go for those government-approved baby drugs," Arnold said.

"No fair!" Keith yelled suddenly. "Look at Bill! He's got all the Marshmallow Fluff!"

They all looked at Bill, who wrapped his giant paws possessively around the blue-and-white jar.

"Bill, you have to share that," Keith declared.

Bill held the jar to his chest.

"Come on, Keith, give the guy a break," Arnold said.

"Do you really want it now?" Cynthia asked in a low voice. "I think Bill's pretty much bonded with it."

"You can have some," Bill said to Emily, surprising them all.

"That's all right. Thanks anyway."

"No. You have some."

"That's—" Emily began to refuse again, but Cynthia kicked her beneath the table. "Well, thanks." While everyone watched speechlessly, Bill rose to plop a spoonful of white fluff into her bowl.

On her other side, Keith whispered, "I think this means you two are engaged."

"Hey, Beldon!" Arnold yelled to their night nurse, who was helping himself to his own bowl of ice cream. "Bill gave Emily some Marshmallow Fluff!"

"My man!" Beldon yelled.

"Emily?"

"Who's Heidi?" Cynthia asked sardonically.

Emily looked up to see Cordelia's sweet face peering around the doorway from the corridor. Cordelia had obviously gotten dressed up for the visit. She wore a Laura Ashley dress of printed, smocked, lace-trimmed cotton, and her long blond hair was braided and tied with red ribbons. She made Emily vividly aware of her mustache of white fluff, which probably made her look insane, like she was foaming at the mouth. Blotting her lips roughly, she rose.

"Cordelia, hi. Come in."

Timidly Cordelia approached, staring at Emily's tablemates with such obvious apprehension that it was insulting. "Am I . . . interrupting something?"

"Yeah, we're right in the middle of electric shock therapy," Cynthia said sarcastically, and with an abrupt shove of her chair, rose and left the table.

"Cynthia . . ." Emily said. "Wait."

"Hey, Emily!" Zodiac flew in the door. She wore jeans and a black turtleneck sweater and a gold stud in her nose. She threw herself around Emily. "God, I've missed you. When are you coming back? What's going on? Are you okay?"

"I'm fine. I'm going to stay here a while. Look, I want you to meet some friends . . . guys, this is Zodiac, my roomie at Hedden, and this is Cordelia, my other roomie. This is Bill, and Keith, and Arnold, and Cynthia." She had to walk over and grab Cynthia's arm and pull her back into the room.

"What are you guys eating?" Zodiac wouldn't be shy if she woke up to find herself on Mars. "Can I have some? Oh, wow, why can't *we* ever make *our* own sundaes?"

"Would you like to make your own sundae, Cordelia?" Emily asked.

"No, thanks." She was still shy, but even so she managed to seat herself next to Keith, who was much more handsome than Bill or Arnold.

Emily sat back down. "So what's new?"

Zodiac slipped off her backpack and opened it on the table. "We've brought you your homework. Cordelia's got your books. And we've got some letters for you. The nurse at the front desk checked it all already. Can you get E-mail here?"

"No."

"Too bad. Everyone wants to say hi, but they're all going crazy with finals and term papers and stuff. You know."

Cordelia gushed, "Merrit Frobisher's been expelled!"

"No way."

"Third time caught smoking pot."

"In the woods?"

"In the boathouse."

"Who was he with?"

"By himself."

"That's sad."

"Yeah, but he's fucked up. Something's going on with his family. He's always bummed after family vacations."

"But *by himself*. Poor Merrit."

"Jorge wants you to call."

"He wants *me* to call *him*?"

"That's what he said. Brought his beautiful body all the way across the courtyard especially to give me the message. Believe me, I tried to sidetrack the man, but he wasn't interested."

"But why doesn't he just call me?" Emily asked, bemused.

"Emily, dope, because the last time you were with him you spazzed out on him."

"Oh. Right. But he still wants me to call him?"

"That's what he said. Could I please ask you to call him. He'd like to talk to you. Here's his number. He's got his own phone."

Emily took the paper but her elation vanished. "I can't. Somebody will answer the phone and know it's me."

"Oh, grow up."

"I just can't do it. It's too embarrassing."

"I'll ask for him," Keith said.

"Would you? That's great."

"*Star Trek*," Bill announced suddenly. He rose, a giant of blubber.

Keith, Arnold, and Cynthia pushed back their chairs.

"Later," Arnold said.

"Coming?" Cynthia asked Emily.

"In a minute. I need to find out about my homework."

"*Right.*"

"She's a little on edge, isn't she?" Zodiac whispered after Cynthia and the others had left the room.

"I should go with them," Emily said, surprised at how much she wanted to.

"You should go with them to watch *Star Trek*?" Zodiac asked skeptically. "Ice cream and *Star Trek*. What is this place, perpetual kindergarten?"

"Emily, we're so worried about you," Cordelia said. "When are you coming back? What's going on?"

She yearned to tell her friends, especially Zodiac, but she'd promised Travis. So, looking at her hands—because Zodiac could tell by her eyes when she was lying—Emily said, "I guess it has something to do with my father. That he never sees me."

"Oh, Emily," Cordelia said, her eyes tearing up.

"So what can they do for you here?" practical Zodiac asked.

Emily shrugged. "Just talk, I guess." She could feel the intensity of Zodiac's scrutiny. "Learn not to feel hopeless," she added, remembering what Travis and Beldon emphasized. "Think about options. Learn to take control of my life."

"Like you can, at age fifteen," Zodiac said skeptically.

"Isn't it kind of . . . creepy? Being with all these, like, psychos?" Cordelia asked in a whisper.

"They're no more psychotic than I am," Emily snapped, and for a moment the desire to do something grotesque possessed Emily. Laugh maniacally like Vincent Price. Jump around grabbing at her armpits and grunting like a gorilla. Or just twitch a little. Maybe roll her eyes. Did this mean she really was nuts? Or was it just that she was sick of Cordelia and her overly sweet, overprotected mentality.

"Will you be able to come to the Christmas party?" Zodiac asked, and before Emily could answer, Cordelia chimed in, "And what about the Christmas trolls?" The trolls were a Hedden tradition; each student drew a name, then bought a present for another student whose name was kept a secret until the presents were given on Troll Morning, the last day of classes.

"I don't know," Emily said. "I'd like to come back, at least for Troll Morning." With a rush of astonishment, she said, "I've been here a week. A *week*. I haven't been in town or in a car. I've just been here."

"What have you been doing?"

"Sleeping, mostly."

"What happened to your face?" Cordelia asked in a little girl voice. "And your hands."

Emily thought the marks were pretty much healed. She stared at her friend without flinching. "I clawed myself."

Cordelia cringed and drew back. Zodiac rose and

came to Emily and wrapped her arms around her in a hug. "Look. You're doing what you need to do. You're my best friend and you're a fabulous dame and you're going to get through this and come out healthier and stronger than the rest of us."

"Zodiac." Emily hugged her friend. She wanted to hug her forever. Zodiac's presence was so comforting. To be this close to another human being, and not to fear the touch, not to instinctively panic, need to get away . . . Emily could almost believe she could trust again.

Then Cordelia, who hated to be left out of anything, ruined it all by coming over and hugging both Zodiac and Emily while trying to squeeze in between them. Emily felt ridiculous and the hugging became a parody of itself.

Zodiac must have felt the same; she rolled her eyes at Emily and stepped back. "So okay, we've got to get back to Hedden. We'll come over as often as we can. And don't forget to call Jorge, okay?"

"Tell him . . . the phones here are usually busy."

"Emily."

"I'll call him."

"Promise?"

"Promise."

In the corridor Emily could hear the murmur of the television, but *Star Trek* would be almost over now, and she didn't especially want to be around people. Going the long away around in order to avoid the living room, she got to the privacy of her room and fell onto her bed, hiding her face in her pillow.

When Owen and Linda arrived home after the session with their children and Travis, they were too numb to talk any more, and with a kind of weary relief they went to their separate studies to work.

But Linda found it difficult to concentrate. She couldn't stop thinking about Bruce and his outburst, his cursing. Bruce's behavior during the conference with Travis certainly lent Emily's story credibility. Obviously Bruce had a dark side, an interior violence, of which she and Owen had not been aware. They would have to face the truth. Owen would have to face the truth.

Where could they go from here? She hated feeling so powerless to change things. It didn't help that things were so strained now between her and Owen. She prided herself on her ability to dig into any problem and work it out, but now she could only wait, wait to hear from Dr. Travis.

That night she said to Owen, "I think I'll call Janet to see if she can go Christmas shopping with me on Wednesday. No matter what happens, we've got to be prepared for some kind of Christmas celebration. Then I can go right to Family Group in the evening."

"Good idea," Owen replied. "But listen, about Emily . . . don't tell Janet."

Owen was in his favorite armchair, a book in his hands. The light falling from the standing lamp behind him enclosed him in a honeycomb of light, and clearly Linda could see how tired Owen looked, how weary. Old. Her heart went out to him.

"All right," she agreed, adding, "I'll be glad to put it all out of my mind for a while."

Gigantic foil bells and elves and candy canes swung from the ceiling. Elvis was singing Christmas songs to a rock beat. Saleswomen wearing red lipstick and plastic holly brooches on their sweaters smiled brightly, offering to spray perfume on Linda as she hurried through the Filene's entrance and into the main corridor of the mall. After the gloomy silence of their farm, all the sensory excitements seemed nearly surreal to Linda, and yet something about it, the enormous Christmas tree spangled with decorations, the scent of cinnamon in the air, the brisk chatter of other shoppers hurrying past, made Linda smile. Made her feel less alone, more optimistic.

And then Janet was there, throwing herself around Linda, giving her a big bear hug, enclosing her in a mist of Joy. "Linda! I'm so glad to see you!"

"And you can't imagine how glad I am to see you," Linda replied.

Janet drew back, studying her friend's face. "Everything okay?"

Linda hesitated. "Everything's fine," she said. "I'm just stuck on a chapter in my book and I can't get started."

"Well, honey, you've come to Dr. Feelgood's Shop Till You Drop Mall and Mood Clinic." Janet laughed. "Forget everything. Just buy. You'll feel better fast."

Linda grinned at her friend's enthusiasm. "Shall we talk first, or dive in?"

"Let's dive in. I've got a ton of things to get."

They decided to split up for a couple of hours before meeting at Legal Seafoods for lunch. Janet had always been Linda's shopping guru, aware of where the best sales and bargains were, the best clothes for Emily and her tribe, the best stocking stuffers. After making a list of Janet's suggestions, Linda tore through the mall, buying presents for Rosie and Riley and lots of presents for baby Sean, for Bud and Irene Burton, for Janet. A cashmere scarf for Celeste. Lots of treats and goodies for their old dog, Maud. At Banana Republic a handsome wool sweater in the window caught her eye, and after a moment's hesitation, Linda went inside and bought it for Owen.

When most of her shopping was done, Linda stood with her bags in the noisy mall, surveying her loot. The corner of a foil-wrapped tin with a Godiva cake protruded from a bag next to a box of long candy canes. An elegant Scottish tartan paper spread over the box holding the sweater for Owen. White stars exploded over deep blue foil; she would use that for the Burtons' books. Santa Clauses cavorted with elves; she'd wrap Sean's Legos in that.

Over the years Christmas shopping had taken on an almost ritualistic importance for her. It was a challenge, a quest: could she find the perfect gifts that in this darkest season would make her loved ones' faces light up with pleasure, that would carry them through the cold season back into the sun? Linda believed in giving lots of presents, lavish presents, and in giving what was unexpected as well as what was wished for.

She hadn't yet bought a present for Bruce, and somehow she couldn't. Somehow she could not conjure up a scene in which she'd be with him at Christmas, handing him a present.

Everything had changed. With every moment she was only getting through the day, forcing herself not to think of Emily, not to think of Emily being raped, of *Emily being raped by Bruce*, or what was somehow worse, Emily lying about it in order to hurt Bruce. She didn't think her daughter was capable of such deception . . . and yet she didn't think Bruce capable of rape.

But Emily was strong, Owen was strong, and Linda would not let her family be defeated. Somehow she and Owen would get through this. *They* would not be defeated.

Linda found herself staring at a display of inexpensive, gaudy, Christmas earrings. Silver bells tied with red bows. Gold Christmas trees with jewels for lights. Gold boxes with red ribbons. At one time Emily would have squealed, "These are so cute!" Would she still? Would this season hold any pleasure for Emily at all? It must; Linda would not let everything be ruined. She swept four sets into her hands, for Emily and for her three best friends. Then another, for Janet. And another, for herself.

And another. For Tina Travis.

* * *

Like my hair?" Janet asked after the waiter took their order.

"It looks great. It always does."

"I had it colored. First time. The road downhill begins."

"Nonsense. You look thirty."

"I doubt it. And I *am* forty-three. Next year Georgia graduates from college. Can you believe it? And Johnny starts. Empty nest."

"You'll love it."

"I don't think so." Janet's eyes teared up. "Oh, Linda, Georgia wants to move to *Seattle*."

"Oh, Janet."

In the fifteen years she'd known Janet, it had always been Janet with her blond hair and long legs and adoring husband whose life seemed more normal, whatever normal meant. Her husband was a lawyer and Janet owned a stationery store but didn't let it take over her life. She just enjoyed stocking what pleased her, having clientele she liked.

"What's up with you?" Janet asked. When Linda didn't answer at once, she remarked, "You seem preoccupied."

"Just trying to think of anyone I forgot to buy a present for. I think I got more presents for Sean than anyone else."

"Let me see them."

Linda lifted out the boxes from the nest of packages and held up the clothing for Janet to admire: red knit Christmas pajamas, a sailor outfit as soft as a cloud.

"Why are babies so seductive?" Janet asked, sighing.

"Nature is very clever," Linda replied. "If we had to start right off with adolescence, the human race would never continue."

Janet caught the tone in Linda's voice. "Something *is* bothering you."

Linda bent over her shopping bags, returning the baby clothes to their boxes, hiding her face until she could gain control of her emotions. "Just a lot of things on my mind, that's all. It's a busy season." She felt angry to the point of tears. She'd known Janet longer than she'd known Owen; *Emily* had known Janet longer. She confided *everything* to Janet in the past; it was a kind of betrayal to their friendship to keep silent now. But what could Linda do? She did not think the spiral of betrayals would stop here.

Chapter Eighteen

❦

That night Linda sat with fourteen other people in a semicircle in the dining room of West 4. A coffee machine bubbled cheerfully away in the far end of the room, reassuring them of imminent release from their metal folding chairs.

"Let's talk about the holidays," Dr. Travis suggested to the group. Everyone groaned. "Let's talk about what it feels like to have a family member in the hospital during the holidays."

"I don't mind saying that it's damned inconvenient!" Linda turned to study the man who had spoken.

"Could you introduce yourself, please?" Dr. Travis asked.

"Bartholomew Wight. Bart. This is my wife, Reba." He was silver-haired and portly, but elegant in his three-piece immaculately tailored suit. His wife was simply beautiful. Enormous blue eyes, a gentle smile. Linda could see where Keith's looks came from.

"I'm a lawyer," Wight said. "Estate planning. Probate. Taxation. Personal injury." He looked around the group as he spoke, nailing each person with a word. "I have a small but successful firm and my good name is worth money to me. We entertain a lot. Have to. People know they can count on me, trust me. I'm reliable. My clients consider me the Rock of Gibraltar. We give a Christmas party at our home every year for upwards of two hundred people and Keith, my only son, should be there. He's a liability when he isn't."

"They choose my clothes for me for the party," Keith said, staring at Travis.

"I wouldn't have to if you didn't insist on dressing like a—a Las Vegas showgirl! Silk shirts! Flowered vests!" Mr. Wight's face was growing red.

"Dear," Mrs. Wight said warningly, putting her hand on his arm.

Linda exchanged a look with Emily. She wished Owen were here to see the other families; their own might not seem so terrible by comparison.

"Just one day a year!" Mr. Wight bellowed. "Hell, not even that! Just five hours a year. *Five hours a year* we ask our son to behave as if he's a normal human being who's come from a decent home so that my fellow lawyers and prospective clients can be reassured that I'm someone they can depend on."

"You didn't mention that you also want me to have a girlfriend with me."

"All right, fine, I *do* want you to have a girlfriend with you. You're eighteen years old. It's time you had a girlfriend. Otherwise you seem odd."

"Dad, I *am* odd."

"Only because you choose to be! Out of some misbegotten desire to bite the hand that feeds you."

"I'm *not* 'choosing' to be gay to torture you and Mom! I *am* gay, and I don't want to pretend that I'm not! I want to be accepted for who I am."

Keith was nearly at the point of tears and Bartholomew Wight was turning purple. Dr. Travis interjected smoothly, "Let's talk about why it is that this particular season pushes so many of our buttons."

"Television," Arnold said. "Television propaganda."

Cynthia's mother nodded. "It is hard, trying to live up to the—the"—she spread her hands as if feeling for the right word—"the glittering perfection of television Christmases."

Linda agreed. "It's like Christmas is the end of a novel, and everything on that one day has to be tied up in a perfect bow."

"Nonsense," Bartholomew Wight growled. "No one achieves perfection, ever. Christmas is about family, plain and simple, we all know that, and once a year I think it's not too much to ask my son to act like one of the family."

"To publicly deny that I'm gay," Keith said.

"You go, boy," Emily said softly and gave Keith a nod.

Poor Keith, Linda thought, shifting in her chair, and was not prepared for Dr. Travis zeroing in on her daughter.

"Emily, how do you feel about this Christmas? Do you expect to spend it in the hospital?"

Emily shrugged and in a small voice said, "I guess. I know I don't want to go back to the farm."

Then where will she spend Christmas? Linda wondered. *And where will I?*

"You're supposed to go home for Christmas," Cynthia's mother reminded her.

"I don't have a home anymore," Emily replied bluntly.

"I hate Christmas!" Arnold's mother burst out. An emaciated platinum blonde, she sat drumming her fingers on the patent leather purse in her lap. "We always fight. Always."

"Because you want me to drink with you," Arnold said.

"A glass of champagne. Is that so awful? One glass of champagne to celebrate the season? Oh, no, you have to become Mr. High and Mighty!"

"Your boyfriends can drink champagne with you."

"And you'll do what? Spend the holiday in a church basement with a bunch of drunks and addicts?"

"Mom, I *am* a drunk and an addict."

"You know I can't stand it when you talk that way."

Frustrated, Arnold folded his arms over his chest and announced to the ceiling, "Man, I am definitely staying here for Christmas."

"The Holiday Bin," Keith quipped.

"You see?" Mr. Wight said, pointing at his son. "He thinks this is all some kind of joke!"

Dr. Travis went to the blackboard and wrote:

POWER

PRIVACY

PEACE

"These are the issues we're focusing on in our group meetings," she said, looking at the parents. "Before we adjourn for dessert tonight, I'd like to propose that we all think about these words over the next few days as we approach the holiday season. Obviously all our problems won't be solved by the twenty-fifth of December. We can't hope to achieve perfection. And when families are under a strain, holidays can push that strain to the breaking point."

She continued to speak, but Linda didn't listen. *Emily said she didn't have a home.* The magnitude of that statement took her breath away. It would be sad if Emily spent Christmas in the hospital, but after Christmas? If Emily really didn't want to come back to the farm, then . . . then what would they do? A void opened before her.

When Dr. Travis finally released the group for dessert, Linda tried to pull herself back into the moment. Theoretically now everyone should mingle, getting to know one another, becoming acquainted with the people and the relatives of the people who shared their lives here in this ward. But each family broke off into its own little enclave. Linda and Emily took their gingerbread and ice cream and sat across from one another at the end of one of the tables.

Linda felt oddly timid with her daughter. *I must go carefully*, she thought.

"Look," she said, pulling the bell earrings from her purse. "I thought you'd like these. And your friends."

"Thanks."

"Would you like to give a pair to Dr. Travis?"

"I guess."

"I got some for Janet, too." She told Emily what she'd bought for the Ryans. "I like the gingerbread."

"We made it ourselves. From scratch. It's supposed to 'engender group participation.' " For a moment the old Emily was back, mischief in her eyes. "Really Keith and I made it while Cynthia sat in the corner sucking her thumb and Arnold searched through the kitchen cupboards looking for real vanilla extract."

"Oh, Emily, that sounds kind of . . . grim."

"It's better than being on the farm."

"Really? *Really*? I worry about you being here."

Emily relented. "It's not a lot different from Hedden. Believe me, we've got just as many nutcases there."

Linda smiled. For a moment the old rapport was between them. "Why do I not feel reassured?"

"Are you going to finish that?"

"Um . . ." Linda realized that at every moment she was judging, gauging, measuring: *will it upset Emily if I don't eat the gingerbread she baked?*

"Can I have yours?"

"Sure." Relieved, Linda shoved her plate across the table. Looking around the room, she said, "Keith's handsome."

"I know. And he's funny. And Cynthia is great, except when she's depressed."

"Is that very often?"

"Only when she's awake." Seeing her mother's face, Emily added wearily, "Just kidding."

The mood broke.

"And you think you're . . . getting somewhere . . . with Dr. Travis."

"Yeah." Emily's face grew serious, grew old.

"Tired?"

In response, Emily yawned.

Some of the other parents were leaving. "I'll go along, then."

"Fine."

She moved to hug her daughter, but Emily shrank away.

"I love you," she said to Emily.

"I know, Mom," Emily said wearily.

Linda left the room, and the ward, and the hospital. She found her car in the echoing lot and began the long drive back to the farm.

$\mathcal{A}$s *she drove* away from Basingstoke, Linda yawned and stretched so deeply she shuddered. Echoes of the evening in the Family Group filled the dark air of her car. She made her living by writing fiction, and yet she had trouble imagining a mother like Arnold's, a father like Keith's. She had immediately, instinctively, passionately loved her child, and this, she had thought for a long time, was the one true quality she shared with all women.

But of course she knew of one exception.

It had been a surprise, even a shock, to become acquainted with Bruce's mother, the beautiful Michelle. Artistic Michelle.

Linda had met Michelle herself at the opening of one of her shows in Cambridge soon after Owen and Linda married. Linda and Emily had just moved to the farm and all four were in a delicate period of adjustment, when each word and look was scrutinized for overtones and the children fell into squabbles over nothing at all.

Bruce was ten, Emily eight, and in preparation for the trip to the art gallery, Owen and Linda had forced them to bathe and dress with care. Bruce wore his blue button-down Brooks Brothers shirt and khakis, just like his father, although Owen wore a navy blue blazer, too. Emily, fortunately, was still in her *Little House on the Prairie* phase and wore one of her adorable ruffled dresses. Linda tied a pink grosgrain ribbon around her head and let her long shimmering honey-brown hair curl down her back. Linda wore a simple little black dress. No jewelry.

As they drove into Cambridge, she noticed that Bruce was nervous. He often drummed his fingers in the air as if playing an invisible piano. He did that then, and at the same time he kept pulling his lips in beneath his teeth and chattering his jaw. This gave him a lipless, idiotic look, and Linda considered gently mentioning it to him, but didn't. It would have only made him more self-conscious. She couldn't tell whether Owen was so quiet out of nervousness or simply out of habit. She had a hunch that it would take her years to coax Owen into the joys of normal conversation. Emily was the only one who wasn't anxious. She was very happily admiring her dress, her shoes, and the little charm bracelet Linda had let her wear for the occasion.

The gallery was a crush of people, all of whom looked glamorous or eccentric or scholarly, all of whom seemed to sustain life from an atmosphere of cigarette smoke and alcohol fumes. Owen took Bruce by the hand and parted the way through the crowd, led—Linda realized—Ulysses-like by an unforgettable, throaty siren's laugh.

Michelle was wearing black jeans and a shirt that on first glance seemed composed of Saran Wrap. It was transparent and she wore no bra, but the material did have a shimmer to it, it seemed to refract the light. She'd had her black hair cut very short, and her slender neck rose from her shirt like a pale column of smoke. Her dark eyes were ringed with black and her lips were dramatically crimson.

"Darling!" she cried, greeting Bruce. Bending, she folded him into her arms. "Everyone, this is my son!" Hugging Bruce to her side, she introduced him to those closest to her. "Bruce, this is Fritz, my agent, and Dominique, who owns this gallery, and my new very special friend, Rodney, and Mr. and Mrs. Delmonico, who are my favorite patrons in all the world."

Spotting Owen, who stood darkly watching, his hand on Linda's arm, she murmured, "Owen." Her gaze settled on Linda. "And this must be your new girlfriend." Before Linda could open her mouth to introduce Emily, she cooed, "I do hope you're taking good care of my men."

They're not your men, Linda silently objected. She didn't introduce Emily, didn't have a chance to, for already Michelle was turning away to greet others coming to pay homage. She continued to hug Bruce to her side for a while, but when a very tall, bearded, rather aristocratic older man approached, she reached up with both her arms to embrace him, and she kept her arms on his shoulders as she inquired, "Darling, how *are* you?" If Owen hadn't moved around to catch Bruce, he would have been swept away from his mother like a grain of sand caught in the irresistible press through an hourglass.

The next time Linda saw Michelle was on the farm, after Owen and she had been married about a year. Michelle was coming to visit Bruce before she went for an extended artistic excursion through Europe. She could only come on a Thursday morning, and so Owen kept Bruce home from school so that he could see her. Linda accompanied Bruce that morning as he waited, sharing small tasks with him in order to make the time pass more quickly. He was nervous, and he wanted his room to look perfect. They had spent the week before cleaning it, Windexing the windows, using Murphy's Oil Soap on the furniture and floors. He had dusted and painstakingly arranged his collections on the shelves: rocks, arrowheads, and fossils; stamps; coins; baseball cards; a few kiln-fired pieces of sculpture that might have been bowls or artistic endeavors and of which he was fiercely and irrationally proud.

Bruce was eleven that year. He was caught in the dreadful prepubescent phase when all at once his body was growing in irregular spurts, his voice cracked, his face was spotted with pimples and three or four ridiculous flossy hairs, precursors to a beard. His hair grew fast and thick, and he wore it in a disordered mane sweeping around his face; he thought he was hiding his bad skin. Linda knew the oil from his hair was only making it worse, but didn't dare mention it to him for fear of hurting his pride.

They heard the car come down the long road, slowing as it hit the first ruts. It was early spring. The snow had melted and rains had swept through, turning the land into mud. Michelle was driving a red convertible. The top was down.

"Whoa!" Bruce yelped, and raced down the stairs. He'd never ridden in a convertible; like most kids, he'd always wanted to.

Linda had planned to behave with dignity. She vowed to herself not to go downstairs nor to stand behind a curtain in her room, peering out the window to watch Michelle's reunion with her son and ex-husband. She would seclude herself in her study even if it meant staring blankly at her computer screen.

But as the red convertible approached, something caught her eye and she remained at her watch post at the window.

Michelle was not alone in the car. A man was with her, and in the back seat, something small . . . a dog? No, a child.

Linda was unspeakably curious. Besides, she reminded herself, Owen was her husband, Bruce her stepson.

She grabbed up a plastic basket of dirty laundry

from the bathroom—there was always a basket of dirty laundry waiting—and carried it downstairs, casually, as if this were any other normal day. The washer and dryer were in the old pantry off the kitchen, and Linda arrived there just as Michelle and the others were entering.

"Bruce!" Michelle cried. "Darling! Look how big you've grown!"

Michelle was wearing jeans, a white T-shirt, a black leather jacket, and enormous sunglasses, which she didn't remove as she bent to embrace her child. Bruce's eyes were as wide and soft as a sponge, soaking in the sight of his mother.

"Hi, Owen, darling!" She kissed his cheek. "And Laura—"

"Linda."

"*Linda*, how good to see you again! I'd like you to meet my dear friend Pierre"—she gestured to the gorgeous man with her—"and Pierre's daughter, Chloe."

They all shook hands. Chloe was slender, like her father, like Michelle, and Linda amused and insulated herself by secretly thinking, *Attack of the Toothpick People.*

"You're twelve now, aren't you, Bruce? I know I should remember, but since I never get any older, it's always such a surprise that you do!" Michelle ran her hand over her son's shoulder and he seemed only too pleased to say, in a voice that cracked with emotion: "Eleven."

"Eleven! That's what I thought!" She beamed at Bruce as if he'd said something very clever. "Chloe is eleven, too! Isn't that great? She's going to tag along with us on this little *Français* jaunt. Of course not every minute. Sometimes she'll stay with her mother or grandparents."

"They live in Paris," Chloe informed everyone with an arch smile.

The blood drained from Bruce's face.

Michelle babbled on. "The Ente Gallery is going to mount a show of my dioramas in Paris. Then I *hope* Pierre and I might be able to escape for a little respite. Chloe will probably come along, too. She's so used to traveling with her father, you see. She doesn't mind having her own hotel room."

You stupid bitch, Linda thought. How could Michelle be so blind? So thoughtless? So heartless? Why had it not occurred to her either to invite Bruce along, too, since they were taking the cosmopolitan Chloe, or on the other hand to keep quiet about Chloe? Couldn't Michelle see how she was hurting her son?

"Bruce, why don't you and Chloe run along and play for a while?" Michelle asked.

"Michelle," Chloe announced in a dry, weary voice, "we don't *play*. We are eleven years old."

Michelle rolled her eyes and collapsed into a chair. "Do you have any espresso? I'm dying for a good jolt of caffeine."

Linda made coffee.

"Would you like to see the farm?" Owen asked Chloe.

Chloe shrugged.

"It's just all mud out there, isn't it?" Michelle asked.

Linda set a plate of date nut bars on the table.

"Did you make these?" Michelle asked, and when Linda nodded, cooed, "How *clever*! Want one, darling?" she asked Chloe.

Chloe shook her head.

"So tell me, Bruce," Michelle said, turning her brilliant gaze on her son, "how do you like school?"

"Fine." He sat on the end of the table, looking close to tears.

Blithely Michelle turned to Linda. "How do you like living out here in such isolation?"

"It's heaven," Linda replied quietly.

Michelle's smile did not dim. "How's your work going, Owen?"

"All right. I have a new book coming out in the fall."

"That's just so exciting. You're lucky you're dealing with words instead of three-dimensional material. I can't tell you the difficulties we're having getting the dioramas properly packed and shipped." She described the problems while Linda and Bruce and Owen sat listening in various stages of misery.

Suddenly Michelle stretched and stood up. "I shouldn't just sit here and complain. I really need to get back and accomplish a few little tasks."

Chloe and Pierre rose, too. Bruce sat staring at the table.

"Good-bye, darling," Michelle cried, swooping over to hug her son. "I'm so glad I got to see you. You're adorable." She ruffled his hair. "Going to be a heart-breaker someday."

Linda and Owen walked the visitors out to the porch. Bruce stayed inside, still staring at the table.

"It might be fun for Bruce to visit you all in Paris," Owen softly suggested.

Michelle looked utterly blank for a moment, as if Owen had spoken in a foreign language, and then a look of delight crossed her face. "Oh, what a good idea! I'll think about it and call you!"

She never did call. Instead she sent three postcards, one from Paris, one from St. Tropez, one from Versailles. She also sent Bruce a picture, taken in front of the Arc de Triomphe, of Michelle, Pierre, and Chloe. Linda found it in the wastebasket, torn into shreds. Later she saw it in Bruce's desk, taped back together. He didn't have many pictures of his mother.

In her deepest heart, Linda had been secretly glad that Michelle was such an absent, careless mother. It balanced out Simon's lack of interest in Emily; both kids, Linda had thought, would feel less solitary in their situation. Less unwanted. They would understand that some parents were just neglectful, that it had noth-

ing to do with their own desirability. And Linda had
heard tales of hideous fights between divorced parents,
situations in which the child was reduced to a pawn, a
trophy, or cases where the child felt torn in half between conflicting rules and demands. As the years
passed, Linda thought that she and Owen were doing
a really good job of parenting and stepparenting. She
thought both children felt safe and secure and equally
loved by both parents. She thought she and Owen
loved both children equally.

Now she vividly realized that this was not true.

As she was coming down the farm's drive, the
horses thundered up to greet the car, their coats shaggy
for the coming winter. They nipped one another on the
neck and pranced, full of beans in the exhilarating air.
Owen had obviously spent the day putting the farm in
order. The tractor was in the shed, the bales of hay in
the barn, the pasture smoothly mown to the pond. He
would be in a good mood, too; he always was after a
day's work outdoors.

The day away had done her good. She felt more
optimistic. And thinking of Michelle had made her feel
by comparison enormously more competent as a
mother and wife. She really loved her family, each person: Emily, Owen, Bruce. She really believed that love
could conquer all.

Her arms full of bundles, Linda shoved the car door
shut with her backside and made her way up the walk
to the kitchen door.

Owen was seated at the kitchen table, reading.

"Hi," Linda said. She crossed the room and kissed
his forehead. "Did you have a good day?"

"Fine."

Something about his expression, his posture, set
alarms off inside her. "What is it?"

"Sit down, Linda. I've been waiting for you."

"Yes. Okay." Letting the shopping bags drop onto

the floor, she sank into a chair across from him. Under the table Maud's cold nose touched her calf, sending goosebumps up her leg. "What is it?"

"I've found proof that Emily is lying."

Chapter Nineteen

What do you mean?"

"Exactly what I said." Owen held up a book. Of pink leather, it was about five inches by eight, with a small leather tab set with a keyhole. "I found Emily's diary."

Linda had not yet had time to assimilate into her mind the very *thereness* of Owen, stocky, redheaded, dark-eyed, stubborn, sweet-smelling Owen, so physically near, wearing the dark green sweater that made him look somehow medieval, gallant, mythic, a nobleman from a tapestry. As always upon seeing him, Linda was struck by love for him. She wanted to be in his arms, to rub her face against that sweater, to hold him and be healed of the ache of being apart from him.

But at his words Linda's body went cold.

"You found Emily's diary? Where was it?"

"At the back of her closet. In a shoe box. Beneath a bunch of shoe boxes."

"You searched Emily's closet?"

"I searched her entire room."

"Owen—without her permission or even her knowledge—that's so *invasive*."

"So is accusing Bruce of rape."

"But Owen, couldn't you have waited until I was home? So we could have searched together? I mean, this seems, oh, I don't know, a kind of violation."

"Linda. Forget that for a moment. The important thing is what Emily wrote."

Shaking her head as if to clear it, Linda said, "I just can't believe that you did that."

Owen put the diary on the table in front of Linda. "I've marked the spots. Read them in order, from the beginning."

Linda looked at the cover. "Owen, this diary is over a year old."

"Read."

Troubled, heavy-hearted, Linda picked up the book. Its weight felt almost sacred. Diaries were such private matters. If she opened this book and read, she was betraying Emily. But did she have a choice?

The first entry read:

> Mom gave me this diary to keep while I'm at Hedden. She says that keeping a diary always helped her through the hard times and made her feel she had a friend waiting for her at night even when there was no one else. When she told me that I thought she was a wuss, but now I know what she means. I don't know if I'll be able to stay here at Hedden. There are so many cool people here. I don't know anyone. I don't know if I'll be able to fit in.

The next entries Linda read according to the markers Owen had made with strips of paper.

> My roommate is named Cordelia. I could just die. She's got this, like, Shakespearean name, and my name is Emily. That tells the whole story right there.

> My biology teacher, Mrs. Lundgrund, is short, fat, and covered with spots, bigger than freckles! And she belches! All the time! Zodiac and I are lab partners and we can hardly begin to dissect our frog,

we can't even look each other in the eye, we start laughing.

I went into the dining hall today, not that I was hungry, I thought I was going to vomit, it's so scary walking into that place, which first of all looks like the Sistine Chapel, not that I've ever been there like everyone else has, but it's so awesome, and plus everyone is there. The seniors get to have all the tables near the windows. Everyone else just sits everywhere, and I don't know anyone. But I got a tray of food and was looking for a place to sit, and there was this, like, eternity of heads of people I don't know, then Bruce came up to me with Terry and Lionel and they all said, "Hey, Emily, what's up?" They asked me how I like it here so far, and stuff, and then they went off, they all looked so cool and then Cordelia was waving at me. "Emily, come eat with us!" So I did, and I met all these girls my age, they were so nice. They all wanted to know about Bruce, of course. He is so handsome. And a junior.

So Angelica and I were talking and she said so Bruce really isn't your brother, and I said right, he's my stepbrother, and she said, well then, you know, you could, like, marry him and stuff, and I said no way, please, that's so geeky, 'cause I don't want her to know. Bruce has changed so much since he's been at Hedden. He's so tall and, like, masculine, and all the girls have crushes on him, and he's so nice to me when he sees me.

"Owen, this is sweet, it's innocent."
"Keep reading."

Cordelia and Zodiac both have boyfriends. I wish I did. The seniors don't know the freshmen exist, and neither do the juniors, really. There aren't enough cool freshmen and sophomores to go around. I'm lucky Bruce always talks to me, that way at least I don't seem entirely snubbed by the male species.

Thanksgiving was really nice. Ming Chu came home and Bruce brought Terry and we played poker until dawn, and Mom and Owen don't know it but the guys drank beer and we took sips of theirs. We had to keep quiet so we wouldn't wake Mom and Owen, but we laughed so hard. It was so cool.

I love school and my friends and I don't think I'm homesick any longer, but sometimes I just can't wait to get back to my room and take a nap. I don't sleep, I daydream. I daydream of the day Bruce will come to me and say, "I never could think of you as a sister, and now that we're both adults, I want you to know how I really think of you," and then he kisses me. I can just feel his long long eyelashes brushing my cheek.

Last night I dreamed that Bruce couldn't wait till we're adults, and just before graduation from Hedden he asked me to marry him and I accepted and he made a big announcement to the whole school.

"Owen, these are just *daydreams*. Just the fantasies of a freshman about an older boy."
"Read the rest."

Mom came and took us Christmas shopping with Janet. It was fun. I wanted to get Bruce this gorgeous black leather coat, but a) I don't have the money and b) then everyone would know how I feel about him. My favorite part of the day is going to bed at night, just before I fall asleep, dreaming of him.

My new favorite dream: Everyone is at assembly. I'm sick with something that doesn't make me gross, not a cold, not my period, maybe just exhaustion, and the dorm is all quiet, the room dark, there's a knock on the door. I'm wearing a scarlet satin peignoir from Victoria's Secret and my hair looks good, and there's a knock on the door, and it's Bruce. He comes in, he comes over and sits on my bed and says, "I was too worried about you to watch the play. Are you okay?" And we sit and talk.

Many pages on:

Bruce comes in my room. "Oh, Emily, I've been so worried about you, my darling." He gets into bed with me and holds me to him. "You shouldn't have gone swimming with Terry, I should have warned you he's not a strong swimmer. I'm so glad you didn't drown. Emily, I love you." He holds me against him and I can feel his heart beating. He kisses me first gently, like he's scared, then hard, passionately, and I kiss him back.

Mom and Owen have driven to Boston to see a play and spend the night with Janet and Bruce says to me, "This is our time, now and forever. I have to go to college this fall, and we'll be separated, but tonight I'll make love to you so beautifully it will be with us for all our life." I will wear the taupe silk gown with hand embroidery from Victoria's Secret, and he will lift it off over my head like the duke did in Dangerous Liaisons *with Uma Thurman. Bruce says, "Emily, you are more beautiful than I ever dreamed." He lies next to me and holds me, and we make passionate love. "Oh, Bruce, my darling," I say.*

"Owen, I can't read any more of this. It's—it's like raping her in another way."

"How else will we get at the truth?"

"But this isn't *the truth*. These are the fantasies of a young girl during her first time away from home."

"Right. And what are her fantasies? That Bruce makes love to her."

Linda took a deep breath. "Owen, first of all, this diary was written a year ago. Look. She stopped writing in February. Obviously by then she was caught up in school activities and with her friends. She stops writing about Bruce. She stops writing about everything." Flipping to the last few passages Linda saw that Emily had made some entries.

This cool guy named Jorge sits across from me in English. He's from Argentina I think, and he's sooo handsome.

Jorge smiled at me today. He looks at me a lot. I know, 'cause I'm always sneaking looks at him.

Jorge walked me from English to my dorm today. Damn! I wish school wasn't ending. He has to go home for the summer, so far away. Maybe I can ask him to write me.

Ming Chu says I should forget about Jorge. He's so much older than I am and more sophisticated. Well, anyone is more sophisticated. Oh, well, at least I can dream.

Reading the last entry to Owen, Linda insisted, "You see? 'At least I can dream'! And that's all she was doing about Bruce."

"Exactly."

"Owen, I *meant* that's all she was doing the first year she was at Hedden. *Not* now."

"I think we should confront Emily with this diary."

"What do you mean?"

"I mean I think we should go back to Basingstoke and have a conference with Emily and Travis and tell her we read her diary and see what she has to say."

"I don't know, Owen. That would embarrass her terribly."

"Linda, she's going to *embarrass* Bruce. How will people treat Bruce at school if this gets out? And you know how rumors get around. It might even affect his admission to college."

"Yes," Linda agreed, thinking aloud. "Yes, I can see that. Still . . . all right, then. Let's ask Dr. Travis what she thinks. If she thinks we should confront Emily with the diary, we will. All right?"

"Fine."

"I'll call her first thing tomorrow." Linda rose. "I'm exhausted. I'm going to take a hot bath. I'll deal with those"—she gestured toward the shopping bags—"later."

As she climbed the stairs, her legs were like lead. She didn't know when she'd ever felt so discouraged. At the top of the stairs she turned toward Emily's bedroom, and when she entered her daughter's room, it was if the floor collapsed beneath her feet, sending her staggering to grasp the door frame.

Owen had absolutely ravished Emily's room. He'd torn the sheets and covers off the bed and tossed them in a heap on top of her mattress, her good old mattress that glared nakedly in the daylight, exposing the brown-red stain of blood from some period that flowed too heavily in the night. He'd pulled her drawers from her chest and emptied them in a pile on the floor. He'd cleaned out her closet, and piles of shoes and shoe boxes of old letters cluttered the floor. The contents of Emily's vanity drawers littered the top of her vanity: old nail polish bottles and emery boards, hair scrunchies, hair pins, powder compacts, lipstick, and eye-liner.

On top of the pile of cosmetics, stationed there stra-tegically, was a small orange box of condoms.

Owen was right behind Linda. "I found those con-doms in her drawer."

Whirling on him, Linda hissed, "Of course you did! *I gave Emily those condoms!* Don't you remember why? *Janet* insisted that I give the children each a box of condoms the summer before Bruce went away to Hedden! So that they could look at them in the privacy of their rooms, feel them, get used to them, so that if they ever needed them they would have them, wouldn't feel too embarrassed by the whole issue! You and I discussed the matter, and you agreed that it was the right thing to do!"

"You're right," Owen admitted. "I'd forgotten that."

"Owen, look at her room! How could you do that to her room?"

"I'll clean it up."

"No. No, I will."

"Linda, we've got to find the truth about all this somehow."

"And what is *the truth* here?" Linda asked, gestur-ing toward the disordered room.

"I'm sorry," Owen said miserably. "I didn't do this to upset you. Let me help—" He moved into the room.

"No," Linda said. "Don't. Please. I'd rather take care of it myself."

Owen looked at his wife.

"I need to be alone now," Linda told him.

Owen turned and left the room. His footsteps sounded like hammer blows as he went down the stairs.

L*inda bunched her* daughter's disheveled linens into a clothes hamper and found clean sheets in the hall closet and made Emily's bed. First, a clean mattress pad, then fresh sheets, an old set, so worn that the cotton had the texture and transparency of petals, covered with tiny pink rosebuds. The hard tight knot of pink, with its sheltering border of green leaves, summoned up before Linda a vision of Emily as an innocent girl.

Once, when Emily was about eight, at another child's birthday party the parents had hired a musician, a thin, artistic-looking man who played the recorder. He tootled merry tunes while twelve children squealed and raced and giggled, playing musical chairs. He played "Happy Birthday to You," and the children sang along. While they sat eating cake, he serenaded them with less effervescent songs, trying to calm the children as they stuffed themselves with sugar. When he played "Greensleeves," the ancient music so suddenly sweet and melancholy and romantic, Emily looked up from her cake and announced to the table, "I think that music sounds how it feels when boys kiss girls." The boys at the table made vomit noises, the girls giggled and tittered, and the parents flashed smiles at one another.

Now the music of "Greensleeves" played in Linda's mind. She sank onto the bed with her hands full of bedsheets and rosebuds. If Emily was not lying, it was here that she was raped. Linda had seen so little violence in her life. Had she ever had violence used against her? Not really. The closest she could come was the remembrance of childbirth. There was a point when she realized she could not escape, could not get up and walk away, could not reason or beg away the pain, could not leave the bed where the agony was holding her.

Also there had been many times when she had sex with Simon even though she did not want it, and did not enjoy it, but took part in it rather than admit the truth. At those times she discovered a wonderful talent in her deepest core, an ability to shut off sensations. She would split away from her body and leave the hapless shell to be manipulated at Simon's fancy, while the essential Linda, her true soul and self, retreated into her mind, pulling up a kind of bridge and shutting off the physical. Had Simon been aware of this? Certainly he never seemed to notice.

Could Emily have done this? Everyone had that power. But Linda feared that Emily must have been too new to the situation to protect herself in this way. It was painful, remembering her words, envisioning the act that took place on this bed.

Emily was held down. She struggled, and her stepbrother hit her. He called her a fucking bitch. He stuck his penis inside her. That must have hurt. She would have been dry and tight with fear; it would have been like a rope burn on one's hands, but more extreme. Like burns on her sensitive, intimate flesh. Emily would have continued to feel the inflammation in her vagina, over the tender skin of her labia, long after Bruce had left her. She would not have known how to soothe herself, with Vaseline or unguents, and when he raped her again the next night, in the barn, it would have been doubly painful, like drawing sandpaper over sunburned skin. So there would have been the physical pain, and there would have been the humiliation and rage of being forced against her will. Of being assaulted. That would have been the worst of it.

No matter how hard Linda worked, she would never be able to make this room clean and pure again. Emily no longer had a refuge here. This room held ugliness.

Linda had always said that she would throw herself under a train or in front of a bus to save Emily's life. She would give her daughter her kidneys, liver, eyes. She would give Emily her heart. Linda had lived her life considering her child's safety and happiness. And she had not been able to keep her daughter safe.

But how could Bruce, whom Linda had watched and

lived with for seven years, whom she had taken into her heart and loved as if he were her own, how could Bruce have changed so entirely, and have hated so deeply, so furiously? So destructively.

Linda had thought of Emily as her angel, her sunshine, her beauty, her darling, her joy. Linda had wanted Emily to enjoy the anticipation and delight of first kisses, first embraces, the tremendous pleasure of early love with all the newness, the gentle trepidation that is aligned to awe and is not really fear, the discovery of physical pleasure so powerful that you can not believe other mortals have ever felt such a thing, the overwhelming love that borders on a kind of reverence. She had wanted her daughter to be with a boy who thought she was beautiful and precious and splendid, who would call her his angel, his joy, his beauty, his darling, his sunshine, his love.

Chapter Twenty

Friday afternoon they met in a small conference room: Dr. Travis, Emily, Linda, and Owen. Dr. Travis sat next to Emily on the dark green sofa.

Dr. Travis turned toward Owen. "Mr. McFarland, would you like to begin?"

"Yes." Owen looked at Emily but did not lean forward, not wanting to seem intimidating. "Emily, I want you to know that I'm terribly concerned about you. I think of you as my own child. I want you to get well, I want you to be healthy and happy, and I'll do whatever I can to help you. But I'm having a tough time believing . . . what you've said about Bruce."

He took a deep breath. Emily watched him guardedly.

"A few days ago I searched your room. I found the diary you kept during your first year at Hedden."

Emily's face went red. "That is just so gross!" She looked at Linda. "Mo-om!"

Linda dug her fingernails into the palms of her hands. "We have to discuss this, Em."

Owen continued. "Emily, there are several passages in that diary—"

Emily's hands clenched and the veins stood out on her neck. "You *pervert*! You sick, disgusting pervert! You're as gross as your son!"

"Emily, please," Linda said.

She was dying of shame; it was like bugs burrowing into her skin, into her organs. Her skin was writhing on her bones. "I hate you, Owen! I'll hate you until I die!"

"Emily," Linda said again.

"What?" her daughter snarled, snapping her head toward her mother. "What do you want to say to me? What *can* you say? You want to defend *your precious husband*, right?"

"I want you to get control of yourself and deal with this, Emily," Linda said firmly. "We *have* to talk about this. Hysterics are of no help."

Emily swallowed. She looked at Dr. Travis. "I'm supposed to sit here and take this shit?"

"Your mother's right, Emily. We have to deal with this."

Emily crossed her arms over her chest and glared hatefully at Owen and Linda. "Fine. *Fine*. Do it."

Owen began again. "There are some entries in your diary in which you seem, well, infatuated with Bruce."

"Well, I was! But that's back when I was a freshman. I'm certainly not infatuated with him now!"

"The point is, several of your paragraphs describe romantic encounters between you and Bruce . . ."

"Oh, God," Emily moaned, "I was such a dork. Don't you understand? They were just daydreams. Didn't you ever daydream? I know it's pathetic. I was just a retard. But I got over it. I got over it a long time ago." She was clutching her arms, digging her fingers into the soft fat flesh.

Dr. Travis leaned forward. "If I could interrupt here for a moment, I'd like to point out that sexual and romantic feelings between stepsiblings are not all that unusual. There is nothing inherently wrong with feeling romantic or sexual love for a stepsibling. Some people manage to hide it, some talk to counselors about it. The important thing is to accept it as something normal, not harmful, as long as it is not acted upon." She looked at Emily. "Emily, you've done nothing wrong by feeling in love with Bruce."

"Perhaps not." Owen cleared his throat. "Still, it seems to me to be some kind of proof that Emily wanted to have sex with Bruce, that she led him on, or, on the other hand, that she only daydreamed this business of the rape."

Emily nearly rose from her chair. "I *didn't daydream* the rape! And I didn't want to have sex with Bruce!"

"Your diary—" Owen began.

"Take a deep breath, Emily," Dr. Travis said.

Emily took a deep breath. Her skin was mottled red. But finally, in a reasonable voice, she said, "All right, maybe I did want to 'have sex' when I was a freshman, but it wasn't sex, really. I just wanted, oh, something dreamy, like music, kissing, and gooey stuff. Not what Bruce did to me. Bruce held me down. He hurt me."

"Perhaps your actions—"

Emily interrupted her stepfather. Now her face was scarlet. "I know what you're going to say. That I *tempted* Bruce. Gave him signs that I wanted him to rape me. Right? Right?" Her glance flew to her mother. "Mom, how can you let him talk this way to me?"

"Emily," Linda entreated, "honey, we're trying so hard to sort through this."

Emily looked at her mother. "I screamed, Mommy! I fought! Bruce just laughed! He knocked me in the chest. He hit me. He choked me with his arm. It was nothing like love! Nothing tender! Nothing romantic. He was mean. He was *hideous*." Spittle was forming in the corners of her mouth as she turned back to Owen. "I just wish someone would rape *you*."

For a moment there was silence, and then Emily cried, "I knew Owen would do this. I knew he'd take Bruce's side. Bruce has always told me that nothing is mine, not the farm, not anything. I don't even have a home! I can't go back to the farm, not when Bruce's there, not with Owen hating me!"

"I don't hate you," Owen protested.

"Bruce *told* me!" Emily shot back. "He told me if I told he'd make my life hell. And he was right!" Sobbing overtook her.

"Emily, please, darling," Linda began, but Emily interrupted her.

"Don't call me 'darling.' Don't call me fucking anything! Not as long as you're married to this—this *shit*."

"Emily—"

"I don't want to talk to you anymore. I never want to talk to you again in my life! Not while you're on Owen's side."

"There are no sides—"

"Oh, give me a fucking break! I don't care anymore, I don't care what you do, search my room, read my private diaries, take everything from me! I'll make my own life, and the hell with you all!"

"Emily." Rising, Linda moved to embrace her daughter, but Emily shrank back as if repulsed.

"*Don't touch me*. Don't touch me ever again while you're married to him."

Linda entreated, "Emily, please don't be this way. I love you, darling. I—"

Emily stuck her fingers in her ears and shut her eyes tight and began to sing nonsense syllables, just as she had when she was a little child and wanted to ignore her mother's words. Now it made her look truly maniacal. It chilled Linda's blood. Helplessly she looked at Dr. Travis.

"I think we should probably end this discussion," Dr. Travis said.

"But I can't," Linda protested. "I can't leave her with things like this!"

"Emily needs time," Dr. Travis said. "Give her some time." •

"But Emily—" Linda felt torn in half. "Emily, I'll call you tonight."

Emily kept her eyes shut, her fingers in her ears. She continued to babble.

"I wouldn't call her tonight, Mrs. McFarland. She probably won't be ready to talk to you. I'd wait a few days."

"But this is intolerable."

"Not intolerable. Just very hard." Dr. Travis rose and opened the door to the corridor, then stood back to let them pass through.

Owen took Linda's arm and together they left the room.

In the car on the way back to Ebradour, Linda and Owen did not speak. Did not dare to speak. Their thoughts rode with them, a bomb, a Pandora's box between them. At the farm they hurried off their separate ways.

At the end of the day they sat down in the kitchen to eat the vegetable-filled omelets Linda threw together.

"Wine?" Linda asked.

"Please."

They ate in silence. For dessert Linda brought out a loaf of bread she'd made the day before and her homemade wild grape jelly. They ate steadily, impassively, hungrily; they'd both forgotten to eat lunch.

"We have to talk," Linda said finally.

"All right," Owen agreed.

Then they sat in silence until suddenly Linda burst into a kind of gentle hysteria that made her cry and laugh all at once. "What can I say? I'm overwhelmed! I don't know what to do! It's too much!"

"I know, kid," Owen said, reaching over to rub her shoulders.

"God, that feels good." Linda shoved her plate aside and lay her head on her arms on the table.

"Remember when we decided to get married?" Owen asked, musing aloud. "How we promised ourselves that our lives were not about our children? That we'd fight, work hard, to keep the business of parenting and stepparenting from eating up our relationship?"

"Of course I remember."

"I thought we did a good job."

"I thought so, too."

"It was tough at first. When we were first married."

"You thought I was too lenient on the kids and I thought you were too tough."

"You used to let Emily get in bed with us."

"She had nightmares. She was eight years old, in a strange house." Linda was beginning to tense up again, and then Owen said, "You made us into a real family. Made us all sit at the table every night, eating and pretending to talk."

Linda smiled into her arms. "And pretty soon we were actually talking."

"Remember the rule we made, that they'd have to settle their arguments *by themselves* by the end of the day, or no TV for either one."

"That was clever of us," Linda said, adding sadly, "I don't think that's going to work this time."

"I know." After a moment's silence, Owen continued: "You taught us how to celebrate. We never had good birthday parties before you came. Or Halloween parties. Or Fourth of July. I was always obsessed with my work."

"And you helped me make Emily more independent. I used to get so anxious when she went off to the pond with Bruce. Afraid she'd drown. Or up into the woods. Afraid she'd get eaten by a bear. Or fall out of a tree and break an arm."

Owen stroked her arm, her back, then ran his hands up her neck and caressed her head. It was wonderful to be comforted.

"We'll work this out."

"I have to tell you I'm pretty discouraged."

In reply, he pushed back his chair. "Let's take a walk."

"Good idea." Rising, she grabbed her jacket from its hook and followed her husband outside.

Linda had always loved the vast mysterious silence of the night air, broken only by a limb cracking, a bird singing out, the wind feathering the leaves of the ivy that twisted and fluttered along one side of the house. The porch lights illuminated the pumpkins she had put on the steps of the front porch. They were beginning to cave in on themselves. It was time to add them to the compost heap. She pulled her coat closed at the neck against the brisk wind. In any other year she would be thinking about decorating the house, inside and out, for Christmas.

The night air was cold, fresh, and full of the scents of crushed leaves, clawed loam, pine, and the sweet rot of apples hidden in the high grass of the old orchard, waiting in winy knots for the animals. The sky was overcast, the stars hidden. But they knew their way.

Over the years the children and Owen and she had worn a trail through the meadow to the pond. Now they followed its sinuous channel past the fenced pasture, the occasional boulder protruding from the ground, and the various sudden hollows and dips, which in wet weather became mushy or slick. On either side of them the hills rose up, dark with forest.

By the pond a boulder protruded, making a perfect bench. Linda and Owen eased onto it and sat staring at the gray water, which looked in the dim light like a soft shadow spreading across the land. Something rustled on the other side, a fox or skunk. Deer came to drink from the pond; she'd seen them often, and tracks of other creatures, too, raccoon, possum, rabbits. It was possible they were accustomed to her after all these years. She'd like to think so. She'd like to believe that in some deep beast way they had come to accept her, to consider her one of them, an occasional night creature. Certainly she had come to feel at home here. She'd learned to let go of the world here, and to listen to whatever lessons the wind and water and earth and air brought. Patience. Acceptance. Gratitude. An appreciation of the variety of acts and accidents that befell even an isolated pond on a cold, cloudy night.

For a long time they stared out at the water. Gradually the black of night shaped itself into different streaks and stripes of gray as Linda's eyes became accustomed to the lack of light, and she thought that perhaps this was how she should see her daughter, not as a golden child, a sunshine, but as a person suffused, like everyone, with a spectrum of radiance and blackness and shadow, and only deepened, not diminished, by her darkness. She should see her stepson that way, too. And Owen, what was Owen thinking?

"Nice," he murmured.

"Mmm," she agreed.

He took her hand in his. "You're cold. Ready to go back?"

She nodded.

They held hands as they walked through the dark back to their house. As they entered, Maud, rumpled and grumbly, staggered out to meet them.

"I'll let her sleep with me tonight," Linda said, lifting the old dog in her arms.

Together they put out the lights and made their way through the house to the second floor and their separate bedrooms.

Linda pulled on her flannel nightgown. She was just sliding into bed, taking care not to knock Maud, when Owen came into the room and climbed into bed next to her, as he had thousands of nights before. He smelled clean and fresh, and his body was like a warming fire. He yanked the covers up and socked the pillow as he got comfortable. He rolled toward her. He reached out his arms.

She moved into his embrace, welcoming his warmth,

but when she felt his heavy leg on hers and his erection pressing like a club against her belly, she was startled.

Usually after an argument both she and Owen needed to make love, to share the wordless affirmation of their unity before surrendering to the separation of sleep.

But tonight her body recoiled. She could not do it. She could not even pretend.

"Owen." She pushed him away. "Not tonight."

"What do you mean?"

"I can't . . . Owen, I can't make love now. Not now."

"Because of Emily?" Owen asked. "You mean you can't make love because of Emily?"

"Because of Emily and Bruce."

"Great."

"I'm sorry, Owen. I don't know why . . . I just don't feel right. It just doesn't seem right."

"How long is this going to last?" He was very angry and punched his pillow hard as he sat up again.

"I don't know." She sat up, too. "Owen, *what if we never know*? What if we live until the ends of our lives with Emily insisting that Bruce raped her, and Bruce insisting that he didn't?"

"Then we'll have to live to the ends of our lives standing by our children."

She felt her breath stop for a long moment. Then with a kind of hopeless sorrow she said, "I love you for saying that. Without hesitation."

"Great," Owen said again. "Ironic, isn't it." Throwing the covers back, Owen rose and strode from the room.

Chapter Twenty-one

The next morning they had just finished breakfast when the phone rang.

"Now what," Owen growled.

Linda waited tensely, unable to move, until Owen mouthed at her, "Celeste." He listened a few moments, then said, "I'll be over in fifteen minutes."

"What's up?" Linda asked.

Owen went out to the porch and returned with his work boots. "Black bears. Celeste was riding in her back pasture and found lots of fence down. Black hair caught in the barbs."

"That must be by her forested land."

"Right. She doesn't feel brave enough to try to mend it herself, even if she takes her gun with her."

"I don't blame her," Linda said.

"It'll probably take most of the morning and some of the afternoon, too. She's always helped us out when we needed it, and besides, I didn't think I was going to get much writing done today anyway."

"Would you like me to make you a thermos of coffee or a sandwich to take along?" Linda asked.

"No, thanks. She'll have stuff there."

He kissed Linda's forehead, then grabbed his old farm jacket and leather gloves and jumped into his trunk and drove down the road toward Celeste's farm.

Celeste was out by the barn, hitching the wagon to

the tractor. "Hey, buddy," she called. "This is great of you."

"No problem. I need the exercise."

The day was windy and cold and vivid. Overhead waves of clouds rushed past the sun, smudging the ground with flickering bands of shadows. Owen turned up his collar and jumped on the wagon while Celeste settled herself on the tractor, started the engine, then steered away from the buildings and toward the hill. The land spread out around them, rolling toward the horizon in the dulled golds and browns of late autumn. He knew this land almost as well as his own. The rocks and hollows held memories of childish games, pleasure, secrets. But he hadn't been out here for a while, for years, he now realized, not since he'd married Linda, really, partly because with his enlarged family he had more responsibilities and less time, partly because Linda didn't understand his relationship with Celeste. He was glad to be back here now. The land was pleasantly familiar, yet made no emotional demands on him, and today he was glad to be free of that. It was good, hard labor. After a while Owen took off his jacket and still, in spite of the cold air, he was sweating. They worked steadily, not talking.

By one the sky was completely overcast.

"Want to stop for lunch?" Celeste called.

"No. Let's get this all done before the rain hits."

*A*s *they headed* back to the buildings, the wind picked up, and they found the horses tossing their heads and bucking. Thunder rumbled overhead. Celeste and Owen shut the horses in their stalls, then kicked off their boots at her back door and entered her house.

Owen loved Celeste's kitchen. Large, with two rump-sprung armchairs in front of a fireplace, it was the heart of her house, and always completely cluttered. The stove was blotched with spilled sauce and spattered oil. Cobwebs laced around the plates on the shelf near the ceiling. The slate floor was gritty beneath his feet. The long table where Celeste cooked and ate and polished her boots and did her necessary correspondence was covered with catalogues and mail, unpacked bags of groceries, dog medicine, a bowl of apples, stacks of books, a box of envelopes, dog leashes, dirty plates and mugs, and now, as she entered, she tossed her work gloves onto the pile.

"Start the fire," she suggested. "I'll make lunch."

Soon they were settled with sandwiches and coffee. The fire threw off golden light and welcome heat, and to make it all perfect, the rain started, lashing at the windows, making the room cozy, safe.

"You're a pal," Celeste told him, sighing and stretching her long legs toward the fire. "I owe you a big one."

"Don't worry about it. I was glad to do it. Needed a diversion today."

She looked at him. "Oh, yeah?"

He stared at the fire. The coffee and sandwich sent a satisfying heat through his belly. If he'd had to bet his life on it, he would have bet that Linda had told Janet about Emily and her accusation that Bruce had raped her. He knew Linda told Janet just about everything. He knew she'd told her what kind of lover he was and even the size of his penis.

So he told Celeste about Emily. "Look," he concluded. "Don't let Linda know I've told you. She'd be furious. We want to keep this quiet."

" 'Course you do," Celeste murmured.

"I shouldn't have told you, except, well, I sometimes think I'm going to lose my mind. I just can't see Bruce—"

"Bruce didn't rape Emily." Celeste's voice was rough with indignation. "How can you even doubt your son for one single second, Owen? Jesus Christ." She slammed her plate down on the slate floor so hard it cracked. Rising, she paced around the kitchen. "This sucks. Jesus Christ. Poor Bruce. Poor you. Owen, listen to me." She knelt by Owen's chair and stared up at him. "Listen to me *good*. I've known Bruce since he was a baby. I've watched him grow up. I've seen him and Emily play games over here; he's told me secret stuff he hasn't told you, I mean really dumb dirty jokes and stuff. There is just *no way* that boy is a rapist. He is a good boy, Owen. He is a *wonderful* boy. Don't you even think for one second about not standing by him. He needs your support now. You give it to him. You give it to him all the way."

Owen's chest filled with gratitude and to his chagrin, his eyes blurred with tears. "But Emily . . ." he began.

"You've only known Emily since she was, what, six? You don't know what could have happened to her before you met her. Lots of shit happens to infants and little kids that works its way out when they're older, and this is exactly what's going on here."

"Linda—"

"Linda may not even know what happened. Hell, think of all the baby-sitters Emily had when Linda worked. Maybe one of them molested her and this is the way Emily's working it out."

"I have a responsibility to Linda—"

"Your first responsibility is to your son, and don't you ever forget that!" Celeste snapped. She rose and settled herself on the arm of Owen's chair and wrapped her arms around him so that his head rested on her breast. "Go on and cry, honey. God knows you deserve to. I won't tell anyone. It's not like I've never seen you cry before."

"We're caught in such a hideous mess," Owen admitted. "I don't know how we're going to find our way out." And feeling like a traitor, he relinquished his pretense of bravery and gave himself over to his tears.

* * *

Linda watched Owen drive away from the house. The morning was hers. She could work, or pretend to. She could clean the house. Or make jam. Or spaghetti sauce.

She forced herself up the stairs, intending to head for her study door. Instead found herself entering Bruce's room.

And why not? Owen had searched Emily's room.

Bruce's room in many ways hadn't changed since Bruce was a little boy. The same wallpaper, a tan background with colorful *Batman* characters, covered the walls, and his carpet was the same noncommittal tan. His bunkbeds were ugly, chunky, reproduction Early American, as was his desk. Over the years Owen had built shelves on all the walls for Bruce's books and general stuff, and Linda sighed as she looked around, wondering when last she'd dusted in here.

Seating herself at Bruce's desk, she began methodically to go through the drawers. What did she expect to find? A diary describing in detail how he raped Emily? No, but something, some sign. He was her stepson, she knew him well, she *thought* she knew him well. He had always been a good, sensitive child. Perhaps something was in the desk, in the room, anything, that would indicate how he had changed.

The top middle drawer held what one would expect: old pencils with the points snapped off, crumbling rubbery erasers, dry ballpoint pens, a ruler, a pair of scissors, a snarl of Scotch tape, some felt-tip pens, and, sweetly, a box of Crayolas. The side drawers were stuffed with junk: tennis balls, a broken Walkman, batteries, pieces of a magnetic chess game Linda and Owen gave him years ago to occupy him during the ride into Boston, packs of baseball cards neatly contained by rubber bands, a Hedden mug with a chipped handle, loose change. Three years of the Hedden facebook, a small paperback with pictures, names, and addresses of all the Hedden students and their parents' names and home addresses. And some letters in lavender envelopes.

She remembered last summer when one had arrived in the mail. Owen had brought it in with the rest of the mail they collected daily from the post office box in town. He'd tossed it carelessly on the kitchen table, yelling, "Mail for you, Bruce." He hadn't waited around to find out who wrote to his son, but Linda had. She'd wiped the kitchen counters—or something, there was always something to do in the kitchen in the summer—hoping Bruce would tell her, but not wanting to intrude on his new adolescent dignity by asking. He'd never mentioned the letters to her. He'd always stuck the envelopes in his back pocket, not caring that the paper got wrinkled, and gone off without a word.

She had never trespassed into either child's private life before, and now she felt a frisson of guilt, but even so, she opened the envelope.

Hi, Bruce,
Isn't it fab to be free for the summer? If you can call spending most of your life crewing for your demented father on his racing yacht free. Dad gets so carried away. Sounds like your parents do too. I've never known anyone who got to ride to the hounds before. I wish you'd send me a photo of you in your red hunting jacket. I bet you look really aristocratic.

I never got to thank you for your help with biology this year. I really do think old Brewster has it in for me, don't you? Besides, why should everyone in the universe have to know what a frog's intestines look like? I've heard so many people say that Brewster hates women. He was the one faculty holdout who would not make it a unanimous vote to let women attend back in 1972, and he tries to flunk out all the females he can. The old fart. I just don't know what I would have done without your help.

Are Terry and Lionel and Pebe coming to stay

*with you this summer? Lucky guys. Maybe someday
you'll actually invite a female to visit you! Until
then, keep cool.*

           XOXOXO Alison

Returning the letter to the envelope, Linda shook her
head, feeling sad that Bruce had felt the need to lie. An
image flashed in her mind: old Babe and Fancy Girl
trotting with Bubalu wriggling goofily along and Maud
waddling behind. Ride to the hounds indeed.

But it was a *lie*. It was proof that Bruce lied.

Still . . . not evidence of anything, not really.

Ruefully she dropped the letter back into the box
and only glanced at the next two lavender letters,
which were notes about how boring Alison's summer
was, how she couldn't wait to get back to Hedden.

The next drawers held nothing exciting: poker chips
and several decks of cards, a wooden Chinese puzzle,
some empty cigarette packs and half-used books of
matches, postcards from Terry and Lionel and Pebe
and other guys off on summer vacations with their
families, a school key chain, a Polaroid camera that she
didn't remember Bruce ever using, his old blue china
piggy bank with the leather tail, books of coins he'd
collected then lost interest in, a half-eaten Three Mus-
keteers bar.

His bureau drawers were all half-empty, and what
was left, not taken to Hedden, were the worn-out, torn,
stained, outcast bits of clothing meant for some emergency or for wearing while doing some particularly
grubby farm chore. When Owen and Linda were married, they held a family conference and agreed that
since Owen and Bruce had done their own personal
laundry all their lives, the fact that a woman was on
the premises did not mean their laundry was suddenly
her responsibility, and the men would continue to do
their own wash. In recent years Bruce had grumbled
more and more about this, and left larger piles of dirty

clothes in the middle of his bedroom, hoping, Linda assumed, that she'd be unable to bear the sight and would start doing his wash herself. It hadn't bothered her at all, though. She would walk right past that pile and on down the hall to her study, and grudgingly, with loud complaints, he'd take the laundry down and do it himself.

Still his clothes were all familiar to Linda, every last torn T-shirt and grass-stained holey sock. She usually helped him pack when he took off for Hedden each fall, and with each changing season she was the one who remembered to bring him the heavy coat or the raincoat, the snow boots or the swim trunks, who brought the other items home to wash and put away.

Nothing hid beneath any of his clothing. Shutting the drawers, Linda turned to his closet.

Why did Bruce's inability to arrange his clothes properly on the hangers fill her with an emotion very like pity? It was the same when she put something into Owen's closet. It was as if they were both just slightly retarded. Her first husband hadn't been this way; he had taken meticulous care of his clothes. Linda's mother had always cared for her husband's clothes, hanging his suit jackets on padded hangers, taking pains to place his pants to keep their crease; she'd even ironed his underwear. Linda had seen to it that both men had plenty of good wooden hangers as well as thick, strong plastic ones, yet Bruce, like Owen, tossed all his clothing over pegs in the closet, or over the closet rod supporting the mostly empty hangers.

On the top shelf of the closet were outcast caps, hats, mufflers, and a sombrero Terry had brought Bruce two winters ago from a vacation to Mexico. Bruce's farm boots, still caked with mud, were on the floor along with sneakers with the toes worn through that he refused to throw out and wore every vacation, bedroom slippers that he never used, dress shoes that had become too small but were too expensive to discard. For a moment Linda was sidetracked, thinking, Perhaps we can give them to Sean when he's old enough.

Then she saw the boxes.

She tugged them out from the corner to the door of the closet, so she would have enough light to see by.

The first box, the biggest, held Legos and *Batman* figures.

The lid of the second box lifted to expose a scant gathering of memorabilia of Bruce's mother, Michelle. There was a photo of her holding Bruce as a newborn baby. A photo of her with him as a little boy, both grinning wickedly as they climbed into the seats of a roller coaster. A photo of the two of them at her opening in Boston. As well there were several postcards, Christmas cards, birthday cards, and two or three letters that Linda read with shameless eager curiosity only to discover that in typical Michelle style they were breezy, affectionate, and devoid of any real sense of Bruce's interests or health or life.

The next box Linda opened made her draw a quick breath of surprise, although she had suspected this was going on this summer. Cradled next to a stack of magazines—*Hustler, Oui, Penthouse*—were three empty half-gallon bottles of vodka. She dragged the box out into the middle of the room where Owen would see, would *have* to see it, the moment he walked in.

Still, it was proof of nothing except that the boys were doing what boys were expected to do.

She returned to the closet.

In the deepest corner, where the light scarcely shone, was a box she had almost missed. A flat box, meant for a tie or a scarf. This one had the lid taped onto it. For a few moments Linda sat staring at the box, considering. She would infuriate Bruce if she cut the tape, but Bruce had harmed her daughter and outraged Linda and turned Owen into an enemy, and so in a spurt of anger Linda rose and grabbed Bruce's Swiss

Army knife from his desk and cut through tape. She lifted the lid.

Inside was an envelope. On the front, in black ink, scrawled so fiercely that the paper puckered slightly around each letter, were the words *For Owen Mc-Farland*.

Bruce's handwriting. Larger than usual, the letters slightly shaky, not connected to one another. As if he had stabbed them individually onto the paper.

How could she not open it?

She slipped her thumbnail under the edge and carefully eased the flap back.

She lifted two sheets of paper thickly covered with words. She sat on the floor, reading.

She read it through again. Lifting her head, she stared across the room, then quickly folded the letter and slipped it inside the pocket of her jeans. Rising, needing to move, to *do* something, she pulled on the box of magazines and vodka bottles, tugging it back into the closet. Shoved it to the back of the closet. Hefted the box of toys on top of it, and the box of Michelle memorabilia on top of that. She shut the closet door. Picked up the flat tie box and the tangled mass of tape and carried them from the room. In her study she tossed the tape into her wastebasket, then found her scissors and quickly cut the box into fragments and threw those in the wastebasket, too. She took Bruce's letter from her jeans and after a moment's quick thought, opened her closet and shoved the letter beneath a stack of yellow legal pads. Owen would never look there.

And she never wanted him to see that letter. It would not help him believe that Bruce had raped Emily, and it would only bring him immeasurable pain. And at the moment, both she and Owen already had more than enough of that.

Chapter Twenty-two

❧

The psych ward was decorated for Christmas with giant paper trees suspended from the ceiling of every room, giving the place a celebratory but disorienting atmosphere. Linda had come early for this Wednesday night Family Group, hoping Emily would talk to her. For the past week she'd called Emily every evening, and every evening when Linda said, "Emily? It's Mother," Emily had hung up the phone.

Now as everyone gathered in the dining room, waiting for Travis to arrive to formally begin the family session, Emily continued to ignore her mother. She sat on a metal folding chair next to Bill, both of them sullen, silent as logs. Emily looked terrible, Linda thought, drained and shadowed, infinitely sad.

Keith approached her. "Do you like the trees, Mrs. McFarland?"

At least someone was speaking to her. "Very much."

"We made them in O.T."

"O.T.?" She was not really paying attention, she was looking to see if Emily was listening to them.

"Occupational therapy. We spread them out on the floor and colored them in. Everyone got to do whatever design he wanted on the ornaments."

"Which did you do?"

"My color scheme was dark blue and silver, and I did stripes and dots."

"I see them. Very elegant." How is Emily, she wanted to ask. Did she participate in coloring the balls? Did she laugh? Did she *talk*?

Dr. Travis entered, and the room came to order. Keith sat down next to his parents. Other people pulled their folding chairs into a loose half circle, and Linda found herself on the end. Bill was on one side of Emily, Cynthia on the other. Had Emily asked her friends to protect her in this way?

Travis was brisk. "Good evening, everyone. It's nice to see you all. Tonight I think we'll stay on the subject of holidays, and I'm pleased to announce that one of our patients has worked out a compromise with his family and will be leaving us in a few days to go home. Keith, would you like to tell us about it?"

"I'm going to attend my parents' Christmas party," Keith began.

"Gala," his mother corrected automatically, then looked around the room with a nervous smile. "Well, you see, it's much *more* than a party. It's an really an *extravaganza.*"

"And I don't have to bring a girlfriend," Keith continued.

"And in turn you won't bring a boyfriend," Keith's father added.

Keith went on. "And I get to choose the clothes I'll be wearing—"

"But they have to be something we approve of," Keith's mother firmly concluded.

Amused, Linda sent a grin toward Emily. But Emily was not looking at her. Emily was not looking at anything, but staring dejectedly at her hands.

"Compromise," Dr. Travis said. She stood up and wrote the word on the blackboard. "Families are a lot of work. Families with adolescents and young adults require a certain kind of work rather like that of any group, from the United Nations to a church committee. Everyone's feelings and point of view needs to be taken

into consideration. Concessions need to be made. Give and take is the necessary tool. Cynthia, would you like to talk about your negotiations with your family?"

Cynthia shrugged. Her mother and father watched her anxiously, desperate smiles twitching on their lips. Like Cynthia, they both looked underweight and exhausted, but unlike Cynthia, they looked eager to please.

Cynthia's mother raised her hand. "Can I tell?" At Dr. Travis's nod, she announced with girlish enthusiasm, "We made a contract! We all discussed it, and I typed it up on my computer at work—I'm a secretary at a dentist's office—and we all signed it."

"And what does it say?" Dr. Travis asked.

"Well, first, that Cynthia's medications will be kept in her room. Not in the kitchen, not in the bathroom, not in Daddy's and my room. Cynthia will have control of her medications. She'll take them every day. But we won't ask her if she's taken them. Instead, she will come to us, find us, and either say, 'I've just taken my medication,' or she'll find us and take the pills with us watching!"

"And if she doesn't tell you or show you that she's taken the medications?"

Cynthia's mother's face fell. She twisted her hands in her lap. "Then we won't ask her. We won't harass her about them. We won't mention it."

Cynthia's father spoke up. "But she'll have no access to our credit cards. Nor to our car keys. She has to gradually earn the right to use those things. Over time."

"And if I continue to stay on my medication for a month," Cynthia said, "I'll get to start looking for my own apartment. And Daddy will pay the rent for it as long as I'm taking my medication. But I'll get a job to pay for everything else. For food and clothes . . . and especially for my medication."

"Good," Dr. Travis said. "Emily? What do you

think about all this? Could making a contract be helpful to you and your family?"

"No," Emily said flatly, not looking up. She was ripping a nail off her thumb.

"Why not?" Travis asked mildly.

"Because my stepfather hates me."

They all looked at Linda. Her cheeks burning, she said, "Emily, that's not fair. That's not true. Owen doesn't hate you, not at all."

Emily stared at her ripped thumbnail. Linda could see the beads of blood speckling the skin.

"Emily?" Dr. Travis asked gently.

"I have nothing more to say. What I say doesn't matter," Emily said, and began to rip at the other thumbnail.

"Emily, it does matter," Linda insisted, leaning forward. "Honey, Owen loves you."

Emily looked up at her mother with burning eyes. "Owen hates me. Bruce hates me. And you're on their side. I'm completely alone."

"*No*, you're not alone."

"Yes, I am," Emily insisted, her voice low and even and defeated. "You've chosen Bruce and Owen. I'm alone now, and I will be for the rest of my life."

Linda's throat twisted. It was Dr. Travis who spoke.

"Sometimes situations seem hopeless. And sometimes that's all right. Sometimes we need to stand back and let our mysterious minds sort things through for us. We all know by now that there are no instant changes. Unlike television situation comedies, we can't find the solution to our problems in half an hour. Sometimes . . ."

Linda listened, desperately wanting to cross the room and grab Emily's hands and hold them tightly, tightly, so she would stop tearing at herself. But she did not move. The group began to discuss another family, and other problems, and finally broke for the night. The patients brought out desserts: sugar cookies cut in

Christmas shapes and iced and decorated with silver balls and red and green sugar. Linda took a cup of coffee and a cookie and went to sit next to her daughter, who was still slumping next to Bill, engrossed in ripping another nail.

"Want a cookie, darling?" she asked.

Emily didn't reply.

Linda took a bite, and as if Emily were a baby, made an exaggerated noise of appreciation. "Mmmm. Did you help make these? They're awfully good." It had worked last week with the gingerbread. Emily had talked, then.

Tonight she didn't reply.

Linda pulled a metal folding chair around so she could face Emily. Emily and Bill. Bill didn't seem to show any signs of leaving them to themselves for a private talk, and finally Linda said, "Emily, I can't leave here tonight knowing you feel so abandoned by me. Sweetheart, you have always been the most important person in my life. You always will be."

Emily did not respond.

Linda went on, thinking her way through it all. "Dr. Travis is right. Sometimes solutions don't come as fast as we'd like. And this . . . this business with Bruce is profoundly difficult. It will take a long time to untangle. But Emily, Owen does love you. And I do love you. You *must know* that."

Emily did not look up.

"I'll tell you one thing I can do. I can spend Christmas with you. Christmas Eve and Christmas day."

Emily looked up. Linda saw the eagerness in her eyes, and her heart lunged with an answering hope.

"I'll talk to Dr. Travis about it tomorrow. I'll take a room at the Academy Inn, and if you can leave the hospital, you can come stay with me, and if you want to stay here, that's fine, too, and we'll have our own little celebration. We'll go out for dinner. See some movies together. What do you think?"

Emily nodded. "Okay."

Linda felt almost as exhilarated and exhausted as she had after giving birth to Emily. "Okay." The other parents were leaving. Patients were drifting out of the dining room. "I'd better go, darling. I'll call you tomorrow." She hugged Emily good-bye. Emily did not return the hug, but neither did she recoil. That was something.

"Thanks, Mom," Emily murmured into Linda's shoulder.

"Oh, Emily, I love you," Linda said. And for once she left the hospital feeling just a little optimistic.

*C*hristmas *Eve and* Christmas Day?" Owen said, incredulous.

"Owen, what would you have me do?" Linda stared at the boxes of tea in the pantry. Herbal or Hu-Kwa? She was tired from the drive home, from the emotional evening with the Family Group at the hospital, her head ached and ached from thinking about all this, and she knew she should drink herbal, the other would keep her awake at night, but she didn't want the list-lessness of herbal tea, she wanted something robust and hot inside her.

Behind her, Owen was talking. "First of all, I think you should have been a little less precipitate. You should have asked Dr. Travis whether or not she thinks it is a good idea. You might have asked my opinion. You might have considered me. Christmas Eve and Christmas Day, why promise both? Why not spend one day with her and one with me? This way, Linda, I hate to say it, but you've let her manipulate you exactly as she wants."

Linda poured the boiling water over the tea. Steam rose around her. She wished it would rise and rise, enclosing her in a cloud. She turned to her husband.

"I can't talk about this tonight," she said.

"What?"

"I'm so tired, Owen. I'm overloaded. I'm going to take my tea and stare at the television."

"I thought we were having a discussion here."

"Yes, well, I'm taking your advice. I'm going to sleep on the matter before we talk about it some more. I won't be so *precipitate* again." She was amazed at how bitchy she sounded. She was amazed at how it didn't bother her at all. As she left the room, she could feel Owen's anger blossoming behind her like a dark cloud.

The administration building of Westhurst College had once been a summer "cottage" for a New York multimillionaire named, appositely, Banks. At the turn of the century Mr. Banks and his wife and children retreated to the relative coolness of the Berkshire Mountains in western Massachusetts, but by the 1970s his heirs had found their own vacation spots, and so they sold the building and grounds to the trustees of the newly created liberal arts school. The great red barn was renovated with skylights and wooden floors and turned into studios. Modern, and not particularly attractive, dorms were built around the circumference of the campus, and miniature replicas of the main building with all its Gothic arches were erected to house theaters, auditoriums, and classrooms.

The founders of Westhurst had been progressive, optimistic, and full of revolutionary ideas about education. Westhurst did not require its students to take basic core courses of science, math, English composition, and history, but did offer those courses in case students wanted to take them. Mostly students concentrated on their particular interest in art—sculpting, painting, acting, composing or performing music, writing fiction. Over the years some of their graduates had achieved prominence in their fields. For every student who gained admittance to Westhurst, twelve applied. It was a popular place.

Bruce knew all this, and it made him nervous. He

had great grades, but in courses that didn't matter here: math, biology, Latin, computer science, physics. But he wanted to go here. He really wanted to go here. Alison was going here, and he wanted to be near her.

He sat now in the waiting room of the admissions office, trying not to look apprehensive. His appointment was at three o'clock. It was two forty-five. His father had picked him up at Hedden after his noon class and driven him here, bringing along a bag of McDonald's hamburgers and fries to eat on the way. Nervous, Bruce had stuffed it all in his mouth, chewing to relieve his tension, and now the food sat in his stomach like a ball of lead. He felt ill.

He'd worn the wrong clothing. It had been a hard call this morning, deciding what to wear, and finally he'd taken the more conservative approach. What every guy wore to a college interview: gray flannels, button-down white shirt, blue blazer, school tie, loafers. Now he was painfully aware of the other guys waiting to be interviewed. One had a shaved head, tattoos, earrings, and a ring through his nose. The other was a flaming gay man with a magenta silk shirt worn long and loose over wide silky trousers. Those two would be admitted just for their looks, Bruce thought miserably.

"Dad?" he asked in a whisper.

Owen looked up from his book.

"Should I take off my tie? Unbutton my shirt?"

"I wouldn't," Owen replied. "Listen, this school is always praising itself for its diversity. You can be their token conservative."

"Dad, I'm not conservative. You know that."

"Not politically. But compared to others . . ."

"Thanks," Bruce retorted. "That's just what I needed to hear right now."

"You'll be fine," Owen assured him.

But Bruce was not so sure. Then a door opened and a young woman came out, her batik garments fluttering. An older woman stood in the doorway.

"Bruce McFarland?" She smiled.

"Break a leg," Owen said. "Break both of them."

Bruce followed the woman into her office. She reached out to shake his hand. "Hi. I'm Annie Sebelius. Sit down, please."

At least the room looked ordinary. Paneled in wood, shelves and desk stacked with catalogues and files, a normal office chair for Bruce and one for the admissions officer. What should he call her? Ms. Sebelius? Or Annie, because this was supposed to be such a relaxed atmosphere? Bruce tried to slouch a bit in his seat.

"I see you're at Hedden," the woman said. She was petite, very blond, with pale blue eyes surrounded by rays of wrinkles. "How do you like it there?"

He was prepared for this and answered honestly. "I like it a lot. Great teachers. A good solid foundation, intellectually, but a liberal philosophy in general."

"We've never had an applicant from Hedden before," the woman said. "Now, this year, suddenly, we have not one, but two."

"You must mean Alison Cartwright."

"You're friends?"

He hoped he wasn't blushing. "Yes. Good friends. She's an excellent pianist."

Annie Sebelius scribbled something on a pad. What the hell is *that*? Bruce wondered. He sat up straighter, anxious. He hated women like this, who were superficially friendly but privately judgmental.

Annie Sebelius opened a folder, studied it, then looked up at Bruce, smiling. "And what is your special artistic interest?"

He'd tried to be prepared for this question, too. "Well, my father is a novelist. My stepmother is a novelist. And my mother is an artist. She makes dioramas, she's pretty well known. Michelle Lourier?"

Ms. Sebelius blinked and shifted in her chair. She

smiled a terrible little smile. "Yes, Bruce, I see that on your application. But we're not interested in admitting your *parents* to Westhurst." Her voice was ever so gently sarcastic when she emphasized the word "parents." "We want to know what *your* artistic specialty is."

Bruce took a deep breath. "I know I've concentrated on the sciences in high school, but this year I've begun to realize that I really want to focus on the arts." He tried to look abashed. "I kind of hate to admit it, but . . . I think I want to be a novelist."

Annie Sebelius stared at him, pursing her lips in odd little jerks. She looked like a goldfish with a bone stuck in her lips.

"Have you published a short story in your school literary review, or written anything for the school newspaper?"

He shifted on his chair. "Not yet. Like I said, I'm just now realizing what I want to do."

"Which authors do you admire the most?" she asked.

Bruce opened his mouth to respond and went blank. He couldn't think of one single writer. "Well, uh, we're reading Whitman in American lit—"

"Contemporary. Someone the school hasn't chosen for you."

His hands were sweating. He wiped his palms on his thighs. Desperately, he changed tack. "I'm also thinking, uh, I'm really good at computers, you know? And I really want to do computer graphics. The art you can do on those things is amazing." He was warming up to his topic, he was on the right road now. This was something he could talk about with confidence.

"I'm not sure we at Westhurst would call the images generated on computers *artistic*," Sebelius said. Again that smug sarcasm tinged her words.

"Look, maybe you don't know it, but computer graphics are a thriving industry!"

She interrupted him. "I'm sure they are. I just don't

think Westhurst is the right place to study them. If *study* is the appropriate word."

She was rejecting him. She had rejected him already. In just minutes, he'd lost his opportunity.

"You're not even giving me a chance!" he protested.

Annie Sebelius looked shocked. "Excuse me?"

"I mean, *shit*! What kind of admissions officer are you? Your mind was made up before I entered this room. You've decided you don't want me, and nothing I can do will change your mind."

She smiled and leaned forward now, her tone earnest. "Well, Bruce, look at your application. The courses and extracurriculars you've taken at Hedden. I really can't see how—"

"It's not that you can't see, it's that you *won't*." She was going to discard him without a second thought. Throw his application in the wastebasket and turn her back on him. Shut him out of this world forever. "Who gives you the right to be God?" he asked. "Who says you have the right to pick and choose and ruin lives? You're just a fucking withered old ice queen bitch goddess, you—"

"Is everything all right in here?"

Bruce turned. A man in a gray suit stood in the doorway. Bruce's father stood right behind him, face grim. Bruce suddenly realized that he was standing, leaning on the desk toward Annie Sebelius, who was cowering back in her chair.

Now she rose. "We're finished."

"No!" Bruce cried. "Wait a minute. Give me another chance. *Please*. What do you want me to do?" His hands ripped at his tie, yanking it open. "You want alternative? I can do alternative. You want me to write a short story? I can do that."

"Bruce." Owen had come into the room and now put his hand on Bruce's shoulder. "Come on, son. We've got to leave."

"But, Dad! It's not fair! She won't even give me a chance! She totally dissed me!"

"Bruce."

"No! Goddamnit!" Bruce yanked his arm away from his father's grasp. Turning to Ms. Sebelius, who stood wide-eyed behind the desk, he said, "Well, fuck you! Fuck you and this whole damned fucking school!" With one sweeping blow, he sent a stack of folders flying to the floor.

"Mr. McFarland, do I need to call security?" Ms. Sebelius asked. Her voice was still cool.

Owen hooked his arm around Bruce's neck and squeezed slightly, pulling Bruce off balance. Pulling him toward the door. "I'm sorry," he said to Ms. Sebelius. Bruce was walking sideways, tripping over his own feet, aware of people in the waiting room staring at him, aware that people had even come out of their offices to stare at him as if he were some kind of freak show. Owen continued to pull him along. They went out through a heavy door and suddenly were in the silent well of the back staircase.

"Let me go, Dad," Bruce said.

"Get hold of yourself, Bruce," Owen replied and released his son.

They stood there, the two men, surrounded by gray plaster, gray linoleum, gray metal railings on the stairs. They looked at one another.

"Dad," Bruce began, and broke into tears.

Owen wrapped his arms around his son and let him cry.

Chapter Twenty-three

Late Friday afternoon Linda was wearing moccasins, and as she came down the stairs her steps made no sound. She entered the kitchen and saw through the door opening into Owen's study Celeste standing there, her hands caressing the old soft leather of Owen's desk chair, her face grave with wistfulness.

It was an intimate moment. Linda meant to slip away, to enter the kitchen again, making enough noise to alert Celeste, but just at that moment Celeste looked up and saw Linda.

Startled, Celeste cried out. "What are you doing here?" She whipped her hands off the chair.

"I live here," Linda replied, slightly amused.

"I thought you were going with Owen. To take Bruce to his interview."

Linda stared. Celeste did not need to know that just that morning Linda and Owen had fought bitterly because Linda refused to go with him to pick up Bruce and drive him to his interview at Westhurst.

"I'm too angry with him right now, Owen," she'd said. "Too confused. How can I stop thinking about Emily? Besides, I would think that my presence would only make him nervous, and today he needs to be totally confident."

So at noon Owen had gone off on his own in the old Volvo. Linda had come as far as the door with him, where she'd said, "Owen. Wish Bruce good luck for me."

She'd gone to her study then, and worked, coming down only for lunch, and for a fresh cup of coffee.

Now Linda thought: how perfectly Celeste-like Celeste was being. Caught intruding, she thought it was her right to grill Linda rather than offer an explanation of her own.

"Is there something you need?" Linda asked pointedly. She took a few steps toward the study door.

Celeste shrugged. "Owen told me about an article in *Outside* magazine. About traveling through the Southwest. I thought I might take a trip in January."

Linda knew the article Celeste meant: hints for women traveling alone. She softened. "His magazines and journals are over on the long table," she said, silently adding, *as you know as well as I.* "I was just going to make a fresh pot of coffee. Want some?"

"Sure."

Linda made the coffee. Celeste came out of Owen's study with a magazine in her hand. With awkward amiability they sat down together at the kitchen table.

"Ready for Christmas?" Linda asked.

"Hardly. You?"

"I've got some gifts. I did a mall run last week."

"When are you putting your tree up?" Celeste asked.

"I don't know." Linda sighed and ran her hands through her hair. "Owen and I always go out in the woods to cut one. But we haven't had a chance even to think about it this year."

"Yeah," Celeste said, stirring sugar into her coffee. "This business with Emily and her rape fantasy must be overwhelming."

Linda stared at Celeste. "Owen told you?"

"Oh, shit." Celeste flinched and grinned. "I wasn't supposed to let you know." She couldn't hide the fact that she was very pleased that she and Owen had shared a secret.

"How long have you known?"

"Just since the bears. He's tremendously upset, Linda."

"We all are."

"Yes, but . . . Linda, he *cried*. I haven't seen Owen cry since he was a child."

Linda shoved back her chair and rose. "I've got to get back to work. Take your time with your coffee."

Celeste reached out her hand. "Don't go. Let's talk a bit, please. You must know I'm concerned. I want to help." She grabbed Linda's wrist. "Linda, *please*. You're going to ruin Bruce's life with this insane accusation."

So angry that she could not trust herself to speak in a voice that did not shake with rage, Linda shook her hand free and left the room.

She assumed Celeste would leave then, and she waited at the top of the stairs to hear the kitchen door slam, but the sound did not come for a long time. Celeste was enjoying her moment of triumph.

When, fifteen minutes later, the door did slam, Linda hurried to look out the window. She watched Celeste climb into her old truck and drive away. Then she dialed Janet's number, and as she dialed, she began to sob. With relief, because it would be such consolation at last to confide in her old best friend. With grief, because Owen had confided in Celeste.

An answering machine clicked on with a recorded message. Janet wasn't home.

Owen didn't return until almost ten o'clock.

She was pacing the kitchen and when he entered, she could not wait for him to take off his coat.

"Celeste was here. You told her about Emily."

Owen stared at her. "Don't you want to know how the interview went?"

"No!" She was shouting. She meant to shout. "Because, you know what, I don't *care* how the interview went! That doesn't matter to me nearly as much as the fact that you went to another woman's house for comfort."

"I didn't go there *for comfort*, Linda."

"She told me you cried, Owen. You *cried*."

"I need a drink." He moved past her through the kitchen, dropping his coat and gloves on a chair, taking down a glass and the bottle of Scotch.

"Owen, you betrayed me."

"Don't be so melodramatic."

"Melodramatic! You made me promise not to tell Janet about the most crucial incident in our entire lives, and then you told Celeste!"

"Well, come on, be honest. Didn't you tell Janet?"

"Of course not! Not when I promised you I wouldn't!"

Owen slugged back his drink. "Then I apologize. I was certain you would tell her. You tell her everything."

"I do not tell her everything. And I don't break my promises to you. I'm amazed that you believe that I do, that you think I take my vows to you so lightly."

"Fine. You can tell her now."

"That's not the point! The point is that you lied to me! You sneaked off and shared our personal family matters with Celeste!"

Owen sighed and sank into a chair. "I did not 'sneak off.' I didn't go over there with the intention of telling her. It just came out." He looked at Linda. "And frankly, I'm glad I did talk it over with her. I need an ally, Linda, you've got to admit that."

"And I don't?"

"You've got Travis. You've got Travis, who believes Bruce's guilty. Now I have Celeste, who believes—and very strongly, I might add—that Bruce is innocent."

"Oh, I see," Linda snapped, "so we're going to line people up and take a vote?"

Owen rubbed his hands over his face. "I don't know how we're going to resolve this, Linda. I wish to God I did."

Her anger was real and justified, but suddenly Linda understood how it also served as a screen, a wall of furious energy, protecting her from the pure pain around her. She sank into a chair across from her husband.

"How did the interview go?"

Owen looked away from her. "I don't think it's the right place for him."

"You're back later than I expected. I've got your dinner ready. I can heat it up in the microwave."

"Thanks, but I've eaten. I took Bruce out to dinner tonight. I wanted to spend some time with him. Emily's accusation . . . has him rattled. He's pretty upset."

Linda studied her husband's face. Owen looked ill. "Did he say anything?"

"Not about Emily."

"About . . ."

"He's just nervous about college acceptances, that's all."

"Did something happen?"

Owen hesitated.

"Tell me."

"I can't. Not while you're so down on him."

"Owen, I'm not . . ." But she let the words disappear unspoken. She *was* down on Bruce. She said, "We're really at war, aren't we?"

"Oh, I don't know . . . *war* . . . that seems a little strong."

"We're on different sides. We have to be. We have to admit it. We're drawing lines. Keeping secrets. Distrusting one another."

"And you're going to leave me for Christmas."

"I'm going to spend Christmas with my daughter. But we have to face the facts. Emily never wants to live here again. What does that mean for you and me?"

"Can Travis give us any idea how long Emily can keep this up? So we can have a kind of time frame to work with?"

"Wait a minute. I could ask how long do you think Bruce can keep up his lie." Before Owen could respond, she continued. "You know what I think? I think Bruce will be able to keep up his lie forever, because he's not losing anything. He's not going to lose a house, a home, a bedroom, neighbors, horses, all that is familiar to him, all that is *home*. Emily on the other hand is losing all of that. No, let me correct myself: she already has lost all of that. Your son has taken it from her, along with her sense of self-worth, and her ability to respond to men, and her—"

"Jesus Christ, Linda, *get off the boy's back!*" Owen rose and paced away from the table toward his study door. "I am sick of you riding the kid all the time. You're wearing him down. You're wearing *me* down. I'd like to remind you that he's innocent until he's proven guilty, and there is *no fucking way in the world* to prove that he's guilty, and I don't see why you don't understand that! Accept it! Tell Emily to get on with her life! I'm sorry she's got emotional problems, but I'm furious that she's playing this ridiculous game."

"Owen, it's not—"

"Let me finish. Just let me finish. You're angry that I told Celeste, but let me tell you, I'm glad I told her. I wish I'd told her earlier. Do you know what she said? Immediately? At once? She said, 'Bruce didn't rape Emily.' Just like that. Without a doubt. Without a second's hesitation. She believes in Bruce. Totally. Absolutely. Now who the hell do you think I want to confide in? *You? You're his enemy.* You and Emily are savaging his life, forcing him to live like a hunted animal! You're trying to ruin his life! If so much as a hint of this rape accusation gets out, he'll be stuck with that for the rest of his life. His friends will drop him. Colleges won't accept him. Girls won't date him. He'll be a pariah.

And I won't let that happen. I won't let you and Emily break him."

With slams of his fist on the table, Owen emphasized his final words.

When he'd finished, it was very quiet in the room.

Linda said, "I'm leaving." She rose and walked out of the kitchen.

After a few moments, Owen followed. She was in her bedroom, packing a bag. Nightgown. Robe. Underwear. He watched her. She didn't speak. She pushed past him and went into the bathroom to collect her toiletries. Then she went into her study and began to gather her papers. She unplugged her computer and disconnected its various cables and cords.

"Linda."

"Could you carry the computer down for me? Put it in the trunk?"

"Don't do this."

She went back to the bedroom, lifted another suitcase from the top of the closet, and began to fill it with sweaters, jeans, socks.

"Linda, it's late."

"I'll stay at the Academy Inn tonight. Tomorrow I'll look for an apartment in Basingstoke. So I can be near Emily."

"Linda—"

Suddenly she stopped, and turned, and stared at him directly, her face taut with emotion. "Yes?"

What could he say to change things? To make things better?

"I'll get the computer." He turned and left the room.

Chapter Twenty-four

On December eighteenth Emily waited by the psych ward doors with a pounding heart. Jorge had called every night for the past week and then he said he wanted to visit her before he left for Christmas break. She'd said: Sure, that would be nice. It had been fairly easy to say that on the telephone, where they couldn't see one another, where he was just an idea, a voice she could easily disconnect. She hadn't realized she would be so nervous when the day finally arrived.

"I want to meet him," Arnold had announced when she told the group Jorge was coming.

"Me, too," Cynthia said.

"Pleeeeeeeeze," Keith wheedled. "I'll give you all my desserts for a week."

"Okay, but you have to promise to be good."

"Are we ever any other way?" Keith asked, pretending to be insulted.

"I mean it. And you have to leave us alone to talk."

"I don't like Jorge," Bill declared.

It was as if a chair had spoken. Everyone stared at him.

"You don't know Jorge, Bill," Arnold pointed out.

"I don't like him. I don't like Jorge."

"Look," Keith said, "Jorge isn't Emily's *boyfriend*. He's just some guy at school. Some foreign guy she was nice to—"

"Hey, that's not true," Emily interrupted. "I mean, he is foreign, but he's not just some *foreign guy*—"

Keith tilted his head warningly at Emily. "But he's not your boyfriend, is he, Emily?"

"I don't have a boyfriend." She saw Bill relax. So it was true, what they were always teasing her about; Bill had a crush on her. She didn't know why; she never flirted with him.

She had convinced the group to give her time alone with Jorge, at least thirty minutes, but now as the actual meeting approached she wished she'd arranged it the other way around, so that they would be there to help her over the first few awkward moments when they saw one another after three weeks.

Would he still like her? She studied her reflection in the night-darkened window. She'd actually lost a little weight recently, without really meaning to, probably because they let her out for walks on the hospital grounds twice a day. Usually she went jogging with Keith, then came in to do exercises in the fitness room. Her mother had brought in more of her clothes. She wore a periwinkle sweater and jeans and when she'd shampooed her hair, she'd just let it fall into its normal loose curls instead of moussing it into spikes.

Suddenly, there he was. He pushed through the ward doors, his long, finely boned face tight with a look of wariness, a kind of brittle guardedness that all first-time visitors wore.

"Jorge. Hi."

"Emily." He had a sheaf of flowers in his hands. Not roses, but spring flowers, tulips, irises, anemones.

He handed them to her; awkwardly, formally, she accepted them.

"Thank you." The flowers gave her a reason to move. "I'll put them in water. Come on. There's a little kitchen down this way."

They had to pass by the living room, where her gang was gathered. Bill and Cynthia and Arnold were watching television, but Keith had leaned himself up against the doorjamb, like a casual observer at a street café, and as Emily and Jorge went by, Keith said in an exaggeratedly macho voice, "How ya doin'?"

"Hello," Jorge replied.

Emily looked back over her shoulder. Keith wiggled his eyebrows, Groucho Marx–style, at Emily.

Emily found the vase—heavy clear plastic, non-breakable—filled it with water, and settled the beautiful flowers. According to ward rules, she could have a guy in her bedroom, if the door were kept open to the hall, but there was only one chair in her bedroom, so one of them would have to sit on the bed, and she couldn't deal with the pure *implications* of that. That left the living room or the dining room and she'd decided to take him to one of the tables at the far end of the dining room. Now she led him to the table and set the flowers between them.

"Oh," she said as soon as they sat down, "I forgot to ask if you'd like something to drink."

"That's all right. No, thanks. I can't stay very long. I need to finish packing."

"When do you leave for Argentina?"

"Tomorrow."

"Are you looking forward to seeing your family?"

He smiled. "Some of them. I'm eager to see my friends. Tell me, how are you?"

"I'm fine. Really fine. I'm getting out of here on Friday."

"For the holidays?"

"No, for good. I still have to meet my shrink twice a week, but I don't have to live here anymore."

"So you'll be back at Hedden for next semester!"

She was flattered by how eagerly he said it. "No, actually, I won't. It's kind of complicated."

"Tell me."

"Well, um, my mother and her husband are separating."

"Divorce?"

"Maybe. Just separating for now."

It was all twisted, all backwards. This was the story Owen had insisted she tell. Insisted Linda tell. This was the country where the accused were innocent until proven guilty, and as far as Owen was concerned, Bruce would never be proven guilty. He didn't want his son to suffer a bad reputation because of Emily's accusations. Finally Linda had agreed. Emily had not been present at all their discussions, but she knew this was as hard for her mother to accept as it was for herself.

"And because they're separating, Mom has to get a place to live, since Owen owns the farm—it's his family's farm. And she can't afford the Hedden tuition and rent as well."

"So where will you live?"

"Mom's taken an apartment here in Basingstoke. I'll go to Basingstoke High. It's a good school. That way I can see my shrink, and also my Hedden friends. If they still want to see me."

"I will." Jorge's sleek black hair had been trimmed, and it hung in glossy sheaves to his shoulders. He was so handsome Emily couldn't believe it when he said, "I hope we are friends for a long time. You know you were the first person who was really nice to me at Hedden. You were . . . genuine."

"You're kidding."

"No."

"But Jorge . . . you're so handsome!"

He shrugged. "What can I say? I'm older than everyone and yet my English is not good, my skin is dark, I'm from South America. People thought I'm either a drug pusher, because everyone from South America is, you know, or a dumb spic."

"Oh, nonsense. I never knew anyone who called you that. All my friends—"

"It didn't help me much with the guys that the girls

liked me." He made a brushing gesture with his hand. "Hey, I don't mean to sound pathetic. I have friends. I like it at Hedden. But you were always so easy to talk to. You have a sense of humor I like."

Something was happening between them, something that had been there from the start, a magic connection, a kind of bridge of sparks. It made her lips tingle, but not in the bad way, like when she was going to faint, but in a good way. In a way that made her feel alive, and something else. *Unique.*

"I'm not crazy, you know," Emily blurted out.

"I never thought you were."

"Yeah, well, being *here* . . . I'm here because of a real event. Something happened to me. Like an accident. Like a car ran into me, only it wasn't that. I'm fine, really, now that I'm mending."

"What happened?"

"I'd like to tell you. But I can't. Not yet. Maybe someday."

They looked at one another in a silence that was not in any sense uncomfortable. All at once it was as if what Emily had been born to do in life was to look at Jorge, and to let him look at her.

"Are you sad about the divorce?"

Emily considered. "I'm sorry for my mother."

"Won't you miss Bruce?"

She longed to be honest, but said, "Well, you know, he'll be going away to college next year . . . we wouldn't be seeing much of each other anyway."

"He's a good guy."

She wanted off that subject. "I'll miss Hedden more than the farm. I'll miss my friends."

"You have funny friends. Did I say that right? I mean you have friends who have a good sense of humor."

"Believe me, honey, I know," Emily said, lapsing into the brash "Lawn Guyland" accent she and her friends affected from time to time. "They were here last night. Zodiac and Cordelia and Ming Chu and some others. We did a kind of Christmas Trolls thing." She flickered her blue fingertips at him. "They gave me this wild polish."

"Maybe I could write you over vacation."

"I'd like that."

"Do you have your new address?"

"Um, yeah, somewhere. In my room. It's kind of embarrassing, the name of the place. The condo itself is okay, sort of small, but okay, but the whole place is named Monet Estates." She saw he didn't get it. "Like the painter, you know?"

"Ah."

It struck her that perhaps Jorge really didn't know who Monet was, and for some reason that made her feel enormously fond of him, as if beneath his handsomeness was a human being who was not as sophisticated and worldly as he looked.

"Each unit is named, like, Water Lilies, or Water Garden. All the Water Lilies have two bedrooms. That's what we have. The place is furnished in lots of wicker and white furniture. It's sort of tacky, but it's temporary, Mom says."

"Can you get E-mail?"

"I wish I could. I don't have a computer. And I don't see one in my future. I mean we don't have the money for it right now."

"Then we'll rely on the government mail service."

"Sounds good to me. How long does it take for a letter to get to Buenos Aires?"

"A week. Maybe a little more."

"I'll get the address. Want to see my room?"

"Sure."

He followed her down the corridor and into her small bedroom. Both beds were made; she still didn't have a roommate, but when she made her bed every morning, she remade the other bed, too. She found the new address in a pile of papers on her desk, wrote it carefully down on a piece of paper, and handed it to Jorge.

Their hands touched. Then he was holding her hand and looking at her.

"Jorge," she said, her voice scratchy, "I'm sorry about the time in the woods."

"That's all right."

"I didn't mean to act like such a psycho. It's just that . . ." How could she tell him?

He tried to help her. "You are very fragile?"

"*No.*" She shook her head. "No, I am not fragile. Well, maybe I thought I was for a little while, but I've learned that I'm not. I'm very strong." She saw that he looked puzzled. "I'm only fifteen," she concluded weakly.

"I'm nineteen."

She smiled. "Very old."

"Oh, ancient."

"Compared to me, you are." She thought that if he would only stay and hold her hand, she would be happy. But those invisible bridges spun out between them were like tiny ropes, tightening around her body, tugging her toward him, tugging him toward her, she could tell by his expression. "I guess I am sort of a geek," she concluded.

"You are lovely."

Then he reached out a hand to touch her face, and automatically, without a moment's thought, she flinched. She felt her face go scarlet.

"I'm sorry," she said. "I didn't mean to . . ."

But he had backed off. Leaning against the wall, arms crossed, he said, "I hope you'll write me."

"And you write me."

"I will." She heard a commotion in the hallway. "Oh, get ready, here they come. My new friends." Seeing a look of consternation pass over his face, quickly she added, "They're harmless."

Then they were all at the door, Keith, Cynthia, Arnold, and sullen, fat Bill. Emily introduced them and Jorge shook everyone's hand, except Bill's, who refused to hold out his hand.

"Well, uh, good-bye again," Jorge said to Emily, a bit discomfited by the group crowding around him.

"We'll see you out!" Keith announced.

"No you won't," Emily calmly asserted. "I'll walk you to the door, Jorge."

Reaching out, she took his arm and led him from the room. Beneath her palm lay the slender length of Jorge's arm, muscles lying beneath wool and cotton. She was aware of his body's movements paralleling hers as they walked. It was as if her senses overloaded; she couldn't talk, she could only appreciate Jorge's presence, like a spoon of honey on her tongue, a sunrise: a promise.

He didn't speak either, until they were at the ward doors. There he stopped and held her hand a moment.

"Good-bye for now."

"Good-bye."

Then he pushed through the doors and she turned to find her friends rushing toward her, oohing and ahhing like children.

And she stood there nearly shivering with awe, because while Jorge had been with her, she had been free of pain.

Chapter Twenty-five

❧

In the early dark hours of Wednesday morning, the lights in Bates Hall hadn't been out for long. Christmas break started today, after the morning's classes, and the guys in the dorm had been wild with the scent of freedom. Their finals were over, their papers were written and turned in, they had only to pack and in the morning they'd be out of there.

Pebe had somehow managed to smuggle in a few liters of vodka, which he'd shared with Whit and Lionel and some of the other upperclassmen, and now he sprawled, fully clothed, on his bed in the dorm, not drunk, just completely asleep.

He came awake at once when the overhead light came on in his room.

"Huh?" he muttered.

"That's not Bruce McFarland. He's in the other room."

Pebe sat up, confused, and looked at his watch. It was Dean Lorimer talking to two policemen.

"It's a suite," Dean Lorimer was saying. "Senior perk. Each boy gets a bedroom and they share the living area."

The men left his bedroom and crossed the small sitting room Pebe shared with Bruce. They entered Bruce's bedroom. They turned on the overhead light and the room seemed to jump into attentiveness.

"Bruce McFarland?"

Bruce was in bed, under the covers. It took him a moment to wake up.

"What's up?" he asked, sitting up, looking at them all: Lorimer, the two policemen, and Pebe peering over their shoulders.

"This is Bruce McFarland," Dean Lorimer told the police.

"Bruce McFarland, we have a warrant for your arrest for the assault and rape of Alison Cartwright."

"I don't understand." The men loomed over him, large and frightening in their uniforms. Several pairs of handcuffs hung from their belts, as well as holstered guns and long nylon billy clubs. He'd seen all this in movies, on television, a million times, but this reality was happening to him, and it chilled his blood. The door was blocked. He felt the panic of a trapped animal. He threw back the covers and rose.

"You have the right to remain silent. Anything you say can and will be used against you in a court of law. You have the right to talk to a lawyer and to have him present with you while you're being questioned. If you cannot afford to hire a lawyer, one will be appointed to represent you before any questioning, if you wish. You can decide at any time to exercise these rights and not answer any questions or make any statements. Do you understand each of these rights I have explained to you?"

"Yeah, I guess," Bruce replied, eager to appease these men.

The other policeman said, "We'd like you to get dressed now and come down to the police station."

Dean Lorimer said, "You have to go, Bruce."

Blinking, he looked around his room. As usual it was a mess of books, papers, clothes, E-mail printouts, empty Doritos bags. On the floor near his bed his khakis and Jockey shorts lay in a puddle, and as he reached for them, a policeman bent over and picked them up.

"We'll take those."

"What?"

"They've got a search warrant, Bruce," Dean Lorimer told him. "They want to take some of your clothing."

"Man," Bruce said helplessly.

He had worn sweatpants and a sweatshirt to bed, and now one of the policemen bent forward and briskly patted Bruce all up and down, then said, "You're fine in that. Just put on some shoes."

"Put on those loafers, son," suggested the other policeman, the nicer one.

"Huh?" Bruce said, and then it hit him. He'd seen it on television. They didn't want him to wear sneakers because he might try to hang himself with the laces.

Besides, the policeman was putting his sneakers into the bag with his khakis and Jockey shorts.

"Why are you taking those?" Bruce asked.

The officer said, "It's all right, son. You just cooperate and everything will be fine."

"I'll call your father," Dean Lorimer told Bruce. "Have him come in right away."

"I still don't understand," Bruce said, and then the officer said, "Put your hands behind your back," and it was as if the wind was knocked out of him. His knees went weak. He caved in over his stomach.

"You all right?" Dean Lorimer asked.

"Can't breathe," Bruce gasped.

"Just an anxiety attack," the policeman said. "It'll pass."

When he could get his breath, Bruce straightened. He could feel Pebe's eyes on him, full of pity, and he averted his gaze from his friend.

He felt the cold metal bracelets click against his skin. His teeth felt scummy and he had to pee desperately. When they left the room, with the policeman's hand on his shoulder, the entire dorm was awake. The corridor was lined with guys in their pajamas or BVDs, rubbing their eyes and scratching their sides and staring at Bruce.

"What's happening, man?" they called out.

"Yo, Bruce, what's up?"

Bruce set his face into a mask of stone and did not speak as he was herded down the hall, down the stairs, out the door and into the police car. The cop put his hand on Bruce's head as he got in. He'd seen that on TV, too. The two cops sat in front, separated from him by a grid of wire.

There were no handles on the inside of the doors in the back seat and the terror of claustrophobia once again swept through Bruce. He was afraid he was going to puke. He looked out the windows as the dark streets and landmarks of Basingstoke flashed past with a surreal familiarity. The Post Office. Antonio's Pizza. The Academy Inn. The town library.

The police station was innocuous-looking. He'd passed it a million times. Red brick, white trim, tidy, squat. They drove around back and entered through a garage door that opened automatically and was completely shut before the policemen opened Bruce's door to let him out.

In the station the light was glaringly bright. They took off the cuffs.

"Nothing in his pockets," the policeman said. "No pockets."

They fingerprinted him, then let him wash the ink off his hands. They stood him in front of a tripod and photographed him.

"You can make a phone call now," the nice policeman said, and jerked his head toward a pay phone on the wall.

For a weird moment Bruce couldn't remember his calling card number and panic seized him again. Then it came back and the phone was ringing and his dad answered.

"Dad."

"Dean Lorimer just called. Where are you?"

"At the police station."

"I'm on my way. Lorimer's getting a lawyer for us. Bruce, don't say anything. You don't have to say anything until we get there, okay?"

"Okay."

When the connection was cut, he felt achingly alone.

They led him into a room. A chipped table sat in the midst of four metal chairs. The walls were blank. They all sat down. The policemen looked at him. He stared right back.

One man leaned back in his chair and stretched. "Late, isn't it?" he asked conversationally.

Bruce just looked at him.

"Son, we just need to get some information from you. Your name is Bruce McFarland, right?"

"Right," Bruce replied.

"Mc or Mac?"

"Mc."

"Good. Birth date?"

"October 21, 1978."

"Okay. Home address."

"Post office box thirty-five. Ebradour, Massachusetts. Oh-one-oh-six-oh."

"Fine. You're doing just fine. This isn't so hard, is it?"

Bruce just looked at the man warily. The other officer, the fat one, was studying Bruce through half-closed eyes and stabbing at his teeth with a toothpick.

"Birthplace?"

"Cambridge."

"Uh-huh. Educational background."

Bruce shrugged. "I'm a senior at Hedden."

"Good. How about employment? Ever had a job?"

"Just part-time stuff for friends in Ebradour. Stacking wood and so on."

Suddenly the fat man leaned forward. "Do you know Alison Cartwright?"

Caught off guard, Bruce replied, "Sure. She goes to Hedden."

"She your girlfriend?"

Bruce stared at the man, whose eyes glittered malevolently within the folds of fat. No wonder, he thought, they used to call policemen pigs. "I don't think I want to talk anymore," Bruce said.

"Oh, don't mind him," the other officer said. "He's just pissed off 'cause he's missing his beauty sleep." Both men laughed. "You were doing so well. How 'bout this: any hobbies?"

Bruce shot the man a look of disdain. "No."

"Going to college?"

Bruce wriggled.

"Where you wanna go? Harvard?"

"I've got to pee," Bruce said.

"Sure, fine, come on." The officer escorted him across the hall to a john, then brought him back into the room. "Want some water? Coffee?"

"No. Thanks."

"See, that's what I thought," the nice guy said to the fat one. "Kid's got manners. He's a good kid. You can tell." He looked back at Bruce. "So what's the deal, here? How'd you get Alison Cartwright so mad at you?"

"She's—" Bruce began, then stopped. "I want my dad. I want a lawyer."

"Just a few more questions," the nice guy said.

"I'm not saying anything else," Bruce said, and folded his arms over his chest.

"You've been a student at Hedden for what, three, four years?" the officer asked.

"I want a lawyer."

"Jeez, kid, it would be best if you'd cooperate."

Bruce didn't reply.

They all sat in an uncomfortable silence then, listening to the fat man suck on his toothpick.

The fat man said, "We got photographs of the bruises on Alison Cartwright."

"I—" Bruce was determined not to talk again.

After a while, grumbling, they rose and led him to a cell. It was empty, as were the cells on either side.

"We'll come get you when your lawyer gets here," the nice officer said.

Then they left him alone with his thoughts.

*S*omeone was pounding on the door. Linda came awake with a start in what seemed, at first, a strange room. Her new bedroom in the rented apartment. Partially furnished, cardboard packing boxes everywhere, shadows in all the wrong places. Disoriented, she looked at the clock on the bedside table: 5:12.

Emily, she thought, and her blood went cold. *Oh, let it not be Emily*, she prayed, Emily could not have attempted suicide yet again, the hospital was a safe environment, was *supposed* to be a safe environment, and besides, more important, Emily was happy now. Was coming home, coming out, to this apartment, in only a few days. It couldn't be Emily. *Dear God please*, she pleaded, and rose and tied her robe around her and hurried to the door.

Owen stood there, shivering in his sheepskin overcoat. He wasn't wearing a hat or gloves, and the December wind whipped around him.

"Linda." It seemed all he could say before his voice broke.

Her heart stopped, then lunged. "Owen. What is it?" She pulled him into the apartment and shut the door.

"Bruce's been arrested. Alison Cartwright claims he raped her last night."

"Dear God."

"He's at the police station. He's locked up. Bruce's in jail."

"How is Alison?"

"She's in the hospital. She's signed a statement, and they've collected—'evidence.' " His voice broke. "They took cuttings of Bruce's pubic hair."

"Oh, Owen."

"Bruce's been at the police station since two. The police woke him up at Hedden, arrested him, handcuffed him. *Led him through his dorm in handcuffs.* Everyone saw him."

"Was someone from the school administration with him?"

"Dean Lorimer. They had to go to him first to find which dorm Bruce was in. He went with them. He called me. Then Bruce called me."

"You've seen him?"

"Yes. But he has to stay in jail until we can go to court at nine for the arraignment. Then a judge will set bail. Then Bruce and I have to meet with his lawyer."

"Come over here, Owen. Sit down. I'll make coffee." She led him through a maze of packing boxes into the tiny dining room/kitchen. The windows were squares of blackness and the overhead light threw a harsh glare on the room. Owen sat at the table. He looked haggard and drawn.

"What does Bruce say?"

"He admits they had sex. But he insists she consented. He swears he didn't rape her."

Linda poured the water into the coffee machine, then turned to face her husband.

"Owen, Bruce is in serious trouble."

"Don't you think I know that?" He caught himself, moderated his voice. "Sorry. I'm just—"

"I don't mean legally. I mean emotionally. Psychologically. Something's wrong. He needs help."

Bleakly Owen looked at Linda. "I know. I know that

now." Bitterly he added, "You must feel victorious."

"Owen, that's not fair. Bruce is my stepson. I love him. This breaks my heart."

"Sorry. You're right, I know that. Jesus, I'm just so fucking confused. This is such a nightmare." He ran both hands through his hair. "I guess I've been an asshole about Emily. But I don't know what else I could have done."

"You don't have to apologize," she said, and yet she was glad that he had. It was a wonderful relief and a terrible burden to know for certain that Emily had not lied, that Bruce had. Owen must be miserable beyond telling.

"There's something else," Owen was saying. "I didn't want to tell you. I didn't know what to make of it. About Bruce."

"Go on." She was taking the mugs down, taking the spoons from the drawer.

"At his interview. Something happened. He lost his temper. The admissions officer, well, it was partly her fault. If she'd conducted the interview differently—"

Linda turned to face him. "What happened, Owen?"

"She didn't give Bruce a chance. She wouldn't let him explain himself, and she was—this is what he told me, you understand, I wasn't in the room—she was haughty. Smug."

"And what did Bruce do?"

"Just yelled at her. Well, he used some profanity. And knocked some papers off her desk onto the floor."

"Sounds to me like he was out of control."

"Yeah, I guess he was, for a moment." Hearing his own words, Owen sighed and admitted, "For more than a moment. We could hear him shouting in the waiting room. The admissions officer threatened to call security. I went in and got him out of there." Owen lifted anguished eyes to Linda's. "He was so *disturbed*. He felt so completely rejected by the woman. He kept saying she hadn't given him a chance."

The coffee was ready. Linda set a cup in front of him, automatically adding the spoon of sugar and drop of milk he always had.

"Drink some of this. I want to get something to show you."

She went into her bedroom, found the cardboard box with the words *Private Papers* hastily scribbled on the side, and dug through them until she found the manila envelope she had hidden in her study not so very long ago.

Returning to the kitchen, she lay it on the table in front of Owen.

"I found this in Bruce's closet when I went through his room, after you went through Emily's."

"When was this?"

"The day you went over to Celeste's. When she called about the black bears. Read it." Wanting to give him emotional space, Linda busied herself at the counter, fixing her own cup of coffee, and then she sat down, facing him.

Owen ripped the envelope open and took out another envelope, addressed in a childish scrawl to *Dad.*

Dear Dad, You Stupid Shit,

I guess you're pretty happy now that you're sending me away to boarding school so you can be alone with your new wife and your new daughter. You think I don't know the truth, but I do. I've seen the way you look at Linda. She's the only thing you care about. And you always take her side in an argument. You just want me out of the house so you can fuck her any time.

What I want to know is why you don't just let me go live with my mother. I don't believe the shit you say that she doesn't want me to come live with her because she's always traveling. I bet the truth is she wants me but you won't let her near me. I bet she's sent me lots of letters and you've thrown them

*away. I bet she's called me lots of times and you
haven't told me. You couldn't control her, you
couldn't keep her, and you won't let me be with her
because that would prove that she loves me but she
doesn't love you.*

*You are a fake and a liar and a loser, the worst
loser in the world and I hate you. I'm glad I'm going
to boarding school because it means I can get away
from you.*

In hate,
Bruce McFarland

"Good God," Owen said. He looked at Linda. "I
can't believe this."

"I know."

"You should have given this to me the moment you
found it."

"You're right; I should have. But I wanted to protect
you. And at the time it didn't seem relevant. Such
venom toward you . . . I thought it would only com-
plicate things and . . . I knew it would break your
heart. Besides, Owen, I don't believe it. I mean, I don't
believe that Bruce hates you. Not now. Or ever, really.
He was younger when he wrote that, and probably
anxious about going away. You know how teenagers
say things they don't mean."

"When were you planning to give it to me?"

"I didn't have a plan. My first thought was to throw
it away, so that you'd never find it. Then I thought,
no, I should keep it . . . so I just hid it with my papers."
She rubbed the bridge of her nose. "Would it have in-
fluenced you if I had shown it to you? Would you have
been more inclined to believe Emily? I don't think so.
I think you would have been angry with me, for dis-
covering it. And Bruce needed an ally. You needed to
be his ally. This would have muddied everything."

"Perhaps you're right. I don't know. I can't say. I'm
so muddled . . . Jesus Christ, Linda, we're good, intel-

ligent, well-meaning people. How did we get into such
a mess?"

"I don't know." She was thinking, selfishly, of how
she would feel when she told Emily, when she told Dr.
Travis, about Bruce's arrest. Now there would no
longer be any doubt that Bruce raped Emily.

"Would you?"

"I'm sorry, Owen, what?"

Owen cleared his throat. His face was flushed with
emotion as he repeated his request. "Will you help me?
Will you help us? Will you go through this with me?"
He flushed and fought back tears. "Please. I don't think
I can get through it alone."

Linda thought of Bruce, his lies, his physical and
emotional cruelty to Emily. Of Bruce disregarding all
the years of their family life and anything the family
might have meant. She thought of Owen's betrayal,
confiding in Celeste, choosing Celeste. She thought of
the contempt that awaited Bruce and anyone who
stood by him, the pity and wrath and abhorrence that
everyone would feel toward a boy who raped. Who
would stand by him? Not the school; of course they
would stand by Alison Cartwright. They would have
to expel Bruce. Not his Hedden friends; the boys would
not want to be guilty by association. She *could* avoid
it all; she could stand exempt from the loathing Bruce
was about to face. She had left Owen and Bruce and
the farm. They were not legally divorced yet, but they
were legally separated. They lived apart. Bruce had
made it clear that he did not love her. Did not love
Emily. In fact, assaulted Emily, destroyed her pride,
and almost destroyed her life. What did Linda owe to
this young man, then, this young man who hated her
and her daughter so furiously? Was her remaining love
for Owen sufficient to pull her back into this approaching maelstrom?

No. Her remaining love for Owen was not sufficient.
But together with her love for Bruce, it was.

For she still loved her stepson. It was there, the love for him, weighing in her heart like a bruise-colored stone. She still loved him, and more than that, she still *claimed* him. Whatever he had done or not done, she had been an integral part of his life for the past seven years. If she had, unwittingly, been part of his problem, or if she were purely innocent, still she would be, she would attempt with all her being to *try* to be, part of the solution.

"I'll go with you," she said.

Chapter Twenty-six

❧

The courthouse was next to the police station; the McFarlands had passed it a million times. An imposing four-square edifice built of large blocks of stone with an appealing, nutmeg-like grittiness, it harbored on the first floor a disappointing warren of small rooms and offices that had been divided up again and again as the town and county government became more complicated.

Superior court was on the second floor; a guard at the door only looked at Linda and Owen as they entered. They found seats in the gallery along with a number of other people, all of whom looked as anxious and uncomfortable as Linda felt. This room was high and wide and paneled in shining oak illumined by the morning light; at another time Linda might have considered it beautiful.

Bruce entered the courtroom with a rotund man in a gray suit.

"That's Paul Larson, Bruce's lawyer," Owen whispered to Linda. "Lorimer recommended him."

Bruce was wearing a rumpled sweatsuit and, incongruously, loafers. Auburn stubble speckled his jawline, which was crisply sharp as only a young man's can be, but he had circles beneath his eyes and his shoulders slumped. Obviously he hadn't slept. He looked confused and nervous. He shot a quick glance at his father, and seemed surprised to find Linda there. Immediately he looked away.

Larson ushered Bruce to the front row of the courtroom seats, then went through the low railings to sit at a table facing the judge's bench. A slender woman in her fifties, clad in a simple business suit, her gray hair short and businesslike, came down the center aisle carrying her briefcase and talking in a low voice to her younger colleague, an attractive black woman. The older woman, Linda learned when the lawyers later addressed the judge, was Donna Sylvester, the prosecuting attorney.

For a long while, it seemed, everyone waited, talking in murmurs. Then the judge entered in his black robes, and everyone stood in respect of his presence, and Linda's heart began to batter frantically inside her chest. Suddenly everything seemed painfully vivid and helplessly real.

She was seized with fear. She could not bear to imagine Bruce found guilty, incarcerated, with all his life cut short. Put among criminals and bullies; locked up with murderers and monsters. How would he endure it? How would Owen? How would she? Was this what she wanted? She was horrified at what he'd done to Alison, and still angry with him for what he had done to Emily, for what he had done to all their lives, but he was not a *bad* boy. He was not a *criminal. This* was never what she wanted, this seemed too much, it was not right, and with all the force of her female strength, with whatever powers of prayer and the primitive feminine might of witchcraft she possessed, she prayed that Bruce might go free, be saved, be given over to her custody and Owen's so that they could help him, heal him, bring him home into the good young man she knew waited in his deepest heart.

The clerk of the court read in a clear voice: "The Commonwealth of Massachusetts is bringing a charge of rape and sexual assault against Bruce McFarland, a seventeen-year-old student at Hedden Academy."

"How do you plead?" the judge asked.

It was Paul Larson who stood and replied. "Your honor, my client pleads not guilty."

"Your honor," Donna Sylvester said, "we'd like to see this tried as soon as possible."

The judge looked over at his clerk. "With the holidays coming it, it looks like the earliest date we can give you is January fifteenth."

"Until then, your honor," Paul Larson said, "we ask that the defendant be released into his father's custody without bail. This young man has no previous record."

"The prosecution has no problem with that," Sylvester said.

"Very well," the judge said. "The court releases you, Bruce McFarland, into your father's custody, without bail. Court date, January fifteenth."

Larson and Bruce rose and came back down the aisle. Owen and Linda followed and they all clustered together in the hall.

"Come to my office," Larson said. "We've got a lot to discuss."

The lawyer's office was on Main Street in Basingstoke, in a pretty clapboard building that had once been a barber shop. A secretary greeted them with a neutral smile and immediately ushered them down the hall and into Larson's inner sanctum. Paul Larson settled them around a small conference table. He opened his briefcase and took out a folder.

"All right," he said, "we've got some work to do. Why don't I tell you where we go from here?"

"Fine," Owen replied.

"We've got a rape charge to deal with here. Let me start with what the prosecuting attorney will have." He opened the folder. "An incident report has been filed by Officer Stakovsky, stating that at one-thirty-six A.M. December nineteenth he was called to the emergency room of the Basingstoke Hospital. There he met with the victim, Alison Cartwright, who had come to the hospital with the school nurse of Hedden Academy. Also accompanied by her friend Rebecca Cooper.

"At that time the officer noted that he observed a swelling on the left side of the victim's face as well as bruise marks on her neck.

"He interviewed Ms. Cartwright, who charged that Bruce McFarland had raped her at about midnight in the music room at Hedden Academy. Ms. Cartwright signed a victim's statement, under penalty of perjury. The examining physician, Dr. Gable, stated that the victim had signs of recent sexual intercourse, including semen in her vagina."

"We had sex, but I didn't rape her!" Bruce blurted out.

"Also," Larson continued smoothly, "Dr. Gable found minor lacerations and bleeding in the vaginal area, which would indicate the use of force."

"*I didn't*—" Bruce began, but Owen shot a look at his son, and Bruce didn't finish.

"Furthermore, the officer took a statement from Rebecca Cooper, stating that Alison returned to their dorm room around midnight, crying hysterically, claiming that she had just come from the music practice room where Bruce had raped her. Rebecca stated that Alison could not stop weeping, could not stop shaking, and vomited several times, until she brought up only bile. Alison said she did not want to get Bruce in trouble, but Rebecca insisted she see the school nurse, and went with her to the nurse's office. They woke her; there's an emergency button at the door to the nurse's quarters. After Mrs. Guera talked with Alison, she insisted they go to the police, and she drove the young women to the emergency room and waited with them while Alison was treated. The statements of Mrs. Guera and Rebecca Cooper will be admissible as 'fresh complaints,' testifying to the victim's state of mind at that time.

"In addition, the police have taken Bruce's clothing, as well as any signs of evidence from the crime scene, and this will be used against him in court.

"Now. The major evidence for the charge of rape is the statement of the victim. Against that we have the statement of the defendant, that sex occurred, but that it was consensual."

"It *was*," Bruce said.

"Against that, the prosecution will have photographs of the bruises on the victim's face and neck, and the physician's report as to the lacerations in the vaginal area. All of which presume violence."

"I didn't *rape*—"

"In your defense, Bruce, several things will help. First of all, you have no criminal history, is that correct?"

"Correct," Bruce answered.

"No charge of rape brought against you before?"

"No," Bruce said immediately.

Linda and Owen looked at one another. Linda felt herself flush, but she did not speak.

"We'll be able to get good personal references for you from teachers and students at Hedden? Especially from women?"

"Well, sure."

"Any other outbreaks of violence of any kind recently?"

"No," Bruce said quickly.

"Wait a moment," Owen broke in. He looked at his son. "What about the fight with Jorge?"

"Dad, that wasn't *violence*. That was just . . . stuff."

"I'd like to know about it," Larson said.

"About a month ago," Owen told him, "Bruce was involved in a skirmish with another boy at school."

"Did Hedden suspend him?"

"No."

"Did they take any disciplinary action?"

"They warned him. It was his first offense. He's been, I think you'll find when you talk to the school, Bruce's been an model student."

Larson was taking notes. "Good grades?"

"Yes."

"We'll get copies of his school records. Friends?" He looked at Bruce. "Who'd be willing to testify on your behalf? As to your character?"

Bruce nodded. "Yeah, I think so."

"All right. Now. Let me tell you the various ways this could go. Bruce didn't sign a statement, which is good. Lorimer got me there immediately, which was a good move, an excellent move, on the school's behalf. And on yours. You should thank Mr. Lorimer.

"The victim's family flew up today. They'll meet with a lawyer and with the police and then we'll know whether or not they'll take this to trial. Sometimes, as I'm sure you're aware, rape victims don't want to face the publicity and intrusion and difficulties of a trial. But one possibility is that they will take this to trial. And we will be pressed to prepare the best defense we can.

"Another possibility is that they'll approach us with an offer to plea bargain. For example, they might suggest that Bruce admit to simple assault. Bruce could admit to that and be given pretrial probation. The court could continue the case for five years, on the conditions that Bruce have regular counseling. This I see as your best outcome."

"And the worst?" Owen inquired.

Larson cleared his throat. "It would depend, of course, on the judge. According to current Massachusetts law, this kind of crime against the person could bring imprisonment for up to twenty years."

"Shit," Bruce whispered.

Linda's fingers went numb with fright. She saw that Owen and Bruce had both gone pale.

"I hasten to add that I don't foresee this consequence," Larson added. "It's a first offense. If it were
a second offense, it would bring life imprisonment."

"Dear God," Linda said.

Larson squinted his eyes, studying her. "I'm talking
about a previous, court-tried, guilty verdict. A record
of offense. Not just a charge." He looked at them
sternly. "There is no former recorded conviction?"

"No," Owen said.

"Good. All right, then. I'd like to get a bit of personal information about Bruce and his family and his
educational background from you."

Linda and Owen looked at each other wearily as
they answered Larson's questions, which were not so
different from those asked when Emily was first admitted to Basingstoke Hospital.

It was $with$ grim efficiency that the three Mc-
Farlands decided, standing in the cold air in front of
Paul Larson's office, how they would proceed with
their day. Owen would take Bruce back to Hedden and
help him pack; Linda would make a run to the grocery
store and prepare breakfast for them all. No one
wanted to eat in a public restaurant. No one was hungry, for that matter, but Owen knew he and Bruce
would need some fortification before the long drive
back to the farm.

Linda moved numbly through the necessary motions
of shopping for groceries and carrying them into her
car and then into her house. While she waited for the
men to arrive, she made a desultory attempt at shoving
the cardboard boxes against the wall. She wanted to
make more room in this tiny apartment. More than
that, she felt a compulsion to move, exert energy, *fix
something*. She wanted *order*. She could not simply sit
down.

She made a fresh pot of coffee, and scrambled eggs,
and cleared the stacks of papers, catalogues, and mag-

azines off the kitchen table and threw a fresh tablecloth over it. She had planned to spend some time making the place look less like a train station and more like a home for when Emily got out of the hospital and came to live with her, but there just was never enough time, and besides, she hadn't cared. It had rather suited her frame of mind to live in a place so obviously temporary.

When Owen and Bruce arrived, their male bodies loomed large in the small rooms. She hung their overcoats in the closet and gestured toward the kitchen.

"Coffee's ready," she told them. "And I made scrambled eggs. And bagels. With strawberry jam. And cream cheese." *This is what you do*, an odd little voice in her head said, *this is what you do when you discover your stepson is a rapist. This is how you continue with your life. This is how you make it through the day.*

Bruce sat at the table. He had shaved and changed into khakis and a sweater.

"Thanks," he muttered when she poured juice into a glass and set it before him.

"You look better," she told him.

He shrugged, not looking at her. He had not looked at her directly yet this morning.

"We saw Lorimer," Owen told her as they sat around the table. "We're going to keep him informed as things develop. He needs to consult with the trustees and with the executive committee, but of course everyone's scattered now with the holidays. So at the moment the school is taking no official action."

"That's good, I guess," Linda said.

"I can't go back there anyway," Bruce said bitterly.

"Yeah, and why is that, Bruce?" Owen asked, his voice suddenly harsh.

"Let him eat," Linda said in a low voice.

"I'm not hungry," Bruce snarled. "I just want to go home." Tossing his half-eaten bagel on the plate, he went into the living room, found the remote control, and turned on the television.

"He needs a kick in the ass," Owen murmured angrily, but his eyes were despairing.

"He needs therapy," Linda said.

"We all need therapy."

"But he needs it the most. The most urgently."

"This will be in the Basingstoke paper," Owen muttered. "Everyone will know."

"That's the least of our problems," Linda said. "It doesn't matter what people think of Bruce. It only matters that Bruce get over this, this . . . compulsion of his. We've got to help him recover the good young man we know is there. We've got to work with him."

"You keep saying *we*."

"I mean it. I must somehow be part of the problem. I want to be part of the solution."

"Does this mean you'll move back home?"

"No. Emily won't be ready yet. And while Bruce is so . . . volatile, I don't think it would be a good idea. We would only be setting up some sort of disaster. But I'll see a therapist with you. With you and Bruce. And I'll come to the farm when I can. I'll spend time with you, and with Bruce."

They looked into the living room where her stepson sprawled on the sofa, his face adamantine and grim.

"I don't think he'll be pleasant to be around," Owen warned her.

Linda laughed briefly. "Oh, really?" But she nodded her head, determined. "I don't care if he's pleasant or not. I'm his stepmother. He can't get rid of me."

Chapter Twenty-seven

*E*mily *was playing* Scrabble with Keith when a nurse entered the ward living room and said, "Emily? Dr. Travis would like to see you a moment."

"What's up?" Emily asked, but the nurse only shrugged and bustled away.

"Now what have you done?" Keith scolded and Emily mumbled, "What *could* I have done in this place?"

She was startled to see her mother sitting in Dr. Travis's office, which now, only five days before Christmas, was cheerfully chaotic with red-and-white poinsettias and cardboard cut-outs of Santa Claus, Frosty the Snowman, Rudolph the Red-Nosed Reindeer.

Dr. Travis, for a change, was in a dull mode, wearing all black, with a gold necklace and earrings. Probably, Emily thought, she had some kind of board meeting today.

"Hey, Mom," Emily said, crossing the room to kiss her. "What are you doing here?"

"Sit down a moment," Dr. Travis directed. "We have something to tell you."

"Don't look so worried." Linda smiled. "It's not bad news." She added, "Well, it's not good news, either."

Emily sank onto the sofa. Automatically one hand found the other and began to tear at the skin around the nail.

"Shall I . . . ?" Linda asked Dr. Travis, who nodded.

"Emily. Emily, Bruce was arrested last night. For raping Alison Cartwright."

Emily could only stare.

"Go on," Dr. Travis said.

"Alison is in the hospital."

"Is she okay?" Emily asked.

"She's not badly injured. She . . . she was bruised on her neck and face, and I guess, I guess there was some tearing in the vaginal area." Linda's eyes welled with tears. She looked at Dr. Travis. "I don't know why this is so hard to say."

"It happened last night?" Emily asked.

"Yes. At the school. In the music room."

The three women sat in a somber silence while the circuits of Emily's brain raced with this new information.

Then Emily said, "It's all my fault."

"What?" Linda was startled. "Honey—"

Emily was tearing at her hands again, her hands that had begun to heal. "It's really all my fault. I hate myself."

"Emily, how can it possible be—"

"If I had made you believe me, you would have stopped him. I did it all wrong, I acted crazy, I should have been calm, I should have made you believe me, then he wouldn't have done it again."

"Em, no, honey, that doesn't make any sense."

"It makes emotional sense," Dr. Travis interjected. "It makes sense to a woman who has been raped. This is not an uncommon reaction."

"But don't you see," Linda pressed, "now everyone knows the truth!"

Emily nodded. She was working on her hands, digging in the flesh, digging, digging.

"Now Owen knows the truth," Linda said. "He knows, he can't *refuse* to know, that Bruce raped you."

Something welled inside Emily, bubbles surfacing, bursting in her chest, space opening up around her heart. She had more room to breathe. She looked at Dr. Travis. "That's right. Now Owen *knows*. Now *you* know. You know I was telling the truth."

"I always believed you," Dr. Travis said.

"And I can tell Zodiac, and Cordelia, and Ming Chu."

"Yes, Emily," Linda said. "Now there is no doubt."

Emily frowned, trying to make sense of the sensations surging within her. *Relief.* She *was* relieved, she felt bizarrely, *desperately* glad that now there was no doubt, now everyone knew she had not been lying. She was not a liar. Yet something was struggling against the rising lightness, something strung of anguish and horror was caught on the effervescence of her relief, clawing it, weighing it down.

"Mommy," Emily cried suddenly, "Mommy, what will happen to Bruce now?"

Linda cleared her throat. "Your father and I, Owen and I, we've just spent the morning with a lawyer, Bruce's lawyer, and we've been in court. Bruce is out on bail. The trial is set for January fifteenth. We don't know what will happen. He could go to jail."

Emily burst into a rage of tears. "What is *wrong* with him! How could he be so *stupid*? So fucking fucking stupid!" She stood up. She thought she would wrench the chair off the floor and throw it through the window. She thought she would claw the paint off the walls. Slam her head against the door.

Linda stood up and grabbed Emily against her. "Baby, baby, it's okay."

"It's *not* okay, Mommy," Emily cried. "I don't want Bruce to go to jail. Oh, Jesus Christ, I hate Bruce. I *hate him.*"

"I know, Emmie, I know, honey," Linda said. "My heart is breaking, too."

T*he next day*, Friday afternoon, Emily sat with her group around a table in the living area. From here she could see through the glass walls to the swinging doors through which Linda would come when she arrived to take Emily home. Keith, Arnold, Cynthia, Bill, even Emily, all were miserable. Bill was so upset he wouldn't even sit with them, but sulked in a chair on the other side of the room.

"I'll call you guys," Emily said. "I'll come visit you, Arnold."

"No, you won't," he replied gloomily. "Your mother won't want you hanging out with an old addict."

"You're not old," Keith said.

"Arnold's right," Cynthia said. "It all changes once you leave. You say you'll keep in touch, but you don't. I know. I've been in and out of hospitals enough times."

"Yeah, but we're different," Keith protested. "We're a really cool group."

"It's true," Emily agreed. "You guys are . . . I'm going to really miss you."

Yesterday she had enjoyed a moment of confused and somehow guilty satisfaction when she told them about Bruce's arrest. She'd been surprised, touched, by their obvious delight, their *congratulations*, as if she had just won an award. They were all so much on her side. Totally. When she confessed her sense of guilt, they'd laughed at her: *What's the matter with you, are you crazy?* Dr. Travis had told her the guilt was normal, she could learn to understand it, she could live with it. When she told them how sad she was for her stepbrother, they had all clamored in disagreement: *Don't be ridiculous! Don't waste a moment's thought on the guy. Remember what he did to you!*

He's not all bad! Emily had wanted to say. *Give him a break!* These emotions were normal, Dr. Travis had told her. Another reason to see a therapist regularly after she left the hospital.

Now Keith said, "It would be too cruel of you not

to let us know what happens with the gorgeous Jorge."

"Yeah, and I want to hear about your party," Emily told him.

"I'm going to be the only one of the group left in here," Arnold said.

"You know Travis would let you go home for Christmas."

"Yeah, well, you've seen Mom. You've heard her. The only way I'm going to stay sober through the holidays is locked in here."

"I'll probably be back on Christmas Day," Cynthia said.

"Nonsense, child!" Keith admonished. "Don't be so pessimistic. You've got great drugs. You've got a good shrink in the outside world."

"Yeah, but I hate the outside world."

The outside world. In the past week Emily had made forays into it, more adventurous each time, once to dinner with her mother, then to a shopping mall, then with her mother to pack up all her things from her room in Shipley Hall.

On their way to the dorm, Emily and Linda had stopped at Tuttle Hall to talk with Dean Lorimer. He was sorry, he told them, that Emily had to leave Hedden, but he understood the financial constraints of a two-household family. Several parents had had to make that difficult choice for one reason or another. They had enjoyed Emily at the school and wished her well in the future.

Emily had listened with a mixture of impatience and sadness, a terrible welling sadness that filled her skin and the membranes of her heart so that it ached with the pressure. She only wanted to pack and get out of there. It made her sad to leave Hedden. She had loved it there. But there was no choice, she knew. She had to go forward into her new life.

Her new life. She knew it would take all of her courage and self-reliance to function. She had not told her mother, though she'd discussed it with Travis, how the few times she'd been out, waiting in line at the movie theater or walking down the street toward a restaurant, the sudden presence of a single man coming toward her would set off danger alarms ringing throughout her body. Her heart would race. Her lips would go cold, her fingertips numb.

The terror will stop, Travis had promised.

But it was an awful thing, that irrational, gripping fear. It made her feel genuinely crazy. A few evenings ago Keith had wrapped his arm around Emily as they stood in the living room singing Christmas carols. He'd smiled at her and hugged her against him. It had been a purely friendly hug. Keith cared for her. He had become her dear friend. He was *gay,* for heaven's sake. All these things Emily reminded herself as she was captured in Keith's embrace, and still as he continued to hold her against him she felt trapped, threatened, desperate to shove him aside, to escape.

She hadn't told Keith; it would have hurt his feelings. She had told Travis, who said, *This will pass.* This is one of the things that only can change with the passing of time.

She wanted it to pass quickly. She wanted to be whole and strong by the time Jorge returned in January. *That might be rushing it,* Dr. Travis cautioned her. Sometimes Emily felt like she contained tornadoes inside her skin.

Now Dr. Travis entered the room, looking exceptionally festive in a multitude of floating red panels. In her ears were the red-bowtied silver jingle bells Linda had given her.

"Are you ready to go, Emily?"

Emily nodded. "All packed. My suitcases are on my bed."

Travis sank into a chair at the table. "Excited?"

"Yeah. Kind of. Kind of scared." They had talked about this for the past two days, how patients often felt nervous about leaving the safety of the hospital.

"Remember," Travis told her, "it will help if you establish a routine as soon as possible. Routines give us a sense of security. And you must remember the various problem-solving skills you've learned here. *They will help you.*"

Emily nodded. "I know."

"There's your mother," Cynthia said. "God, she's pretty."

Through the glass window Emily saw her mother approaching. She was wearing jeans, a black turtleneck, and a black blazer, and her face glowed the way it did when she was especially happy: at birthday parties, at Christmas, when she got good news from her agent on the phone. She's happy because I'm coming out, Emily thought, and affection flooded her chest.

"Hi, Mom." Emily rose and went to the living room door.

Linda gave her a quick hug, then stepped into the living room. "Hello, everyone!" She had a bag in her arm, and she approached the table and began to pull out brightly wrapped packages. "I brought little presents for you all. Nothing fabulous, just little things; you all have been so great to Emily."

"Does it matter who gets which package?" Cynthia asked suspiciously.

"Oh, yes, of course. There are cards."

"Can we open them now?" Keith asked. "Pleeeeeeze?"

"Absolutely not. You have to wait till Christmas morning."

Bill rose out of his chair like some kind of hulking monster and plodded toward the table. He was kind of growling, the way he did when he was upset, and Emily moved toward her mother protectively. He might get violent if there was no present for him. But Linda picked up a package and handed it to him.

"This is for you, Bill."

He didn't say thank you. He said nothing. But he took the package and returned to his chair and held the present against his chest like a baby.

"We just need you to sign one more piece of paper," Dr. Travis told Linda.

"Fine. Well, good-bye, everyone."

Suddenly Emily found herself hugging everyone, Keith and Arnold and Cynthia. She approached Bill, who didn't show any signs of noticing her, and leaning over, pecked a sisterly kiss on the top of his head. He did not respond.

Then her mother took her arm and led her from the room, chatting all the way.

"I was going to make a reservation at the Academy Inn for a celebratory dinner, but then I thought you probably don't want to sit in some stuffy old-fart place this evening, so I thought we'd go to Luigi's Pizza and then to a movie. What do you think? Good idea?"

"Cool."

Emily heaved her duffel bag and backpack over her shoulders and Linda picked up the suitcase.

As they walked to the nurses' station, Emily said, "I can't wait to see our apartment."

"Oh, you'll *love* it!" Linda exclaimed. "It's so clean, and the bathtub and sink and everything is all brand new and sparkling." She knew how much Emily had hated the stained, faded appearance of the farm's appliances and bathrooms.

"Sign here, please," Dr. Travis said. Then she turned to Emily.

"You're a wonderful young woman, Emily. I know you'll do just fine."

"Thank you."

"And I know you'll like Dr. Srivastava," Travis said, naming the shrink Emily would see twice a week for the next few months. "She's the best there is."

"Thank you," Emily said again.

"Thank you," Linda echoed. "We can't say it enough, can we?"

Travis hugged Emily and shook Linda's hand and then Emily and Linda walked to the ward doors and left the psych ward together.

Their new apartment was too small for much of a Christmas tree. All the lights and ornaments were at the farm, in boxes in the attic, Owen's ornaments and Linda's so mingled over the past seven years that it would be hard to claim ownership of any one item. So Saturday Linda and Emily went out to buy a compact little evergreen and a new stand and tiny twinkling lights, and Sunday they sat watching television movies and stringing popcorn and cranberries to ornament the tiny evergreen they'd managed to wedge into a corner of the apartment. They were going to spend Christmas Eve and Christmas at Janet's house, but they both loved the sight and smell of a tree. It made them feel at home.

They had just finished decorating the tree and were congratulating themselves when the phone rang.

"Linda," Owen said. "I've had a call from the Cartwrights' lawyer. They want to meet with us tomorrow afternoon."

"Why?"

"Larson says they might consider dropping the charges against Bruce."

"I'll be there. What time?"

They sat in a large conference room, uneasily looking at one another, Linda and Owen and Bruce and Paul Larson on one side of the mahogany table, Bert Cartwright and Donna Sylvester, the prosecuting attorney from the district attorney's office, on the other. Alison was not present.

Bert Cartwright was handsome, wealthy, impatient. He wore his gleaming black hair cut close and his skin glowed with a tan of someone who had just spent a week skiing. His suit was beautiful and expensive, and cut to flatter his full chest and shoulders. His blue eyes flicked over Linda with an appraiser's ruthless skill. *I wouldn't want to be married to this man*, Linda thought.

Cartwright looked at Bruce and then at Owen with clear, steady, direct contempt. Owen sat between Linda and Bruce; she could feel the tension in Owen's body.

Ms. Sylvester spoke first. "I've called this meeting at the behest of the Cartwrights. I want to say in advance that I have tried to prevent them from taking this action, and I think they are making the decision in haste. They, acting on the wishes of their daughter, have asked the Commonwealth not to prosecute Bruce."

Linda heard Owen catch his breath.

"We have more than enough evidence to prosecute and to win a conviction," Ms. Sylvester continued. "The evidence is strong. It is clear that Bruce Mc-Farland raped Alison Cartwright. However, Miss Cartwright has decided that she does not want to take this to trial. This is not, I must add, because she is afraid of the stigma and the publicity, the future disagreeableness this would cause her. This is because she says she cares for Mr. McFarland and does not want to see him incarcerated. I have told them that I have no doubt we could win this case, and we could see Mr. Mc-Farland jailed for his assault. In addition, I have brought before them the option of pretrial probation. The defendant could agree to become part of the court system; as long as he saw a therapist regularly he would not be brought before the court. In this instance, therapy would be enforceable, and I believe we all can agree that therapy is necessitated in this case.

"However, the Cartwrights are reluctant to proceed with any kind of legal action. They like Bruce. They know he has no previous record. They do not want to see his life ruined. They believe there is a good possibility of redemption if there is therapy. What they are asking, then, are three things:

"First, that Bruce withdraw from Hedden Academy. Obviously Alison doesn't want to live with the fear that a rape or other violence might occur, as well as with the embarrassment Bruce's presence might cause her.

"Second, they would like your word of honor, Mr. and Mrs. McFarland, and yours, Bruce, that Bruce McFarland will enter into a long-term program of therapy with a board-approved psychiatrist or psychologist who specializes in working with men who rape.

"Third, that Bruce will never contact Alison again. Will not accost her physically, will not telephone her, will not send her mail or E-mail."

Linda stole a look at Bruce's face: he sat with his head down; it was impossible to read his expression.

"I must add that without the testimony of Alison Cartwright, the major evidence in this case disappears. The Commonwealth could continue with prosecution, however. We do have the evidence of the doctor who examined Alison, the written statements of the nurse and her friend, who helped her get to the hospital and spoke with her after the rape, as well as the physical evidence of the photographs of the bruises on Alison's body and the pubic hair match. The crime of rape is one the Commonwealth does not like to see go unpunished. But Alison made a strong case on Bruce McFarland's behalf. Because of that, we are willing to drop the rape charge, as long as you agree to the three items we mentioned."

"Certainly," Owen said, but Paul Larson cut him off and leaned across Bruce to whisper in Owen's ear.

Then Paul Larson spoke. "My clients agree to the stipulations."

Owen leaned over to whisper to Linda. "Larson says we cannot thank them. To do that would be to admit to Bruce's guilt."

"But he *is* guilty!" Linda whispered back.

Ms. Sylvester said, "Mr. Cartwright would like to say a few words."

Cartwright looked at Bruce. "I didn't have to be here today," he said. "I could have let my lawyer handle this. I didn't have to incur the expense and take the time from my work to fly up here, but I did, and I'll tell you why. I wanted to get a good look at you. I'm looking at you, young man. *I see you. I know what you did. I know what you are.* If I ever see you near my daughter again, I will personally make you sorry. Is that understood?"

Linda felt Owen's entire body go rigid.

Bruce nodded, looking miserable.

"My daughter still cares for you, insane as that may be. It is solely because of her compassion that we are dropping this case. I'd like to see it proceed. I'd like to see you tried. I'd like to see your name dragged through the mud. I'd like to see you in jail for the rest of your life so you can never assault another woman. But I'm bowing to my daughter's wishes. She's had enough pain out of you. I don't blame her for wanting to let the whole thing go, but I will not forget. Do you hear me, Bruce McFarland? *I will not forget.* And if I ever hear of you so much as standing on the same street as my daughter, I'll personally make your pathetic, disgusting, pervert ass sorry you were ever born."

Bruce sat looking at the table, his face flaming red.

"Do you understand me?" Cartwright asked, each word sounding like a curse.

Bruce nodded.

"Answer me. Look at me, and answer me."

Bruce raised his head and met Mr. Cartwright's eyes. In a shaky voice, he said, "I understand you."

Cartwright looked at Owen and then at Linda. "As for you two . . . I can't imagine what you two did to turn this boy into a rapist, but you're both beneath contempt. You're *lower* than this boy. I hope you're ashamed of yourselves." Abruptly he turned to Donna Sylvester. "That's all I have to say."

Everyone stood. The lawyers shuffled papers into briefcases. Bert Cartwright stormed out of the room, leaving a cloud of hostility behind him. Sylvester followed. Finally, in miserable silence, Bruce and Owen and Linda and Larson went out of the room.

Chapter Twenty-eight

❧

Dr. Ingersall's office was on the second floor of an elegant old Victorian house on a side street in Northampton. Two days after Christmas, Linda arrived early and found herself in a waiting room furnished rather like any family's den, with a television and VCR and two cushiony couches and three cozy armchairs, with glossy magazines on the coffee table and on a low shelf a stack of bright plastic children's toys.

Dr. Ingersall, clad in jeans and a tartan flannel shirt, no jacket, no tie, came out from his inner office with an open, hearty, country sort of ambling walk. He wore tooled leather cowboy boots.

"How are you both today?" he asked.

"Fine," Linda replied politely, and everyone shook hands, and then they went into Ingersall's office and he closed the door.

They settled in a room brightened with many windows and on the wall, impressionist prints. Linda and Owen sat side by side on a sofa, Ingersall next to them in a chair. The coffee table held a vase of fresh daisies, a large bowl of pistachios, and a box of tissues.

Dr. Ingersall began. "I've spent several sessions now, as you both know, with Bruce. I like him. He's a likable boy. Bright, engaging, good-looking, too. On the surface, a fortunate young man. Inside, however, he's churning with emotions. He feels helpless. He feels powerless. He feels he's facing challenges for which he is not adequate. He feels inferior."

Linda was shocked. "Bruce feels inferior?"

Ingersall nodded. "At my first meeting with your husband, he told me about Bruce raping your daughter. So I'm sure you are acquainted with the literature on rape. You know that rape is not about sex or love. It's about power. All our studies show that the act of rape stems from a sense of inferiority, powerlessness, inadequacy, and desperation."

"How could Bruce be desperate?" Owen asked.

"Well, look at what's been going on in his life. He's finishing his senior year. He knows he's got to leave the familiarity of boarding school. He'll be separated from his friends, his teachers, and in a sense from his entire self-image. He's being asked to test himself against new criteria: how good is he now? Can he gain admission to a first-rate college? Can he get into the one college he passionately wants to get into? A college, I might point out, for which he is not particularly well matched."

"Alison Cartwright wants to go there."

"Yes. Alison. The young woman who Bruce feels love for, the woman whom Bruce believed was beginning to love him. They've just begun to realize they're in love, and suddenly he sees that before they can really become a couple, she'll be torn away from him. She is choosing a school that rejects him."

"He didn't know until the interview that the school would reject him," Owen pointed out.

"I don't think that's quite true," Ingersall replied. "Bruce's read the school description. He's read the catalogues. He knows Westhurst is an unusual school, appealing to strictly artistic types. He went into that interview knowing that he would fail, knowing that he would be rejected. It made it even more devastating, and even more exactly what he projected, that the person who interviewed him was a woman."

"But still," Linda cut in, "still, I can't grasp that Bruce feels inferior."

"Feelings aren't always logical," Ingersall reminded her. "Adolescents certainly aren't. And in Bruce's case, his sense of inferiority stems not from school, where his grades are good, where he has friends, where he performs well. I think we're going to discover that it stems from an old and powerful and primal wound: Bruce was rejected by his mother."

"But he had me," Owen pointed out. "And he had Linda. And if he was hurt by Michelle's lack of interest, well, then why didn't he talk to me about it?"

"Bruce was a little boy when his mother left him," Ingersall said. "He couldn't articulate all his emotions, all his confusion. He's been carrying this around with him for a long, long time. Other things have contributed: he is conflicted about Linda, for instance. On the one hand, he likes her, even loves her. On the other hand, he still harbors the childish belief that if she weren't there, in his mother's place, his real mother would be. And as he's grown older, he's developed a sense of pride as well as a broader and superficial understanding of the dynamic between him and his mother. Can he come whining to you, to anyone, because his mother's deserted him? Of course not. He's almost eighteen years old. He's got to be a man. Intellectually, he knows that Michelle is like any number of women and men who have no instinctual affection for their offspring. He can read stuff like that in any magazine. He can hear that on TV. But emotionally, beneath all those protective layers of intellectualizing, lies an opening, bleeding, tormenting wound. He has to face it, he has to come to terms with it, he's got to go through it, if he's going to live with himself and with others in this world."

Linda said, "This sounds pretty grim."

"It is pretty grim. You've got an anguished, deserted

child in a man's body. You've got a young man who's tried to suppress an enormous amount of trauma for most of his life."

Quickly Owen said, "You sound as if you think he'll . . . rape . . . again."

"I think it's certainly a possibility. While he is in such turmoil. That's the act that makes him feel powerful."

"But can't we do something? Can't you?" Linda asked.

"I can help. We can make a start. I think Bruce likes me all right, is beginning to trust me, and that's crucial. But even at two sessions a week, this is going to be a long process. It's not going to be over in a few weeks or even a few months. And Bruce is going to have to put himself through some pretty tough emotional stuff if he's going to get well. He's facing an enormous challenge. A lot of hard, painful work. This will cause the same intense stress that Bruce faced when he knew he was returning to Hedden for his senior year, and when he was facing the interview at Westhurst, and when he was about to be separated from Alison for Christmas break. He's volcanic, your son. We don't know when he'll erupt, we only know that there is a destructive fire rumbling inside him."

"He's starting at the Ebradour public high school in January," Owen said. "He's got some friends there—"

"Lilibeth," Linda murmured, concerned.

Owen looked at her. "I guess I'll have to keep a pretty close rein on him."

"Yes. And as we discussed before, keep him busy. Keep him busy using his body and his mind. Keep him occupied, so that he's exhausted by the end of the day."

"I've started him refinishing furniture in the barn," Owen said. "He seems to enjoy that, and I told him when we sell it he can keep the profit, use it for spending money."

"Good. There's another thing I want to suggest. It's a form of chemotherapy."

"Chemotherapy," Linda repeated, her heart lurching.

"Like Valium is chemotherapy," Ingersall said reassuringly. "Like antidepressants and antianxiety medications."

"What are you recommending for Bruce?"

"It's called Depo-Provera. It's a weekly intramuscular injection that suppresses the release of a pituitary gland hormone, thereby lowering the male's level of testosterone. This brings about diminished sexual arousal. It is being used on repeated rape offenders."

"Chemotherapy alarms me," Owen admitted.

"Perhaps it will help to know that this same drug is issued commonly as a birth control device, and to regulate menstruation in women, to help adjust irregular menstrual cycles."

"Are there any side effects?" Linda asked.

"The common ones are mild: rashes, acne, nausea, that sort of thing. There have been extremely rare episodes of liver toxicity, jaundice, and blood clotting, but let me remind you that any woman taking an oral contraceptive faces these odds."

"Have you talked this over with Bruce?"

"I've mentioned it. We need to be careful with Bruce right now. He's volatile. He's a mixture of painful emotions. On the one hand he knows what he's done, and he feels lacerating, hideous shame. He hates himself. He believes himself to be a hateful person. This makes him respond to others with anger, like a wounded animal. On the other hand, he doesn't want to believe that he actually raped two young women. He is still openly protesting, declaring his innocence. I realize these are contradictory states of mind, but they both exist within Bruce at this moment. He is very angry. Very frightened. He has just lost everything, or what is everything to him: his school, his friends, his world for the past three and a half years. His girlfriend and the chance to be really loved by a woman. His home situation has changed dramatically: he's lost his stepmother and his stepsister. He certainly feels that he's also lost his father's love, and he feels he deserves this."

Owen cleared his throat. "I tell Bruce I love him every night."

"Yes. Keep doing that. I know he's not very likable now, but he needs to hear that from you."

"I love Bruce, too," Linda said.

"Yes. And in some part of his deepest soul he knows this. But right now he's angry, angry and cornered. He's hostile toward you, and toward Emily. That's why I suggested that you wait a while to join us in the family meetings. I suggest that you and your husband meet with me once a month, to discuss Bruce's progress. But for the rest, it's Bruce who's got to spend the time." Ingersall looked at Owen and Linda steadily. "We need to be very clear about this. You can't change the world for him. It's up to Bruce now. It's Bruce who's got to do the work."

*T*he man facing Emily stood no more than an arm's length away. She could smell his sweat. He was taller than she was by a good four inches, and heavy. He was not smiling, and he was breathing heavily. He was in his twenties, perhaps. Older than she was for sure.

Her body told her to run away. To move away. Get back. Leave.

The man reached out his arm toward her. At once she grabbed his right wrist with her left hand, and suddenly he slid forward, grabbed her left arm with his left hand, twisted her left arm over his head, and Emily found herself on her back on the floor. His shin pressed against her armpit and he kept the pressure on her wrist.

For one long frantic moment she was paralyzed with

fear. Then she remembered, and she tapped the mat twice with her free hand. The man stood up. Emily stood up, too, and they faced one another again.

"Now you try it," the man said.

She reached out her left arm. The man grabbed her wrist with his right hand. With her right hand she grabbed his arm, slid forward on the mat, and as if executing an eccentric dance step, lifted his arm up over her head and turned her body, pulling downward so that the man fell to the floor. She put her shin on his armpit. He tapped the mat twice.

"You're getting it," he said as he rose. "You need to put more pressure on my wrist."

They faced one another again. He reached out his hand.

They were working on katate tori shihonage, same-side four-corner throw, the first technique one learned in aikido. During Christmas vacation Emily had studied the brochure listing the Basingstoke Community School's second semester offerings, and of all the defense arts taught, aikido was the one that most interested her, because it was based on the idea of nonaggressive self-defense. She liked the idea that she could learn to protect herself without harming someone else. She saw no need to add any more violence to the world.

Grandiose thinking, perhaps. Sometimes when she was just walking down the small-town streets of Basingstoke, the sudden appearance of a group of men just leaving a café or bar would make her seize up with fear, would make her nauseated, and she'd have to lean against a wall, dropping down to pretend to tie her shoe, until some distance was gained between them and her. Then she thought: I should carry a knife. I should carry a gun. She did have a can of mace in her shoulder bag. It was one of the things her new shrink had suggested, that and the whistle she wore around her neck.

She knew she wouldn't hesitate to hurt someone if he came toward her with malicious intent.

But aikido would teach her self-protection, and more. The instructor—sensei—had told the class that ai meant harmony; do meant the way; ki meant your energy, your life force. One of her goals for this year was to come to some kind of peace with her self, the self comprised of her body and her mind. She wanted to feel stronger, emotionally as well as physically. She wanted to feel more graceful, not to those looking at her, but inside her skin, in the relationship between her nerves and her bones, her instincts and her movements. She wanted to feel that her body was strong and capable. That her mind was clear and ready. That her soul was scarred, but healed.

It helped that aikido was such a formal martial art. All students had to wear the white, pajamalike gi, which sensei told them must be kept clean. Emily wore the white belt of a novice wrapped twice around her waist and tied in a knot. Of the ten other students, four were yellow belts, five were green belts, and one was a brown belt. Their instructor was a black belt, and at first Emily had found him an intimidating sight. Short and stocky, with his black hair tied back in a low ponytail, Lyman Rice wore a hakama, a long black skirt over his gi, and the effect was oddly powerful, making him seem otherworldly, even regal. Before stepping onto the mat, everyone had to give a formal bow of respect to the center of the mat, and when class began and ended, everyone had to give a formal bow to sensei. The students even had to bow to one another, formally, before and after working out, and after she got over the embarrassment and self-consciousness of this, Emily discovered that it helped her see her partner as a comrade, not an adversary.

Which was good, for the world seemed full of adversaries. It was the end of February. She'd been out of the hospital for two full months. She saw her therapist twice a week. Yet sometimes after a day at school she was so exhausted by her own timidity that she hid in her bedroom and cried.

Not that her mother didn't know. Their dumb little apartment was too small and the walls too thin for secrets. But her mother came now and then to the counseling sessions at the Basingstoke Mental Health Clinic, and Dr. Srivastava had warned them both that Emily's recovery would take time and would be spotted with occasions of depression and feelings of failure. So Emily understood, as she walked the long modern halls of Basingstoke High, why it was that she flinched when a strange guy came too close, why her chest held her breath in a vise when Tom Hudson or Mark Stephens stopped to talk to her, both of them so tall, seeming to hover over her like giants. She knew they liked her; she liked them. She didn't want to be afraid of them and absolutely she did not want to display any fear. She hadn't told anyone at the high school, not even Bridgett, her new best friend, about the rape. She did not want to be stared at and gossiped about.

Sometimes images fluttered through her mind like a pack of cards thrown by the Red Queen. Rooms and faces. So many rooms, so many faces, in the past few months. Her bedroom on the farm, at Hedden, in the hospital, now in this new apartment. Her mother, Cordelia, Cynthia, Bridgett. Sometimes it was like being on a train, looking out the window at the countryside, and then the train rushes forward at jet speed, blurring the images into disorder.

Hedden. When school first started in the new year, Cordelia and Zodiac and Ming Chu had been good about calling her and meeting her in town for lunch, but as the days went by they called less, and when they did get together, they had less to talk about. Her Hedden friends couldn't get interested in the public high school gossip, and Emily found herself wanting to place some distance between herself and the private school. She had to move on with her life.

The hospital. Just once in the month since she'd left the hospital had she gone back to visit her friends there. Cynthia had been right. Everything changed once you were out.

Her mother had dropped her off at the front doors of the hospital, promising to pick her up in exactly one hour. As she went through the heavy swinging doors into the psych ward, a rush of anticipation mingled with anxiety passed through her, and then there she was, back in the familiar corridor.

"May I help you?" A strange nurse coming down the hall with a clipboard in her hand had greeted Emily.

"Um, I'm a visitor. I mean, I used to be a patient, and I just wanted to see some friends . . . Is Cynthia still here?"

"She's in the dining room." The nurse took Emily's purse to hold at the desk.

Emily had planned on their being in the dining room. When she'd discussed the visit with her mother, Linda had suggested this time, because if things were awkward, they could all go watch *Star Trek* at seven.

She'd made her way along the halls, surprised at how small and overheated and crowded the psych ward seemed, even compared to the dinky apartment she shared with her mother. When she stepped into the dining room, she'd realized with a jolt that she knew only two of the people there. Fat Bill. And Cynthia.

Fat Bill had seen her come in, but his eyes had registered no emotion. He'd been at his usual place at the end of a table, an empty bowl in front of him. Cynthia had sat at the table next to him, and three new patients had sat at the other end, not speaking.

"Hi, Bill," Emily had said.

He hadn't replied.

"It's me, Emily. Remember? I brought you some candy."

At the word candy his eyes had blinked. He'd looked at her hands. She'd put the Whitman's Sampler box on the table in front of him.

"How are you doing?" Emily had asked.

Bill hadn't answered but had frantically torn at the plastic wrapping, then wrenched the lid off the box. He'd put three chocolates in his mouth at once. A brown dribble of chocolate had leaked down the corner of his mouth.

Emily had pulled a chair up next to Cynthia. The other girl had sat listlessly, thin arms crossed in her lap, her hair lank and unkempt, her eyes dull.

"Hey, Cynthia, it's me, Emily. How are you?"

Cynthia hadn't responded in any way.

Beldon had come into the room then.

"Emily! Hey, girl, you're lookin' good!"

She'd been both glad to see the man again, and oddly defensive. He had seen her at her worst, her most pathetic, and she hadn't wanted to think about that. She hadn't wanted him saying, "Remember the time you clawed your face?" But she'd risen and given him a hug, and Beldon had hugged her back, then asked, "How do you like your new school?"

"It's okay. I'm meeting some people." She'd looked at Cynthia sitting inert in front of her. "Cynthia seems a little down."

"That's putting it mildly. It's the same old story. Third, maybe fourth time she's done it. Left the hospital, felt great, stopped taking her meds, had a great manic time during the holidays, then crashed. Back to the hospital for a while."

"Poor baby," Emily had said. She'd bent over Cynthia, wrapping her arms around the other girl's shoulders, stroking Cynthia's greasy hair.

"Nice," Cynthia had said. "That's nice."

Emily had continued stroking her hair.

"Heard from Keith?" Beldon had asked.

"Yes. We talk on the phone about once a week."

"How is he?"

"Back in school. He likes that. His parents are giving him some breathing space, and his mother has agreed to see a counselor with him."

"His father?"

"Refuses to. But the mother is a start." Emily had told Keith about aikido, and Keith had told her about the extracurricular course he was taking. "He's taking ballroom dancing."

"Ballroom dancing. I can just see him."

Beldon and Emily had laughed together. Emily was glad she'd met Keith. She could imagine he would be a good friend for the rest of her life.

"*Star Trek*," Bill had said.

Bill had risen, Cynthia had risen, and to Emily's surprise, the other three patients who had been sitting so unanimatedly at the other end of the table had risen, too.

"I'll come see you again," Emily had called to Cynthia. But Cynthia hadn't replied, and as Emily went back through the ward and out the swinging doors, she had known the words were a lie. She wouldn't come back.

Emily didn't think about the hospital much these days. She was lucky, she knew, not to have the serious psychiatric problems others had, and some days she was simply grateful for that, and that was enough.

The farm. She really didn't miss it that much. She missed Barn Cat. She missed seeing baby Sean and Rosie. Someday, her mother said, they would drive out to Ebradour and visit the Ryans. Someday, perhaps in the spring.

Linda had really loved the farm and what Emily hated most of all was that her mother and Owen were living apart. That her mother no longer lived on the farm. Emily burned with guilt about that, even though

Dr. Srivastava told her she should not feel guilty. How could she not feel guilty? She was guilty. If she had just not told about the rape, if she could have just gotten over it without making such a fuss . . .

Sometimes the guilt was so mixed with anger she could not tell them apart. When she thought of what Bruce had done to her, to them all, when she thought of all the consequences, the way she and especially her mother had had their lives totally, completely altered forever . . . she could not bear it. She could not bear it, and her anger was like acid inside her soul. Her new shrink told her that it would harm only herself, no one else, and so she tried her best not to dwell on it, but when she did, she found herself in the same state she'd been before she went into the hospital: nearly wild with rage. And with nowhere to put that rage. Certainly she couldn't keep harping on about it to her mother, who put on a good front for Emily's sake, Emily knew, but who also, Emily knew, because of the thin walls, cried herself to sleep at night.

So twice a week, in the evenings, she tried to channel that rage into this discipline. She arrived in her gi, bowed, did the thirty minutes of warming-up exercises with the others, then faced her partner and practiced the techniques of aikido.

There was only one other woman in the class, a rather flabby older woman who seemed as determined as Emily to learn this martial art. The few times Emily had had her as a partner, Emily had been vividly aware of the woman's femininity, how her wrist was softer, plumper, her movements more supple and languorous, and less precise. The woman was gentler, almost apologetic, and Emily supposed that was the way she was, too. They were not good partners for one another.

It was the best for her when she practiced with one of the green belt men who knew more, whose movements were quicker, smoother. It was frightening for Emily to work with a man. Each time it was frightening, as the man stood before her, always taller, always heavier, sometimes somber and intense, sometimes insulted and bored by a woman partner, sometimes amused. But male.

Run, her body told her.

Stay, her mind told her body. Stay. And learn.

Chapter Twenty-nine

In a small town off the Mass Pike, almost exactly halfway between Ebradour and Basingstoke, a colonial mansion had been turned into a small guest house named The Bayberry Inn. On this cold February night the lounge did smell of bayberry, and of cinnamon-scented candles and apple wood crackling in the fire-place.

Linda was curled up on a deep sofa, staring at the fire. She had arrived early because the weather fore-casters predicted snow and she hated driving in snow. Owen would be there soon.

Until then, it was balm for her soul simply to sit in this luxurious room. This peaceful room. With each passing second she was thankful that Owen had sug-gested they come here. It was expensive, but they had decided such an indulgence was necessary. Once a month, dinner here, the night here, time together away from their busy homes. Time away from their work, professional and familial. Time away from their chil-dren.

"Been waiting long?"

She looked up, and saw her husband standing there. He'd lost weight recently and his blazer hung on him, and the collar of his button-down shirt was loose. Still he was breathtakingly handsome, and just for a mo-ment all the delicious electricity of their early meetings broke over her, flooding her with desire and with delight, because this man was hers.

"Not long," she said. "How was the drive?"

"All right." He sank onto the sofa next to her. "Have you seen the suite?"

"Yes. It's wonderful. A four-poster bed. Wood-burning fireplace. *And* a clean, modern bath."

"The best of both worlds."

"Yes."

"You look good."

"Thanks." She was glad he noticed. She'd lost weight, too, an accidental consequence of the recent events in their lives, and for tonight had bought a dress that showed off her figure. Owen liked to see her in a dress; how long had it been? She lived in jeans and sweaters and boots or fleece-lined moccasins.

For tonight she'd had her hair cut and shaped. Her hairdresser had suggested tinting it. "Goodness!" Maxie'd exclaimed. "Look at all the gray !"

"Leave it," Linda said. "It's my badge of courage."

"What?" Maxie asked, puzzled. "Honey, it makes you look old."

"Never mind," Linda said, then to placate the other woman, "I'll think about dyeing it."

"Darling, we don't dye. We cellophane. We color."

"Fine, but not today."

Owen, she noticed, had more gray in his hair, too. And the skin on his face had begun to hang down from the bones, just slightly, but enough. The curved lines between his nose and mouth were more deeply engraved, and when he was in repose, as he was now, staring at the fire, the sides of his mouth turned down. They did not use to do that.

"I brought a bottle of champagne," Owen said.

"Lovely! What kind?"

"Perrier Jouët."

"You're kidding."

"We can afford it once a year. We deserve it this year."

They had spent New Year's Eve separately, at home with their children. Linda nodded ruefully. "When shall we drink it?"

"Well—how soon do you want to eat?"

It was lovely to discuss such inconsequential matters. For the first time in weeks they could think only of themselves and their immediate pleasure.

Bruce had been invited to spend the night with a bunch of guys, Ebradour friends he'd known since he was a child. He and Owen had discussed this with Ingersall; the host parents—and all of Ebradour as well—knew that Bruce had left private school, but nothing more, and Ingersall thought there was no reason to tell them. Bruce was taking low doses of Depo-Provera; he was working hard in school; he spent all his spare time in the barn, refinishing furniture; he saw Ingersall twice a week. At home he was sullen but placid. Tonight he and the other boys would watch videos and eat pizza. The parents would be around the entire time; it seemed a safe enough bet.

It would be the first time Bruce had spent away from his father since the night he was jailed.

Emily had also been invited to spend the night, with a new friend from the Basingstoke public high school. Bridgett was a somber girl, with braces and glasses and her hair in braids. She was seemingly uninterested in boys, which was probably one of the reasons Emily liked being around her. Bridgett wanted to be a journalist when she grew up and her conversation was packed with information about injustices, especially against women.

Linda had driven Bridgett home several times, and met Bridgett's parents, both college professors, serious intellectuals, strict disciplinarians. She found them rather dumpy and overearnest, and she could tell they found her, a novelist separated from her second husband, a wee bit alarming, but all in all they had passed each other's inspections.

The important thing was that Bridgett was Emily's friend. Now and then Emily met Cordelia and Zodiac and Ming Chu in town for ice cream and coffee. But the other three girls were always engrossed with Hedden gossip; Emily felt left out. She *was* left out. She was in a different world now, but doing all right, Linda thought.

Emily saw her therapist once a week. Sometimes she voluntarily told Linda about her session; other times she'd simply shrug off Linda's queries. "We just talked about life and stuff. Nothing exciting." It was the therapist who'd advised Emily to take a course in self-defense, and that, more than anything else, seemed to be imbuing Emily with a stronger sense of self. A kind of grace was slipping into Emily's bones, a slight ease in her posture, her chin held a little higher, her shoulders straighter.

The truth was, Linda had to face it, Emily really loved living in Basingstoke. On the farm she had missed the daily serendipitous exchanges with people; Emily liked being around people. She had begun to baby-sit for a family who lived in the condominium. Eleven-month-old Greg was a picture-book baby, with wisps of white-blond hair and huge blue eyes and fat rosy cheeks and very fat thighs, and he was a cheerful baby, too. When he saw Emily come in the door, he squealed and bubbled with glee and waved his arms for her to pick him up. She carried him with her everywhere, and took great pains to keep him perfectly clean, and never let him cry for more than a millisecond. As Emily joked to her mother, he was one nonthreatening male.

Owen knew all this, just as Linda knew how Bruce was doing. They talked to each other on the phone every night, just before they went to sleep. They talked about their children, and they talked about other things, too, their work, the farm, their friends.

Linda was scheduled to attend a joint family session with Dr. Ingersall once a month. At some point in the future Emily would be invited to join them for a session. Bruce needed to apologize to Emily, Ingersall said, if their relationship was to continue at all. It would be healthy for both of them to confront one another again, he said. But Bruce wasn't quite ready for that yet. Probably Emily wasn't, either.

Tonight, Linda and Owen had agreed in advance, they would not discuss their children. Life did hold other elements. They had not been attracted to one another because of their children nor had they married for that reason. Their lives would go on when the children were grown.

"Let's go to our room," Owen said now. "I have something for you."

"Oh, yeah?" Linda responded archly.

Owen grinned. "That, too, but not till after dinner."

They went up the winding staircase and down the hall to their suite. Linda put a match to the kindling while Owen popped the cork on the champagne. They settled into the small armchairs in front of the fireplace and toasted one another, and then Owen reached into his pocket and took out a piece of paper and handed it to Linda.

Linda looked at it. It was a check, for one hundred thousand dollars, made out to her.

"Owen?"

"I sold the south woodland."

"Owen, no."

"You know the Huntingtons have been pressuring me to sell it to them for months now. When Bruce was arrested, I knew I'd need money for a lawyer, so I called them and did it. Now that we don't need a lawyer, I want to give the money to you."

"Won't you need it for Bruce's therapy?"

"I've kept enough from the sale of the land for that

and other expenses: medication, an old pickup for Bruce when he gets his driver's license. But this is for you. I want you to buy a house in Basingstoke. That should be a good hefty down payment on something, something small but nice."

"I don't know what to say."

"I've been thinking a lot about us, the future, the next few years. Emily has two and a half years of high school left. She'll probably want to stay in Basingstoke, right?"

"I'm sure of it. She's moved enough; she won't want to leave Basingstoke. Her old friends are there, her new ones. Her therapist."

"And God knows how long Bruce is going to be living with me. I hope next year he can live at home and attend U. Mass in Amherst. I really can't predict what will happen with him. But whatever happens, I am still your husband. You are still my wife. You've got to have some kind of life, something better than that dinky apartment."

"I do hate paying rent instead of putting it into a mortgage."

"Right. If you come back to the farm to live . . . *when* you come back to the farm to live, you can sell whatever house you buy, and we can use that money to do the work you've always wanted to do on the farm. Until then, well, you'll have a decent place to live."

"Owen, this is so generous of you. I don't know what to say, except thank you. And honestly, I'll be so glad to leave that apartment." She looked down at the check, and then with a sigh she looked up at her husband. "But perhaps you should save this money. In case . . . in case Bruce needs a lawyer in the future."

"I've thought of that. I can't live my life that way. I don't want *us* to live *our* lives that way. It's hard enough that we're living apart. We'll probably live apart for three or four years. At least. That's enough.

We are doing enough for our children, living apart this way, so that we can be good parents to them. We need to think of ourselves as well. We need to have some quality of life or we'll become such miserable cranks everyone will suffer."

Linda nodded. "That's true." Leaning over, she held out her glass. "Well, then, let's drink to my new home. Our new lives."

Owen touched his glass against hers, and they drank.

"Now tell me," he said, "have you read any good books lately?"

She loved him utterly. She wanted to weep with joy and sympathy, but she rallied and said, "Actually, yes . . ."

They talked about books and movies and music and videos, all the pleasures of the world they'd foregone over the past few weeks. Their conversation carried them down to the dining room for a delicious meal of grilled salmon and the celebratory richness of cherries Jubilee. They talked about their own work, too, and Linda told Owen about a section in her book she was stuck on, and he discussed it with her, helping her turn it over and over, like a crystal ball into which they both could see, and gradually what she needed to do with the book became clear. They had always talked to one another like this, and it was bliss to talk this way again. As they looked at one another, they saw it was still there, after all they had gone through. It was still there, the love, the admiration, the understanding. The desire.

We are still married, Linda thought. There were so many different ways to be married. Women in earlier times took separation from their husbands in their stride. When men went off to war. When men went off to try to make their fortunes, in the gold rush, at sea. Marriage was not defined by location; a marriage did not arise from the fact of two people living in the same house. It was more complex than that, and more elementary. Linda and Owen were not living together, and would not for years, but they were still together in every way that mattered, and that was what counted. That was the bedrock of their lives. Emily, watching, would come to understand this. Would come to appreciate it, to learn how to make a marriage herself. And perhaps in his own time, in his own way, Bruce would, too.

They went into their bedroom. The fire had burned down and only a few embers glowed, fiercely orange amid the ashes, but that was enough, that provided sufficient light. They undressed one another. They held one another, standing together, naked flesh against naked flesh, all up and down, thighs touching, chests touching, lips touching, warm breath and warm breath mingling, their souls mingling, so that they seemed enclosed within a translucent cocoon of desire and possession.

Their bedcovers had been turned back. The room was warm, luxuriously so as the cold winter wind rattled against the windows. They lay in the bed together. They did not speak, except to say endearments. The lives waiting for them, the difficult lives they would return to the next day, were as much a part of this night as the wind outside the window, but for now they could forget all that, let it wait for them, held apart from them, while they focused on one another, and on what had brought them together and would keep them together, growing richer and more profound with each burdened day of each new year; Owen's body, Linda's body, brought together in an act of love.

In January, when he returned from Argentina, Jorge had called Emily, and then he called her every night, and then they began to meet on Saturdays for lunch at the Basingstoke Café. She had like that, sitting across the booth from him, drinking coffee; she'd felt grown-up. And day was a good time for her, full of light, even if it was only the thin January light. She felt less threatened.

One day when the snow was falling in wet smacks against the café window, Emily had confided in Jorge. Looking at the plastic red geraniums, she had told him about Bruce raping her. Asked him to keep it a secret. He promised he would and as the days and weeks passed, she knew he'd kept his promise, for Zodiac or Cordelia would have called her in a fit if they'd heard any kind of rumor.

"That's terrible," Jorge had said when she told him. "I'm very sorry."

"I wanted you to know," Emily had said. "So you'll understand if I act weird."

"You don't act weird."

"Well, I did. When I freaked out at you in the woods."

"That wasn't so bad."

"Sometimes I still get scared. Mostly of guys. It comes up inside me without my control, just all at once, for no reason, like a cough or something."

"I can understand that."

"I'm taking aikido. To learn to be brave."

"I think you're already brave."

"You probably think . . ." She hadn't known how to say it. All the things she felt, still felt, although the doctors said she shouldn't, her mother said she shouldn't, still she felt them: soiled, sullied, damaged, not just by the rape but also by the fact that she had been in a mental institution. She wanted him to know he didn't have to hang around with her now that he knew. She was strong. She wouldn't fall apart. "You probably think . . ."

"I think I like you," Jorge had said. "A lot." He was leaning on the table between them, his arms crossed behind his plate.

"Doesn't it make a difference that . . . ?"

"It only makes me sorry that it happened. It only makes me wish that I could help."

He'd asked her to go to the movies with him the next Saturday night. He'd call a cab, he said, since Hedden students weren't allowed to keep cars at school. That appealed to her. It seemed adult, plus she wouldn't be alone with him in the dark, not with a cab driver present.

That first evening when he arrived at their apartment, he presented himself with an old-fashioned, almost geeky courtliness that, Emily could tell, amused her mother as much as it pleased Emily. He brought a box of Godiva chocolates for "Mrs. McFarland," and a sheaf of pink roses for Emily, who felt her cheeks flush with pleasure in spite of herself.

The movie had been *Phenomenon*, starring John Travolta, who was a guy with sudden special mental gifts and aberrations, and halfway through the movie, Jorge leaned over to whisper to her, "I didn't know this was what the movie was about. Do you want to leave?"

"No," she'd whispered back. "It's fine. I like it." And to her own surprise, she'd patted his hand, reassuringly, and somehow he took her hand in his and held it for the rest of the movie.

And she had liked that. A lot. She had not been at all afraid.

Now, at the end of February, they had gone to the movies three times, and for the past two Sundays she and Jorge had gone ice skating at the local pond, and then he had come over to the apartment for a pizza dinner with her and her mom. They had watched television together. Her mom had gone into her bedroom to read, coming out now and then for a cup of coffee, not really coming out to check on them, like Emily knew other moms would constantly, checking on two people sitting side by side on the sofa.

Jorge did not try to kiss her. Did not try to get his arm around her. He only held her hand. That was enough, that was like honey in her blood, when he held her hand.

"Mom," she'd said one night, "I need to talk to you." It was night and Linda had come in to kiss Emily good night. She sat on the side of Emily's bed and waited. "Mom. Jorge says he likes me."

Linda had smiled. "Well, of course he does. How can he not? Look at you. You're perfectly adorable!"

"Mom. Get serious."

"I am serious. You *are* adorable. You're smart, and witty, and you listen to people when they talk, and you are turning into a beautiful young woman, especially now that your hair is growing out."

"But I feel so . . . confused."

"Is Jorge rushing you?"

"No. Not at all."

"So you don't feel that he's pressuring you."

"No. No, it's not him, it's me." She felt like she was made of a pack of cards, a pile of leaves, a lump of snowflakes, and sometimes any old wind would come up and blow her thoughts and feelings into a blizzard.

"That's understandable. After all you've been through. Good Lord, a new school, new friends, not to mention your old friends at Hedden, and at the hospital, and in Ebradour. Cut yourself some slack, Em. Give yourself time."

"But do you think he means it?" Emily had asked.

"That he likes you?"

"*Really* likes me."

Linda had reached over and softly smoothed Emily's hair. "Jorge seems . . . reliable. Steady. He certainly *acts* as if he likes you. He looks at you so fondly. He treats you well. I think you can trust him. I think you *should* trust him."

She was trying. She was trying to trust him, and their new and growing intimacy was both delicious and frightening, like skating on a pond when she wasn't quite sure the ice would hold.

This Sunday afternoon they skated together at the pond across from the Basingstoke high school. It was exhilarating, the movement, the brisk air, the bright scarves and mufflers, the comedy of novice skaters, the chatter and giggles of children. Jorge held her hand sometimes when they skated. He was not particularly confident on his skates and Emily liked it that he didn't mind trying, learning, in front of her.

As the lavender sky turned dark, they sat together on the bench, undoing their laces and tugging on their boots, their breath billowing into the air around them like steam.

"Ready to go?" Jorge asked.

"Yup."

But they stayed there, looking at each other.

"Could I kiss you?" Jorge asked.

The night air was soft and sparkling with cold. Nearby in the distance children shrieked and giggled as they made their way from the pond up the hill to the street.

Emily nodded. Slowly Jorge stretched his hand toward her, softly he put the palms of his hands against her cheeks. His skin was warm. Instinctively Emily turned her head just slightly so that her lips touched his hand and she could inhale the scent of his skin. What caused this sudden elixir of happiness to flow through her veins? As he bent to her, his dark eyes were so serious it nearly stopped her heart.

He tilted her head just slightly, and bent to put his mouth on hers. It was the softest of kisses. It was an exhalation. He pulled away.

"So."

She had never been so happy in her life. "So."

"That was okay? That didn't scare you?"

"No. I liked it." She put her hands to his face. "Do it again."

This time she kissed him back.

TODAY JOANNA HAS THE LIFE SHE'D ALWAYS DREAMED OF...

Joanna Jones, the successful host of *Fabulous Homes*, a New York-based TV show, seems to have it all. Blessed with great looks, she has a successful lover and a job that gives her fame and money, while allowing her to indulge her passion for beautiful homes.

TOMORROW SHE MIGHT LOSE IT ALL...

Suddenly and shockingly, Joanna will discover what she doesn't have: a committed relationship she can depend on. Now she faces a stunning discovery alone and makes the tough decision to leave her glittering life for an old Nantucket house on the ocean, new friends, and unexpected enemies. The choices ahead will test her courage; the surprising twists of fate will challenge her faith as she faces a day of ashes, a time of sorrow, and one extraordinary new chance for love, happiness and.....

~ *Belonging* ~

BY NANCY THAYER

"Nancy Thayer has a rare talent for conveying the complexity and richness of women."
—*Publishers Weekly*